THE

OTHER
CASTLE

A Xiinisi Trilogy
Book II

by

KIT DAVEN

Kelly,
This one has a mystery
as its central theme. Enjoy!
Missing you & Lee. Look
forward to our paths crossing
again soon!

xo
Kit Daven

THE OTHER CASTLE
© 2016 by Kit Daven Books

ISBN: 978-0-9919827-3-8

First Edition: June 2016

Also available as e-book:
ISBN: 978-0-9919827-2-1

Cover Art by Sean Chappell

Books written by Kit Daven:

A Xiinisi Trilogy
The Forgotten Gemstone (Book 1)
The Other Castle (Book 2)

For more information on the writer, visit **KitDaven.com.**

For

Sean

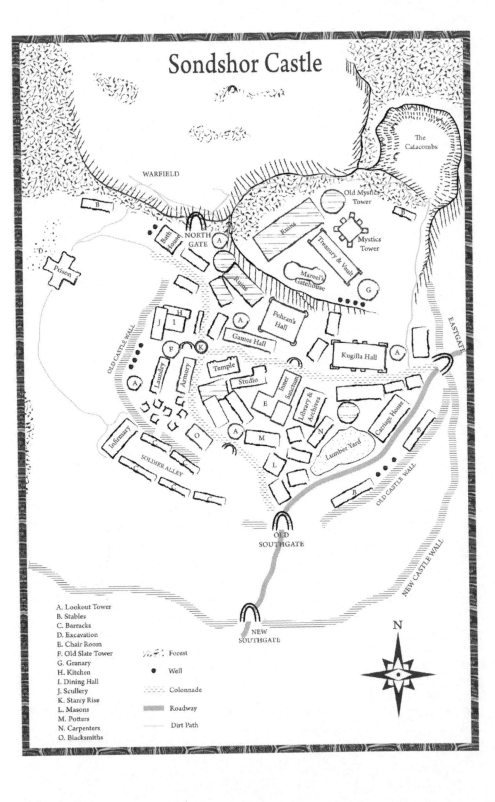

Sondshor Castle

The Catacombs

WARFIELD

Old Mystics Tower

Mystics Tower

Ruins

Battle House

NORTH GATE

Treasury & Vault

Prison

Marvel's Gatehouse

G

EASTGATE

Fohran's Hall

Games Hall

Kugifla Hall

Temple

Studio

Inner Sanctum

Library & Archives

Carriage House

Infirmary

Lumber Yard

SOLDIER ALLEY

OLD CASTLE WALL

OLD SOUTHGATE

OLD CASTLE WALL

NEW CASTLE WALL

NEW SOUTHGATE

A. Lookout Tower
B. Stables
C. Barracks
D. Excavation
E. Chair Room
F. Old Slate Tower
G. Granary
H. Kitchen
I. Dining Hall
J. Scullery
K. Starry Rise
L. Masons
M. Potters
N. Carpenters
O. Blacksmiths

Forest

Well

Colonnade

Roadway

Dirt Path

N

Ule held up a blanket woven of violet cotton and white wool—a favorite of hers and Bethereel's. Nights in Eastgate had been chilly and the blanket warm, but now that they lived within Sondshor Castle, they'd never feel cold again.

Their room was small compared to others on the third floor of Kugilla Hall. The ceiling hung low, trapping warmth from the hollow between the plastered stone walls, where heat rose from the hearths on the main floor. And come mid-morning, sunlight blazed through the only window, which faced southeasterly and overlooked the eastern Colonnade.

No, she and Bethereel had no need for the blanket on the bed anymore.

Ule grew frustrated. If any of their belongings had a dedicated place in the room, surely a blanket on a bed seemed an easy match, but she resisted setting it there. She had to put it somewhere, though; she had to bring order to their room eventually.

Neither the straw bed nor the round sitting table with its wobbly chairs, neither the wardrobe in the corner by the window nor the dresser by the open door resonated with her in anyway. Clothes and trinkets were piled here and there, and Ule struggled with how to dress the room in their belongings. No matter how hard she tried to visualize her and Bethereel living in this space, it remained just a room—

"This castle holds secrets."

She flinched at the voice, clutching the blanket to her chest. At the sight of her superior standing in the doorway, her nerves settled.

The arch scribe had a way of filling a room with his presence despite his diminutive stature. His white hair jutted at odd angles from beneath a crimson turban that hugged his ash brown face. His amber eyes darted all about the room as though he expected to find a spy crouched behind the piles of gifts on the table or hidden behind the open door to the wardrobe.

When he spoke, the careful intonations within his temperate voice were accompanied by clicks and nasal hums. He knew languages from Sondshor and Sondmid, Eesshor and Eesmid, as well as several Woedmid dialects, yet he always liked to speak to her in his native North language, Diminished Eelsee. If she had to guess why, she figured that her being the only scribe familiar with the language offered him a chance to be reminded of his home.

"What castle doesn't have secrets, Mbjard?" she answered in the common language of Sondshor. The utterance of his personal name slipped from her mouth before she realized the impropriety of addressing him that way.

She stood at attention, nearly dropping the blanket. "Sorry. I meant Sir."

He shrugged off her worry. "Mbjard's fine. I allow it on occasion with my other adepts. You're no different from them now." His nostrils flared, and the flesh across his pointy nose bulged slightly.

She detected his annoyance. "You disapprove of my new appointment?"

"It'll take some getting used to," he admitted.

Others had expressed their disapproval of her promotion to adept, but Mbjard's surprised her. Immediately, she defended herself. "The Magnes thinks I'm capable—"

Mbjard waved his hand as though he intended to wipe her out of existence. "Lyan fancies you." A flash of mirth and a chuckle blurred the bitterness in his gaze. "If I had the choice..." He fixated on the wardrobe across the room behind her.

Ule grew embarrassed at the spill of clothes there. She'd begun to sort things and put them away, but then second guessed where they ought to go. Eventually she gave up. She imagined the disarray failed to inspire any confidence in Mbjard regarding her abilities to fulfill the responsibilities of her new position.

Whatever Mbjard had intended to say remained within his thoughts. Finally, he mumbled, "There's so much you don't know."

Everyone has secrets, Ule thought. Hers involved hiding her Xiinisi origins. Display of her ability to manipulate energy on a quantum level was certain to startle and frighten most of the people in the world of Elish.

She'd had a lot of practice keeping this secret. After bidding farewell to her Master in the desert, she found it difficult being alone at first. Eventually, she managed herself well until he returned, transformed from a tall, bald blacksmith with a long skinny beard into a young man of average height and average build, whose face was the kind you felt drawn to; then once it was gone you forgot how it looked. He hid his Xiinisi and previous Elishian identities well.

She, however, struggled to keep his secret, experiencing a bit of difficulty with the transition from calling him Avn, his true name, to calling him Navalis, or Nav for short, as was the custom in the castle these days.

Secrets were at the heart of their existence, and though she hated to admit it, hiding her Xiines side became a little easier knowing there was another of her kind in the world.

Quietly, she began to fold the blanket, irked by something else Mbjard had said. His comment regarding Magnes Lyan bothered her.

Her relationship with Lyan was one of mutual respect. Everyone knew that. Besides, had there been any truth to this persistent rumor, he would have stuffed her in a cannon and ejected her from the castle after she and Bethereel wed two months ago. Someone who was jilted or jealous wouldn't promote her to ensure she was eligible for living quarters within the castle grounds.

Mbjard was wrong. Lyan's need for her was purely professional. He promoted her because of her ability to understand all languages, even codes and ciphers. Because of her skills, she enjoyed the privileges they provided her and had grown accustomed to the jealousies of other scribes. She seldom cared what they thought. She did, however, care what Mbjard thought. He was more like a friend than a teacher, and she felt unprepared to defend herself against his disparaging attitude.

"I know more languages than any other scribe," she finally blurted.

She'd grown tired of using this argument, but at the moment her focus was split between this undesirable conversation with Mbjard and figuring out what to do with the blanket. She'd been so sure about simply throwing it over the bed, and now she wasn't sure of anything.

"Yes, and you've been fulfilling your duties well enough," Mbjard agreed. "There is, however, more to being an adept than copying old books and being Lyan's personal interpreter."

She struggled to find another argument. "What about...?" Her mind latched onto a recent memory involving a visit to the artist studios. "Did I tell you? I found three more portraits of Adinav to destroy."

"Ah! Yes, of course." Mbjard nodded. "You've been effectively fulfilling Lyan's mandate of expunging all evidence of that scourge Adinav."

She felt her mood lift.

"Yes, well done," he approved. "Now, if you could convince the artists to willingly destroy their own works of Adinav, then I'd be truly impressed."

Ule dug her fingers into the blanket and squeezed.

"You see," Mbjard began, "having ability isn't nearly as valuable as how you control and use that ability."

For the briefest of moments, Ule felt as though Mbjard was Navalis lecturing her instead. She felt incapable of achieving the kind of self-control either of them possessed.

Mbjard must have sensed her self-deprecating thoughts and defeat, for he said encouragingly, "What you do best of all is assist other apprentice scribes."

"Thank you," she said, reminding herself she was Xiinisi, a race of world builders. Her powers and insight far exceeded Mbjard's imaginings, ones that if he had even a limited understanding of, he'd be on his knees worshiping her. When she had been younger, a gesture of this sort would have delighted her. Now, she grew at ease knowing she no longer needed that kind of adoration.

Her responsibility to observe and protect the world of Elish on behalf of the Xiinisi had helped her to regain some respect among her kind. More importantly, she felt she belonged again. Her past crimes of destroying a few worlds had finally seemed to be forgotten.

She was only an ill-appointed adept in Mbjard's eyes, but her own kind had seen in her the potential to be a world Sentinel. She was powerful, and the thought settled her mood yet not her indecision.

She turned the blanket in her hands and considered the possibility of draping it somewhere, anywhere, if it meant at least one possession had been put away.

"Assisting me requires a certain kind of insight," Mbjard continued. "The kind that comes from experience. You've only a few years as an apprentice. There are others who've been studying much longer than you. I only hope you're prepared."

Mbjard had been quick to take her under his supervision when she first began working there, as per Lyan's orders. Mbjard had always been supportive without being smothering; for that she was grateful. He had always seemed genuine and sincere, too, but given the revelation of his resistance to her new position, she wondered if Mbjard would have taken her on as an apprentice had he not been forced to.

"Is there something the matter?" he asked her.

"Not to sound unappreciative of your concerns," she told him, "it's just that I'm trying to figure out where to put this blanket before Bethereel returns from Sondshor Market."

He stepped into the room and looked about. "There's always the bed."

"Too warm I think," Ule mumbled. She stared down at the blanket and considered putting it there anyway, just for now.

"Or you could always hang it," he suggested. "There. Cover that ugly thing." He pointed to the wall above the bed. A long jagged crack interrupted the smooth plaster.

She considered his suggestion. Having the blanket she and Bethereel had enjoyed so much hanging above their new bed as a reminder of their previous home, invoked a deep sense of joyful nostalgia.

She climbed on to the bed and held the blanket against the wall. The scent of jumble stew clung to the fibers, and she realized she'd no longer smell the wonderful spices that had emanated from the flat below them, or hear their neighbors argue over which wine to drink first.

Mbjard hummed his approval, then added, "A little to the left."

She followed his advice.

"Yes, very good." He snapped his fingers. "Reminds me of the old tapestries in Fehran's Hall. I'll have a carpenter make you a rod, if you'd like."

Pleased by the idea, Ule gathered the blanket in her arms again and stepped down from the bed.

"I'd need to discuss the cost with Bethee first," she told him.

"My wedding present to you both, not that you need any more." He wandered into the room further and sat in one of the wobbly chairs at the table, near a large basket filled with of wrapped cheeses, jars of jam, and bread. In the middle of the table, a stack of small boxes, some wrapped in ribbon and others in plain brown paper, threatened to tip over.

"That's very generous of you." She sat in the other wobbly chair. "Thank you." His gift seemed like an afterthought. It made her uncomfortable, and she wondered if Mbjard had wanted something else from her. "Not to sound ungrateful," she began to ask, "but is there another reason you're here?"

He nodded. "I'm not here to make sport of tearing you down about your new position," he said. "I've accepted that some things are beyond my control. I'm more interested in knowing how the translation is coming along for that old journal I gave you a few days back."

"I've made progress," she lied, as usual, for she had already reviewed the contents of the journal using her Xiinisi abilities. As an Elishian, she had to give the appearance of working slower.

"Good," he said, growing a little uncomfortable himself. "Very good." He coughed. "Is there any mention of a... treasure?"

Treasure was a broad term, usually denoting something of value to someone. "What do you mean by treasure?"she asked.

"Now don't mock," he warned. "There are stories about a treasure in this castle. These stories are told throughout the shors. Even up North, in my hometown, we've heard them. Have you?" He drew a finger to his lips awaiting her response. After she remained silent, he leaned forward. "You haven't then, have you?"

"I swear," Ule began, "I *will* vomit if you start telling me a love story."

He laughed as he shook his head. "No, no, nothing like that. You've read the old texts, the ones recorded on feralwood parchment?"

She knew the parchments well. They were primarily historical in content, and contained vivid, detailed accounts of events of the ancient past.

"All of them," she replied. "Although, the world has changed a lot since then or... maybe people's views have changed. The world's pretty much the same, isn't it?"

"Past perceptions are beyond our experience so we can't say for certain." He stared at her momentarily before continuing in a solemn voice. "I say this with respect for your skills," he began, "I think perhaps you should keep your sensitivities to yourself. Discretion will serve you better now that you're an adept. Understand?"

She forced a smile.

"But, be sure to tell them to *me*." He winked at her. "I do value your insights." Lowering his voice, he leaned toward her. "According to the old texts there is rumored to be a great mystery buried somewhere in the castle, locked away beneath chains, staked to the earth with daggers and steel pins and swords."

The story began to sound familiar. She gasped as she recalled bits and pieces of the myth. "I know that story. Something about being locked in a cage and immersed in tar." She paused a moment, then added, "Who'd do that to treasure?!"

Noticing his excitement, she leaned forward and gave him her full attention.

Mbjard licked his lips and with the motion of a finger, invited her to lean in a little closer. "Oh, I agree, I agree." He rubbed his hands excitedly. "As you have discovered, documented history isn't always accurate. Sometimes we interpret descriptions as literal, when they were intended to be figurative, and vice versa."

He leaned back, his gaze searching the air. "What were the exact words of that description? Let's see, let's see... Ah, yes! *Lined in gold and silver and sapphires, and within a shimmering reflection, a rolling sea of mystery.* That's it. And!" He raised a finger to emphasize the word. "Did you know the tales passed down through song suggest the original castle was built by..." He paused for effect.

She leaned in a little closer, anticipating how he would finish the sentence.

"A demon."

She rolled her eyes. "I truly doubt that!"

He seemed amused by her comment. He could've easily been annoyed, and so she sucked in her breath and slapped her hand over her mouth to prevent any further blurting. After a moment, she lowered her hand.

"I'll work on reigning in my outbursts as well," she promised him.

Mbjard nodded, smiling. "At times it isn't appropriate, but not today, not when we're alone, understood?" Then he laughed.

She nodded, feeling camaraderie return to their relationship, as he recounted what he knew about the treasure. The subject brought a levity to his personality she'd never seen before, and she enjoyed the childlike side to his temperament.

The story he told about a demon building the castle unsettled her, though. She knew from her childhood, nearly two eons ago, back when the world of Elish was young and primordial, that the Elishians who flourished in the forests and veldts were the ones who started building temples, towers, and castles.

Although Xiinisi law demanded she not directly influence or coerce the beings she created, she had planted images in their dreams, drew pictures of buildings on stones, and with those same stones began building a tower. Those beings mimicked her at first, until they began to understand the nature of construction and continued experimenting on their own.

At that time, most demons were vaporous, unable to influence matter in any way. She knew that, but no one in Elish was supposed to have retained that memory. Mbjard's knowledge of such an idea made her wonder what kind of information had been retained in the Archive, and she tried to deter him from discussing it further.

"We both know the old stories were written by people who understood the world in a very different way than how we do now," she insisted. "Who's to say demons even existed back then?"

"Who's to say they haven't always existed?" Mbjard countered, eager to debate. "Who's to say they didn't exist before us? What if we are descended from them?"

She bit her tongue. The primitive humanoids and other creatures which populated Elish in the beginning came before the demons, woven out An Energy and matter—fine black threads which took form in either simple or complex patterns.

Prototypes were always built in mature form, prepared to reproduce in the manner designed within them. They multiplied, grew more aware of their world with every generation, and always the first of their emotions was fear. Fear of the darkness, fear of the earth, of the sky and trees and other creatures, until familiarity with their world began to stir within them the desire to understand, compelling them to wonder and ask and explore.

For some, fear subsided; for others fear persisted. Fear of nearly anything, for they chose to quake instead of question, and thus demons began to manifest, created by and thriving on a primal reaction.

These vaporous representations eventually passed through a nexus into another realm, the Chthonic Dimension, leaving the Root Dimension to all corporeal beings.

Except the demons hadn't done that in Elish. Somehow, they had remained behind. Over time they had become material in form, influencing their bodies to appear more humanoid than whatever object people collectively feared, whether it be cactuses or cats.

Mbjard lifted his hand, gesturing with an open palm. "There is, of course, no evidence to support either argument, but they are worth considering... another day." He rose from the wobbly chair. "There are secrets in this castle, Ule. And many of them are... rules, the kind everyone knows," he told her.

"There are lesser known rules, the kinds created by groups of similar people, and the kinds created by those in power which give them permission to behave in ways others aren't permitted to. Men have their secrets and women theirs. Guards know things the cooks don't. Then there are rules so old they rarely get used. We forget they ever existed at all."

She sat back in her chair and listened, feeling as though Mbjard were lifting the corner of a great tapestry. Something visible could be seen just beyond, something she couldn't quite discern entirely yet. She hoped he granted her access soon.

"I'm not supposed to tell anyone, not yet." He stood before her, peering down through his spectacles. "But you'll hear the rumors soon enough."

"What is it?"

"Lyan has made decisions that some believe are reckless." He began to pace the room. "People talk and spin ideas, and those who were once allies are now enemies, because they let others into their minds; they can't think for themselves." His smile faded. "As of this morning, and I'm not surprised, not really... The people have officially called for Protos."

She stood abruptly. "They can't make Lyan step down! After everything he's done—"

"They aren't," he assured her. "He'll maintain his position until a new Magnes is elected, one who will officially begin a new reigning lineage. Adinav made sure to obliterate his family. According to accounts, he was convinced they were working against him and killed every last one of them, including distant cousins. Now is the time for a new family. Protos is a rare occurrence, but it is the right of the people to call for this election."

Whatever she had thought she'd known about the state of affairs— her general mood toward Sondshor Castle was quietly shattered. She had believed people were content and happy, satisfied even. Sondshor had recovered well from the war and flourished in ways other shors hadn't.

She considered the fate of Lyan, whose brothers had died in the war. He had no family of his own either, no other examples to indicate the nature of his future children. He didn't stand a chance at being re-elected even if he did campaign.

"I may not agree with your new position," Mbjard said, "but consider this. The newly elected Magnes may very well get rid of us all for security reasons, so heed my advice." He reached up and placed both of his hands on either side of her head. She bowed to his will and he placed a soft kiss on her forehead, then let go. "Make the best of being an adept while you have this opportunity."

He crossed the room and paused in the doorway.

"We are on the eve of an election, the first this castle has observed in over six hundred years," he told her. "For the next six months, you'll be working among those with great privilege. It will affect you. It'll affect all of us. If you're not prepared, you'll suffer for it."

Upon his departure, Ule breathed deeply, unsure if Mbjard's parting words were meant as a caution or a threat.

✳ CHAPTER 2 ✳

News of the election buzzed throughout the Dining Hall. The vaulted building came alive in a way Ule hadn't experienced before, as conversations bounced back and forth along the long tables, row after row. For once she was grateful to be at the table along the south wall, for it was quieter and less boisterous than the others.

At the next table over, fellow apprentice scribes eager to show off their translation talents began conjugating foreign words in the oddest voices they could muster, and it was clear that none of them desired to run for the election or took it seriously.

Ule tried her best to ignore their banter and laughter, knowing full well that all of them, including her, would be spending a lot of time writing accounts as the election unfolded. Until then, she preferred sitting with her wife, Bethereel, and the clothiers.

Some of the clothiers began explaining to their superior, Rozafel, about the election and how, according to Protos Law, anyone was eligible— former Magnisi, generals, merchants, farmers and artisans. What promised to make the election so highly entertaining was watching all the men and women who had decided to run for the position of Magnes and considered themselves worthy of occupying the High Chair.

Ule settled into eating dinner, trying hard to catch her breath as she admired the dressings of the head table, which was fashioned of oak wood stained sea green with legs carved into the shape of serpents. It ran the width of the room, opposite the main doors where the castle's staff flowed freely into a courtyard beyond.

The head table was set on top of a stage, which permitted everyone eating dinner there to gaze down at the assembly, and offered a clear line of sight to the Magnes for anyone who wished to speak with him directly.

The other tables, the ones dedicated to staff, were stained black to conceal pockmarks and scratches. They ran the length of the room toward the main doors, equally spaced from one another with seating on either side.

Ule delicately pinched the stem of a crystal glass with her gloved hand and raised it. The wine inside remained an even level of thick red nectar. She struggled for breath, felt a shudder through her chest as her rib muscles trembled.

"It's warm," she mumbled to Bethereel, who was sitting beside her.

After a moment, the comment registered in Bethereel's mind, and she nodded in agreement. "A little bit. Sitting at your desk has made you feeble. We should race to dinner more often."

And they had run, down two flights of stairs and along the Colonnade.

They cut through Fehran's Courtyard, then along the narrow alley behind the Games Hall which always came alive later in the evening. They skirted a lookout tower and the ruins of a former Magnes, crossed the northern Colonnade, and behind a small storage building, they slipped through the side door of the Kitchen.

There, they had ducked and dodged around cutting tables, fire pit stoves, and iron cauldrons, careening through the doorway of the service counter, out into the Dining Hallway, where they abruptly stopped, turned about, and entered a line at the counter.

As Ule stood there, an ache had pushed against her skull, one which she associated with the fast double-beat rhythm of her heart. Now, as she sat and rested, she thought it odd she hadn't recovered yet.

The wine glass slipped between the white silk fabric of her gloves. She squeezed her fingers tighter and her deltoid and bicep muscles spasmed. Dark red wine splashed about the inside of the glass, but she held on to it with all her strength.

Laughter roared and receded, momentarily deafening her. Corks popped from wine bottles, sharp explosions that made her head throb. Knives scraped ceramic plates, making her cringe.

Something's wrong, she thought.

The clothiers who sat around her hadn't noticed her shaky hand. Couldn't they see something was amiss? No, she realized, they couldn't. They were too busy imbibing. For some, dinner in the Dining Hall was their only significant meal during the day and their only chance to socialize. Even Bethereel was looking the other way, engaged in conversation with Rozafel.

The table seemed wider suddenly, as though everyone was at an unreachable distance. Ule set down the wine glass with great effort. The spasm along her arm eased. She glanced at her half-eaten meal, bits of roast chicken swirled together with chunks of salted potatoes and heavily seasoned mashed turnip, and she grew concerned when the food began to move about on her plate.

She was on edge, her entire body vibrating. The sensation reminded her of the time she had been submutated into a gemstone by the cactus demon, Istok. Though it had happened long ago, the memory of it still made her shiver as she wiped her damp upper lip.

Bethereel giggled.

Something Rozafel had whispered in Bethereel's ear had amused her, and Ule wondered what it was the woman had said to make her lover laugh that way.

Now's not the time for jealousy, Ule scolded herself. She knew this, but she glared at Rozafel anyway, wishing she'd sit somewhere farther away from Bethereel.

Suddenly, Rozafel's short stature shortened more, her ample bosom grew, and her dark ash dreads lengthened. Bethereel also changed, every part of her elongating and stretching.

Complete opposites, Ule mused, blinking profusely to help readjust her visual focus. Yet no matter what she did, her sight remained skewed and distorted.

Something, maybe the wine, is affecting my perception, she thought.

Her upper lip began to twitch. Pain rose from within her body, sweeping through her nervous system. She grimaced until the pain subsided. Catching her breath again, her eyelids fluttered as everything around her brightened.

This, she realized as her arm began to tremble, this was something else. Her body—it was dying.

Her immediate thought was a simple one: regenerate. She'd make some excuse to leave, find a closet somewhere, deathmorph into the same form, then return with no one knowing anything had happened. But she wasn't certain she should. Her instincts faltered. Something about what was happening unsettled her, and she needed guidance from her Master.

Navalis always knew what to do. All she had to do was ask, except she risked being detected by the arch mystic and a few of the master mystics, who could perceive surface thoughts in others. For that reason alone, Navalis insisted they stop projecting their minds.

He sat two tables over, at the far end, his back to the main doors of the hall. He was engaged with other mystics and she saw little hope in catching his attention without others noticing. She decided to break the rule and calmly projected her thoughts, pushing back the rise of another blast of pain.

"Nav?"

Eager for his attention, she stared at him. He was surrounded by fellow apprentices and remained engaged in discussion, his hands gesturing emphatically until he began reorganizing cutlery to illustrate whatever point he hoped to make.

Ule caught her breath and waited for his projected response, a soft vibration she usually felt within the base of her skull. Her heart beat faster. Perspiration seeped through her silk undershirt. She pushed her thoughts again, more urgently this time.

"Navalis?"

During a pause in his conversation, he glanced briefly at her.

She pushed her will, freezing the next seizure at the base of her skull. Another pulse of pain reared up behind the one held in check. To impress the urgency of his attention, she projected again, this time using his true name.

"Avn!"

His green eyes met hers and his voice, earthy and strong, entered her mind. "What have I told you? Someone might hear." He scanned the room.

Ule followed his lead, then looked for the arch mystic.

Kerista sat at the head table, where she squinted in pain. Beside her, Mbjard poured water into a cup and placed it near her plate. Knowing Kerista was in pain meant she couldn't focus well enough to listen in on their communications, at least not until her migraine passed.

Ule took advantage of the moment and projected. "I've been poisoned." She waited for a response but when none came, she continued. "Should... should I heal myself, pretend like nothing's happened? This isn't like before, in the desert; that was so quick, I barely felt it. But, this. I don't know what to make of it."

Next to Navalis, a friend of his began to rant. Boriag was an unusual fellow whose timing couldn't be worse. Those nearby found it difficult to ignore him. As far as Ule could tell, Navalis concentrated on both conversations, the one beside him and the other in his mind. He still had yet to respond to either one.

Navalis had been quite adamant about both of them reserving their inner reservoir of energy—*No healing, no phase-shifting or shape-shifting, no willful expression of any of their abilities while in the world of Elish... unless absolutely necessary.* She'd thought he meant their physical reserve of energy, the one that drove the functions of their bodies, allowing them to heal themselves without the presence of the An Energy.

Now she knew better. Not only did time move faster in this world compared to their realm, but every time she healed herself, regardless of how much she endured the backlash of pain and eased it by consuming food or water, she drained time from her current generation, too. Every time she called upon the An Energy to express her will or shift, these acts also shortened her lifespan. That was what happened when any of her kind stayed for an extended amount of time in a created world.

Back in their own realm, where the An Energy was abundant, they could call on it at any time with ease. The amount of time drained from their lifespan might be mere seconds. In Elish, where very little An Energy remained and time moved much faster, their lifespans could be diminished by days or weeks from simply healing a cut.

Ule loved her current generation, her present form; so many wonderful things had happened, and she'd grown so much. Even though she could keep herself the way she was after deathmorphing, she still had difficulty with the thought of letting go.

She had just started to develop an awareness of that temporal aspect of her life, her inner clock, and she felt her generation aging quickly from staying the poison. If she acted now and restored herself, she'd still have plenty of time remaining to enjoy the rest of this phase of her life.

She felt the fierce presence of her Master within her mind, and it calmed her.

"Determine the type of poison," he told her.

She scanned deep within her body, narrowing the scope of her mind to see the molecular components of what was coursing through her. As a third pulse of pain reared at the base of her skull, she increased her efforts to discern the pattern of the poison.

"I see repeating amino acid residues connected by disulfide bonds," she reported.

"How many amino acid residues? How many bonds?"

She began counting. A bead of sweat rolled down her forehead and onto her cheek. "Forty two residues, four bonds, and..." She paused a moment as she saw something unusual in the toxin. "And one cystine knot."

Her mind warmed again as Navalis projected his thoughts. "You're dealing with a polypeptide neurotoxin. Venom. Specifically, spider venom."

"I don't recall being bitten by a spider." She scanned her body for the smallest prick, cut, or bite, yet found none. "There's no point of entry on my body."

"The venom must've been slipped into the food or wine..."

"But no one else is getting ill!"

Navalis paused. His sudden absence chilled her until he projected again. "Then we have to consider the possibility that someone meant to poison you or someone sitting nearby."

Ule regarded Bethereel, looked for any signs of distress or pain in her lover's face. Bethereel was flushed, possibly from the wine, and she smiled politely while listening to Rozafel tell stories from her childhood.

"Given your close proximity to Lyan," Navalis continued, "He might have been the intended target of another assassination attempt."

Her mind froze. The head table seemed a long way away. Her neurosystem remained in an arrested state, providing her a cushion from the ill effects of the poison: nausea, agitation, spasms, pain. She'd been poisoned once before, and died within minutes. This poison was different—slow moving, painful—and if it had been intended for Lyan, someone didn't just want him dead, they wanted him to suffer.

"What am I supposed to do?"

She hated the way Navalis avoided her eyes. Peering down at the table, he frowned deeply. After what seemed like forever, he raised a grim countenance and regarded her.

"Someone was meant to die tonight. They're watching, waiting for a potent venom to take effect," he solemnly told her. "If not Lyan, then who?"

"I'm..." Her heart sank at what he suggested. "I'm to die? Is that what you're telling me to do?"

Navalis's mind receded again.

A sidelong glance, and she saw Bethereel hunkered over her finished meal, listening intently to Rozafel tell the story of when she had chased a goat and mistakenly herded it into her mother's kitchen. This time around, Ule didn't find the story funny.

Death is only an illusion, she reminded herself. If she died now and here, the life she knew was over, unless...

Unless she deathmorphed into a form similar to what she was now, different enough to seem like another person yet one that reminded Bethereel of her lover. They'd start over again.

Perhaps she should confide in Bethereel, tell her about the Xiinisi. She had wanted to at times. It seemed the natural thing to do now, for the knowledge would spare Bethereel much grief.

All that mattered was they stayed together.

She hurled her thought at Navalis. "I don't want to hurt Bethee!"

"If Lyan's the intended target, your death will alert him of danger. He'll take better precautions with his safety. Something good will still come from this," Navalis assured her.

Heaviness consumed her. She knew she must yield to both her Master and the poison. Taking in one long last look at Bethereel's olive complexion and long dark hair, inhaling the scent of her lavender perfume, Ule released her neurosystem.

Several seizures hit her at once. She lunged forward, the muscles in her face twisting her mouth wide. Froth spilled from her lips as she struggled for air. Two clothiers sitting across the table screamed, throwing themselves from their stools.

"Ule?"

She heard Bethereel's soft consternation, felt her lover's hands wrap around her shoulders.

Her head snapped back, wrenching her throat. The pain seized her, took control, and she likened it to a force transforming her into another state—just like when she had become that damned gemstone.

"Ule!" Alarm quavered in Bethereel's voice, making Ule want to cry. Her lover didn't need to see her this way, dying.

Ule's jaws tightened. Her teeth bore down and bit into the soft tissue of her tongue. Warm blood gathered in her mouth, pooling along her teeth and sputtering onto her lips.

Everything she saw looked bright and harsh; everything she heard changed. Laughter fell away to gasps and shouts. Screams erupted. People ran toward her, some away from her. Somewhere a glass fell and shattered. Nearby, people shouted: *What's with her? She's been poisoned! It must be in the food!*

And a flurry of ill ease stormed the hall.

She fell backward, her legs stiffening. Her body convulsed as she spilled onto the floor. Her back arched, and the base of her skull cracked against the hardwood.

The world tipped at an odd angle, lights dancing before her eyes and fading away. She saw the ceiling, a distant puzzle of interlocking timbers. The people seemed like giants, towering above, looking down at her.

She thought it odd that the woman next to her desperately stuck a spoon down her throat. She gagged several times, her eyes watering, then she turned away to vomit. Others nearby did the same. Ule heard their retching, all of them frantic to save themselves from whatever they believed to be in the food.

The rancid smell of partially digested chicken, wine, and stomach acid rose from the floor. Those frightened by the prospect of being poisoned, swooned and fainted, falling forward onto their dinners or worse, backward into puddles of half-digested food on the floor.

Ule's seizures degenerated into muscle twitches. Immobile, she pushed past the pain, beyond her physical body where the increasing pressure on her brain threatened to distort her vision even more. Switching to her Xiinisi perception helped her stay aware of what was happening around her.

On her right, Rozafel knelt beside her. With stern determination, she clamped her thick hand down on Ule's chest and leaned in. On her left, Bethereel pressed Ule's shoulders to the floor while calling out for help first, then she called to her.

"Ule?" Bethereel's voice wavered. Panic welted the softness of her face. Her lips pinched and opened, moving in strange, contorted motions.

Ule's body continued to deteriorate. Her eyes began to dilate. With her perception, she locked onto the distraught countenance of her lover.

Bethereel hunkered forward and shook Ule, then turned her ear toward Ule's mouth.

Ule wanted very much to kiss Bethereel's lobe, one last kiss until they could be together again. Instead, she breathed a final breath.

Bethereel sat backward, slumping against a chair behind her. Legs curled beneath her, she sagged. Tears welled in her eyes and clung there. Whatever carefree spirit had possessed her, the very essence which gave Bethereel grace and strength and beauty, slipped away.

"No, I'm here!" Ule wanted Bethereel to hear her projected thoughts, but another presence blocked the message.

"Why'd you do that?" Ule complained. "She needs to know I'll return to her."

"No. I won't let you jeopardize our work here or our safety by telling her we're Xiinisi. You must let her go."

"I won't!"

Disobeying him, she began examining her form, determined to push it back to life. The large store of energy within her, even with the addition of the heavy meal she had just eaten, had begun to diminish rapidly. Reviving her body would be a slow endeavor, but if needed, she would willingly waste a generation's worth of energy to ensure she returned to Bethereel intact.

Refocusing on her form, Ule sought out her brain to begin repairing the damage done by the poison. There, she discovered billions of cells had already decayed and her core temperature was dropping rapidly. Whatever cells still remained alive in her body had aged considerably and were starving for oxygen. Her body was on the verge of deathmorphing.

The presence of Navalis returned. This time he was outside of her, his body in proximity to hers. He knelt next to her, pushing Rozafel aside. Boriag accompanied him, and in the distance, she heard the familiar raspy voice of the arch mystic, Kerista, barking orders at her charges.

"Bring the body to the Infirmary," she commanded, no longer crippled by headaches. "Don't let anyone touch the body."

Ule glimpsed Bethereel one last time.

Bethereel wept, caving into herself. Rozafel knelt beside her, uncomfortable and self-conscious as she patted Bethereel's hand. Beyond them, chaos escalated as soldiers stormed the Dining Hall, shutting down the serving counter to the Kitchen and ushering everyone outside into the courtyard.

I will return, Ule promised Bethereel. I will show you who I truly am, and you'll never need to cry again.

✳ CHAPTER 3 ✳

Ule's eyes remained partially open. The transmission of energy along her neurological pathways had started to slow down, conveying little to no information. She was physically blind yet still saw using her perception, preferring to stay close to the confines of her body.

She, or rather her body, was being carried by two men. On her left was Boriag, a tall and lanky man. His thinness was painful to look at, and his long arms and legs struggled as he helped carry her through the main doorway of the Dining Hall and out into the courtyard beyond.

On her right, Navalis struggled less with the weight of her body and more with Boriag's awkwardness, pulling and pushing against him as they carried her through an uncooperative crowd, one that preferred to stare rather than get out of the way.

She waited for Navalis's thoughts to pervade her mind. She was certain he'd project again once Kerista and her master mystics were far enough away, even though Kerista was the one they worried about the most. Her ability to read others' thoughts far surpassed those of the master mystics, which meant that when she was nearby, they both needed to control their thoughts and project fake memories.

Most of the time Ule let her mind wander, unfettered by laws and codes; it was the only part of her existence that truly felt free. Creating fake memories to support Ule's life story as an Elishian proved difficult for her.

"Don't project!" Navalis warned.

Ule might very well have gasped had her body been alive, for Navalis's words arose not from the base of her skull, but from another unexpected place deep within her solar plexus.

"Listen," he commanded.

She had known some of the Xiinisi were privileged to a covert form of communication, but she hadn't known it possible to project thoughts this deep within their forms. She listened, the force of his words soothing her.

"Kerista can't perceive my thoughts channeled this way," he explained. "This is a difficult skill to learn. It requires tremendous focus, and there's an understanding and trust regarding how it can be used. Still, I think it's time you learned. When the time's right, I'll teach you. For now, you need to slow your regeneration. After you're interred, I'll come for you and guide you in deathmorphing."

Relieved by his instructions, she regarded the flex in his shoulder, the way it hitched while he carried her. A light sweat broke out on his cheeks. On the other side, Boriag huffed, his cheeks deeply flushed. Occasionally they shouted at others in the courtyard to move out of their way.

She wanted to ask Navalis how long she'd have to maintain stasis.

Then she heard his voice again, advising her as though he knew what question plagued her mind.

"There'll be an examination," he told her. "Possibly an autopsy, if external clues to your death aren't found. Preparation of your body, then the funeral and procession... three days? Maybe four."

That long, she thought, until she remembered that in parts of Elish, they still honored the ancient custom of eviscerating the dead and drying out their organs and flesh with salt and sun. The process often lasted as long as two months. At the castle, however, the dead were prepared differently, then tucked away in an endless maze of catacombs with an environment which naturally preserved bodies.

The buildings on the castle grounds had always seemed a mess of craziness, as newer buildings were built on top of older ones. Now, at this angle, she discerned a pattern. The wooden cornices of leaves and vines delineated the newer upper levels of some of the buildings, while terra cotta shingles roofed some of the older ones.

She passed beneath an archway of stone that bridged the Old Slate Tower and the remnants of a building enclosing a fountain and a garden. Passersby stopped and leaned against the railing to stare down at her, and she hated how self-conscious she felt.

She turned her attention to the tower on her left. From her vantage point, it was a true giant with serrated slate peaks which looked out of place next to the less ornate multi-leveled rectangular buildings nearby—to her left, a laundry facility made of wood, and to her right, an armory made of stone.

Everything appeared to bow toward her in mourning, grim and sombre against the partially clouded sky. She fought a strange emotional array of irritation, embarrassment, and shame for the graceless and violent nature of her death. She wished it had been more private, more discreet—elegant.

Navalis and Boriag carried her through the yard between the buildings, then wove through the cottages of the generals, instead of hauling her out onto the southern Colonnade. At the break in the old rampart, her body tilted at a gentle incline as they walked down a grassy slope at the edge of a field.

She swayed slightly as they picked up momentum and turned down into another courtyard. She noted the iron gratings on windows, an architectural feature unique to Soldier Alley. The oblong stretch of land was lined with two-story wooden barracks built along a portion of the old rampart, where soldiers kept a lookout on the new wall being constructed across the field in the south.

She glimpsed soldiers and guards dressed in leggings, leaning against their lodgings, looking haggard from intense drills. She felt helpless as they stared at her.

Navalis and Boriag steered her toward the end of the yard, where a long building of white stone offered her privacy. The Infirmary was dedicated to healing the injured and sick. She was neither of these things, but they carried her through the front door, into a short hallway, then veered sharply to the right and squeezed through a second doorway into a large chamber, where they clumsily set her onto a hard surface of well worn stone.

As her head lolled to one side, Kerista marched into the room. Lips pursed, neck strained, she pointed toward the windows facing Soldier Alley and called out to the soldiers lingering nearby.

"Close the shutters!"

She snapped her fingers at Navalis and Boriag. "And you two! Guard the inside of the room. No one's allowed in here until the physician arrives. When he does, one of you come for me. I'll be conferring with the Magnes and General Gorlen. Understood?"

Navalis acknowledged Kerista's command with a nod. He took up position near the door, while Boriag slipped outside and watched for anyone attempting to enter from the yard.

Outside, shutters clattered as they were shut by soldiers, and when the secured room met Kerista's approval, she departed in silence.

Several moments passed before Navalis stirred from his post near the door. He stared at Ule with little expression. She didn't know what to make of the twitch of his mouth—a grimace? Perhaps a smile? Regardless, he seemed genuinely affected by her death.

They stared at one another, and after several minutes, he peered over his shoulder through the doorway. When Boriag wasn't looking, he walked over to the table and swept his fingers down her face; her eyelids yielded.

She saw the backs of her lids lined in veins. Pushing her perception beyond her body, she saw Navalis resume his position near the door, his expression unchanged.

"My advice," he projected to her, again through her solar plexus, "is to find something to focus on."

She chose to focus on him, preferring his appearance in this form compared to his last. Course brown hair stopped at his shoulder. His face was smooth and flawless, no longer weathered by battle scars. His arms were free of forge burns. Not quite as muscular or as tall as the blacksmith he once was, Navalis had chosen a nearly symmetrical face with bland features, and he would have been forgettable (as was his intention no doubt), if not for those eyes which always remained the same color, always a pale green that reminded her of saplings.

He smirked. "Perhaps you'd make better use of your time focusing on something else."

Something else, she wondered. All that consumed her was death—staying the decay of her cells, holding onto diminishing vitality, cringing at the stillness within, searching her molecular structure for a familiar hum of energy, anything that indicated she was still alive.

At the heart of her discomfort, she did have a question. She heard herself ask: Why? Why had she been murdered? Of course it also mattered *who* had murdered her, but more importantly, she needed to understand their reason.

Heeding her Master's advice, she began examining the nature of her death. Unsettled and disappointed, she turned her mind inward, noticed millions of cells releasing energy and the increasing chill within her form.

She despised the lethal toxin for forcing her to give up control of her body. The spasms within her muscles, the way her spinal cord had whipped about, they had been her system's way of reacting to the venom. But there had been other symptoms, she realized: breathlessness, tingling around her mouth, sweating, an elevated heartbeat.

She had been out of breath before then, not quite keeping up with conversations, pausing between mouthfuls of chicken for an extra gulp of air. Her thoughts reconsidered every subtle gesture, half-heard comments, even her own conversation, from the moment she arrived in the Kitchen...

Ule veered to the left, Bethereel to the right, darting around raised square fire pits topped by grates and filled with glowing embers. They collided into counters as they ducked beneath ceiling racks filled with strainers and pans. Occasionally they dodged a ladle or two hurled at them by angry cooks.

At the service counter, they pushed one another through the doorway, but they weren't quick enough. From across the Kitchen near the meat counter, a powerful voice rose above the din, and Senaga, the head cook, bellowed, "Stay out of my Kitchen!"

Before Ule caught her breath, Bethereel pulled her into the Dining Hall, where they stumbled into the shortest line at the serving counter and laughed at themselves.

Ahead of them, Navalis leaned against the counter while Boriag leaned across it, determined to get more potatoes added to the heap of food already on his plate.

Regaining her composure, Bethereel clutched her stomach and stuck out her tongue. "How can he eat all that and stay so skinny?"

Ule fanned her face with a hand, as she examined the strange expression that overcame Navalis as he suddenly stood upon noticing her.

"Don't look so surprised," she told him, struggling to catch her breath. "We've been early before."

Navalis shrugged, half-smiling. His eyes wandered to Bethereel and back to Ule again. "You're only ever here once dessert's served. Figured you two preferred eating with the servants."

Boriag slowly turned about, eyes wide as he stared at the mountain of food on his plate. "This chicken smells delicious," he sang.

Navalis snorted and smacked Boriag on the shoulder. The impact caused Boriag to stumble forward. He shielded the food to prevent it from spilling. Hunkered over the plate, he snarled and growled like a feral animal protecting its kill.

Bethereel giggled at his performance.

Ule hadn't laughed then the way she wanted to now, for she remembered that in this particular moment, she had been annoyed about not being able to catch her breath.

"Seriously?" Boriag had said. "You're joining us to eat tonight instead of hanging out with the owls?" He hunched a bit, but it did little to conceal his skinny frame. Every time he gulped, the bulge at the front of his neck bobbed grotesquely.

"Funny!" Bethereel pushed ahead of Navalis. She ordered meager portions of chicken and a pile of vegetables from a server, who scowled once he recognized her and Ule as the ones who had upset Senaga.

"And you're going to eat with those on?" Boriag pointed to Ule's hands.

"What's wrong with them?" She held up her hands to display finely embroidered gloves. Swirls of white thread created a subtle effect against the white raw silk.

He shook his head, mirth threatening to consume him.

"They're a gift," she fired at him, "left behind in our new quarters." She turned her hands around, holding them at odd angles.

In her peripheral vision, she became acutely aware of Navalis staring at her and of Bethereel pulling away from the window with a plate of food as Boriag leaned into her and whispered, "What's she doing?"

Bethereel shook her head. "Her mind's spun dizzy."

Ule threw her arms down in frustration, finding her disgruntled mood melting in the presence of Bethereel's beauty. She sucked in a deep breath, felt a pressure on her chest and her heart that she associated with love, but now saw she had been struggling to breathe because of the poison.

Navalis took his turn at the serving counter.

"Did you know he wants to study demons," Boriag announced to Ule and Bethereel. Then he smacked Navalis on the back while balancing the plate of food in his other hand, and asked, "Any luck with that yet?"

"No," Navalis replied, his mouth slightly pinched in annoyance. "It's just a matter of time till I get Kerista's go ahead."

"Yeah. Can't it be a hobby? Do you have to make it your specialty?"

"I can only do so much tiptoeing around her." Navalis scowled. "Besides she's likely to sniff out my thoughts eventually."

Boriag grimaced at the suggestion, then slowly nodded. "Perhaps, you need to persuade her." He made kissing sounds and chuckled. "You know she's sweet on you, right? A little wooing, a bit of booze, more for you, eh? Work those charms of yours, you know, offer her a bouncy-bounce." He grinned. "I'm sure it's been a while for her."

Navalis cast his friend a dark look.

Ule admired her Master's ability to blend in with everyday life among the Elishians, after everything she'd put him through. He had been trapped in Elish for hundreds of years, and he had fought in a hundred year war as a soldier in one form or another. Back then, he'd found comfort in personal relationships, but this time around, he showed little interest in interacting with anyone romantically or sexually. His focus seemed devoted to training her as a Sentinel.

"Why do you even want to study demons, Nav?" Bethereel's lament was sore. She disliked demons immensely.

"To learn about the world," Ule answered on behalf of Navalis. "And ultimately about ourselves, isn't that right?"

Boriag laughed. "You're such a ghoul, Ule."

She hadn't meant to be, she thought as she lay on the examination table in the Infirmary and continued remembering.

Her heart had still beat fiercely, her breath labored, yet she had thought it a reaction to Boriag's criticism.

"We're not anything like demons," Bethereel complained. "We don't go around scaring everyone to feel alive."

"I don't know about that," Boriag said. "I think some of us do. Remember Ilgaud, that murderer they put away? And what about Kerista?"

"There must be a reason why demons live in the world with us," Ule continued arguing. She didn't know why the subject interested him and he'd never bothered to explain. She only wanted to support him, the way he had supported her in the past. She owed him that.

"Oh no, here we go again!" Bethereel slapped her forehead.

Ule had wanted to remind them of how demons fought alongside Elishians to overthrow Adinav. Many of them had been co-opted the way the Elishians had, used as soldier-puppets to fight a war while Adinav tried to escape the confines of the world.

"You do remember a lot of them fought in the war," she finally said, "helped us defeat the Grand Magnes, don't you?"

Boriag began to step backward. "Don't engage!" he warned everyone.

"No politics," Bethereel begged, clutching her plate. "New subject, please." Before anyone could protest, she turned to Navalis and changed the subject. "Sabien's been asking about you."

Navalis flinched. Ule noticed the slight gesture and a hint of remorse in his eyes.

"You remember my cousin, don't you?" Bethereel's tone turned sharp.

"Tall, beautiful man with dark hair? Runs the curiosity exhibit in Sondshor Market at the old smithy? He liked you, you liked him; then you didn't."

Ule remembered a time when Sabien had fallen into a deep depression. His health had deteriorated a little, but he came back from whatever illness had struck him, and after he recovered, Navalis no longer visited him in Sondshor Market.

Exasperated, Bethereel shook her head. "You're hopeless," she mumbled, then walked away.

Ule inhaled deeply, her lips tingling from the sensation. She hurried after her lover, growing breathless again. Her cheeks grew warm and perspiration dampened her neck, as she skirted the tables and met up with Bethereel near the main doors, where a crowd of soldiers had gathered.

Bethereel darted around clusters of people, Ule following at her heels until she suddenly halted. Ule swerved to avoid barreling into her. Then she swerved again to avoid Kerista, and nearly spilled food onto Magnes Lyan, who were both making their way to the head table.

"My apologies!" She sniffed a little, and as she bowed her head, she rubbed her upper lip.

Had her lip been itchy? No, it hadn't, Ule remembered. She'd wiped sweat from her upper lip, while she gazed at Lyan's grim, bearded face.

"Kerista and I were discussing your new promotion," he told her.

Uncertain what to say, Ule nodded.

"Under my counsel," Kerista interrupted. "I wouldn't have approved." She wore a teal robe instead of a leather tunic like the other mystics, and the color cooled her brown eyes and intensified the silver in her short curly hair.

Of course not, Ule thought and focused on a false history of herself should Kerista's unpredictable new mind reading ability suddenly start functioning.

Ule nodded again, uncertain how to respond. Her lungs ached and her heart beat extra hard.

"Your thoughts are inconsistent," Kerista stated coolly.

Lyan frowned. "Have you considered she may not have fully recovered from her amnesia?" he countered swiftly. "Show some compassion."

Kerista stiffened. Clearly, she was deeply offended by the suggestion. Hands folded in front of her, she insisted on barring Ule's way. "Mbjard doubts her ability to function in her new role."

"The appointment is assured, my word is final," Lyan stated. Before Kerista could object, he spoke again, addressing Ule. "Congratulations on becoming an adept." Then, in a softer voice so no one else might hear. "And your new quarters."

Both she and Bethereel nodded again, bid him a joyous supper, and continued searching for space at a table.

"That was weird," Bethereel said as she clung to Ule's side. A second later she mumbled, "Gosh you're warm."

Ule gasped for air. "What's weird?"

"Oh, I don't know, it felt like Lyan wanted us to invite him to our room."

"It's only polite we invite him for drinks."

"Na, he wants something... sexual."

"What?! Why?"

"It's obvious he fancies you."

"Favors," Ule corrected Bethereel. She coughed to clear her throat of phlegm. "He *favors* me."

A slight woman darted in front of them, carrying a plate of partially eaten food. Head bowed, stray strands of black hair dangled in front of her sandy face. When she looked to see who blocked the way, her pale complexion flushed. Tears welled up in her brown eyes. The gentleness of her girlish face hardened as she let out a wail and dashed her plate on the floor.

A collective cry from other diners boomed throughout the Dining Hall, blessing the broken dish, an ancient custom of grace within the castle. Bits of food rolled around Ule's feet.

"Laere!" Bethereel scolded the woman.

Laere glared at her, darted between two soldiers, and disappeared.

Stunned, Bethereel stared after her. "What was that about?"

Ule coughed, her eyes watering slightly. "I destroyed a few more of her paintings last week."

Years ago, Laere, like so many others, had understood the necessity of destroying all renderings of Adinav, but as time passed, the artists had become more and more resistant to relinquishing their work, forcing Ule to be firm with them.

What she had done to Laere's portraits hadn't made her feel sad, so why had she cried? Now, she understood. The poison had caused the tears. Bethereel hadn't noticed, for she pushed ahead through the crowd toward the table on the south wall and found two empty seats next to Rozafel.

Ule had been out of breath, sweating, her heart racing, which she had never thought to associate with anything other than hurrying. Now, she knew better.

Other than servants, no one had touched her food. No one had intentionally touched her in any way except for the occasional shoulder nudge. Even more peculiar, it seemed her symptoms, so subtle at first, had started manifesting by the time she arrived at the Dining Hall.

The poisoning, Ule realized as she lay lifeless within the Infirmary, had happened much earlier, perhaps when she had been alone with Bethereel.

✳ CHAPTER 4 ✳

Night must have settled over the castle, for Ule heard the hollers of soldiers and guards returning to their barracks. Coming off long day shifts, they loitered about the fire pit in the courtyard, where drink and vulgar insults were bandied about. Others departed for the night watch.

Those who remained outdoors grew louder and louder, occasionally bursting into song, and as midnight approached, their revelry diminished into fatigued, drunken slurs. Eventually, they fell quiet.

By early morning, dampness thickened the air, silencing the usual chorus of insects as a storm approached. Ule didn't care for the way the humidity revived mildew spores hidden in the cracks of the stone table yet couldn't revive her dead body.

She tried to shake the image of Bethereel's distress, but the sight of her lover stuck in her mind like an axe in a stump. She recalled when that had actually happened, a couple years back when she worked a farm and chopped wood for the first time. The axe got wedged in the wood, but she'd wriggled it free quite by instinct. The image of Bethereel, however, remained fixed—a blade buried so deeply it had become permanently entrenched in Ule's mind.

Bethee. She wouldn't. Ever the na!

The old world expression failed to dispel Ule's doubt.

She couldn't have poisoned me. Not my Bethee.

Anxiety snaked through Ule's thoughts. She hated suspecting someone she loved so deeply of being capable of murder, but there had been no one else with her, no one else with whom she had come into such direct and intimate contact in the hours prior to dinner.

Ule quieted her mind and reviewed memories from earlier in the day.

Subtle scents of rose and sandalwood had drifted through the open door to their new room. No matter how softly Bethereel tiptoed, her fragrance betrayed her stealth long before she customarily pounced. In the memory, the collective scents reminded Ule of Bethereel's softness, of her strength and biting wit.

Half smiling, Ule had reached across the table, her fingers dancing over the assortment of gift baskets and unopened boxes. She and Bethereel had made a promise to each other; after unpacking and arranging their room, they'd open them all.

Some were belated wedding gifts, others housewarming tokens. She settled on a flat box, not much wider or longer than her hand, and tore the red satin ribbon free. She paused, head tilted, as she listened for Bethereel's reaction.

"You beast!" Bethereel's warm body collided into hers. She didn't mind how the edge of the table dug into her flesh as Bethereel grabbed for the box. "How dare you open our presents without me!"

Holding the box high above her head, Ule twisted about. Leaning into Bethereel, she smothered her lips, forcing their tongues to dance.

Breathless, Bethereel pulled away. "The dinner bell's going to toll any moment. I'm already half starved."

Ule ignored her. With her free hand, she began unbuttoning the back to Bethereel's marigold clothier overdress.

"The door's wide open," Bethereel mumbled.

"Hasn't stopped anybody in this castle." Ule tried to discard the gift on the table, but the box caught the edge and toppled to the floor. The lid popped open and something white and silky spilled out. Ignoring the mess, she gave up on Bethereel's buttons.

Great strides propelled her across the room toward the wooden doorway. The black iron brackets creaked and the latch clicked into place as she shut it. She spun around and leaned there, rivets digging into her back. She shivered at the sight of Bethereel slipping out of the patchwork overdress with its many pale orange pockets, and then her white under dress.

Bethereel seemed out of place among the hard shadows cast by the evening sun. Amber light caught the edges of the narrow window behind her. Against the gray brick and plaster of the room, Bethereel glowed. Peach stockings and a coral slip clung to her olive skin. A living flame in the stillness of the sterile room, Bethereel flicked a dark strand from her forehead and tucked it back into the braid coiled about her head.

They wore their hair the same way this evening, and although Ule preferred Bethereel with long flowing curls, there wasn't any time to undress her further. She hastened toward her, eager to warm her hands. Her fingers danced over sheer fabric heated by Bethereel's flesh, and Bethereel struggled with the hooks on Ule's dress, and won in the end. They chased one another naked around the room, and Ule ignored her braid as it unraveled and fell down along her backside.

They never bothered with the bed, pausing now and again for deep kisses and even deeper caresses. On the table. On the chest. On a wobbly chair. Maybe this way they could make the room their own, instead of relying solely on their possessions.

Near the window, she pinned Bethereel against the wall. Bethereel's head rolled to one side and she gasped at the release of pleasure stirred by Ule's touch. Ule moaned with her own arousal, trembling from an orgasm stirred by Bethereel.

Bethereel sighed, her eyes gazing out the window at the fading sun while she tugged at Ule's braid. "We're going to have to stand in the Dining Hall to eat now."

Ule caught her breath. "They'll make room for us. They have to. I'm an adept now."

Bethereel moaned. "Promise, no politics tonight?"

"I can't." Reluctant, she pulled away, letting the cold air come between them. "Does this rule apply to you, too?"

"What?" Bethereel spoke sharply, her innocent eyes narrowing. She shook her head in response. "Of course not."

Ule laughed, turning toward the wardrobe. "You're the one who starts rallying against demons every chance you get." When it came to demons, that was a topic of debate on which they disagreed, passionately.

"I'm—" Bethereel held up her hand and turned away, her cheeks turning as flush as her lips. "I don't want to start anything with you, not tonight."

"Fine, no politics." Agreeing to the arrangement irked Ule. Every time they made this promise, they broke it. "That goes for you, too."

Smiling coyly, Bethereel kissed her lightly on the lips. She tended the wardrobe, thumbed through folded garments stacked on the shelves first, then sorted through the rack where an assortment of clothing hung from many hangers.

She chose blue—a long, flaring dress with a plunging neckline. Ule wore mauve; a pant suit consisting of a tailored jacket with tapered leggings and high brown riding boots.

"What's this?" Bethereel dove beneath the table. Her eyes melted at the sight of two silk gloves, which she turned over in her hands several times before trying one on. Frowning, she held one up and tugged at the delicate white fabric. "My fingers are too long," she complained.

"I like your fingers," Ule whispered in her ear. She pulled the gloves free from Bethereel and slipped one on, then the other, and ran her fingers over the delicate patterns of fine silvery thread sewn into the fabric. She held them up to the last of the evening's amber light. Although they were a bit snug through the palm, the gloves fit perfectly.

"They're beautiful," Bethereel cooed. "We must thank Rozafel for her gift."

"There's no tag on the box." Ule searched the ribbon and examined it for any markings. "Are you sure they're from her?" She held up her hands again to admire the gloves in the dimming light.

"See here." Bethereel pointed to the stitching along the cuffs. "I'd recognize her feathered chain stitch anywhere. She makes her loops long and narrow." Bethereel tightened the sash high on her waist. "Hmm, come to think of it, someone could have purchased them from her, too."

"Did you see that?"

Bethereel glanced up from adjusting her dress.

Ule shook her head. "I thought I saw something. Must be the sheen in the fabric, a trick of the light."

"Come," Bethereel tugged on Ule's arm. "I'd like to eat early for a change."

Ule had grinned, goosebumps dimpling the backs of her arms, her heart quickening. In that very moment, she poured her love into Bethereel, embracing her impatience and tenacity.

In hindsight, Ule understood that moment differently. Laying on the hard stone table within the Infirmary, her body's eyes beginning to cloud, she saw clearly. The goosebumps she had experienced were not an indication of her love for Bethereel. They had been her body's warning system. An unwanted intruder had begun invading her being.

In her memory, they had hurried along the corridor, nearly knocking over residents who occupied other living quarters there. They swept down the main stairs of Kugilla Hall, dashed onto the Colonnade, and ran to the other side of the castle grounds. Her racing heart and breathlessness, the tingle in her lips, had all been the result of the poison, and she'd been infected well before dinner. Running had merely sped up its effects.

Had Ule known, she would have slowed down, enjoyed her time with Bethereel; dinner, their conversation, their lovemaking. She'd have taken the time to unwind Bethereel's braid. Everything had all happened so quickly. Instead, Ule lay immobile in the damp and cold as night passed. Nearby, Navalis sat slumped in a chair, lightly dozing.

Rage whipped through her.

It's not fair!

Navalis bolted from the chair, looking around the room for an intruder. Catching his breath, he regarded Ule. "Are you all right?" he projected.

She ignored him.

Bethee's strong, she thought. She'll grieve. She'll... fall in love again.

This notion saddened Ule. She didn't want Bethereel to move on. She didn't want Bethereel to suffer either, or be alone.

"Ule?"

I'll make her feel better. As soon as I deathmorph, I'll woo her. She'll know my love again, even if I look a little different. I... I could come back looking very similar to what I was. Or, I could be Ule's twin, a long lost sister returned to Sondshor in search of family.

"Shhh." Navalis intended to calm her, but the intrusion annoyed her.

He returned to the chair and sat there, propping up his head with a bent arm. He shut his eyes and began to breathe heavily.

When her thoughts threatened to rile her again, she focused on her Master's deep breathing, growing more grateful for his presence and the way his meditation helped ease her rage and desperation.

The first rays of dawn slipped through the cracks of the shutters, and she realized that no matter what happened in the future, her relationship with Bethereel had been forever changed.

A new sense of purpose took hold like a seed. It sprouted and grew steadily throughout the night.

I will find out who did this, she promised herself and Bethereel, so we can know the truth.

✳ CHAPTER 5 ✳

Navalis hadn't wanted to intrude on Ule's thoughts, but she'd been quietly raging. He pulled her mind inside his. At first, a roaring whisper advanced and receded, then an image came into view. Ocean waves perpetually rushed against a shoreline, and he recognized the world as one Ule had created in her youth.

A hazy lilac horizon and three white suns crowned an ocean warmed by underwater volcanoes. The vision indicated the state of the world in its infancy, before it had evolved into a terrain of cracked clay pocked with murky lakes. The land crawled with *Iilverd*, eel-like moss beasts that were evolutionary by-products from earlier creatures.

In this younger version of the world, a gaggle of avian creatures must have been nearby. He heard their separate voices caw and chatter in unison. He searched the beach and winced at the fine black sand reflecting rays of white light.

Two races of beings had populated the world then, but neither the Gypsums nor the Granites were anywhere to be seen. He wondered why Ule still clung to this younger vision of the world.

Such a shame, he thought. If Ule hadn't destroyed it, she wouldn't have been imprisoned for most of her youth.

"Quickly!"

The word cut through the shared vision. The vista dissolved and the rush of water faded into the familiar rhythm of his meditative breaths. Behind him, shuttered windows radiated with warmth from the morning sun.

Something stirred in his immediate environment. His eyes snapped open and scanned the cabinets across the room. The shelves stored jars which were crammed with pale specimens floating in amber fluid. To his left, surgical tools and vials covered several small metal tables. The medical paraphernalia remained intact, unmoved, impartial.

He'd been in this room and tents just like it far too many times during Adinav's war. Every soldier he had become was different yet ended up with similar injuries. His appreciation of the medical facility outweighed his desire to push away his memories of that time.

In the middle of the room, Ule remained on the table, her arms turned outward, her jaw slack. If he didn't know her the way he did, he'd think she looked innocent. Perhaps she had been at one time, before the Xiinisi Council locked her away in Isolation.

Her mind stirred at the disconnection between them, yet she continued to obey his instructions and prevented her thoughts from rising.

A commotion outside prompted him to stand.

Boriag ducked his head through the doorway and whispered, "Heads up! Her Holy Nightmare's a-coming."

"She's in here." Kerista's words punched the silence, arriving well before she did. "We must determine cause of death. We must squash any rumors before they breach the castle grounds."

Inside the doorway to the room, she stopped to make way for a small entourage led by Magnes Lyan, then pushed past his guards and addressed him. "Can you imagine how your opposition could spin this unfortunate event?"

Boriag began stepping backward, bringing a finger to his lips as he retreated into the hall and sneaked outside into the yard.

"People die every day," Lyan told Kerista, his tone solemn as he stared at Ule. "I don't care what my opponents think. This has nothing to do with the election."

"If she's been murdered..." Kerista's mind wandered. She, too, stared at Ule's body, eyes narrowing. She snapped her fingers at Navalis.

Unsure of her intention, he approached her.

"Was anyone in here besides you and Boriag?"

He shook his head. "Only me."

"Then you closed her eyes, did you?"

"I..." He flinched. He had, hadn't he? Impressed by her powers of observation, he began to explain. "I—"

"You took a risk at being poisoned yourself from touching her." She eyed him suspiciously.

Anyone else would have squirmed and stammered, roused to defensive anger by her accusatory tone. Navalis stayed calm despite her brashness.

"Boriag and I carried her in here," he softly countered. "Neither of us are ill."

Kerista gripped his arm. "You carried her like this." She gave a squeeze, her fingers digging deeply into his bicep. "Touching only the clothes she wears, not her flesh." She pointed to Ule's face. "*This* was a foolish gesture on your part."

If he wasn't powerful enough to unwind the very fabric of Kerista, reduce her back to a mass of black threads, he might find her intimidating. Being trapped in the world had made him anxious once. Now, knowing he could return to his realm at any time, made him feel invincible, secure. Nothing she said or did phased him.

"Hush," Lyan urged with a heavy breath. He skirted the table. "I'd do the same to keep her soul safe, until she's prepared for her journey to Mxalem."

Navalis had heard different pronunciations of the Elishian afterworld during the past century, the most common being *meez-ale-em*. The Magnes spoke it accurately—*m-zall-em*—according to Ule. She knew that language changed over time, but still insisted on referencing what she originally created. Eventually, somehow, she'd need to learn to embrace change.

Kerista winced at the name, a clear indication of her disbelief in a realm beyond their own. Navalis was relieved by her attitude, for the last person who nearly drained the world dry of natural and supernatural resources had spent over a hundred years figuring out how to punch a hole in Elish's Root Dimension.

Kerista pointed past Lyan's guards and toward the last of the entourage, an army physician. "Osblod, you must work quickly," she demanded.

Osblod was a thin older man with a mahogany complexion and a bald head heavily marked by dark scars. He pushed through the crowd, towering above everyone.

He had been a soldier during the war. His quick thinking and resourcefulness in treating the wounded had saved many lives, and predetermined his future. On several occasions, he'd patched up Navalis when he had been a Blacksmith.

Lyan backed away from the table, nearly flattening himself against the specimen cabinets. He sneered at what was about to be done to Ule. His anger and discomfort were strong.

Osblod removed a pair of thin leather gloves from the white apron he wore. They'd been treated with layers of beeswax and burnished smooth. The leather flexed and expanded, folding into fine creases at every finger joint, as he squeezed his large hands inside each one.

He raised his head slightly, gesturing toward the Magnes. "I can't work with so many here. This isn't a curio show," he complained, wedging a monocle scope over his left eye. "Please!"

Lyan waved away his guards, and they retreated into the hallway and out the main door of the Infirmary. As they bottlenecked during their hasty exit, Navalis joined them.

"Not you!" Kerista pointed at him. "Stay. Observe and learn. You will be studying the body very soon. This is a good opportunity for you."

Navalis had learned to act on impulse when opportunities arose. It was a skill he had honed while fighting a hundred-year war. When he considered Lyan's recent behavior of vetoing the decisions of some of his advisers, he saw that it was possible to undermine Kerista's authority regarding his choice of specialty, which he had declared and she quickly rejected.

"Is this to do with my specialty? Am I to study demons after all?" he asked, feigning curiosity.

Kerista blanched. Her heavily creased lips trembled. "Forgive my apprentice's lack of social propriety," she begged of Lyan.

Lyan remained pensive, then finally replied, "Under the circumstance..." He failed to finish his thought and slumped against the cabinet until

Osblod wielded a pair of scissors and began cutting along the inside sleeve of Ule's mauve jacket. Alarmed, he jolted upright and asked, "Is that necessary?"

Osblod raised his squarish head and cocked it to the side to peer around the monocle scope.

"Yes," he replied then resumed cutting the jacket sleeve along the upper arm and over the shoulder. "I've detected nothing to explain her death yet, but there may be something beneath her clothes. Still..."

He paused a moment, poising open scissors above her body. "Everyone's assumed poison but some conditions can cause seizures. She suffered amnesia for a while, correct?"

Both Lyan and Navalis nodded.

"Physical trauma to the head can cause amnesia," Osblod explained. Using his free hand, his fingers lightly brushed over Ule's brow toward the crown of her head and rested there. "The injury may have caused scarring or some other damage which now has fully shown itself. The only way to know is to look inside."

"We must know the truth," Kerista insisted. Her motives were usually political in nature, but this time she softened. "It's the least we can do to offer peace to Ethera..." She snapped her fingers. "What's her name?"

"Bethereel," Lyan answered.

"Yes, pretty girl," Kerista said. "Any word how she is?"

Eyes raw from lack of sleep, Lyan tensed. "Inconsolable."

Osblod resumed cutting and removed the jacket in pieces, carefully setting them aside on a nearby table. On the stone slab, Ule's sheer yellow camisole brightened against her pale flesh. Lyan averted his gaze, stared at the floor for a moment, as though he needed to acclimatize. When he had grown accustomed to whatever turmoil he suffered, he resumed looking at her.

"Come now," Osblod called to Lyan. "You've never been squeamish. We've seen worse."

"We're not at war," Lyan hastily countered.

"We're always at war, friend," Osblod said.

Navalis was struck by the nuanced way Osblod spoke to Lyan, as though a vein of hostility threatened to rupture their friendship.

"Especially now," Osblod continued. "Campaigning against you will be an intriguing venture, yes?"

"Not you, too," Kerista blurted. "I swear, anyone with a decent trunk of money's campaigning."

Lyan remained solemn and stared at Ule.

"I've not nearly as much as him," Osblod admitted, "but enough to persuade people, I'm sure."

As long as Navalis had known Osblod, he had possessed an awareness most soldiers didn't. Though Osblod seemed to enjoy goading Lyan about the election, he realized cutting away Ule's clothing was distressing him, so he set down the scissors and began undressing her the traditional way, beginning with her boots.

One at a time, he tugged on the heels until the stiff brown leather slipped over her feet. He thoroughly examined each foot and the insides of the boots, and still found no evidence.

Next he tended to her gloves. Her body had begun to stiffen, so when he bent an arm at the elbow, it stayed that way. He yanked at the delicate fabric covering each finger until a glove slipped free.

Blackened finger tips pointed into the air. Along each finger the black lightened into dark purple then faded to red as it approached the palms of her hands.

Osblod backed away, carefully laid the glove in a tray on a nearby table, then returned to examine the fingers. "You? You're the one to be taught, eh?"

Navalis nodded.

"What do you make of this?"

Navalis immediately recognized the condition as necrosis of the flesh. "Point of contact and entry," he answered.

Osblod shook his head in confusion. "What does that mean?"

"It's poison."

"Very good," he acknowledged Navalis's sound judgment. He carefully pulled off the other glove to discover a similar pattern of necrosis.

"What type of poison does that?" Lyan asked, pained by the sight of Ule's marked flesh.

"Venom," Osblod replied. "Someone must have milked a snake or spider and saturated the fingertips of the gloves."

"There are venomous demons as well," Navalis added.

Kerista sucked in her breath. The vein across her left temple swelled in size. If he ever needed to annoy her, he knew exactly how. For now, he contained his amusement.

"She was murdered." Lyan spoke softly, raising his head as though startled awake.

"Possibly," Osblod agreed. "I'll know more once I identify the poison. You can relax, my friend. From what I've seen, I won't need to look inside her. She'll be whole for her journey to Mxalem. Bound so tight Mneos won't be able to touch her."

After a moment of silence, Lyan mumbled, "Demons."

Kerista pinched her lips together.

"Demons," Lyan repeated. "They've been a topic of interest lately." With a huff, he addressed Navalis. "Ule was always advocating for them.

Got my advisers riled on many occasions. You're one of her sympathizer friends, aren't you?"

Navalis nodded curtly. "Not sure I sympathize with demons, but their presence is worth investigating."

Kerista tutted.

"Please!" Fatigued, Lyan struggled for strength. "I'm... curious, a quality I've learned from Ule." He addressed Navalis again. "Tell me why you think demons should be studied?"

Navalis had spent hundreds of years on Elish, hiding his true agenda which involved helping Ule restore herself. Doing so had taxed his strength, patience, and will. The stress and the risk at pretending to be something else while stealthily stalking around, working undercover, keeping track of lies and secrets, had depleted his spirit and energy. This time, he decided to hide his agenda in plain sight by having a similar one as part of his Elishian identity.

"They have abilities and powers," Navalis replied. "And we do nothing to understand these powers so we can defend ourselves." This part was, at least, why the Xiinisi had taken an interest in the phenomenon. A demon had shown itself capable of imprisoning and restricting the powers of a Xiines, as well as setting them free.

To make the subject an issue worth pursuing for the Magnes, Navalis needed to make it matter within the context of Elish. "People go missing, turn up dead, even more so since the war ended. Demons attack remote outposts and farms. There's rumor they may be uprising. Some of them don't want to return to their caves. They believe the world is just as much theirs as it is ours."

Lyan frowned deeply. His mood turned dark. "Is this how you—"

"I've heard this argument too," Osblod interjected. "I'm curious to know where you stand on this issue, Magnes, you know, for our campaigns."

"To know your enemy is to defeat your enemy," Navalis interrupted, hoping to keep Lyan focused on the topic of demons instead of the election. "Isn't that how you won the war?"

"Ever the wise one, eh?" Osblod laughed, as he resumed removing Ule's clothing, piece by piece, in preparation for the funeral rites. "What did you ever do during the war?" He craned his head to examine Navalis. "I don't see a scar on you!"

Kerista let out a long sigh, her attention focused on her charge. "This discussion is best left for after the election." Then she addressed the Magnes. "We need to determine *why* Ule was murdered. Her death may have bearing on your health and safety. You've already had two attempts on your life so far. This castle can't afford to lose you at such a crucial time. It's time to establish a lineage, not replace you with another temporary Magnes."

Lyan shuddered. "Do you think this was an attempt on my life? That the poison was intended for me and she died instead?"

"Not likely," Osblod said, removing the last piece of her clothing and examining it. "So far, the only source for the poison is the gloves. I doubt they'd fit your sausage fingers." He returned to the metal table where the gloves had been discarded and began sorting through small vials. "Her death could be a warning perhaps."

Lyan glanced at Ule's naked body. It was pale and unmarked except for her hands, and he grew uncomfortable, which reminded Navalis that he, too, should be made at least a little uncomfortable by the sight of her nakedness. As Xiinisi, he knew her well and her body was just another form, but as an Elishian, they were casual friends and nothing more.

"Perhaps the intent of her death was to weaken communications in the castle," Navalis suggested, hoping to turn the conversation.

Kerista leaned in toward him and whispered, "What are you up to?" She searched his face for clues, possibly attempted to read his surface thoughts. Pain pinched her face, and she retreated.

"She was our best translator, wasn't she?" Navalis challenged Kerista, hoping Lyan recognized his resistance to her intimidation. "Take away the one person capable of speaking to foreigners, and your leverage with the other shors is gone."

Lyan remained grim.

"Interesting idea," Osblod said. He uncorked a vial of yellow solution and dipped a fine glass rod into it. The solution clung to the rod until he dribbled it onto the white silk gloves. He directed his monocle scope toward the fabric and after a moment, he spoke. "Any of your opponents stand to gain from that. Even demons wanting to stir up fears."

Kerista whirled about. "Why do you say that?"

"The poison, it's spider venom, I think." He stood. "It's not any species I'm familiar with. There are, how would you describe it, absences in the tissue, voids perhaps?"

"I don't understand," she said, her irritation increasing. "Do you mean shadows?"

"No, there'd have to be something there to cause shadows. The solution I use enhances cellular structures. What I'm seeing?" He shrugged. "They're just little bits of... nothing."

"Let me see!" Kerista held up her hand, demanding the monocle scope. Osblod complied. She donned the equipment, began to examine the gloves, and reeled backward. The scope fell from her eye. She pressed her hands against her forehead and grimaced.

Navalis caught her, kept her upright until she regained her balance. With a moan, she pushed him away. Too proud, perhaps? Or maybe just arrogant. He couldn't tell.

"It affects perception too," she said, her voice diminished and shaky. Fear momentarily consumed her. "The distortion is... profound."

"I've never seen the likes of it before." Osblod recovered the monocle scope from the floor. "It appears only in the fingertips and nowhere else on the gloves. The poisoning was intentional, there's no doubt about that."

"I concur," Kerista said. "Given the venom's unusual quality, we need to start an investigation. We're dealing with someone who possesses great knowledge and ability, in the same league as Adinav."

"No offense to you, Kerista," Osblod interjected, his mood shifting. "We're making assumptions that her death is connected to Lyan. What if it isn't? Could be Ule has her own enemies. She was involved with Adinav, wasn't she? Perhaps she knew something and someone found out. Could be someone's protecting our Magnes."

"Enough!" Lyan's outburst shook him. He squared himself and stood tall. "It occurs to me that we know very little about Ule." His lids grew heavy. Weariness creased his brow. "Kerista, work with General Gorlen and conduct an extensive investigation of Ule and her death."

"Of course," Kerista replied. "We'll uncover the truth. You have my word. I'll instruct my best apprentices to assist me."

Lyan pointed toward Navalis, a gesture that seemed to take great effort. "Is he one of your best?"

Kerista hesitated, as though she weighed the consequences of answering yes or no. Finally, she answered, "Y-yes, he is."

"Good! Be sure he begins his studies with Osblod as soon as possible."

Navalis hid his disappointment, searching for more arguments, scheming to have his way. Before he could speak his mind, the Magnes spoke again, to Osblod this time.

"Be sure to teach Nav everything you know, everything you've learned about anatomy so he'll be properly prepared for studying demons."

Stunned by the revelation, Navalis nodded curtly. "Thank you."

Kerista's face flushed. "If word gets out we've got an apprentice studying demons, people are certain to regard the Magnes as a demon sympathizer." She addressed Lyan, her fierceness returned. "No one wants to instate a family line that associates with demons. No one will vote for you," she urged. "As sure as the sun sets, they won't."

She redirected her tenacity toward Navalis. "And nobody will be studying anything when our Magnes is no longer in power. Did you think of that?"

"His is a good idea, Kerista," Osblod defended the Magnes's decision.

"First Mbjard and now me." Frustration bloomed across her face. "Why do you undermine the wishes of your advisers?"

"Because you refuse to embrace change," Lyan replied. "The kind of change this castle needs to thrive."

In a fit of dread, Kerista closed her eyes. "Magnes—"

"Help lead the way, Kerista. Permit Navalis the opportunity to at least try. Do this willingly," Lyan suggested. "Show everyone you have the type of thinking required to push this shor into an era of abundance."

She struggled with herself for several moments then finally agreed. "Fine!" The word was sharp and final, and as soon as she had said it, she calmed and began issuing instructions.

"Navalis, as of today, you'll begin specializing in demons. All I ask is that you be discreet, at least until after the election." Then she turned on Osblod. "Election or not, you are bound by your oath to the Magnes not to divulge any of what you heard here today. Do I have your word?"

Osblod nodded. "Yes, my word."

"And you," she addressed Navalis again, "will you speak of this to anyone?"

"No, of course not," he responded.

By the way she shook her head and avoided looking at him, he knew she still disagreed with his pursuit. Perhaps when he started reporting his findings to her, she'd begin to think differently.

✳ CHAPTER 6 ✳

Ule emerged from her happiest memories to discover night sky above. The air looked thick and jaundiced, the clouds ill. Occasional tirades belted across the sky, followed by grumbles, and she was grateful the storm had the freedom to express its bitterness when she couldn't.

Light drizzle dampened the brown burlap tightly bound around her body and gusts of wind buckled the stiff fabric. Her body dipped and swayed, carried along by something firm yet flexible beneath her. A stretcher, perhaps?

Near her feet, she made out a dark silhouette: broad shoulders, sinewy arms, a glistening bald head. Osblod steered the stretcher along a foot path which wound down along a steep hill and into a small quarry.

She recognized the shadows and contours of Navalis hovering above her. His face glistened with mist and sweat, and his hair stuck to his cheeks. She was about to project her mind when she sensed someone else nearby, following close behind.

The path inclined briefly, then leveled out. Jutting from the sides of nearby hills were numerous buildings, a collage of simple square tombs and ornate crypts contrasting with the organic rock face of the hillside. The Catacomb entrances reminded her of carvings still trapped in blocks of stone, not yet fully formed, not yet freed from their source to stand on their own.

At the base of the hillside, large stone archways marked several entrances to rooms where the dead were prepared. She'd never had a reason to attend the Catacombs until now, so she wasn't sure what to expect.

The floor of the quarry had been paved with flat stones. In areas less traveled, weeds and grass poked up between them. In the middle, two rectangular fire pits glistened black, embers occasionally flaring red.

The other person who accompanied Navalis and Osblod brushed past them in a flurry of rippling teal fabric. Kerista hurried toward the first archway, where General Gorlen stood at attention waiting for her.

Wiry silver curls stuck to his forehead made damp by the light rain. His broad olive cheeks glistened. The glint in his eyes reflected a stern, bitter disposition.

Gorlen wasn't like the other advisers and generals whose authority was respectable. No, his authority made Ule's flesh crawl. Perhaps it was the kind of attention he gave her during council meetings—a casual dismissal of her intellect yet not her body. Or, perhaps his constant contact with criminals as head of the Prison and the guards had sullied his good nature. Or, because he possessed a rare power, one that when combined with the authority of the arch mystic permitted him to remove a Magnes from power if they felt the shor was suffering under his rule. Or, perhaps he was simply a cockwart. Regardless of the reason, she disliked the man.

The nearer she came to the archway, the easier it was to overhear his conversation with Kerista.

"Has anyone come? Is the wife here?" Kerista asked.

He nodded. "She's not alone," he said as he pointed inside the low archway. "Rozafel refuses to leave her side."

Ule wondered what business Rozafel had with funeral preparation or consoling Bethereel, until she remembered what Bethereel had said— the gloves had been made by Rozafel.

So she's come to gloat then, Ule thought until her logical side interjected. But why? Why would she want to kill me?

Kerista paused. "Has Rozafel done or said anything... peculiar?"

Gorlen peered over his shoulder a moment, as though the matter of her death was of the utmost confidentiality. "Under my watch, she's only made efforts to comfort the wife. Nothing more. I'll keep an eye on her, but she seems an unlikely suspect, if you ask me. She's never shown an interest in politics."

"Ah!" Kerista leaned in a little closer. "You think as I do, Ule's death has something to do with the election."

Gorlen nodded. "Someone's trying to unsettle everyone, maybe distract Lyan and anyone else campaigning for the Chair. They've done a good job of it." He grimaced. "Protos is just the beginning of a whole lot of nonsense. People'll do anything for power. Who's to say someone won't simply kill the new Magnes for the Chair once this is all over, eh?"

"A Magnes hasn't been overthrown for several hundred years," she told him. "I like to think we're more civilized now."

Gorlen lowered his voice. "We could prevent all this from happening, you and me. We declare Lyan unfit, remove him from the Chair, be done with Protos, and rule together."

Osblod and Navalis turned toward the archway. Both Gorlen and Kerista acknowledged them as they ducked to clear the top of the wide entrance and steered the stretcher toward one of several red sandstone slabs.

Kerista stood silent a moment longer, then patted Gorlen on the chest.

"I've no desire to rule a shor, my friend," she said. "I only want to hone my skills, which requires a laboratory funded by a Magnes. Besides, we don't know for sure who killed Ule or why. Until we do, we must consider all possibilities and protect Lyan's reputation."

The gravity with which Gorlen had suggested his idea melted into a loud laugh. "The criminals must be rubbing off on me."

Their words diminished in volume now that Ule was well inside the hillside, in one of the Mortuaries. Despite the low entranceway, the chamber arched high above. Chipped plaster painted long ago in bold primary colors had faded, and what remained of the mural depicted the perils and adventures of a deceased man making his journey to Mxalem, the land of the dead.

Osblod and Navalis kicked up puffs of orange clay from the hard packed ground untouched by the drizzle. Although the place had remained colorful over many hundreds of years, it lacked vibrancy.

Kerista called out to Rozafel, but the clay floor dampened her voice. "This is the time for Bethereel to tend to her wife. Now if you please?" She motioned to the door.

Bethereel, distraught and withdrawn, gaped at the unceremonious way Osblod and Navalis set the stretcher on the ground. In both hands, she squeezed a familiar blanket—the violet and white keepsake of warmth they had shared together in Eastgate.

She squirmed when they unwrapped the burlap from Ule and lifted her naked body onto a large slab of red sandstone. By the time they had each retrieved a basin filled with lavender infused water, Bethereel's eyes had stopped blinking.

Navalis set his basin of water near Ule's head and Osblod set his near her feet.

"No! Don't look!" Bethereel implored. Her arms trembled as she shook out the blanket, determined to cover Ule's body.

Navalis and Osblod both nodded once and silently retreated from the Mortuary. Ule panicked. She wanted Navalis to stay and tell her what to do next. She didn't want Bethereel to see her this way—without life, without passion.

Rozafel leaned toward Bethereel and told her, "You shouldn't cover the body. We've got to start preparing it."

Bethereel shook off Rozafel's attempt to touch her, pain and anger pinching her beauty as she forced back tears.

Rozafel rushed to Kerista as quickly as her stubby legs would permit. She leaned forward, her thick dreads bouncing all about. "See," she said, her sandy complexion flushed from the exertion. "Oh, she's a frail thing. She needs my help."

Kerista frowned. "This is the time for family to wash and seal the body, to speak their final private thoughts."

"Oh please!" Rozafel batted her eyes, waving her hands in front of her. "Oh no, no, no, I'm very close with Bethee. Very close." She stopped and lowered her voice. "I don't think she's... capable."

Unaffected by the woman's pleas, Kerista replied, "I'm sure she'll manage."

Bethereel suddenly withdrew from the sandstone slab. Hugging herself, she moaned. "She must have a dress! Yellow, like corn silk.

Like, like her hair—"

Rozafel rushed to her side and tried to embrace her. "Yes, yes, I'll make one for you," she insisted.

Again, Bethereel twisted away, not wanting to be touched. Her discomfort was evident in the shudder that wracked her body.

Yes, be cautious of her, Bethee. Ule's silent warning was interrupted again by her voice of reason. What exactly did Rozafel have to gain from my death?

Bethereel, she realized.

Rozafel pleaded with Kerista in a loud whisper. "She needs help. If I leave, will you see to it Ule's body is sealed?"

Kerista hesitated. She stared long and hard at Rozafel.

Ule sensed Kerista's mind prodding tentatively at Rozafel's mind. Her mental abilities were significantly more powerful than the last time she had used them.

Kerista's eyes fluttered, breaking her focus. Even in the dim light, her eyes grew sensitive, and she rubbed her brow to work out the pain. "Very well," she said sullenly, motioning to Gorlen.

He entered the Mortuary at her command and strode toward the slab. His knuckles popped as he squeezed the grip of his sword and awaited her instructions.

"I must tend to the apprentices," she told him. "Keep watch over these two until I return." She retreated from the cavern, orange clay swirling at her feet.

Gorlen stood watch several feet away from the slab. Even in death, his eyes roved over Ule's naked body as they had when she had been alive and clothed. Unlike other men who appreciated her beauty that way, he took no further interest in her. No other aspect of her mattered, only her body. She was insignificant otherwise. An inconvenient distraction.

Rozafel gently slipped the blanket from Bethereel's hands and set it down on a mourning bench along the wall behind them. Then she removed a spool of coarse black thread from a pocket in her skirt. "Come now, Bethee. There isn't much time." She patted Bethereel's wrist and offered her the spool.

Bethereel flinched.

Ule longed to wrap her arms around her Bethereel, whisper words of love in her ear. To caution her. To comfort her. To undo the heinous act and return their world back to the way it had been.

Rozafel would pay for what she had done.

"The needle won't hurt her." Rozafel's words failed to comfort Bethereel, and she grew a little impatient as she removed one of several fine needles stuck in the collar of her overdress.

"You must protect Ule, " Rozafel said. "See, she's curled up deep inside, frightened by what might steal her away. We must seal her now, before Mneos covers her with his shadow and sucks out her spirit, before a mystic tricks her into telling secrets not meant to be heard by the living. "

"I... can't!" Bethereel sniffed. "I don't want to ruin her beauty." She began to weep again.

Rozafel unwound the spool, using the length of her forearm to measure a piece of the black thread before cutting it on the edge of her tooth. "I'll do a nice wide feather stitch, not a boring cross stitch like others usually do. She'll be beautiful, you'll see. "

Bethereel sniffed again, dabbing at her cheeks with a yellow handkerchief. She stood back from the slab, from Rozafel too, who deftly threaded the needle.

Rozafel leaned over the body, unaffected by touching dead flesh, and began stitching Ule's lids together with staggered, hooked loops. Sweat beaded on her upper lip as she sewed with great care, dabbing at the stitches where the flesh seeped a little.

Ule cared little for the closeness of the woman and projected her perception well above the slab where she lay. Bethereel stood at a distance, hugging herself, growing paler and grimmer the more she stared at the stitches.

"It'll be pretty when it's done. Wait and see," Rozafel assured her. Bethereel's lack of response prodded her to glance upward. She ceased sewing. "What's wrong?"

On the verge of crying, Bethereel shook. "Why don't you show any remorse?" She clenched her teeth. "Did you—"

Gorlen grunted. "Come now, girls, tend to the deceased. I've no desire to spar with Mneos today." His words seemed to be intended for Bethereel, for he scanned her from head to toe.

Bethereel retreated, keeping her words and thoughts to herself. Any accusation she intended had been quashed by his intimidation. But had he meant to intimidate her, or was he cautioning her? Did he, too, consider Rozafel the murderer?

After a deep breath, Bethereel lowered her head. "I meant nothing."

"I *am* sad." Rozafel reached for her, then reconsidered. "Mostly, I'm sad for you."

Bethereel nodded, indicating she understood.

"Come, do you want to do a stitch or two?"

Hesitant at first, Bethereel took the threaded needle. Her fingers shook and the needle jabbed Ule's upper eyelid just above her lashes. Bethereel inhaled slowly as the flesh resisted at first, puckering beneath the point, and once it slid in, she held her breath. Her eyes fluttered and she began to sway.

Rozafel tried to grab her before she fell, but Gorlen lunged and caught her instead.

Ule seethed at her current state of powerlessness, and her one and only thought nearly became a projection—*Get your lecherous hands off my wife!*

She wanted to project her thoughts or rise from the slab and give the general something truly worth seeing—the animated dead. She'd scare Rozafel to death, too, for doing what she'd done. But she thought about Xiinisi laws, their codes of conduct—she'd already broken them once and suffered. She wouldn't dare do that again.

Gorlen lifted Bethereel and placed her on a mourning bench.

"Get on with it," he told Rozafel.

Nodding exuberantly, Rozafel caught the edges of Ule's eyelids and began to sew. Based on her skill, Ule knew she must have sewn the eyes and lips of many corpses. True to her word, wide feather stitches decorated each eye. Her lips, however, were sealed with a nearly invisible stitch.

When Rozafel finished, she tended to Bethereel, who had managed to sit upright. "You must whisper in Ule's ear now, tell her that her spirit is safe," she urged gently. "Then we must bathe and oil her body. Do you think you can do that?"

Back on her feet, Bethereel approached the slab. The turn of her nose and the curl of her lip reminded Ule of all the times they had tried strange, exotic food. Bethereel was disgusted by most of it, and in this moment she was disgusted by the tradition she was forced to participate in.

"You..." She licked her dry lips. "You did a wonderful job."

It was a lie. Ule witnessed Bethereel's rage—in the way it made her neck tense along the nape, how it pulled at one corner of her lips and made her hands tremble.

She leaned forward and whispered into Ule's ear. "You're safe, my love. Soon you'll be on your journey to Mxalem, where you must make space for me next to you."

The words were intended to ease the spirit of the deceased. Instead, Ule vibrated with anxiety, as Bethereel tended to the basin near her head and began to lovingly wash her body. Fear nibbled at her thoughts slow and steady.

Afterward, Bethereel rubbed Ule's flesh with lavender oil. The ointment was intended to be sacred, but Ule knew the oil helped slow down decay and the lavender kept the insects away, all for the sole purpose of preserving her in a life-like state until the funeral.

Finally, Bethereel retrieved the blanket from the bench, unfolded it, and pulled it over Ule's body, concealing her nakedness yet keeping her face exposed. They had always done so much together, mimicking and mirroring each other in many ways—

Wait! What had Bethereel said?

Ule panicked.

What had Bethereel meant by making a space for her in Mxalem? She didn't mean... She couldn't... No, not my Bethee!

Then Ule realized Bethereel was capable of anything.

Don't you hurt yourself, she warned her. Don't you die!

❋

Throughout the night the storm grumbled. Ule wallowed in its tempestuous mood, and both of them eased into a bright morning made all the more cool by Kerista's crisp orders.

At each corner of the slab a guard stood. All four of them jolted at her command.

"Clear out, all of you!"

They obeyed her, vacating the Mortuary in two by two formation, and Ule laughed at their stiffness and nervous coughs.

From the shadow of a doorway, Gorlen advanced.

Kerista frowned. "What are you doing there?"

"Patrolling the tunnels," he answered. "And the other entrances to the Catacombs and tunnels that go into the castle."

"A waste of time, if you ask me." Kerista shook her head and rubbed her neck. "Now, give me your report. Did anything happen yesterday evening?"

Gorlen relayed in detail what had happened under his watch. Ule was surprised at the accuracy of his account—not once did he exaggerate or diminish what had happened or what had been said.

Nodding every few seconds, Kerista hmmed and uh-huhed, then asked, "What are your thoughts on Rozafel?"

"Difficult to say," he replied. "She seemed more worried about the wife."

"And Bethereel, is there any reason to suspect her of Ule's murder?"

He shrugged. "She did faint at one point, but women, especially the ones from Eastgate, they tend to be good at acting, you know? Then there's that blanket. I wonder what it is she doesn't want anyone seeing on Ule's body."

Ule had known Kerista to be a pillar of reserve and stoicism. This time, something slipped through her professional facade. She sneered. It was slight and it mirrored Ule's sentiment, as well as the sentiment of many other women who had had the misfortune of meeting Gorlen.

A wave of grief doused Ule. There had been others since she gave in to the poison, smaller ones that rolled away quickly, but this wave nearly pulled her under.

Kerista suddenly peered over her shoulder. She stared at the slab. Ule worried Kerista had sensed her grief, until Kerista turned completely about, her attention gravitating toward the entrance.

Bethereel trudged under the archway. At her side, a familiar man accompanied her.

Ule climbed the wave, reaching for the man whose stories had entertained and warmed her on many a night. He had brought laughter, joy, and mystery into her world, and she loved Sabien like a brother. She reached the crest of the wave, the swell of grief diminishing.

Sabien supported Bethereel as they walked, their arms linked together. Bethereel looked paler than she had the day before. Even the basket filled with yellow fabric looked too heavy for her to carry.

Sabien's usual pinched eyebrows were relaxed for a change, and Bethereel's round joyful demeanor had deflated. At first glance, they didn't appear to be related. Sabien had black hair and Bethereel's was dark brown. He bore a cherry colored birthmark on his forehead, yet she didn't. Beyond these differences, their similarities were many: the arc of their brows, the curve of their hairlines, their gently lopsided mouths. Even the straight-backed way they walked indicated they shared the same ancestors.

"Anything you need," Sabien told her. His voice was as soothing as Ule remembered it.

"I don't want to keep you from your shop," Bethereel insisted.

Sabien's reputation for storytelling and showing strange artifacts had garnered him much success. He hadn't the need to travel with his show anymore, and his curio shop was very popular. Anyone else might have let that kind of success go to their head, but Sabien somehow managed to remain his humble self.

"I've hired someone to watch the place," he insisted. "Anything of value is on me." He patted the pocket to his blue pin-striped vest.

As they neared the slab, Bethereel balked. She tried to slow him by pulling back on his arm. "Don't. Not yet," she pleaded. She pushed ahead of him, turned and shoved Sabien backward. "Don't look at her, not until I get this dress on her." She dug through the basket, fumbled with the yellow bundle of fabric and pulled it free. Sheer and lightweight, it ran through her fingers like water.

Sabien caught the bulk of the skirt. Only the hem grazed the dusty ground, and he briskly shook the clay from the fabric.

Bethereel pouted. She snatched the dress from him. "We must get another one made." She started toward the archway, fingers clenched around the cloth.

Sabien grabbed her by the arm, turning her back around. He braced her shoulders. "Bethee." He forced their eyes to meet.

"I... " She sagged her head. "I can't breathe."

He spoke softly as he hugged her. "I know."

"I'm so tired. I haven't slept—" She collapsed against him and cried.

"Let me help you dress her," he said, guiding her back to the slab. He reached for the edge of the blanket to pull it back, but Bethereel stopped him.

"I don't want her to get cold."

Sabien scooped her hand into his and held onto her. "It'll only be for a moment. Once she sees that dress, I'm sure *she* won't mind either."

Ule longed to ease Bethereel's suffering.

Soon, she thought. I'll be there for you. It'll be another version of me, but the same, just... *different*.

A masculine voice suddenly cut through Ule's mind. There was a hollowness to it; an ethereal quality, too. The voice was disembodied, and she hadn't heard its disdain in a very long time.

"Is she dead?" it asked.

Sabien removed the blanket, folding it several times, and placed it on the mourning bench nearby. Then he gently flexed Ule's arms, testing the degree of rigor mortis remaining in her body. Carefully, he folded her arms across her chest and eased her into a sitting position.

The disembodied voice laughed, made joyful by her demise. "She is. The cow is dead. How's that for a wonderful surprise?"

She sensed the voice's proximity. She pushed her perception and found the source within Sabien's vest pocket. A stone. A kornerupine to be exact, mostly dark green except for a fine line of pink through the middle.

"Shhh," she urged.

"What? You're alive?" Istok's stammering was brief. His tone turned harsh. "Fuck!"

"There, there," she consoled him, searching for any indication Kerista was sensing their conversation, but she was far too busy speaking with Gorlen. Still, Ule didn't want to chance it. "See that woman over there? She can read people's thoughts, so stop talking!"

"What do I care?" His voice was chiding in nature, laced with malice and rage. That much about the cactus demon hadn't changed. Istok was as bitter as ever.

To this day, she delighted in remembering how she had used his submutative magic against him, beating him with his own severed arm. Magic infused spines which ran the length of his forearm had pricked his flesh multiples times and turned him into a stone.

Better him than me, she thought.

She recalled all the women he'd changed into stones and how it had taken three of his spines to kill Elishevera, her flower beast friend who was made of flesh, plant life, and stone. As she considered his brand of magic, which always turned plant life into bone, she wondered how it was possible that he, a demon that looked like a plant, had been turned into a stone. Had his magic interpreted his corporeal form in the same manner as it had hers?

The thought unsettled her, and she asked, "Why aren't you in your iron box?"

"He lets me out at times. My anger keeps people away. He likes that!"

"Sab wouldn't do that."

"Oh no? Well, maybe I'm too bulky," Istok snapped. "Maybe I clash with his vests. Who knows why that gash does what he does?!"

Incensed by the comment, she lashed out at the demon, pouring her anger into every word. "Watch your mouth!"

"I have no mouth thanks to you!"

Kerista turned abruptly.

Ule froze. She reigned in her anger. She wanted Istok to do the same. Instead, he spewed a string of profanities.

Sabien frowned and rested a hand on his chest, covering the place where the stone was. Bethereel backed away from him, visibly affected by the emotion Istok expelled.

Kerista must have felt the rage and hostility, for she approached the table cautiously, scrutinizing Sabien as he pulled the yellow dress down over Ule's torso.

"This is a difficult time," Kerista said to him. "A *sad* time."

"Yes," he agreed as he eased Ule from a sitting position and laid her back down on the table, smoothing out the dress over her belly. Next, he lifted her legs while Bethereel pulled down the skirt in the back.

"An unexpected death," Kerista continued. "The sort of death that might stir up a lot of *anger?*"

Sabien straightened to his full height and smoothed out his vest. Ule noticed his hand linger on the vest pocket where the stone lay hidden. "Yes," he said again. "It was sudden. Undeserved. I hate to watch my cousin suffer. It makes me... *very* angry."

Bethereel clutched desperately at his arm. "It tore." Her voice was plaintive, on the verge of tears again. "The dress, it tore."

"Where?" He directed her toward the slab, urging her to show him. "It's small," he told her. "We'll mend it. No one'll ever see."

Always a problem solver, Sabien's assurances calmed Bethereel. She grew even more at ease when they replaced the blanket over Ule.

Kerista retreated, overcome by a calm of her own. Satisfaction scarred her stoic expression, and Ule wondered just how much she had heard of Istok, mistaking the thoughts for Sabien's.

Tired of Istok's vileness, Ule began diminishing her perception, retreating into her dead body. She hid there, mindful of the increased cell decay, millions of cells disintegrating. Beyond her body, every now and then, she sensed the demon raging.

✳ CHAPTER 7 ✳

"I had this fantasy..."

The solemn male voice stirred Ule. She latched onto the spoken words, little hooks that reeled her beyond the confines of her body, where millions of cells congealed with one another.

"...that you knew Avn well, perhaps were related. You were similar in many ways."

A memory of her Master arose. He had worn a heavy black leather apron and cradled a horse's hoof in his lap, picking at black gunk with a small knife. As soon as the visual came to her, it slipped away again.

She transcended into the world beyond her body to see who spoke with her. Sabien stood nearby. He was alone, except for Gorlen standing in the shadows keeping watch.

Sabien's brows were furrowed again. He laid his hand against her arm, dragged his fingers over her oiled skin.

"I figured you'd been exchanging letters," he continued. "Any chance you did? Do you have them stashed away somewhere? Did you keep them from me, to spare my feelings, maybe? No? I guess not."

He waited, as though he expected her to answer. In the silence, he focused on the sleeve of her dress and began rubbing his fingers over the ridges of the embroidered edge.

The lavender shirt beneath his black vest made his olive skin glow, and Ule missed basking in his energy as much as she missed sitting beneath a midday sun. There was an effervescence about him that reminded her of her home realm.

"I never told you my private thoughts. You and I were such great friends, eh?" He crinkled his thin lips. "If not for Bethee or the desperate notion of Avn coming back, I'd wouldn't have bothered with you, I think. "

Disappointment rattled her as she considered how much she admired and cared about Sabien, only to discover he didn't share her feelings. Not keen on hearing any more, she began to withdrawn into her body again.

"But you were the last to see him and speak with him," Sabien said, then laughed. "I imagined you telling him everything I told you, that you were trying to convince him to return so we could be together again." He stopped fussing with Ule's sleeve and pressed it gently against her. "Why else would I talk to you so much? You're usually such a nuisance and a bother." He lowered his gaze to the floor. "All those questions of yours. Endless..."

Squeezing his eyes shut, he shook his head.

Though Ule was convinced Rozafel had poisoned her, she wondered if she should consider other possibilities. After hearing how Sabien truly felt, she wondered if he had any reason to hurt her.

As she was about to fully submerge into her body, Sabien's eyes glistened.

"I miss you, here," he confessed. He touched the middle of his chest, over his heart. "You silly girl."

A spark of hope stayed her. She saw the tremble in his lip when he spoke. And it pained her to see him grieve.

She didn't know what became of a person once they died, only that their energy transformed into another kind of energy, moved on to another dimension, and she wondered if they were meant to linger and hear such confessions.

In the shadows, Gorlen yawned. The sound annoyed her. He annoyed her.

Sniffing, Sabien wiped his eyes. He leaned over her and lowered his voice. "I know you can hear me," he said. "I know what you are!"

Ule shivered. How could he know she was Xiinisi? It wasn't possible, she assured herself. No one here knew, except for Istok, and he was... silenced. At least to the Elishians, he was.

"You're a stray cat Bethee brought home, and now, after all your scratching and biting and purring, you made me care for you." He shook his head. "And know this: I hate you for leaving Bethee behind and... I love you, like a sister."

An aching coursed through Ule. She tried to subdue it. Being anchored to a corpse felt too much like being trapped in a gemstone again. Anxiety churned and panic swelled. She recognized the early symptoms of cleithrophobia. Though their kind experienced many kinds of fear as they evolved during their existence, very few experienced the fear of being trapped.

She pushed her perception beyond the confines of the Mortuary and the layers of galleries within the hill and the mausoleums on top until she saw sky, pale blue and flawless, where she expanded into its openness and the anxiety began to dissipate.

✻

Ule hovered above herself. It was better than retreating into her body, where she felt alone and the need to call out to Navalis felt urgent. Besides, this way she could keep watch over Bethereel as she slept on a mourning bench, and be sure that Gorlen didn't try anything untoward with Bethereel even though Kerista stood nearby.

At the Mortuary entrance, a shadow appeared. Ule hovered high above, surprised to see Mbjard. He approached the slab. Upon passing General Gorlen, he bowed, then plodded across the ground, clay sticking to his riding boots. He wore black and gray silks embroidered with gold quills, the traditional formal robe of the scribes reserved for formal events.

Now that she had died, she wondered what words of advice he'd offer her. He had warned her after all, hadn't he? Perhaps he was her murderer, but she didn't know what he could gain from her death. The notion made her feel ill, for she deeply liked the man. While Navalis schooled her about being Xiinisi, Mbjard had taught her how to be Elishian, even though he hadn't any notion of her being something else.

Mbjard acknowledged Bethereel, who softly snored as she sat slumped on the mourning bench, her face pressed against a wooden support beam. He acknowledged Kerista, too, who stood alert and rigid on the other side of the chamber. What truly absorbed his attention was the body on the slab.

Mbjard stood a while, bowing over her. Then he lifted an arm. Ule examined the object he held. It was a long thin glass tube filled with dark black fluid, and it had a fine glass nib at one end.

"I..." Mbjard sighed, and she saw his eyes were red-rimmed as though he hadn't gotten any sleep. "I knew you weren't ready," he whispered.

Kerista stepped forward, straining to hear him.

"If only Lyan had listened." Mbjard lifted Ule's hand and gently posed the pen between her blackened fingers. Then he pulled from his pocket a length of twine and gently bound it to her.

Kerista craned to see what he was doing.

"She'll need this," Mbjard told Kerista. He stepped aside and lifted Ule's hand to show how the pen was poised to write. "For her travels to Mxalem, so she can record her adventures among the dead."

Kerista's smile failed to conceal her disgust.

Mbjard remained quiet as he gazed at Ule. She saw his lips move, and realized he was mouthing words, yet not uttering any sound. She considered projecting her mind to read his thoughts, to understand his intentions, but refrained for fear that Kerista might detect her.

Kerista stepped closer to better examine the glass pen. "Such delicate craftsmanship," she said.

Mbjard stiffened.

"The nib is as fine as a syringe needle," she praised. "How do you fill it? Such a dark ink, so similar in hue to Ule's wounds, don't you think?"

Ule didn't care for the insinuation, neither did Mbjard.

"If you would like instruction," he told Kerista, "come by the library and I'll be glad to demonstrate how to fill a pen with ink." His smile was forced. "For now, if you don't mind, I'd like to make my confession to Ule."

Kerista chuckled. "You believe in Mxalem less than I do."

Mbjard, who had always maintained a calm exterior, cracked a little under Kerista's scrutiny. "Grieving is a process," he snapped. "Literal interpretation isn't as important as people letting go of their greatest mistake or ill wishes toward the deceased, so they can feel closure.

Confession allows everyone a final chance to make their peace with the deceased. *That* is what matters. You should try it some time."

Ule had never heard Mbjard raise his voice or show irritation, even toward the most bumbling of his apprentices. She was as stunned by the outburst as Kerista, who struggled to speak yet said nothing and exited the Mortuary.

Resuming his confession, Mbjard solemnly rested his hand on Ule's forehead. "I regret," he said aloud, more for the benefit of General Gorlen. "I regret I didn't prepare you more."

Sagging slightly, he bowed his head. From his sleeve, he withdrew a small metal cap which fit over his forefinger. On the tip was a fine point of steel. Discreetly, he began scratching symbols on the inside of her wrist while continuing to speak.

"That I didn't believe in you more. I should've helped you understand."

Ule focused on his slight movements, the tics and dots and arcs and how they were connected, and recognized the writing system as an abjad of ancient Eelsee, an obscure consonant alphabet which had once thrived among criminals—thieves, murderers, and assassins.

When Mbjard had finished, he hid the needle away again. Leaning toward her, he lowered his voice. "I warned you." Then he, too, departed the Mortuary.

Ule began to decipher the tiny characters incised into her wrist. They seemed to be two statements that mirrored each other yet contained contrasting sentiments.

The only tongue you need.

Beware, the multi-tongued beast!

She didn't know what to make of it. It seemed to allude to Elishian beliefs of the Afterworld. If she had truly died and Mxalem did exist, she wondered what multi-tongued beast awaited her on the journey to the land of the dead.

The mural in the Mortuary showed no depiction of any creature with many tongues. If what Kerista said was true about Mbjard *not* believing in Mxalem, then what did the message mean and who was it intended for?

Was it a coded message to someone else, someone who robbed the dead? Did Mbjard work with criminals? And if so, had he killed her to facilitate a plot of some kind?

Ule was unaccustomed to asking these kinds of questions, and searching for answers about her murder was becoming increasingly more confusing.

❋

Ule floated high above, studying Mbjard's cryptic message and wondering what he might gain from her death, until she heard Boriag's distinctive chortle.

She looked down as he ducked into the Mortuary, Navalis following close behind. Their black leather boots had been polished, their indigo tunics washed, and their faces freshly shaved.

"You sure you want me along?" Boriag asked.

"She was your friend too," Navalis said.

Ule had many questions for her Master, but as long as Kerista was present, she had to be satisfied with their one way communication. Thankfully Kerista had responsibilities elsewhere.

Out of habitual respect, Navalis and Boriag both nodded at Gorlen, as they walked side by side toward the slab. In return, Gorlen ignored them.

Discreetly, Navalis scanned the room.

"Kerista's not here," Ule projected to him. She waited for his voice to resonate inside her skull or solar plexus, but felt nothing.

"She was a kind of friend," Boriag mumbled. He blinked lazily, as though trying to understand a complex formula. "Don't expect me to confess anything though." He pointed a long, skinny finger at her body on the table. "She already knew I thought she was weird."

Navalis nodded, stifling a smile.

Boriag loped around the table, staring down at her. "I didn't think you two were that close."

"We worked together," Navalis said. He scanned her body in a calculating way, and though he didn't have any reason to confess to her, she knew he still needed to pretend a confession, to maintain his Elishian identity.

"Huh! Why'd you never mention anything to me?" Boriag stood upright, his mouth slightly ajar. His eyes widened, making him look innocent. "Oh, you and she, together were you?"

"Not like that." Navalis sighed. "On occasion I helped her destroy some of the more complex artifacts which belonged to Adinav. We had... an understanding."

Ule remembered the times she and Navalis had worked together briefly, under the guidance of either the arch mystic or the arch scribe. They had decoded and dismantled some of the strangest inventions she had ever seen in any of their world building projects.

"Oh." Boriag shrugged. "I thought we were here to, you know, *talk* to her. And I was, you know, your look out."

Navalis frowned. "I'm making confession. It isn't a crime."

"Oh!" Boriag nodded his head and touched his nose. "Gotcha!" Leaning into Navalis, he lowered his voice. "I've got your back."

Ule shared Navalis's confusion regarding Boriag's meaning. It was as if he and Navalis were having two separate conversations.

Dampened footfalls neared the table, stirring the orange clay. Gorlen approached, a smile on his lips. "You two!" He pointed to Navalis and Ule. "Always tucked away in the shadows, some private corner. I guess there'll be no more hushed conversations between you two, eh?"

Navalis remained silent, unmoving. His stony expression refused to flinch or twitch.

"What were you two up to? Plotting to seize the Chair? Perhaps you had a secret affair. Poor Bethereel, she didn't even suspect, did she?"

Saddened by the suggestion, Ule didn't want to hear any more confessions. Navalis, Mbjard, Sabien, Bethereel... These were all people she cared for and though she entertained the possibility that any one of them could have killed her, she couldn't believe any of her theories. Perhaps she was wrong about Rozafel, too.

As she was about to retreat inside her body, Navalis responded to Gorlen's accusations.

"Jealous?"

Although Gorlen snorted, the comment riled him. "What, did your love affair go sour? Seeing Ule in another woman's arms must've spun you crazy! Enough to kill her maybe?"

Boriag gaped, first at Gorlen then back at Navalis, both horrified and amused by their conversation.

Sickened by their banter, Ule reacted defensively. Her Master would never hurt her that way. He'd done everything within his power to keep her safe and protected. It wasn't in the Xiinisi nature to destroy one another; they were creators. Punishment for forcing the end of a generation in another Xiines involved a lengthy stay in Isolation.

A slight smile curled Navalis's lip. "It wasn't anything like that."

"Then perhaps you're here to find out what she knows so far about the afterlife," Gorlen suggested. "Would be the better explanation, if you ask me, given how unaffected you were during her autopsy."

Boriag quickly defended Navalis. "He, we wouldn't—"

Gorlen addressed Boriag. "*You've* never done it before?"

"I, umm..." Boriag sagged and pointed toward Navalis. "Well I'm sure *he* hasn't."

"Hasn't what?" Navalis frowned.

Gorlen reached down and where his leggings were exposed from beneath leg plates, he squeezed the bulge of his crotch. "*Talked* to the dead."

Ule watched the expression on her Master's face. His eyes widened, only a little, enough for her to recognize he understood what was meant by the gesture. She, however, remained confused.

"And you have?" Navalis asked of Boriag.

"Y-y-yes, but it wasn't to steal secrets from the dead. I-I was... curious."

No matter how loud Gorlen howled with laughter, the Mortuary diminished its ferocity.

Boriag shrugged. "Turns out a dead one's as non-responsive as a live one." He shook his head again, the burn in his cheeks turning raw. "And so what if we want to speak to the dead. We are mystics after all. It's none of your business."

Gorlen's temper flared. "Not this one!"

"Please," Navalis interjected softly. "I just want to say goodbye to my friend."

In the silence that ensued, Gorlen retreated and stood on watch only a few feet away this time. "Go on then," he urged. "Make your peace with her."

Navalis approached the slab and stood there in silence. He bowed his head, stared at Ule for a moment, then called over his shoulder. "Isn't confession supposed to be a private matter?"

Gorlen laughed again. "If you think I'm leaving her alone with the likes of you, think again."

Ignoring them, Navalis leaned over Ule. "I miss you already," he said. "And yes, my feelings for you ran deeper than friendship."

Ule squirmed at the notion. His words felt stiff and rehearsed, and she realized they were for the benefit of those standing nearby and not her. Their lack of veracity unsettled her. She expected a better performance from her Master, so what he said next stuck in her mind.

"You're to be laid to rest in Erzo's Gallery, the one that depicts the turret reaching toward the sun. It's a perfect fit. The color of the sky in the mural matches your eyes."

He sighed deeply, feigning a morose sadness. "I miss you threefold. Not two or four or five times over. Threefold. Remember that."

He stepped away from her, bidding her a formal farewell. Boriag followed his example; his grief, although genuine, was fleeting compared to Navalis's.

She pushed her perception, following him until she'd felt her discomfort ease. Three, she repeated, something to do with the number three. She listened for any more clues to secret messages hidden in his strange, awkward performance, yet when he spoke, his tone had returned to normal, as though he hadn't been affected by grief at all.

As he and Boriag crossed the Mortuary, he asked his friend, "Have you considered dating men?"

Boriag nodded vehemently. His lips tightly pinched together, he finally let out a long whistle. "No luck there either."

* CHAPTER 8 *

Far away voices broke the silence and disrupted Ule's boredom. Beyond the Mortuary entrance, many talked at once. They laughed at times in a loose, silly manner. Someone whooped, and the sound echoed around the cavern and eventually faded. She heard music, too, in the form of soft strumming on a zither.

"What's this?" Gorlen abandoned his post by the slab. He motioned to a guard at the door. Before the guard could respond, voices flooded the room—a cacophony of slurs and laughter spurred by alcoholic fumes.

Ule projected her perception and regarded the gathering. They were familiar. Cartographers, illustrators, painters, and sculptors. Even a musician had joined them, pressing a small zither against the round of his chest, a pick squeezed between his fingers.

Artists. She'd had heated arguments with every single one of them regarding the destruction of certain artworks, mostly those depicting the Grand Magnes Adinav, who had been transformed by death into some living eternal creature. He and the devastation he had inflicted needed to be deconstructed, hidden, so no one in the future might be curious about following in his footsteps. The world's safety depended on it, and as a Sentinel to the world Elish, Ule would burn a thousand paintings of the man if she needed to.

Laere staggered forth, bits of hair stuck to her flushed cheeks. She held one arm tucked behind her back, concealing something, as she roamed the room. Finally, her gaze settled on the slab where Ule rested.

"By my eyes!" She stepped forward and lost her balance. Gorlen reached for her, but she recovered and stood upright. After inhaling a deep breath, she asked, "Smell that everyone?"

The musician strummed the zither from the lowest note to the highest. The ascending pitch echoed her question.

The other artists followed her lead and inhaled deeply. One of the cartographers gagged and complained.

Gorlen nodded toward the guard posted at the entrance, and in some secret way must have conveyed a command, for the guard exited outside.

"That," Laere pointed at Ule's body, "is the smell of rot and decay and *justice.*"

Gorlen squeezed between her and the slab. "Move along. This is no place for your celebration."

For once Ule appreciated his sentiment.

"But is this not the time for confession?" Laere asked. Leaning forward, she thumped her chest with her free hand. "I have *need* of confession."

A half dozen guards gathered at the entrance to the Mortuary, and Ule waited with great anticipation for them to escort the drunken fools away. She might have been bored, but she had no interest in listening to Laere's defamation.

Gorlen ordered the soldiers to maintain their positions, to await his command. The soldiers obeyed, standing at ease, side by side, blocking the entrance.

"Do you deny us our right to confess? To make our peace with Lyan's pet monkey?"

Gorlen smirked at the comment. "Mind your mouth." His tone remained serious. "Be respectful. That's *Magnes* Lyan to you." And he stepped out of her way. "Be quick about it."

Laere stumbled forward, her eyes glazed. She kicked up a puff of orange clay, then tried to wave it away. Her friends gathered around the slab, and she walked between them, clinging to the red sandstone until she stopped near Ule's right shoulder.

Laere tilted her head. Lips slightly parted, she raised her hand and poked Ule in the arm, just above the edge of the blanket that covered her. When she saw Gorlen was unable to detect what she was doing, she poked Ule in the arm again and smiled.

"Ah yes!" She nodded vehemently. "My confession."

The musician strummed across the strings again, this time descending the scale and lingering on the lowest string for added dramatic flair.

Laere sucked in her breath. "I confess that you, Ule, are an idiot, and I don't feel bad for saying this. *That* is my confession. I don't feel... *bad*."

The other artists clapped in agreement, occasionally patting one another on the back and laughing.

"I just feel," Laere began, but her intoxicated thoughts drifted away. She swayed a moment. "I just feel... whiskey." And from behind her back, she revealed a glass bottle filled with amber fluid.

Her friends cheered as she raised the bottle to her lips. With a jerk of her head, she downed a mouthful of the alcohol, and this cued the musician to begin a lighthearted song.

She passed the bottle along to the cartographer who had gagged earlier. "Here, drink some more," she told him. "It'll help clear your sinuses of the smell of her stupidity."

He drank deeply, then passed the bottle on to another artist.

Laere began to circle the slab again. Her eyes danced over Ule's covered body, her hands trailing along the edge of the slab.

The soft melody issuing from the zither was upbeat. The musician's thick fingers moved quickly, grazing the strings.

Ule watched Laere in return, unnerved by the woman's mirth. There was a twisted kind of joy in the delight Laere expressed, in the way she smiled, in the way she laughed. She sensed something else, and perhaps she was imagining it or being hopeful, but she detected a profound sadness in Laere she hadn't noticed before.

"I don't care if you know every language in this world," Laere began to rant. "You know *nothing* about being an artist."

Oh no! Ule thought. She couldn't be! Not Laere! Was she the one who murdered me?

Laere seemed happy enough about her death. If anyone had reason to hate Ule, she did. In fact, every single last one of the artists did. And Ule suddenly considered the possibility of all of them conspiring to poison her.

"If you knew just a little of what it's like to create," Laere continued. "The thrill of taking something, turning it into something else entirely, you'd think twice about destroying our work. The skill and labor, the *love* involved in painting, in drawing a map even." Her voice began to rise. "That portrait of Adinav was... real. The truest rendering anyone could achieve of the man, and you burned it!"

The cartographer took another swig from the bottle. He nodded silently, his face turning pale.

Laere leaned into Ule, spoke directly into her face. "You got what you deserved," she whispered. "You heard me right, you... you... *monster.*"

She flung herself backward, breaking through the gathering around the slab. She spun around and began to dance. The musician plucked the zither a little louder, his cheeks flushing from the effort.

The cartographer joined her, and together they kicked up small clouds of orange clay while they passed the bottle back and forth between them. After another swig, he buckled over and vomited onto the ground.

"That's enough!" Gorlen ordered.

The artists ignored him; the musician, too, who stumbled sideways and regained his footing without missing a note.

Gorlen motioned to the guards. Immediately they obeyed, their leather tunics rubbing against metal mesh leggings, creating a cacophony of noise that clashed with that of the merriment. They paused just inside the Mortuary, some of them squeezing the grip of their swords with anticipation.

Laere lunged toward Ule again until their faces were close. Clumsily, she climbed onto the slab and laid next to the body.

"Every piece of artwork, like..." Laere trailed off. She licked her lips as she played with the collar of the yellow dress Ule wore. "Like children, going out into the world only to get slaughtered, by *you*." She pulled hard at the collar, but the fabric slipped through her fingers undamaged.

"You're no better than Mneos snatching the souls of babies."

Your paintings aren't children, Ule thought.

Stunned by what she heard herself think, she remembered a time when she would have agreed with Laere. She, too, would have held dear every one of her creations, no matter how poorly they functioned, even the dysmutated kind. But, she had also destroyed the products of her labor simply because they had not matched her vision for them.

She had witnessed the same destruction in Laere once. When the under sketch and blocked colors for a portrait of a young boy failed to satisfy Laere's aesthetic, she took a knife to the canvas and slashed it in a fury, upsetting both the child who sat for the portrait and his parents who had been nearby.

"Get down!" Gorlen raised his hand, palm down, to signal the use of physical force without weapons. The soldiers marched into the Mortuary, their weapons remaining sheathed.

A painter screamed. Artists began shoving at the guards. The musician played on, and every now and again, a note squealed from the zither as he was jostled.

On the table, Laere clutched at Ule. "It's my confession, I can do what I like!"

Gorlen marched toward the slab, his eyes alight. A smirk tilted his mouth. He peeled Laere from the table despite her resistance, and Ule didn't understand why he found amusement in the situation. It was sad and unfortunate the artists felt this way.

Logic defied them all in their drunken state, and Laere was no different when she decided to twist her hands into the blanket to secure her position. Gorlen picked her up by the waist and pinned her against his chest. Laere held on to the blanket with all her might, dragging it with her.

Not our blanket! Ule seethed.

The blanket cleared the slab and hung from Laere's grasp, trailing in the orange clay. With her other hand, she reached out and grabbed Ule's arm, her fingers grasping at the girth of the bicep and slipping down to the wrist. Gorlen pulled her farther away from the slab, and she held on, dragging the body with her.

Gorlen set her down a moment and leaned forward to pry her hand free. She wielded the blanket like a shield, and Gorlen laughed when he bound her in it and pitched her over his shoulder. Laere, like the other artists, didn't share the same conditioning or training as the guards, except when it came to drinking, but that didn't stop them from trying.

The first to throw a punch was a sculptor. Perhaps, in her inebriated state, she believed she was invincible when she tried to drive her knuckles through the guard's metal chest plate and instead bent her wrist at an odd angle.

She buckled over and cradled her hand as it began to swell. The guard laughed at first until he saw her in pain. Overcome with concern, he inquired about her welfare, then was struck by the cartographer, who had the sense to aim for the guard's face. Regardless of how tight the cartographer's fist had been curled, he stumbled backward and clutched his hand, too. As for the guard, he remained fixed to the ground where he stood, and wiped a spot of blood from his nose.

"You're not cowards, I'll give you that much," Gorlen told Laere, as he watched other guards struggle to restrain themselves from seriously hurting anyone.

Some of the artists had wrapped themselves around a guard's torso or leg and struggled to pull them down to the ground, as if somehow lowering the guards promised the artists a better chance at defeating them.

"It's our right," Laere screamed. She kicked out her legs and tried to wriggle free from the blanket. She tried to threaten Gorlen, too. "I'll report you!" But her words were muffled by the blanket.

Ule watched in dismay as the scene unfolded around her.

The cartographer lunged forward again, his arms raised high. He'd gone manic, his hands curled into tight fists as both arms began to flail, but Ule couldn't make out what he wanted to punch. His eyes bulged. From deep down within his trembling body, he began to scream at no one in particular.

The guard with the bloody nose grabbed the cartographer by the wrist and twisted. He slammed the cartographer to the ground and pinned him there, where he struggled to pull free, then eventually gave up and laid still.

"We have rights!" Laere's shouts rose an octave. She kneed Gorlen in the shoulder.

Unaffected by the blow, he ignored her.

"Get them out of my sight now," he instructed the guards. "Lock them in the Core for the night. " He smiled, pleased by the objections he heard. "A night in Prison ought to sober all of you up."

To the guard carrying Laere, he added, "And bring back that blanket. I don't want to have to deal with the wife crying if she sees it's gone."

Among the chaos, one last attempt to fight back was made by the musician. His zither gave off strangled sounds as he swung it at the head of another guard, who deftly ducked and dislodged the instrument with a sharp blow to the musician's chest.

The zither hit the ground in an explosion of dissonant notes. A cloud of orange clay rose into the air, causing everyone to cough as they fought.

The artists quickly lost strength and energy. One by one, they were pushed and pulled and eventually steered through the exit of the Mortuary, where they ambled about stunned, bruised, and bloodied.

Gorlen handed off Laere, still wrapped in the blanket, like she was a package being delivered. While she hung off the shoulder of another guard, he pulled back her hair from her face and said, "You have the right to be drunks, but that's about all."

Laere fumed. Ule wasn't quite sure what Laere had intended when she took a deep breath and pursed her lips, hollowing her cheeks slightly.

"Don't do it," Gorlen warned her. "You'll only make it worse for yourself."

Laere swallowed hard.

"That's a good girl." He released her hair and gave the guard a final nod.

The guard ducked through the exit and joined the aerie of artists who had resorted to hurling vulgar curses instead of punches.

Inside the Mortuary, a haze of orange clay hung in the air. Gorlen returned to the slab, where Ule's upper body teetered on the edge of the sandstone, ready to spill onto the ground.

In the silence that followed, sadness overcame Ule at the unfortunate behavior of Laere. She watched as Gorlen replaced her body on the slab, adjusting her arm and head back into their previous positions. Then he coughed to clear his throat, and waited.

Once the air had cleared, he leaned over her and ran a finger across her collar bone. She wasn't sure why he did that, or why he sighed, until he stripped her down, bathed and oiled her with an unexpected gentleness. When he shook out her dress, she saw the orange fabric return to its former yellow hue.

After the slab was dusted and she was dressed again, he laid her out and straightened the fabric. He stared at her long and hard. She wanted to move, just a little, enough to spook him, but she'd just witnessed either a softer side to his personality or, perhaps, his deep fear of Kerista upon seeing the body sullied and disheveled under his watch .

He shook his head and let out a long whistle. "You sure know how to make enemies."

Yes, she thought. My enemies are many, and they're creative and resourceful and clever...

She imagined Laere siphoning venom from a spider, then soaking the fingertips of a pair of gloves in the harvested poison. She certainly had good reason to kill Ule. They didn't see eye to eye on the necessity of destroying artwork depicting Adinav. But, was Laere's malice enough to compel her to murder?

When I come back, Ule vowed, we're going to be good friends, you and I.

❋

"Leave us. "

The command was firm, absolute, far too gritty to have come from Gorlen.

Ule pushed her perception out of her body. The panorama of the Mortuary flowed through her mind until her focus anchored onto Lyan in the middle of the room. He stood several feet away, his gaze fixated on her.

Sadness dulled his eyes. His brown curls had been cropped short and his beard shaved, making him look more gaunt than usual and more battle-scarred than she remembered.

"I said, leave us."

Lyan expected his commands to be fulfilled immediately, as any Magnes should. He even gestured for Gorlen to exit, but the general joyfully disobeyed him.

Mbjard had told her about people in certain positions following *other kinds of rules*, and she wondered what privilege Gorlen possessed as head of the Prison which permitted him to disregard the command of a Magnes.

"Under the circumstances, you know I can't." Gorlen said. He shifted his weight and rested both hands on the pommel of his sword. "The body must be watched at all times. No exceptions."

"What do you expect?" Lyan snapped. "For her to rise from the dead?" The muffling effect of the room undermined the authority he projected.

"The investigation," Gorlen reminded him. "We still need to find who did this to her. And to protect her from..."

"From what?"

"There was an unfortunate incident, an attempt at vandalism," Gorlen began. "They were drunk."

Lyan strode across the room. "Yes, they were, but no harm came to Ule's body. Can't say the same for the artists."

Given the way that Gorlen smiled, Ule wondered if he was amused by Lyan's concern or, perhaps, the memory of breaking up the revelry.

"They shouldn't have resisted," he declared. "They asked for it."

"They were *drunk*."

The men stared at one another in silence. Ule waited for one of them to break the standoff. For as long as she had been at the castle, some strange hostility existed between them. She always considered Gorlen the source of their tension, since he wasn't the friendliest or most likable of men. Now that they were together, she saw how different they were.

Gorlen had a darkness to his mind. Though capable and physically strong, he lacked a luminosity—the illumination that comes from being self aware, of learning about oneself. He knew what he needed to survive and nothing more. She wondered if he had been born that way or if that awareness had been beaten out of him.

Lyan, he was capable too, and strong, yet he was always learning, about the world around him and what everything meant. He asked questions. He engaged all parts of his existence—mind, body, and spirit—and that's what made him stand apart from men like Gorlen, who valued very little of anything. Lyan had what Gorlen didn't—introspection, an awareness of being a part of a world much bigger than himself, and she admired him for this quality.

Lyan broke the silence.

"There's no doubt Ule was murdered. It wasn't a random act. She's dead because of me. In an indirect way, I'm to blame."

She hated that he blamed himself. He wasn't accountable for her murder.

"With all due respect Magnes," Gorlen said, "Ule wasn't well liked, even among the advisers. We tolerated her at most because of your... *needs*."

Lyan backed away, squaring his shoulders. His eyes darkened.

Gorlen smiled. "No matter how much you gave her... appointments, gifts, and new chambers... she loved someone else." He bared his teeth. "There were many times I wanted to remove you from power for it, but love isn't a crime now, is it? You've just as much motive to kill her as any Chair hungry adviser."

Ule resisted the gossip. She loved Bethereel, not Lyan, and she didn't want to consider that even he might have had reason to kill her.

"Go! Now!" Lyan pointed to the archway. "Before I split your skull where you stand."

A sheen of sweat broke out on Gorlen's upper lip. He clenched his hands and glared, but it failed to intimidate the Magnes. After several moments, he bowed his head.

"This threat will be noted," he said quietly. "There was a time before *she* came when you were less impulsive." He marched away and chose a post just outside the entrance, which provided him a full view of the Mortuary.

Lyan turned pensive, and after a moment, he approached Ule. The sternness in his eyes softened, his mouth remained rigid, and he sighed.

"I grew up with death all around," he began.

His voice was full and earthy, and she found herself wanting very much to hear his thoughts, but after Laere's imparting of insatiable rage, she no longer wished to be afflicted by another's bitterness. If there had been any truth to the rumors regarding Lyan's affection for her, she imagined his surpassed Laere's.

"I've watched men dismembered and gutted on the battlefield," Lyan continued. "Run down and crushed by the weight of armored horses. I've seen them bleed out and die from infection in the Infirmary. Their deaths affected me, urged me to fight in the war. Every death I saw gave me strength."

A deep sigh escaped him, deflating his rigid stance.

"But you. I've never seen anyone poisoned 'til now."

He clutched the slab, his fingers turning white as he leaned over her. His lips trembled. "Watching you die, I've never felt so helpless."

He shook his head. "I can hear Kerista now. What would the people think if they knew you made me weak? How my enemies would laugh." He chuckled. "They'd spin my weakness into their negative campaigns."

Lyan stretched his neck, making the tendons crack. She wanted to ease whatever burden made him so tense just so he might relax. Resigned to being dead, she re-examined his scars and discovered others that had been hidden beneath the beard he had worn. Most were fine faded lines, except for a thick one across the top of his throat just beneath his chin. It ran the width of his neck and was accompanied by rows of raised dots where stitches had been sewn.

"In the war, we fought for our existence in this world." He grimaced. "I didn't kill Adinav, but I fought him with every breath. Now, I fight for power, in a war against other people who have little regard for others' lives."

Reaching forward, his thumb grazed the sleeve of her dress near the edge of the violet and white blanket, which had been returned to her during in the early morning. A fold gave way under his touch, and his fingers slipped beneath the blanket and pressed against her oiled flesh.

"I'm to give your eulogy tomorrow." His eyes lowered. "What am I supposed to tell everyone? That you were intelligent and strong, courageous and vibrant. Do I say, *I loved you?*"

The confession struck Ule with a strange mingling of sadness and dread.

"Or do I say, *I love you*, because I do still love you. It's odd. My feeling hasn't gone even though you have."

His eyes roved over her features.

"You were never mine to have, I accepted that." He nodded more to himself than to her. "Know this, Ule. Many disliked you. Only a few loved you. I consider myself one of them."

She spun around in her perception, hovering slightly above her body, as Lyan leaned forward and gripped her chin.

Gorlen stormed the Mortuary. "You mustn't touch the body!"

Lyan frowned. Leaning forward, he kissed her sewn lips. It wasn't a chaste kiss or an almost kiss. His lips met hers and lingered, and for a moment, she wondered how his passion might have fired her nerve endings had her flesh been alive.

"Magnes," Gorlen blurted. "Don't give me a reason!" He leaned toard Lyan until their faces were close, and he whispered, "If not for the circumstances, I'd turn the other way and let you do what you desire, but I can't. There's an investigation—"

The kiss ended abruptly. Lyan raised his head. A ferocity sharpened his cheekbones and his chin jutted forward. He speared the general with his look. He straightened, his features ironed by righteous anger.

"What!?" Gorlen straightened, too. "Mystics are the worst for it, finding any way they can to speak to the dead."

"I'm aware of their practices," Lyan seethed. "I'm not a mystic, I'm your Magnes. Remember that."

Gorlen conceded to him. "I meant no offense."

Ule wasn't convinced. Neither was Lyan, for he crossed his arms over his chest to create a barrier between them.

"How do you expect your lineage to be instated if you can't handle such talk?" Gorlen asked.

"Words of wisdom? Coming from you?" Lyan skirted the slab, keeping a respectful distance. "A shame really," he continued. "Such intelligence gone to waste. I'm surprised you're not campaigning for the privilege of being Magnes. Oh, but then you didn't think to save your war loot, did you?"

Gorlen's face twisted, as though stung by a slap instead of words. Ule enjoyed his discomfort and expected Lyan to as well, but he departed in haste.

Gorlen began to pace the room, his arms twitching. He stopped and swiped the air with his fist. Ule imagined his invisible target was Lyan. Eventually, Gorlen's agitation calmed. He stood at the head of the slab and stared down at her.

After a moment, he said, "There are other ways to acquire the Chair." He pressed a finger against her sewn lips. "Shhh," he said. "Don't tell."

She wasn't sure what his words meant but they were certainly suspicious. Don't tell what? That he hated the Magnes? Everyone knew that. That he wanted the Chair for himself? Almost everyone wanted it. That he conspired against Lyan?

Ule considered the ramifications of such an idea. She had been Lyan's most valuable interpreter, but she had also been the object of his affection. Remove her from the picture, and Lyan is doubly struck, made weak and vulnerable during an election.

She added Gorlen to her growing list of people who had good reason to kill her.

✳ CHAPTER 9 ✳

Navalis descended the stairs toward the landing of the main floor of the Mystics Tower. He crossed the uneven slabs of gray stone and stood in the doorway, scanning the laboratory. Struck with a vision of long ago, he remembered the old tower, one quite different from what existed now.

The old tower had been circular and not as tall, and after it was destroyed by whistle bombs, the mystics abandoned the site and rebuilt a new one next to it, behind the Treasury, diminishing the field north of the castle that bordered on a woods that ran along the precipice of a steep hill. The new tower was square in structure, with rectangular extensions around its base which helped reinforce the tower walls and doubled as private laboratories on the inside.

The main table in the laboratory was longer than the old one, the workbenches wider, the bookcases taller. Sleeping chambers and the odd workspace filled the floors above, and at the very top, the new Observatory was partially domed.

Oddly, what hadn't changed in the past several hundred years were the behaviors of the mystics. They still studied long hours and pilfered elements whenever the desire struck them, cultivating their perception and their paranoia, too. Except for a pervasive melancholy due to Ule's approaching funeral, the mood was fundamentally one of inquisition and experimentation.

Navalis strode into the main laboratory and skirted the end of the long table. Near the main doors, Boriag looked up from a workbench. His eyebrows arched wide, his mouth opened. He looked as though he were about to say something but instead returned to reading his book.

Accustomed to Boriag's eccentricities, Navalis ignored him and slipped through a narrow doorway nestled between two wrought iron bookcases by the main door.

In the long, narrow room, slatted windows cast shadows, indicating the sun was at its apex. He still had plenty of time to show Kerista the laboratory he had selected for his studies. However, come morning, they were all expected to gather at the Catacombs to witness Ule's final funerary rite, after which he could resume his studies uninterrupted.

At the far end of the room, Kerista stood in front of a wide oak table before the windows. On either side of her, makeshift shelves, bookshelves, and cupboards lined the quarried stone walls.

When they last spoke, she had been reading a stack of parchments. Today, he saw racks filled with glass vials and tubes containing pale green liquids. She held up a glass tube and swirled the colorless contents. After several moments, the fluid turned pale green like the others.

He knocked once on the door frame to get her attention.

She stopped, her arm poised. She glanced over her shoulder before resuming her experiment.

"Any progress yet with the poison?" he asked.

She placed the tube in a rack and turned around. "No," she replied. The silence between them persisted, and when she spoke again, she did so reluctantly. "Can't seem to figure out the nature of the voids in the spider venom."

"About the other day, during Ule's autopsy—"

She raised her hand, and he immediately stopped talking.

"What's done is done." She tried to smile. Her lips pursed instead. "We need to discuss your methodology for studies. Please sit." She pointed to a stool near the table.

Preferring to stand, he approached her. "I have suggestions."

She glanced at the stool, then back at him again. Her cool smiled faded. She was clearly irked by his decision to ignore her, for he sensed in her whips of anger desperate to lash out.

"Since you're so anxious to start studying on demons," she said, ignoring him in return, "begin by examining their bodies first."

Her suggestion mirrored his Xiinisi mandate. At great length he had discussed with the Xiinisi Counsel what areas to focus on first. All of them— Hethn, Gur, Oaxa, and even quiet Veht—expressed their curiosity regarding the corporeal quality of demons. They agreed that in addition to learning how demon vapors were formed, they also needed a better understanding of their physiology.

"I couldn't agree more." He smiled at Kerista, hoping his charm might warm her to him again. "I've been gathering texts and anecdotal evidence—"

"Anecdotal?" She laughed. "All this push for studying demons, and you want to interpret myths and rumors? You're a mystic, not a scribe." She resumed examining the vials on her desk. "You're to acquire primary scientific data, not folk tales."

She moved gracefully, gathering a half dozen clean tubes. They chinked against one another as she arranged them in an empty rack.

"You're to begin a series of *dissections*, using your fundamental anatomy skills." She took a deep breath before continuing, and Navalis observed her sag—a moment of fatigue, or perhaps defeat.

"You're not the first to pursue this area of study," she said. "There have been others. They, too, began with anecdotal evidence, then ended up with little to show for their effort." She slid a tube into a wooden rack and faced him. "I suggest you focus on facts, not fictions. Be prepared to evolve according to the demands of your subjects. Osblod has agreed to guide you as best as he can. Just be forewarned, his knowledge is limited to people, horses, and cows."

She could have withheld the knowledge of the previous demon studies or found some way to deter him, but instead she co-operated, so he kept quiet instead of pushing further regarding his agenda.

"I'll need a demon to dissect," he said.

"One's already been caught for you. When you're ready to show me your lab, I'll have it delivered there." She turned toward a side table piled with stacks of parchment and pointed to a stack of thin leather bound books tied together with a black chord. "Those are for you."

He retrieved what appeared to be about twenty thin volumes. Familiar symbols etched along the edges of the worn covers and spines stirred memories. A name surfaced in his mind—Goyas.

He remembered the tenacious man with the long red beard. On his deathbed, he'd channelled a thought through a powerful lens and pierced the heart of the general Navalis had once been.

"These are the journals of a most prominent and powerful mystic," Kerista explained. "His methodologies are... creative. You should find his approach helpful."

He recognized some of the journals from a time when Goyas had started writing in them, back when Navalis had deathmorphed into a bird, and later a cricket, then a cat.

Goyas had displayed a thorough and meticulous manner while documenting his research and findings. Reading his notes promised to be mind numbing, but Navalis welcomed anything to help facilitate his understanding about the molecular structure and energy of demons in corporeal form.

Then he could focus on the other part of his mandate—determining if anything in the environment contributed to demons achieving solidity. Therein was the true challenge: Locating places where demons took corporeal form.

"What about the other mystics?" he asked. "I'd like to read about their findings."

She nodded at the journals he held. "Goyas makes mention of them in his journals. By all means, search for them in the Archive if you'd like, but do so on your own time, understood?"

"Thank you." He turned the bundle over in his hands, recalling when some of them had been newly bound, the dyed leather vibrant and unmarked. Now they looked worn and faded.

"I don't want you working alone on this, for your own safety," Kerista admitted. "Select someone to be your assistant, preferably an apprentice mystic of similar experience to your own; someone who you trust won't blather to others about what you're doing. Be mindful to choose someone who can stomach anatomy."

Navalis nodded in understanding, and as he was about to depart the laboratory, Kerista stayed him with a question.

"Would you do me a courtesy, since my authority doesn't seem to matter to you? Tell me your true reason for wanting to study demons."

His mandate was simple. He wanted to understand how demons came into existence and how they functioned biologically. This was his Xiinisi mandate and it was his Elishian mandate, too—they were one and the same. Though he could be honest to the Xiinisi Counsel about the reason for his studies, he hadn't given a lot of thought to what he'd tell Kerista.

Kerista's mind pulsed. Navalis felt her searching for his thoughts, and recognized her ability was improving. He forced is mind to recede. In response, hers reached a little farther, then collapsed from the effort.

She sagged against the workbench and rubbed her temples.

"During the war," he began to lie, "up near Eelsee, my parents were killed by snake demons." He grimaced for good measure. "I was lucky enough—"

"Nonsense!" Her cool exterior grew more frigid. "You may have the Magnes fooled but not me."

Shades of Goyas, he thought. She even sounds like he once did.

Her ability for Clear Sight was developing just as Goyas's had. Eventually, she'd grow more powerful, and the vulnerability Navalis had felt from being stabbed by a pin of an idea long ago returned. The anger, too. His cheeks flushed, yet he remained in control—always in control. He turned that anger to his advantage, channeled his truth into it.

"I fought a filthy cactus demon." His voice strained, holding back a torrent of true rage. "He impaled me on a tree branch." He touched his chest where the wound had been when he had been a blacksmith.

As proof, should he need to verify his story, beneath his tunic he pushed his flesh and muscle about, forming a massive scar just below his sternum. He did his best to mask the pain which resulted from manipulating his molecules so quickly.

"The demon left me there to die." He gave into his anger, played with the drama and its intensity. "Somehow I pulled myself from the branch, and just when I thought I was free, he pricked me with one of his spines."

She struggled to find her voice. She flinched, and he knew she believed him now.

"When I woke, I was something else, immobile, caged. No matter how much I begged, he wouldn't let me free, yet somehow I escaped." The anger subsided. Navalis shook his head, regaining his composure. "Demons have abilities, a kind of magic we need to understand, so we can protect ourselves."

The Xiinisi Council had agreed unanimously on this point. Even Veht, with her multitude of eager eyes, urged him to learn about demon magic, should the phenomenon occur again in another world of their creation.

"And you lived?"

"You don't believe me." He laughed. Without hesitation he slipped his tunic over his head.

"This isn't necessary," she insisted.

He ignored her, let the tunic fall to the floor. Hastily, he unbuttoned the white cotton shirt he wore beneath and yanked it opened.

She winced at the sight of the ugly scar. At first she averted her gaze, but she looked again, first at the scar and then at his face.

He took a risk projecting his emotions so whatever surface thoughts she read in his mind at least matched his words. He buttoned his shirt and gathered his tunic from the floor, quite satisfied with himself, for he had maintained his charade as an Elishian by telling the truth.

"This is why you aren't so easily intimidated," she said, softening with remorse. "You fought a demon and survived. I guess that makes the rest of us seem weak by comparison. We're just no match for you, are we?"

Navalis considered her comment. He thought of all those he had met who had possessed uncanny perception.

Almost a match, he thought and considered the strength he had encountered in Goyas, then Adinav, and now her.

He nodded and said, "Perhaps."

✳

Navalis examined the serpentine creature. The length of its tubular body filled the rusted examination table. Its flesh was covered in green scales flecked with gold and maroon, which were vibrant in comparison to the dusty chamber tucked away beneath the castle grounds.

"It's a blessing they can die," Kerista said, as she began to pace about. The heels of her boots struck the stone floor, channeling her dissatisfaction into a slow clump, clump, clump. "I can't believe this is the laboratory you chose."

The room had been plastered long ago. Deep fissures and cracks marked the sullied walls, and near the bricked up window, broken patches revealed gray stonework beneath. Along the ceiling ran clay pipes with holes, which filtered in fresh air from above.

Several stools and a table had been abandoned along one wall. He'd need more tables, a bookshelf or two, and a cupboard to store his tools. Otherwise, he was quite fine with the room.

"I'd prefer you at the old excavation, along with the others, under lock and key," she admitted. "Will this be enough space for you?"

"Yes, it'll do," he assured her and resumed examining the demon.

Near the demon's jaw, bulbous protuberances indicated the beginning formation of shoulders. From the planes and indents beneath the scaled flesh, he determined well formed clavicles, acromions, and the beginning of humerus bones.

Kerista grew more rigid the closer he leaned over the table to conduct his initial examination. He leaned forward a little further, enjoying the way she twitched.

Midway down the demon's tubular body, another set of wide, scalloped protuberances suggested a well-formed pelvic girdle, and he was eager to see if the structures beneath the flesh were made of bone or some other element.

"Very well," she said. "I'm sure there are more of those out there. Snake demons are as common as cat demons. Some of them are walkers, the ones that claim to be as old as time. Most are crawlers, like this one." She nodded toward the mass on the table. "Young enough to still look like snakes, and easy to trap."

"When was it killed? I'd like to keep notes about the rate of decay."

"Explain your reasoning," Kerista demanded.

Navalis stood upright again. "All biological matter contains energy," he began to explain. "If we can determine the rate at which decay occurs, we should be able to determine the nature of their essence, then compare it to the essence of other animals and ourselves. The color and frequency might indicate how old they were when they died, maybe even something about their magic and their origins."

Kerista nodded slowly at first, as she considered what he had said. "For the record," she said, "demons aren't similar to us in the slightest. However, your treating them like any other animal is an intriguing approach." She paced a lap around the room before continuing. "I approve, so to answer your question: The snake demon was trapped yesterday morning and brought to the castle just before breakfast."

She retreated to the far side of the subterranean room. There, she folded her arms across her chest and shivered, no doubt from the chill of being underground.

"They discovered it at the edge of a wood beyond Eastgate, near the quarry," she further explained. "They'll do their best to be swift with returning any specimens they find, but if they fail, we do have another source, but permission from the Magnes will be required, and the specimens might be... problematic."

Navalis didn't much care how they acquired the demons, as long as someone kept supplying them, and for now, he was content with dissecting the snake demon.

Kerista paused by the door. "I have instruments, designed by Goyas as a matter of fact, which measure color and frequency in the finest of increments," she told him. "Be sure to come by the lab later, and I'll have them ready for you."

"Absolutely." Navalis eyed the demon, examining its great length, which coiled once at the far edge of the table and draped over the side onto the floor.

"I must applaud your ability to look past your hatred for them, to want to learn from and understand something that caused you so much suffering."

"Everything can teach us something," Navalis mumbled, offering a Xiinisi philosophy on the issue.

"They're fear mongers!"

Kerista's harsh words broke his concentration. He gave her his undivided attention.

"They're foul!" Her cheeks and lips flushed with heat. "They slink in the shadows and for a good reason!"

Navalis retreated from the table, curious about why demons incited such a visceral rage within her. He'd witnessed a similar response in other Elishians, like Bethereel. Demons were feared and avoided and banned to the dark places. Perhaps on some level, Elishians knew demons reflected their darker aspects and couldn't tolerate what they saw.

"I hate them as much as anyone," he told her. "I feel this hatred all the time, it's difficult." He hoped to appeal to Kerista's authority through a bit of naive idealism. He was, after all, playing the part of an apprentice— young, not quite innocent anymore, struggling to make sense of the world. "Knowledge will help ease the wound, I know it."

She blanched at the suggestion. "Interesting notion," she mumbled. With a shaky exhale, she turned at the doorway. "I look forward to your first report." After a slight hesitation, she departed the room.

Navalis turned to a side table near the head of the demon, and released the buckle on a roll of black leather. He laid it out flat, unfolding the edges to reveal an assortment of fine blades and hand drills, oddly curved saws, pincers, needles, and twine.

He sensed Kerista lingering nearby, just beyond the chamber door on the stairs. He waited, hovering above the tools, admiring the pristine edge of a scalpel, until he sensed her ascend, following the slope of the steps as another presence descended. Brief, muffled words drifted through the open doorway, a gentle prelude to Boriag, who burst into the room with manic exuberance.

"Ho, there you are!" He paused in the middle of the room to catch his breath. "It's a downright maze beneath the castle, eh? Got lost twice getting here. I've not been around these sub-levels before. What do you make of the windows? Nothing but solid earth and stone beyond. Crazy, isn't it?"

"This is the original castle," he told Boriag.

"Really?!" Boriag stared around the room again.

"Yeah, before the floods filled in the area with sediment."

"And it's still holding it together," Boriag marveled. "Says something about the old architects, doesn't it?"

His gaze settled on the snake demon. "Eck!" He lifted a trembling hand and pointed. "It's so small," he whined. Squinting, he hunched forward for a closer look. "Wow, what's that smell?"

Navalis chuckled. Boriag's ramblings could be both annoying and amusing, but his keen ability for observation, lack of inhibition, and unusual loyalty to friends made him a valuable assistant. And given Boriag's comfort level around the dead, Navalis anticipated Boriag had a strong stomach for this kind of work.

Navalis raised a scalpel above the demon's chest and sniffed the air. "Smells like... moldy cheese, doesn't it?"

Boriag nodded enthusiastically. "Yeah, shades of last week's stew if you ask me. Well this certainly reeks!"

"Could be its magic scent," Navalis conjectured, lowering the blade and resting it lightly on the scaled flesh.

Boriag wiped his nose, his upper lip curled in disgust. "Can't believe you want to do this. It's so..."

Swift and assured, Navalis pressed the scalpel against the snake demon's flesh.

"Eeew!"

Navalis ignored Boriag's complaint as the blade slipped easily into the scales. Pale green fluid oozed along the incision. He wasn't sure what to expect of a demon's biological structures and examined every detail of the thick epidermis.

"Oh!" The shift in Boriag from disgust to shock was followed by a moan.

Doubt about the man's constitution halted Navalis's hand. He regarded Boriag as he began to sway slightly.

"Oh my," Boriag said, blinking profusely.

Navalis retracted the blade from the demon and rested it on the surgery table, ignoring an additional odor of vinegar emanating from the opening in the demon.

"And yet you have no qualms over bucking with a corpse," Navalis muttered.

Boriag slumped. "No! I can do this. I *want* to do this." Catching his breath yet again, he tore his gaze from the demon's body. "Maybe... if I just, you know... Don't look!"

"Hmm, maybe." Navalis pointed to a stool across the room "Sit. Before you keel over and crack your head on something. One corpse in here is enough."

Dazed, Boriag obeyed. He sat abruptly onto the cracked wooden seat. Dust jetted out from beneath him, lingered in the air a moment, then floated away. He sneezed.

"Better now?"

Boriag nodded as he wiped his nose with the sleeve of his tunic.

Navalis resumed the dissection. "Take notes. Start with a detailed physical description of the demon and a note about its magic scent."

"I can do that."

Navalis heard the crinkle of parchment, the *tink-tink* of nib against inkwell followed by scratches on paper. Once the sounds softened, indicating Boriag had relaxed into the process, Navalis focused on the snake demon.

"The epidermis is thin, soft in texture, easy to cut," he began to dictate notes. "The dermis is thick, dark gray, soft as well. There's a smell of vinegar and moldy cheese exuding from the incision. The tissues are smooth. There aren't any glands or follicles. Hold on..."

He deepened the gash and strained to see inside the cavity. The light from the crystal lantern nearby failed to illuminate the details. "There doesn't appear to be a hypodermis."

"Are there any blood vessels? 'Cause that green stuff needs to be coming from somewhere," Boriag suggested.

"Can't see any veins in the dermis yet," Navalis replied, examining how the flesh gave way to a layer of black connective tissue, which appeared like a mass of fine threads.

Navalis regarded the similarity between the black fibers in the demon and the ones his kind used to create worlds—An Energy infused with matter.

"I don't see..." Words faded from his mind as he peered into the demon.

"What? You don't see what?"

Navalis ignored the alarm in Boriag's voice.

"You know,I could be working on my strengthening potion instead of helping you," Boriag complained. "Come on, out with it."

Navalis wriggled his fingers inside the demon, slipping past the scaled outer flesh. The opening slopped and clung to him. He pushed through the black connective tissue and stopped. Though he felt nothing of substance under his fingertips, something caused his flesh to tingle, then a blast of plain jolted him.

Once the initial shock subsided, he tried to stop the searing ache but couldn't. It radiated along his arm, like hot flames licking along the underside of his flesh.

Grimacing, he reeled backward, his hand slipping free from the demon. Green fluid sprayed across the wall and floor, spattering the front of him. He bellowed and collapsed on the ground, grinding his shoulders into the wall desperate for any other sensation. His fingers flexed uncontrollably, and the scalpel fell and clattered against the stone floor.

Dimly aware of Boriag hovering nearby, Navalis cried out again, his focus dedicated to stopping the searing pain in his flesh. He pushed his body to resist the fire coursing within his fingers and arm, but it failed to respond. He flicked his hand, tried to dispel the agony with force, but the skin along his fingers and across his knuckles bubbled and bled regardless.

Boriag grabbed him by the elbow, far from his wounded hand.

As Navalis was about to try halting the relay of pain to his neurosystem, the burning suddenly stopped. He caught his breath, regained his senses. All that remained was a raw ache from the blistered skin. Shakily he stood.

Boriag's voice was unnaturally high when he asked, "What did you touch in there? Are they full of acid or something?"

"I'm not sure," he muttered.

"Enough poking around for now." Boriag urged Navalis toward the doorway. "Come on, to the Infirmary with you. See if Osblod's got anything to say about these burns. Besides, it's almost time for... you know."

Navalis regarded the snake demon for a moment, expecting something to rise or ooze from the wound. Nothing happened. As hard as he tried, he couldn't think of a reasonable explanation for what had just transpired; or why, for the briefest moment, he'd lost touch with his innate power—the ability to control and heal his body.

* CHAPTER 10 *

No one else came to confess their feelings or thoughts to Ule in the day that followed. By nightfall, the placidity of the Mortuary bored her, so she withdrew into her mind, where she mulled over past events and everyone she'd recently been in contact with.

Each of them, she speculated, had a reason to end her life. Magnes Lyan, out of spite for unfulfilled love. Mbjard, out of jealousy, maybe, or perhaps to guard a secret. Even Kerista had a motive—her pursuit of power—although what that had to do with Ule failed to make any sense. She was certain if she listed every single person she knew, she'd find some dark corner in their psyche cluttered with motives.

She became acutely aware of suddenly feeling distrustful toward everyone, a reflex of self-preservation that affected her reasoning until a vibration actually tore through her body. The sound was loud and fierce.

She expanded her perception, pushed past the decay of her body, expecting to see the worn edge of the lavender and white blanket covering her and the mural of the Gates of Mxalem above her. Instead, she discovered sky, clear and blue and real, the sun blazing white hot, indicating mid-morning.

She lifted her perception until it was high enough to see the immediate surroundings. Her body had been moved near the fire pits, not far from the entrance to the Mortuary, and by the look of the way in which many were dressed, in shades of gray, a ceremony was well underway.

She found the uplifting weather delightfully traitorous, a perfect betrayal of this sombre gathering—her funeral.

Down below, she noticed a circle of soldiers stood with their backs facing the altar where her body had been laid out. Gone was the blanket that had covered her, and since it wasn't considered apart of the death rite, she imagined it had been returned to Bethereel.

Although she was mostly cast in shadows by the soldiers surrounding her, her yellow dress shone. Indeed, engulfed in a circle of steel armor, dark leather, and shadows, her body appeared like a star in a night sky.

She listened for a recurrence of the sound that had interrupted her thoughts but heard only the crowds muttering and moving about, and the soft reverberation of a phantom noise drifting along the nearby hillside.

She pushed her perception farther and higher, until she hovered above the ancient quarry where the dead were interred. There, she waited for the sound to recur.

Her lover's sadness pulsed within her mind. She scanned the grounds and found Bethereel standing among the importants, near the entrance to the Mortuary. She tried her best to overlook Bethereel's gaunt, pale face and the unflattering slate gray dress she wore. Once tall and proud, Bethereel now appeared shriveled and diminished as she clung to Sabien, who wore a charcoal gray suit.

Ule forced herself to disengage from Bethereel's mourning, and mused over the uneven patterns in the flat stone of the ground, speculating that soil had long ago been unevenly deposited there by torrential water, possibly a flood.

At the farthest outskirts of the landscape, where steep hillsides marked with doors and stairs and tomb entrances arched around, slabs of abandoned stones poked through the ground.

Near the Mortuary entrance, she saw Lyan. He stood among his advisers yet was separated from them by his guards. He, too, seemed to be waiting, his gaze fixated on the altar where her body lay.

Ule examined her body. In the crevices made by her arms hugging her body and where her legs touched, small tokens had been placed: hand carved statues of cats and dogs, sachets of lavender, flowers and other trinkets intended to accompany her to the land of the dead. Beneath her, draped over the sides of the altar, was a large piece of brown burlap which would later be used to bind her tight.

And the crowd grew larger.

Some of Lyan's advisers directed the funeral instead of the usual clan of priests, who had fled the castle grounds several weeks ago after being caught for committing fraudulent crimes. The advisers looked nervous, and probably preferred to be with their counterparts near the entrance to the Mortuary.

Among the stoic faces of those who stood there, Kerista's and Gorlen's stood out from the others. Both were stern and alert. Occasionally, Kerista leaned into Gorlen to speak a few words, and he'd nod in return.

Nearby, Mbjard stood, maintaining a cool composure. Occasionally his lips twitched and he dabbed at the corner of an eye.

Any one of them, she began to speculate again, was capable of murder. What of Gorlen? He had always detested her. Which of the other advisers secretly hated her? There must be many, if there was any truth to what Gorlen had said.

The crowd squeezed down the path and gathered around, keeping at a respectful distance from the soldiers surrounding the altar. Within the crowd, a figure moved faster than the others. Laere barreled her way, forging a trail among the people, and Ule wondered what drove her with such haste.

Laere stopped a moment, huffed as she was forced to make way for an elderly woman who hobbled along. Craning to see above everyone, she lightly patted a sprig of lavender tucked behind her ear. Her face was pale and grim, too, as though the night in Prison had wiped the smirk from her face.

Behind Laere, a solemn Boriag loped along and when he spotted her, he called out. "Is it true?"

Laere looked back at him and glared. "Is what true?"

"That you nearly made Senaga, the old girl, piss herself with fear." Boriag matched Laere's pace. "Those portraits you stashed in the pantry made her scream something fierce. According to a baker, she swore Adinav was peering at her from behind the cheese bin. You know, we can't have her set on edge every time she's about to cook. She'll sour the pies."

The discovery of more hidden paintings came as a surprise to Ule, for she was certain she'd found them all. Laere was proving to be more prolific and slippery than she let on. Why was she so determined to preserve the memory of a monster? Did she secretly worship him and his ways? Did she want someone like him to return?

"Don't worry," Laere snapped. "They made sure to cut 'em up and burn them right before my very eyes." She returned to scanning the crowd. Her mouth twitched. "At least Ule was decent enough to do it behind my back."

Oblivious to her growing irritation, Boriag lingered nearby, moving along slowly with the crowd. "So," he said, "rumor is you spent a night in the Pit 'cause you defiled Ule's body. Is that true?"

She sneered. "Can't deny it."

He let out a long whistle. "You know, I admire a girl who can push boundaries as well as buttons. I'd love to hear all about it."

Quite suddenly Laere called out and waved at the young cartographer who had joined in the celebrations at the Mortuary. Ule searched the crowds, passing over his bruised face twice until she finally recognized him. He scowled. He slumped and ducked between two other people, rushing ahead of them. He clearly wanted nothing to do with Laere.

Both Laere and Boriag gave in to the flow of the crowd, streaming past the altar and the soldiers surrounding it, pushing toward the fire pits, where everyone took turns throwing lavender and sandalwood onto the metal grating over glowing embers. Laere pulled the sprig of lavender from her hair and threw it down on the pile of flowers.

Smoke wove in and out among the people, saturating the air with sacred scents. The Gatekeepers of Mxalem, giant lion-men feared for barring the way into the land of the dead and stranding the dead elsewhere for their amusement, were meant to be honored and subdued by these smells. That was what Elishians believed. Ule, however, knew these plants were burned as a way to mask the stench of decay, as well as prevent insects from gathering around dead flesh.

The soldiers surrounding the altar suddenly shouted out in unison. Ule recognized the strength and ferocity of the vibration. They were what she had heard earlier and what had interrupted her attempts at reasoning.

The crowds moved a little quicker now, piling into the far side of the fire pits, where the facade of the arcing hillside changed. The rock and earth looked cut and blocky, receding into long, wide steps chiselled into the steep incline of a stony hill. People gathered at the lower steps, sitting quickly to observe the soldiers around the altar.

The soldiers shouted again. Their voices thundered and reverberated along the hillside. When there was silence once more, they unsheathed their swords.

None of their blades bore the mark of Sondshor Castle on their swords. Their armor, too, lacked any distinct insignia or crest.

The strange soldiers stepped forward, brandishing their swords high above their heads. The crowd roared back in return, and she saw part of the crowd step forward carrying simple masks, some painted black, others white, and still others red or blue, the colors associated with the four beasts of Mxalem.

Ule recognized some of their faces just before they were hidden by the masks. She'd seen these men and women before, now and again, whenever she visited Eastgate for dinner and a night of entertainment with her old flat mates who were both actors. She searched for them and found them as they both donned blue masks.

There were at least thirty actors from the many playhouses in Eastgate. Those with the same colored masks came together, flailed and loped in unison, mimicking a beast.

The white beast growled and panted in the manner of a dog, and the black beast hissed and mewled like a cat. The blue masked actors swooped like a bird, moving in unison toward the soldiers, while the red masked ones slunk, the black eyes painted on the foreheads of their masks becoming more prominent as they neared the altar.

The beasts advanced. The soldiers, also actors Ule realized, fought them off on her behalf, enacting for onlookers the perils of her upcoming journey to the land of the dead, and showing what she must do to appease the Gatekeepers of Mxalem. She appreciated their fierce cries of triumph and the melodramatic moaning of each beast as it died.

The crowd remained solemn. Some people looked bored, a few exchanged jokes, others sniffed and dabbed at their eyes. She wasn't at all surprised to discover Boriag lightly applauding the performance and then stopping when mourners nearby shot scathing glances at him. Next to him, Laere stared fixedly at the altar, neither sad nor happy.

Ule had always observed the tiniest of nuances in gestures, tones, and expressions, not always understanding what was meant by them. As hard as she tried, she found it difficult to discern who cried from grief and who cried from mirth.

She always needed to disregard or overlook the constant snark, misery, and bitterness within others. She developed the skill of focusing on their positive attributes to cope. Now, she wondered if by doing so she had blinded herself to a part of reality worth paying attention to, the part where hostility lurked and dissatisfaction veiled the world in ugly, muted shades. Maybe then she could read Laere's and Boriag's moods. In actuality, perhaps Laere was cruel and beneath Boriag's silliness lurked a sad, bitter man.

There were too many suspects to watch. Overwhelmed, Ule pulled back again. Below, she was vaguely aware of Lyan addressing the crowds. His tone was eloquent and graceful, and she was certain he had said only good things about her. Something about him felt vulnerable, and she wondered if it had to do with his love for her.

Everyone grew more solemn. Many bowed their heads. As Lyan's words ended, the advisers raised their voices. The swarm of old men and women with their weathered faces began singing an ancient dirge about battling the Beasts of Mxalem, and Ule was reminded of the primary members of the Xiinisi Council.

She was responsible for imparting a memory of them into the Elishian culture. Long ago, during the early stages of Elish's evolution, she'd told many a scathing story about Gur, Oaxa, Hethn, and Veht. She had been young and angry at being condemned to half an eon in Isolation, and she made them out to be monsters. What surprised her was that her bias toward the Council had remained intact since ancient Elish. In the eyes of the Elishians, they were still monsters, but over time they had become associated with death.

Soon the crowd joined in the mournful singing. Ule watched everyone's mouths move, heard their voices crescendo, even Boriag's broken soprano. Everyone sang except for Laere, who pushed forward to the front of the crowd.

Her mouth twitched. Her eyes grew dark and glistened. At first Ule thought Laere was fixated on the altar, but now she saw—Laere focused on the importants instead. More specifically, she stared at Bethereel.

Ule's instincts kicked in. More than ever, she wanted to return to protect her Bethee.

The dirge crescendoed, signaling a group of mystics to approach the altar. Navalis led them. Usually stoic, a strange energy swept upward through his face instead of downward in the expected manner of mourning, and Ule realized he was in physical pain.

When he helped the others wrap the burlap tightly about Ule's body, leaving her face exposed, she saw his bandaged hand. She wondered how he had been injured and if the reason he hadn't mended it was because someone else had seen it happen. Still, blocking the pain was well within his ability, unless he was keeping up appearances to maintain his Elishian identity.

As the dirge ended, a few children rushed forward to slip flowers into the folded burlap around Ule's face. The same men who bound her, all mystics, hoisted her into the air. They made it seem so effortless as they carried her body on their shoulders toward the Mortuary entrance.

Ule imagined them carrying her body through the maze of tunnels deep inside the hillside, where walls were lined with mummified remains, browned and withered by time. Somewhere in a gallery, preferably one that hadn't caved in, they'd set her body on a shelf or lean her against a wall with others and bid her farewell.

Ule chose to remain outside, and began to release the tether on her perception, giving it a bit more slack. She planned to explore the tunnels and chambers of the Catacombs later. For now, she observed the crowds, searching for clues.

Bethereel fell in behind two guards, following them into the Mortuary accompanied by her cousin. A small procession followed next, led by Magnes Lyan with guards attached to him like limbs, then Mbjard and Kerista, along with General Gorlen and the advisers.

The crowd began to disperse, retreating along the path back up toward the eastern grounds of the castle.

Laere remained behind, her gaze lingering over the empty altar as she waited.

The sky darkened, clouds rolling in low along the horizon.

Bethereel emerged from the Mortuary, still accompanied by Sabien and the rest of the procession.

"Bethereel!" Laere called and rushed toward her.

The first drops of cold rain began to fall.

Leave her be, Ule nearly projected in a sudden panic.

Dazed at first, Bethereel turned. Eyes glazed, she said nothing.

"I—" Laere struggled to catch her breath as she stood before her. "I want to apologize, for what I did in the Mortuary. I—"

The slap was sudden. It stunned Ule as much as anyone else who saw it. In all the time they had spent together, Bethereel had never portrayed a violent side. Passionate, yes, but never vicious.

The slap stunned Laere, as well. She clutched her cheek. Through her fingers, a bright pink mark began to emerge.

Sabien called to Bethereel softly, tried to calm her, but she ignored him. What chilled Ule the most was the intensity of her rage, the way it both animated and stiffened her body as though she was possessed by someone else.

"P-please." The word hitched in Laere's throat. A sob began to choke her. "I didn't mean it."

"But you did," Bethereel seethed. A strangled cry erupted from her as she lunged her frail body forward. She struck Laere across the chest.

Laere pitched backward onto the flat rocks, falling gracelessly. She flinched as her hip struck the ground, and she stayed there, the rain dampening her skirt.

Sabien and a nearby retired general struggled to subdue Bethereel's flailing arms without hurting her. She cuffed randomly at the air in a frenzy until Sabien and the general secured her arms. As Bethereel grew fatigued, she slumped in defeat. Escorted on either side, she was nearly carried along the path toward the castle.

Ule had never seen Bethereel so distraught. Again, she began to question if she truly knew Bethereel as well as she had thought?

At the first rumble of thunder Laere stood, not bothering to wipe the dirt from her skirt. "I *am* sorry," she said to herself, for no one was around to hear her. "And I'll prove it." She limped back toward the castle, nursing her hip and her pride.

Ule lingered behind, struck by how genuinely remorseful Laere had been for what she had done.

No one is ever what they seem, Ule thought, as she tightened the leash on her perception and withdrew back to her body within the Catacomb, where she dwelt on the subject of perception, wondering if she could trust hers to discover the truth.

✳ CHAPTER 11 ✳

Navalis sat alone. When he had been called to the Consilium by the Xiinisi Council, he expected the others to be waiting for him in the cella, the room at the heart of the round temple-like building. There, the Xiinisi Council gathered to discuss policy, create laws, and conduct briefings, hearings and interrogations.

Navalis waited, taking turns examining the pits and cracks in the evenly spaced pillars that encircled the structure. They, like the walls and balcony were clouded with white and lined with streaks of black in the manner of marble. The building lacked windows and doors, and a roof, too. If not for the opening high above, he might have felt trapped again, the way he had for hundreds of years in the world of Elish.

Instead of sky, he looked up into an energy field that was created by the collective Xiinisi as a way to delineate their realm from the void beyond. The energy field pulsed and shimmered with thousands of colors, each representing the signature essence of a Xiines.

The idea of a sky with suns or stars or distant worlds was a construct they'd devised, a cosmic environment called a Mirari that changed to reflect how a world's inhabitants evolved in thought, awareness, and understanding as they pondered on their observations of themselves, the world they lived in, and what might exist beyond.

The Mirari extrapolated on energy emitted from nearby planets contained in their Vault, interpreting that energy into fixed pinpoints of light, something to catch the eye and excite the mind, so that one day those lights might be called stars, suns, or galaxies by the inhabitants of the worlds they had built.

For more than a hundred years, while trapped in Elish, Navalis had watched stars rake paths across the sky, counted the new ones that emerged and the constellation patterns that evolved. All that time he wished for ways to break through the illusion and Ule's accidental barrier which kept both of them trapped there, so he could return home to Xii.

Now he enjoyed the truthfulness of the energy field and the ethereal spaciousness of being Xiinisi. His heart lazily pulsed a single beat now and again, instead of a quick double heartbeat. His nerve endings were diminished, too. Had he remained humanoid and returned to Xii, the stimulation from their energy-saturated realm promised him pain more severe than what he experienced within a world.

He needed to remain alert and strong, as he tried to figure out a way to keep his thoughts separate from the minds of the Council. He searched for the best words to make *them* listen. Otherwise, his efforts and sacrifices, his reason for being in Elish would be for nothing.

He didn't want to reveal what had happened to Ule, not yet at least. Otherwise, they'd insist she return to Xii and be rehabilitated, her training as Sentinel terminated. If he opened his mind to the Council, they'd know everything, and he needed to find some way to prevent their minds from uniting.

He sensed other presences in the room. The four primary Council members shifted to transcend the walls and emerged from the shadows cast by the balcony.

On his left, a black feline creature with a mane of virescent vipers slunk toward him. Oaxa's wide, blood orange eyes blinked lazily as she sprawled across a marble bench. Her flattened triangular nose sniffed at him, long whiskers twitched, and he sensed her judgment.

Behind her, a giant white wolf padded across the floor. Gur settled onto a dais. Forked tongues slid over thick tusks curled along either side of his maw, and he stared hungrily at Navalis.

In front of him, Veht, a humanoid with a multitude of black eyes freckling her salmon pink flesh, slid onto a marble stela worn smooth from much use. With fluid grace, she crossed her legs and began examining a crimson talon with patches of tiny black eyes set into her brow and cheeks. Simultaneously, she watched him with her other eyes—those which dotted along her collarbone and her left arm.

From the shadows behind him, Hethn lurched. He was the oldest of the Council and towered over his peers. He turned his bird head and shoulders thick with indigo feathers toward Navalis and nodded. Above his pectorals, his feathers ceased, and the remainder of his form was humanoid, masculine in stature, with thick arms and legs covered in brilliant tangerine flesh.

Hethn nodded to each of his companions, and eased himself onto another marble stela. Indigo eyes specked with bronze settled on Navalis. His beak split and moved, grinding together. Words slipped through.

"In such a short time," Hethn began, his ancient voice raspy, "your mind has become sealed again. Must we pry it open? Come now, give us your report."

"Before I begin," Navalis began, his nerves on edge, "I formally request... *quarantine.*"

Gur snorted and growled. "The new rank's gone to his head."

Oaxa, orange eyes narrowing, bared a fang. Her voice calm and reasonable, she urged him to open his mind. "Come now, share your information with us."

Navalis bowed his head momentarily. "I... I might be tainted. While dissecting a demon, I came into contact with... something." He maintained eye contact with them, each in turn, hiding what he needed to behind the truth.

"What is this something? Open your mind. Tell us about the demons," Gur demanded.

Veht shifted on the stela, sitting upright. She bit her lower lip, the eyes along her arm staring at him, occasionally blinking with milky nictitating membranes instead of eyelids.

"I implore you, grant me quarantine," Navalis insisted. "Let us speak today instead of linking minds. I don't want to contaminate the collective with false speculations and uncertainty, or any other unforeseen element that is the result of recent events."

Complaints arose from Gur and Oaxa. Even Veht, who seldom spoke, tilted her head and contributed a soft lilting complaint of her own.

Hethn raised his hand. Silence settled over the Council.

Oaxa shook her head. Her mane of vipers hissed and recoiled. "He means to withhold information. He's a liar."

"I mean only to protect you," Navalis insisted. "At least until I understand more about what it is I've been in contact with. I can just as easily tell you everything with careful, reasonable words."

Hethn cleared his throat. "Am I to understand that you have some knowledge of demons already? Is this true?"

Navalis nodded, knowing what criticism awaited him as Hethn asked, "So you have discovered what environmental factors assist in their becoming corporeal?"

"My initial intent, was to study their environment. Due to circumstances, I felt it necessary to postpone this path of enquiry. I've gone ahead and dissected a demon."

Hethn frowned. "You willingly put yourself at risk by dissecting a demon without knowing something about its environment first? How can you understand your observations of their physical structure without first knowing what in their environment is stimulating their solidity?"

"I'm aware of the importance of determining their habitat of origin." He tried to assuage the Council's concern. They had, after all, entrusted him with the responsibility of studying demons. The least they could do was give him some leeway.

"If I push my agenda too far," he continued, "I may compromise my position with the arch mystic who is my superior in this world. She too wants to learn about demons, but doesn't understand the importance of my approach. She's insisting on hers."

Hethn cocked his head. His eyes blinked slowly. "You discovered something unexpected then?"

"Yes." He inhaled deeply. "I've discovered a substance. It might be another energy form." He shook his head. "Its behavior was unusual, unpredictable. Oddly, it bore a striking resemblance to..."

"To what?" Gur barked

"And you think it dangerous?" Oaxa interrupted. Her tail whipped about and curled around the base of her stela, gripping the marble stone tightly.

Navalis shook his head. "I don't know what to make of it," he replied. "There was a layer of tissue beneath the demon's skin, like... black filaments—"

"An Energy?" Veht guessed, excited by the discovery.

"Demons are solid," Gur stated. "Why wouldn't they consist of An Energy? All our creations do."

Inside, Navalis laughed at the nature of the substantiative evidence he wielded. "The An Energy doesn't behave the way this energy does," he explained. His nerves settled as he lifted his injured hand. Burn blisters had scabbed and begun to heal across his knuckles and palm, down to his wrist.

Veht covered her mouth and gasped. A patch of eyes on the back of her hand blinked in unison.

Hethn frowned, crinkling his feathered brow.

Uncertainty trembled in Veht's soft voice. "Can you heal yourself?"

"At the time of the injury, no. The energy resisted my will. Since coming here, there's been a change. I've been able to replenish the missing molecules with new ones," he answered her. "For the sake of continuity, though, I need to appear injured and heal naturally so I don't alarm those closest to me."

Gur snorted loudly. "Where exactly do your new friends think you are?"

"Visiting family."

"Of course," Hethn agreed. "Yes, we are family, aren't we?" Pensive, he stared at the wounds for several moments. "There is very little in nature that evolves without some stimulus from its environment. You must find a way to pursue this enquiry."

"I will," Navalis agreed.

"I trust your judgment," Hethn told him. "Until we know more, I grant you quarantine."

Oaxa moaned. "He'll never tell."

"There's little to report," Navalis told her. "The demons are approximating humanoid form to the best of their understanding. The ones who look the most humanoid..."

"Go on," Veht softly urged.

"They're the oldest."

By talking the matter through, he now understood what he had been observing all this.

"Time," he said, "factors heavily into their evolution. Becoming solid doesn't happen over a few days. The oldest, the most humanoid of the demons, have been walking the Root Dimension of Elish for millions of years."

Veht tilted her head. "Are you referencing Istok, the demon Ule destroyed?"

Navalis took a moment to recall his exchanges with the cactus demon several years ago. He'd twisted Istok's arm. He had heard something snap inside, just before Istok had bellowed in pain. Unlike other demons, Istok was made of something similar to bone, and he possessed something that felt like muscle beneath his flesh.

"Ule didn't destroy him," he corrected her.

Veht's eyes blinked all at once.

"She used his own magic against him," he explained. "He transformed." He expected Veht to retaliate in some way. Instead, she remained transfixed.

"So," Oaxa interrupted, "perhaps the oldest specimen of demon worthy of close examination is now a stone." She opened her mouth wide, fangs glistening, and yawned. "How unfortunate. Perhaps if he were still a demon, you'd know more about them?"

Hethn raised his voice to silence them. "We are all treading on new ground here." He stood and began to walk about the Consilium. "You say time is a key element?"

Navalis had consider the element of time, based on his observations. "Perhaps," he replied. "The specimen I dissected was very young in comparison to Istok. It was still more snake then humanoid."

"I like snakes," Oaxa commented, the vipers about her face hissed and flicked their tongues.

"Time is a product of the mind," Hethn explained. "This means demons have high functioning minds." Then, as an afterthought, he mumbled, "And powers."

He fell silent again and roamed about the Consilium with taloned hands clasped behind his back and head bowed. He passed through shadows, and when his indigo head and shoulders faded into the darkness, all that remained visible was his orange body wandering about the cella.

Eventually, he returned and asked, "Are there any other demons as old as Istok?"

"Yes." Navalis recalled one in particular, a cat demon that had helped him fight an army of the undead, watched his back, and slew Adinav. "There is one I've mentioned before, Kaleel the Rex."

"Oh yes." Gur shook his head. A growl grumbled in his throat. "A savior of despair. He's the one who harbors a death locus the size of a forest within a woods. Can all demons manipulate reality this way?"

Navalis shook his head. "I'm not certain yet. I'd like to continue with the dissections. Give me time to discover the environmental conditions for their origins. I assure you, I'll find answers."

Hethn lowered himself onto the stela and folded his hands in his lap.

"Agreed."

Gur sucked at his tusks. He cocked his head backward, snuffled. "And what of Ule?"

"Yes," Oaxa said. "How is her training progressing?"

"She's still too preoccupied with her Elishian life," he reported. "My concern is she's... lost objectivity with respect to her Sentinel duties."

Hethn mumbled, then spoke aloud. "This is a problem with our kind. Immersion. It gets the better of us when we're in a world we enjoy. It's a compulsion of curious creatures, but done too often or to obsessively, we can forget who and what we are. We've lost too many to Immersion. I hope you are taking measures to curb her tendencies."

Navalis nodded. "Yes, but it has been difficult. Recently, the arch mystic has started developing what their culture refers to as Clear Sight, just like another mystic I once knew, and Adinav. Ule and I must curb our telepathy, speak discreetly, to avoid detection."

Veht clutched her knees, patches of eyes on the backs of both hands bulged. "Should we be concerned about this mystic?"

"No," Navalis assured her. "She isn't anywhere near as powerful as Adinav, and she's certainly more reasonable than he was."

Satisfied with his answer, Veht relaxed.

"Let us end our meeting here," Hethn said. He stood and stretched, the feathers on the backs of his shoulder lifting and settling flat again.

"I expected more," Gur barked. He dropped from the stela, landing on all fours. He padded across the floor and returned to shadows, where he shifted into a ghostly apparition and disappeared through the marble wall.

"Perhaps for the next meeting, it will be safe enough for us to link minds," Hethn suggested. With a curt nod, he returned to the shadows and disappeared.

Veht returned to the north wall, her footfalls quiet, her movements fluid. She too slipped through the marble and was gone.

Only Oaxa remained.

She slipped off her stela, claws scraping against the marble floor. She slunk toward him, her orange eyes narrowed. She sneered as she peered up at him. "I don't know why you do it, or why Hethn trusts you when he knows just as well as the rest of us do. You're a liar."

"I've told the truth."

Oaxa tilted her head. "*Your* truth," she corrected him. "*The Truth* will show itself eventually." Silently she padded across the Consilium and disappeared.

What little he did tell them was the truth. Perhaps one day, he could tell them everything.

✳ CHAPTER 12 ✳

Ule remained in stasis, her energy fluctuating and surging, seeking to regenerate. The decay within her form sought transformation. Her impulse to create swelled rapidly. She fought against honoring these sensations and instead directed her focus outward.

She propelled her perception into the small gallery where she had been laid to rest. Soft blue light pulsed from crystals clustered along the base of the walls. She heard their hum, detected a residual magic scent, and knew they were the work of the mystics.

Above her, a white sun in a pale sky had been painted in tight brush strokes onto the plastered dome ceiling. The sky ended in a sharp horizon all around the room just above the stone shelf where her carefully wrapped body had been placed. Next to her, rising up along the arced ceiling and pointing toward the image of the sun, loomed a turret expressed in sharp brush strokes that threatened to conquer the sky. Up close, fine cracks marked its bronze and terra-cotta paint, making the painting look like a mosaic.

She had been interred in Erzo's Gallery after all, and although the room was older, it wasn't as old as the subterranean ones below. The room was still, and she needn't be alive to know the air was stale. Hallways twisted and turned and had been designed that way to reduce and, in some instances, prevent airflow, which helped reduce oxygen and moisture to create the perfect conditions for preserving the dead.

She remembered the repeated number three from Navalis's confession. At first she thought the number referred to three hours, but after she expanded her perception to explore the Catacombs and found no activity, she reinterpreted the number to mean three days, and hoped it didn't mean three weeks. She simply couldn't wait that long to deathmorph.

Time had reduced the other bodies around her to thick skin shrunk over bone. In some instances, the bodies were plump—the recent dead—and they appeared frozen in mid-breath.

She waited for what seemed an eternity until one evening, faint footfalls disturbed the stillness. She wondered if Magnes Lyan had come to gaze at her, or perhaps Kerista to re-examine her body for more clues.

Her Master's voice resonated deep within her solar plexus. "You've gotten too used to being comfortable."

Before she could respond, he ducked through the door of the gallery.

"I'm anything but comfortable," she projected through her mind, relieved by his presence. "My energy is about to explode."

Navalis nodded. "Before you begin to regenerate, keep in mind this time you'll be leaving behind your matter. You'll retain only your essence.

The An Energy will support your essence in the interim, you'll see, so hold off on taking a new form immediately."

She panicked. "What? Why?"

"If you deathmorph using your current molecular array, your corpse will disappear and raise suspicion. Your new form needs to be made from other harvested matter. I'll guide you, don't worry."

Ule worried anyway.

She had imagined herself returning in a form similar to what she had always been, perhaps a little taller, a little skinnier to compensate for the elongation, with tawny hair and a longer nose. Little adjustments here and there, except for her eye color.

Her eyes would always be sky blue, her Master's light green. She had no control over what hue they emitted. None of her kind did, for it indicated their signature energy which remained unchanged no matter the shape their forms took.

She reeled at the prospect of leeching elements from the environment. She had been immersed in her current molecular array since inception, having never swapped her molecules for new ones or changed her form into something else for any great length of time.

Had she not been incarcerated, she might have practiced at taking other forms the way her kind did at that age, but she had been stuck in a void and never thought to play with shape shifting. She'd only ever done it when it was necessary and returned to her preferred form as quickly as possible.

Early in life, she had aligned all her particles and molecules into a pattern that flowed with ease. Anything else had felt odd and... uncomfortable.

Now, as a corpse, her spirit flopped about like a fish lying at the side of a river. Eager for creative release, relieved to finally relinquish the state of decay, she saddened at what her Master meant by being comfortable for too long.

"Let go."

His thoughts were encouraging but she resisted, tension building within her. She had beckoned and rode the An Energy thousands of times with the power of her will, her molecular form always in tow, decreasing or expanding in tandem with whatever dimension she moved toward. How was she to release her essence without summoning the An Energy? If she let go, what would stop her from spiraling away into oblivion?

One molecule at a time, she told herself. Reluctant at first, she began disengaging from the matter of her current form. Each release felt like a whisper, a fine hair being plucked free. As the movement felt less strange, she braved the task and began to let go of millions of molecules at once. The sensation of severing caused a tide of anxiety within her. She paused, then returned to releasing the bonds a few at a time. Regaining her confidence, she released billions of molecules at once; then, in a fit of bravery, she tore free.

The An Energy rushed to engulf her. She was shocked at first by the sudden embrace. She hadn't summoned it, yet it responded as though she had.

"That's weird!"

Navalis smiled. "Without matter, in our purest state, we're something of a magnet for the An Energy. We are children of the An Energy, don't forget that."

Feeling confident, she oozed from the corpse wrapped in burlap as an amorphous mass of azure energy—her essence. The An Energy continued to surround her as she poured from the shelf and slithered across the clay ground. Glowing tentacles reached out before her as she positioned herself in the middle of the gallery. She waited there, undulating and swirling.

"Before you begin to harvest, follow me."

Her intention was to follow her Master's instructions, but elements from within the clay stuck to her, the way the An Energy had. For a moment, she worried the An Energy might abandon her, but it didn't.

Navalis motioned her toward the door. "This way, down below where the lack of oxygen stops anyone from lingering long. No one'll see us there."

She pooled around his feet and followed, the start of her next generation well underway. Although she lacked form, her inner clock had begun to count down in her current generation, and she hoped to complete deathmorphing soon, before too much time had passed.

"Avn?" She hoped he felt the depth of her conviction when she called him by his true name. "I've given much thought to what's happened. No matter what I'm to become, I need to find a way back into that castle."

They turned a corner in the narrow hallway. No crystals lit the way. Only the glow of her essence and their naturally keen perceptions guided them. She discerned a small flight of well worn stone steps and poured down them. As she did, iron and aluminum and dioxide molecules bolted toward her. Trace amounts of silicon and magnesium also adhered to her, and the An Energy continued to embrace her.

Navalis's voice soothed her creative compulsion. "Do you know who murdered you then? Are you looking for revenge?"

"No," she replied. "Nothing like that." Although she did feel a vengeful rage on occasion, she wasn't truly willing to act on it. Given the temptation in the right set of circumstances, she might. Of course, she wanted to find out who had murdered her and why. Mostly she needed to see Bethereel again.

She followed Navalis down a decline, along another passageway. He ducked beneath a small archway. The darkness made her energy look brighter even though her blueness was being dulled by churning matter—the beginnings of her new molecular array. What few molecules she possessed began to cling to one another in a familiar pattern.

"I won't keep you from pursuing your murderer," he told her. "If that's what you're up to. But you can't lose sight of your training. The castle is as good a place as any for your next generation."

"What will I learn?"

"Given what happened to you, you'll learn how to think instead of panic in unusual situations."

Nothing could be worse than what she had recently endured. She likened her experience of being poisoned to that of being transmuted into a gemstone—unique, painful, and disempowering. She felt herself agreeing with her Master's wishes for the first time. She *should* learn more self-control. Training her mind to think creatively—to think at all!—in unnerving situations was a beneficial skill to possess.

The Catacomb tunnels narrowed, forcing Navalis to turn sideways at times. The galleries grew smaller in size and changed shaped, with rooms built off of other rooms like honeycombs. And every one of them was stacked to the ceiling with withered centuries-old corpses.

"In here." Navalis ducked inside a gallery.

Ule's tendrils of energy pulled her along the ground through a doorway supported by rough wood beams. Carbon atoms flew toward her from the wood, and despite the million or so she gathered, she needed a lot more for an Elishian form and wondered how much of it was required before the luminous quality of her essence was grayed by matter.

"I'll do whatever training you require," Ule offered, "as long as I can find my killer. I've been over every detail a hundred times. I've suspected almost everyone, I even suspected Bethee. Why would anyone want to hurt me?"

Her Master laughed as he leaned against the wall near the door, stooping slightly to avoid the ceiling.

She was struck by his demeanor.

"What's so funny?"

He regained a serious composure. "There *are* plenty of reasons to kill you."

"Name one!" From the moment of her outburst, she realized she didn't want to know.

Her Master stiffened. "Political ambitions come to mind first." His jaw sharpened as his thoughts persisted within her coalescing form. "You've been erasing part of the world's history. Revisionists aren't usually well liked no matter how noble their intentions. Then there's your close relationship with the Magnes."

"You make it sound sordid. It wasn't like that."

She recalled Lyan's confession of love, which made her doubt how well she knew him. He had stopped showing romantic interest in her once she'd married Bethereel, and she had believed he had changed his mind afterward, the way so many people do when they discover they aren't desired in return.

"What's actual isn't nearly as important or interesting as what's perceived." He smirked. "And how you handle *what* people think and *how* they think will affect how well you navigate society in that castle. Remember this when you are pursuing your killer."

Her doubt began to swell, exerting an unusual effect on the infinitesimal matter which zoomed across the long, dark room toward her. Elements wobbled as they entered the horizon of her essence instead of diving directly into it. As she passed by another glowing crystal along the wall, its blue light was dimmed by her darkening energy.

"Regardless of what your relationship was," Navalis continued, "if someone wanted to hurt Lyan—"

She hovered a moment, her form bubbling into wisps which floated and lingered in the air. Time from her new generation was draining quicker than it should, and as long as she held off deathmorphing, it would continue to do so. Her compulsion to gather matter intensified. Her Master hadn't said to, not yet, but she wanted to try.

She hesitated, wondering which bodies to harvest first. They must have all lived at the castle some time long ago. So many of them packed away, nearly forgotten. There was a young boy, still wrapped in burlap, shriveled lips pulled back to reveal crooked teeth. Next to him, a woman dressed in a long fluted dress and corset lay in a provocative way; the turn of her broken hip and dark, empty eye sockets beckoned to anyone who gazed upon her.

The mummies in this gallery were very old, and Ule found their calcium resources lacking compared to the ones in the previous gallery, where the recent dead were plump with traces of hydrogen and oxygen.

Among the older mummies, she recognized a style of tunic that resembled those of the modern mystics. She stared at the slight form and its thin white beard which was loosely braided all the way down to its waist.

"He's familiar," she stated, willfully pulling carbon, calcium, phosphorous, and what sulfur and magnesium she found from what remained of the man's bones. More black filaments knitted together, and she realized that despite the new matter, she could still rearrange it into any form she desired, even her previous self.

"That's Goyas." Her Master frowned. "Magnes Fehran's Mystic from long ago. He chose not to make the journey to Mxalem, I see."

"What do you mean?"

Her Master approached the body, his flesh paler than it had been a few minutes ago. When he knelt before the mummy, his knee joints creaked.

"He isn't wrapped like most of the others." He examined the body, fully absorbed in analyzing his observations. "Not surprised. He didn't believe in Mxalem. He considered it a comfort tale more than a sacred one." He pointed to the corpse's face. "See here, he hasn't undergone the usual ceremony: Open eye sockets and mouth. Sometimes the thread gives way over time and the lips'll recede, but there's no evidence of needle marks. He wasn't sealed."

Navalis paused a moment then mumbled, addressing the corpse directly. "Why are you here, my friend, and not with the other mystics?"

✳ CHAPTER 13 ✳

What matter Ule harvested from the mystic's body moved more swiftly with every moment. Even worse, several days of her new generation had passed since they'd left Erzo's Gallery and relocated to the gallery below it.

"I don't remember much of Goyas," she projected. "He seemed kind in his own way."

Navalis glanced up from the body of the old mystic.

In the dim light, Ule detected a light perspiration across his brow as he scanned the gallery, and she realized the lack of air in the chamber was beginning to affect his body. Why was he taking so long to instruct her? It benefited them both if they hurried now.

"He doesn't belong here," Navalis said. "The corsets, the long jackets, they belong to the fashions from the latter part of Adinav's reign. Goyas died long before Adinav was born."

"A-are you saying his body was moved?"

Navalis touched the areas along the corpse's neck, where bits of mummified flesh were striated and frayed. Lost in thought, he denied her an answer.

Suddenly, Goyas sagged and crumbled into dust.

Navalis stood abruptly stood and glared at her. "What have you done?!"

Ule balked at his ferocity. "I'm harvesting matter. It started on its own, like instinct I guess, a-and it's... easy."

As she finished the last word, the corpse of the provocative woman crumbled into dust too.

"You were to take only a little bit from everywhere, to avoid complete decimation," Navalis explained. "To avoid *suspicion*."

"Who could possibly survive visiting the dead here?! I mean, look at you; you're nearly dead yourself."

Navalis grunted. "Someone is, using some kind of portable air supply." He folded his arms across his chest. "Whoever it is moved Goyas here."

He kept some thought guarded from her. She waited for him to speak again, and heard only his labored breath. His lungs failed to breathe properly, which meant his body had begun to suffocate.

"Come Nav, we don't have much time before you'll need to regenerate," she urged him. "Let me take form."

"You don't have enough matter."

"I have the same amount I had before."

"You're to be taller this time."

Ule's heart rejoiced. She wanted to be as tall as Bethee.

"Of course, and I'll be a little thinner for it. So what?"

The roiling mass of her matter sought permanent form. Edges and surfaces emerged momentarily before sinking into her essence again. About the periphery of her energy, smoky tendrils swirled about.

"Gather more," he commanded. "A little bit from everywhere, and go easy on the pillars. We don't want the room to collapse." He stopped a moment and considered the idea. "At least not yet."

Ule did as she was told, gathering more matter, waiting for her Master's cue to stop. At this rate, she'd be rather bulky or perhaps taller than Bethereel, and that might make her too distinguished, too noticeable. She wanted to be more like Navalis—vague and unassuming.

She began forming bone and ligaments, then tendons, tissue, and an outer shell of flawless skin. The black filaments knitted together until she was humanoid, the last of her molecular array solidifying. She started creating details into the form. Her hair grew long and blond. Small mounds appeared on her chest.

"Stop!"

Ule froze. "You know, with the extra matter my breasts will be more full—"

"No breasts this time."

She shook her head and leaned forward, cupping the shell of a rudimentary ear. "Sorry, what did you say?"

"You're to be my in-law," he told her. "Married to my sister until she died from a pox. You're from the North, from a merchant family who looked to expand their connections by marrying off their—"

"Daughter!" She finished the sentence she hoped he intended. "I'm to be a woman, right? Flat-chested daughter. Some of the Eelsee women are like that."

Navalis approached her and she saw his lips were tinged blue.

"You're to be my *brother*-in-law for this generation," he told her in words instead of thoughts. His lips cracked and both eyes clouded over. "As relations, no one will be suspicious of why we speak to one another in private."

"Wait! No!"

"Listen carefully," he continued. "This is your new history for your new form. Memorize it!"

Of all the variant forms she had imagined taking, she hadn't considered the other gender. Reluctant, she spoke using the voice of her form, the tone sounding hollow, neither feminine nor masculine.

"So I'm to be a-a-a *man*?" Her throat ached. She hated the idea. "What about a ghost? You were a ghost once?"

He must have expected resistance, for his response was swift and automatic. "The mystics will detect you!"

"What about a child?"

"They've very little privilege in the castle. They're expected to be naive, innocent, and are restricted from most areas."

"Not if I'm with you—"

"No, I need you as an adult, someone with intelligence and independence. Your mind is what opens doors usually shut to most."

Ule's non-distinct head reared back and she snarled. "I have no knowledge of what a man is or does!"

"Precisely," Navalis said. His muscles were growing hard from lack of oxygen. The veins in his arms were darkening and bulging too. "You said you wanted back in that castle. As a man, you'd have access to other areas you wouldn't as a woman. The inverse of this is true as well. You need to broaden your experience."

"I'll be the same on the inside, I will."

"On the very inside, yes," he agreed. "You are and always will be Ule. However, you'll perceive and experience the world through a different pattern of hormones and this will affect the expression of your character and personality."

She loathed the idea of becoming the other gender. It felt wrong. There was no way she could convince anyone she was a man, even if she possessed male anatomy.

"Now, reduce the breasts," he instructed her.

Reluctantly, she obeyed and her form responded. Mounds of fatty tissue flattened, the areolas and nipples diminished in size, and as she pushed her hormones to rise in testosterone and lower in estrogen, she grew lightheaded from the strange shift.

"Increase the pectoral mass here and here," Navalis began, touching her on either side of the chest. With his fingers, he outlined the edge of where the muscle ended on both sides of the torso.

She continued pushing her body into a fundamental humanoid male form, guided by her Master. The tilt of her pelvic girdle decreased. The flexibility in her hip sockets diminished. Her spine straightened. And when Navalis explained there need be no rules as to the size and shape of genitalia in either gender, she formed a penis proportionate to her height, straight in posture, and unblemished. Since she would be the one seeing it and handling it the most, she might as well appreciate the sight of it.

When she was finished, Navalis asked, "How do you feel?"

Ule looked down at her thick square hands and her naked athletic body, alive yet desperate for oxygen. If they lingered much longer, her new form, which felt like it belonged to someone else, would begin to suffocate, too.

"Weeeird," she responded, her voice undeniably masculine now. Her words felt harsher than she intended. She most certainly wasn't a woman anymore.

When she grew hair, Navalis explained how to shift genetic coding to inhibit its growth and mimic the men of a tribe in the North, who were known for being bald. Ule obeyed, and she shifted other genes as well, a receptor gene and a number of its variants responsible for increasing the amount of melanin within her skin. When she had finished, her flesh was a cool shade of brown, more ashen than earthy, just like Mbjard's.

As a man, she felt anchored to a massive ship that required great strength and will to steer. Her essence didn't feel big enough to fill the space within the body and maneuver it, until the perception she had been accustomed to for so long suddenly shifted. In an instant, everything around her appeared smaller and farther away.

Ule hated the way being a *he* felt—being tall and thick and heavy. Though she understood why the change was necessary, she wanted to complain.

Ule, or rather *he*, also wanted to punch something.

Navalis backed away until he was beneath the archway to the gallery.

"Have a go at that pillar, if you need to," he suggested. "Make the room collapse. This way, whoever was ingesting poor Goyas over there can't come back for more of him. If they saw his body was gone, they'd only get suspicious anyway. Oh, and be sure to run. Don't waste energy on shifting."

On peering inward, Ule was relieved to find that his inner clock had slowed down again. Satisfied, he practiced channeling strength into his fist and punched the nearest pillar with all his might. The plaster cracked and so did his knuckles. The wood beams across the ceiling groaned. Ignoring the pain in his hand, he punched a second pillar and a third and backed away, standing just within the entrance to the gallery, next to Navalis.

Pillars shifted. The ceiling buckled at one end, and thick orange dust exploded into clouds. Stone slabs and bodies from the gallery above pitched through the earth.

Ule delighted in the results of his ability, the ease with which he mustered physical strength, for the exertion required less effort than when he had been a woman.

After Navalis stepped out into the tunnel, where he began healing his body, Ule resumed his destruction. He pushed on the doorway supports until the wood snapped. The entrance to the gallery caved in with a thunderous rush.

In the settling orange dust, Ule grinned.

❋ CHAPTER 14 ❋

Navalis lingered inside Kerista's laboratory, waiting for her to comment on the sample of biological matter he had harvested from the snake demon, and hoped that what she saw might facilitate his request for another specimen.

She toiled at the far end of the room, bent over the oak workbench, where she adjusted a series of aligned concentric lenses.

He perused the nearby shelves and spied glass containers filled with fluid and strange objects. There were piles of notes and tinted lenses coated in a thick layering of dust as though Kerista had abandoned them to play with other experiments.

Quite by reflex, he scratched his injured hand. An itch persisted, and he scratched it again, curling his fingers into a fist to ease the prickle in his flesh. Although plenty of time remained in his current generation, he didn't see any need to waste more of it by healing the wound. He'd already aged enough by bringing his body back from asphyxiation, and his hand was healing well enough on its own.

He still hadn't sorted out what exactly within the snake demon's body had caused the injury, but when he resumed examining the beast, this time with a pair of leather gloves provided by Osblod, he had found deeper layers of tissue that reminded him of the black filaments his kind harnessed to create their worlds and creatures.

Demons originally began as vapors, and he wondered what had made matter stick to them. The only energy capable of doing that was the An Energy. Before he could analyze the snake demon's anatomy further, it collapsed and softened, decaying into a gelatinous green mess, which he examined on a microscopic level.

"Am I expected to see something here?" Kerista remained bent over her work table, her right eye pressed against the eyepiece of her makeshift microscope. "The voids have disappeared. Nothing is playing with my perception." She flicked one of the lower lenses out of alignment to adjust the focus.

Navalis strode toward the workbench with haste. "They have a cellular structure similar to ours," he told her.

She straightened immediately, overcome by confusion. "There's not a cell here. No structures of any kind."

A chill coursed through him. She stepped aside, permitting him to look through the eyepiece of the scope. What lines and dots he had seen before had gone. No remnant remained to indicate the cells he had seen in his laboratory less than an hour ago.

"The specimen degraded quickly," he mumbled. He stood upright and scratched his chest. "I'd like another demon."

"Another?" Kerista tsked at him, as she reached for a set of scrolls and leaned into the sunlight that streamed through the east-facing window. Instantly she looked younger, softer, malleable like gold. He knew otherwise.

"I have a theory I'd like to test," he urged, determined to bend her will to his anyway.

Her smile was grim. She began stacking the scrolls onto a high ledge of a bookshelf on the other side of the narrow room.

"Don't follow every whim," she told him. "Theories are best left to sit a while. Always, without fail, their weaknesses will show."

"Really, I'd like another," he insisted. "An older one this time?"

She laughed.

Unintentionally, he squared his shoulders. He expected a lack of cooperation from her at some point, but so soon? How could she justify withholding the very item he needed to do the dissections she insisted he do?

Determined to keep moving forward, he considered offering a compromise. "If it's going to take a while to find another, I can always go to Woedshor and investigate their libraries for stories," he suggested. "I've exhausted the libraries here."

"Again with the anecdotal evidence." Kerista's mood shifted in a heartbeat. Her eyes lost their glassy sheen. "Focus on the science!"

What the mystics did wasn't entirely science, at least not yet, but he couldn't tell her that. Before he could counter her, there was a commotion at the open door. A chink of chain mail. The scraping of thick heeled boots. A heavy breath.

Kerista winced. "Boriag, what are you doing?"

"Oh," Boriag replied. "Didn't mistake me for a guard, eh?" He winked and flashed a toothy smile, then held out a piece of parchment.

Kerista glared at him, examining him from head to toe. She stepped forward and took the parchment, glanced over it, and shook her head. "This..." She waved a hand over the mathematical formula printed there. "Has to do with strengthening metal?"

Boriag nodded, his armor chinking from the slight movement.

Kerista leaned toward Navalis and muttered, "How am I supposed to make sense of this?"

Navalis had seen Boriag's equations. To all but a few of the Masters, Boriag's mathematical and chemical expressions seemed like the rantings of a mad man, but they were actually quite advanced for an Elishian.

"If the experiment works," Navalis told her, "you can always assign the adepts to study his formula for you."

The idea seemed to please Kerista, and she addressed Boriag again. "And this..." She pointed to his armor. "This is part of the experiment?"

"Yeah." Boriag shifted in his spot, setting off a cascade of clinks in the over-sized suit of armor. "Waiting for the imbuing of my first attempt to settle. It's a guards uniform from the old days. Made of tin actually. If the imbuing works the way I hope it will, the tin won't buckle from impact. The applications could be astounding. Make our soldiers safer with better armor and shields." He looked upward, a somewhat proud expression on his face. "We could build with the treated metal too, reinforce the stonework of the castle—"

"Thank you for your insights." Kerista held up the parchment. "I look forward to perusing this."

"Hey, Nav." The visor on Boriag's helmet began to slide forward but he grabbed it before it fell shut. "There's a fella here asking for you. Wouldn't say his name. Says he's your brother, but he doesn't look a speck like you, friend."

Navalis frowned. Ule had arrived a day early. Could his Student not follow the simplest of instructions?

"What does he look like then?" Kerista asked.

"He's very, very... tall." Boriag shuffled setting off the armor again. "Oh, and he's as dark as night and Nav's about ten shades lighter than a green olive. You really need to get out in the sun more."

Navalis folded his arms across his chest and frowned. "Sounds like my brother-in-law."

"Has he traveled far?" Kerista asked him, her face softening.

Navalis nodded.

"Must be important," she said, then ordered Boriag to fetch the man.

Instantly, Boriag played the part of a guard rather than an eccentric mystic. He turned on the spot and waved frantically, setting off a rattling with his armor that incurred a series of complaints from the main laboratory: *What's that awful noise? Boriag, you cow's tit. Shuuutuuup!*

A dark shadow towered next to Boriag and looked about anxiously. Ule was taller than Navalis remembered, until he realized Ule's form had lost some girth and muscle mass, which created the optical illusion of a longer body. Ule definitely looked more effeminate since the last time they spoke.

With a shaky hand, Ule swiped the baldness of his head. He looked into the room, ducking through the doorway. "Brother!"

Navalis noted Ule's anxious twitches, the nervous glance, and the way his body froze at the sight of Kerista. His discomfort in the new masculine form was evident.

Kerista stepped forward. "I'm the arch mystic. It's always a pleasure to meet the family of my apprentices and adepts."

"Hi—" Ule coughed to clear his throat. "I-I'm Ul—"

Navalis bit his lip at the error. He had given Ule another name, made him repeat it several times.

"Ul?" Kerista squinted her eyes, waiting for a response.

Navalis recognized her expression. She was suspicious and did what any perceptive mystic with any degree of ability would do—she began to prod his mind, searching for his surface thoughts, except she stopped as soon as she started. No pain, no exhaustion, just defeated as though the ability was inaccessible.

"It's Ulmaen," Navalis told her. "Being at the castle must have his brain addled." He hoped Ule would pick up on the suggestion to explain his behavior.

Ulmaen cautiously nodded his head. "So many people here." Wiping his hand on his shirt, he extended his hand toward Kerista. "My name's Ulmaen."

Smiling weakly, Kerista extended hers. When they shook, she winced and pulled her hand free, shaking it vigorously.

"So sorry." Ulmaen nearly knelt on the ground before her. "Don't know my own strength."

Navalis detected a much higher tone in Ulmaen's voice than what he last remembered, and he speculated that Ulmaen's hormones were in the process of shifting back to being estrogen dominant.

"Brother, if you didn't come here to cripple my superior, then why are you here?"

"Huh? Oh! Your sister!"

At last, perhaps his Student remembered something of what they had discussed. "What about her? It's been less than a year since your wedding. Is she complaining about how no good you are already?"

"Ah... no!" Ulmaen stopped and wiped his bald head. "Nothing like that. I... it's um... bad news."

Navalis smirked. Ulmaen's acting was horrible. "How bad could it be? Did my sister kick you out of the house? What'd you do?"

"S-she's dead." Ulmaen's nerves eased at the announcement.

Boriag gasped, and his chain mail lightly clanked.

"A pox got her," Ulmaen explained.

Navalis grew silent, just as he had practiced—a blank look, to depict his shock at the news, followed by a deep sigh.

Kerista approached him, arms folded in front of her. "My condolences," she told him. "Perhaps you two should speak in private."

He nodded, his solemn expression masking his irritation. He urged Ulmaen from the room, and as Boriag shifted aside to clear their pathway, he set up a clatter.

Once outside, Navalis and Ulmaen walked side by side through the grassy field, distancing themselves from the Mystics Tower. To the north, the woods concealed the steep hillside and the paths which led down into the old quarry as well as toward the Catacombs.

Out of earshot of anyone, Navalis leaned toward Ulmaen. "Your temperament and personality are too fluid for your own good," he said.

"What's that supposed to mean?"

Navalis remembered an instance from several years ago, when he had watched Ule deathmorph, moving from one form to a new one without the need to revert back to an immaterial state. The ability to shape-shift like this was rare. Ulmaen was doing it again, subconsciously.

"You've lost muscle mass," Navalis explained.

"Oh, I hadn't noticed."

Navalis quieted as the clatter of armor filled the air. He looked over his shoulder and spied Boriag walking with great difficulty into the middle of the field. Nearby, two adept mystics walked side by side and upon noticing Boriag, both shook their heads.

"Your hormones are shifting back to a feminine state," Navalis continued. He directed Ulmaen farther away from the tower to be certain no one overheard their conversation. "I can hear it in your voice, see it in the way you move."

"It's difficult," Ulmaen complained. "I'm used to moving in a certain way. Generally, I'm accustomed to my arms laying flush against my torso and my knees pointing forward when I walk. Then there's the swing of my hips. Oh, and crossing my legs when I sit is impossible now on account of the new parts. I could go on."

"There are physical restrictions in both gender forms," Navalis explained. "You observed the other day in the Catacombs what having increased physical strength can feel like."

Ulmaen's face relaxed at the memory.

"Yeah, but I feel like a rock *all the time.*" Ulmaen snorted. "And the last time I was an actual rock, I didn't much care for it."

Navalis detected a softness and even higher tone to Ulmaen's voice, suggesting that the hormones were steadily shifting.

"Restore your biochemistry," he demanded. "Make sure to maintain the appropriate ratio of testosterone to estrogen."

Ulmaen winced. "I don't know how to gauge the world around me anymore."

"You need to focus." Navalis steered Ulmaen away from the stables, where several horses were being attended to by stable boys. Among the half dozen horses, a couple began to wander into the field to graze.

Ulmaen sighed. "I guess I didn't realize just how much I used my feelings to gauge the world around me, and without estrogen, I feel like I'm looking at my emotions through a fish bowl. How do you do it? How do you live in the world like this? I mean they are there, I can still feel them, if I want to. When I'm a woman, there's no indication there's a choice sometimes. I always use my emotions."

Struck by the sensitivity of his Student's insight, Navalis stopped and Ulmaen mirrored him.

"As sentient beings, we have three ways of interacting with and interpreting our environments."

"That many!"

Navalis nodded. "Our intellects, our emotions, and our gut instincts."

A clatter resounded through the air, compelling Navalis to look toward the source. Boriag adjusted his armor as he continued across the field, the weight of the protective sheath slowing his stride. In the doorway of the Mystics Tower, Kerista stood with her arms neatly folded across her chest as she watched Boriag.

"Why are there so many ways to approach the world?" Ulmaen wondered.

"When one doesn't work, the others take over," Navalis replied. "Some of us gravitate more toward intellect while others prefer their intuition and instincts, and some of us have learned to use all three simultaneously."

Navalis wanted to smile, but knowing he was expected to be mourning, he remained firm in his solemnity. Kerista might be watching him as well as Boriag.

"From what you've described," Navalis said, "it seems your new form is calling you to cultivate your reason and logic, perhaps even your instincts too. This is an excellent development."

"Says you."

"Come on, shift your hormones," Navalis urged.

Ulmaen closed his eyes. After a long moment of concentration, he opened them again. "How's that?"

"Good. I can hear the difference in your voice already. And remember to adjust your form. Be sure to focus on maintaining your masculinity. It'll take a little effort at first, but eventually being a man will start to feel natural."

"I'll do it right now—"

"No!" Navalis stopped. "Do it slowly over the next couple of days. Be sure to be seen eating a lot. People will eventually find out the distance you traveled and realize you look the way you do because of a long, hard journey. They'll see you putting on weight again. They'll believe that."

"And I won't raise suspicion." Ulmaen sighed. He stopped and stared down at the ground. "At any moment, anything I do or say could reveal my true identity, couldn't it?"

"You're doing fine." Navalis smacked Ulmaen on the shoulder, a gesture he wouldn't have thought to do in his previous form. "You just need to practice covert behavior more. And following instructions."

"Oh, about the name, I'm sorry. I figured being a man, Kerista would be less intimidating, but as soon as I saw her, whoosh! The name was gone from my memory."

"She's a force to be reckoned with," Navalis agreed. "Don't ever underestimate her." He hoped Ulmaen would heed his words of wisdom better than he had his instructions. "Now, explain to me why you're a day early?"

Ulmaen shrugged. "While waiting around in Eastgate yesterday, I overheard Senaga chatting with a fish vendor about how the castle was hiring on additional servants. Seems as though Protos has brought more people to the area. I figured, if I got here today and you put a good word in for me, I'd have a chance at getting hired on."

Navalis was struck by the simplicity and brilliance of Ulmaen's plan. "As a servant, you'd have access to places in the castle most don't," he thought out loud.

"My thinking exactly," Ulmaen agreed. "I'd be in proximity to all social strata within the castle."

Navalis nodded, although he recognized some restrictions. "You won't be able to go everywhere," he said. "But someone of your size and strength might be offered privileges. If you gain enough confidence with the importants you serve, they may provide you plenty of opportunities."

"If I play the game well enough, right?"

"Something like that."

Ulmaen huffed. "I don't know if I can play *The Game*." Then he laughed. "I'm going to make a terrible Sentinel, aren't I?"

Despite the difficulties Ulmaen was experiencing with maintaining form, his instincts were proving to be powerful. They were the kind that caused or solved any variety of problems.

"I'm sure you'll make a fine Sentinel," Navalis assured him.

As the field gently sloped down toward the eastern rampart and Eastgate, they turned around and trudged back up the hill toward the Mystics Tower. As the field leveled again, a sharp whinnying reverberated off the Treasury and a nearby granary.

A horse rose high in the air, its front legs curled and poised. Before the horse, Boriag stepped up, arms wide open, and he let out a holler. Gravity took hold, and the horse dropped back toward the ground, both front hooves striking Boriag square in the chest and slamming him into the ground.

"Should we help him?" Ulmaen asked.

Navalis shook his head. "Give him a chance first."

From all corners of the field, mystics, groundskeepers, and stable keepers ran toward the fallen man and tried to regain control of the horse.

Boriag moved, only slightly at first. Then, with great effort, he dragged himself back to his feet. He staggered, clutching his chest. It was remarkable he remained conscious. Even more remarkable, there wasn't a dent in the chest plate of the armor. He shook off anyone who tried to help him and nearly fell to the ground again. Tottering, he let out a weary whoop.

Ulmaen laughed. "That horse should've killed him!"

Navalis agreed, noting the shift in his Student's personality. Ule would have worried and fussed. She'd have run to Boriag's aid, fretted, and ignored Xiinisi law had there been any injuries to heal.

The emotional shift involved in switching genders was perhaps the most difficult part for their kind to manage. Ulmaen didn't lack emotions, not really, he was merely accessing them differently than he would have in female form.

His stress triggers would differ. So, too, would his response to other stimulants—arousal, anger, joy. Most importantly, his instincts and reasoning would develop quickly.

Now that Ulmaen was well on his way to becoming a more experienced Xiinisi, Navalis returned his attention to demons and wondered how long he'd have to wait for another specimen.

✳ CHAPTER 15 ✳

The Inner Sanctum moved and breathed. Little space remained as advisers settled about the central table, sitting in high backed chairs. The old and the swelled, both in body and mind, assembled twice a month to share their expertise.

The advisers were grand people, large in stature as well as status. Accountants, merchants, generals, strategists, mystics, artists, scribes— anyone with unique insights and opinions was welcomed to voice them.

Back when he had been Ule, she felt small in comparison, both in size and in mind, and had learned to keep her opinions to herself until Lyan asked for them. Now, as Ulmaen, he scanned the room easily, seeing past anyone no matter their height or station. Everyone and everything appeared smaller as a result of a simple yet distinct change—Ulmaen was physically larger and taller than Ule.

The new experience of bearing height was unsettling. When smaller in form, the proximity of people hadn't been a bother, and the intimacy was welcome. Now that he was taller and broader, he occupied more space. As a man, nerves fired off at the slightest touch. What had once comforted him now unsettled him, and he much preferred to keep at a distance.

Perhaps what amused Ulmaen most about being a man was his natural physical strength. In female form, Ule relied on accessing her Xiinisi ability to compensate for a lack of strength. In male form, he had no need for it. The small wine cask he carried on his shoulder weighed a substantial amount yet his body naturally resisted its weight with ease.

Familiar faces glanced at him, yet no one recognized him for who he used to be. To them, he was simply a new servant. The notion of being simultaneously seen and hidden caused his mind to somersault. He nearly laughed aloud as he realized the amount of leverage he suddenly possessed, knowing what he did about these people, and how they were convinced they knew nothing of him because they regarded him as a stranger.

At the urging of a fellow servant, he tipped the round cask forward and set it on its side onto a table. Carefully observing who was in attendance, he failed to hear the clunk-clunk of wood rolling across wood until a companion servant waved wildly at him from across the room. Struck by the antics, he glanced down in time to see the cask rolling toward the edge of the table.

Nearby, a few advisers stared in anticipation, waiting to see what would become of the wine cask, but Ulmaen's reflexes snapped into action. He clutched the small barrel as it pitched over the edge. A loud cheer erupted from the advisers, as his arms strained to recover the keg and set it back onto the table, upright on end this time, where it stayed put.

"Nearly lost that one, eh?"

Ulmaen recognized the acrid tone, the sharpness of the snort that followed. He turned and grinned at Gorlen, whose wide face and steely eyes had always evoked a violent compulsion. As Ule, she always wanted to slap him. Now, as Ulmaen, he'd rather punch Gorlen instead.

Without thought of his new status in the castle, Ulmaen offered a humorous retort. "The wine or my pride?"

Immediately he was admonished by the other servant. Despite the scolding, laughter erupted from some of the advisers.

"A sense of humor," Gorlen hollered. "We can use a bit of that in here." Then his face twitched and eventually settled into a sneer.

Ulmaen found the expression difficult to read. Had Gorlen meant to be appreciative or sarcastic? He tried again to think of something clever to say in return. Recalling something of his back story, he remembered a passage from a chronicle he'd read.

"There's a custom among my tribe," he began. "When there's a gathering of many people, pouring wine is done while dancing."

Laughter again, at the absurdity of the custom. Even Mbjard, who sat near the Magnes, nodded deeply and smiled, no doubt familiar with the practice. Lyan and Kerista appeared mildly amused. Only Gorlen seemed agitated.

"Not to piss on your people," Gorlen said, "but most of us want to drink our wine, not wear it."

Ulmaen faked a smile easier than Ule ever had. He mimicked the other servant and began filling fluted glass decanters with wine from the cask.

"This is going to be interesting," he muttered to himself.

The other servant begged him to stay quiet and Ulmaen finally conceded, realizing that if he talked all the time, he wouldn't hear what was being said by the advisers as they discussed their issues.

There had never been a formal routine for speaking. Their orations had always been organic. This time around, the topic returned to the new rampart wall being built in the south beyond the old one.

Generals commented on the security of the new ramparts, then accountants pointed out the cost for materials, followed by master masons suggesting recycling stones from the ruins by the Treasury.

Conversation easily digressed into a series of historical anecdotes offered by a master scribe regarding examples from the past concerning which wall designs did or didn't work.

Administrators who dealt directly with the farmers complained that yet again the farmers were rebuilding their markets and shanties near Old Southgate and that they needed more men to tear everything down to keep the field clear until the new south wall was completed.

Upon pouring wine for Magnes Lyan, he overheard Gorlen comment on the clan of priests that had been run out of the castle grounds by young women who had been impregnated by the head priest.

"We still haven't located those scum priests," Gorlen grumbled. "According to the financiers, they took off with a lot more money than just alms. They pocketed the admissions they collected for hosting those sacred plays, and they didn't pay a single actor."

Kerista tutted at the information. "We should close the Temple."

Mbjard shook his head at the suggestion. "People need a sanctuary."

"Assign some guards to watch the Temple," Lyan ordered.

Mbjard shook his head again. "How are people to feel safe and at ease surrounded by menacing guards?" Then he told Gorlen, "No offense."

"Huh?" Gorlen replied.

"Then assign a few mystics," Lyan said, amending his demand.

"Even worse," Mbjard mumbled.

Kerista scowled at him.

Lyan rapped his knuckles against the table. "Find someone to look after the temple. I don't care who."

Mbjard quickly nodded and made note of it.

Ulmaen's mind ached as he tried to keep track of who was saying what. When he was Ule, none of it bothered her; she'd had a way of going with the flow. Now, he felt less patient of it, less flexible. He found himself extracting facts and wanting to organize them, label them, and file them into little boxes, if he could.

At the mention of Ule among the advisers, Ulmaen's heart skipped a beat. He felt like he was trespassing as Gorlen reported on an arrest he had made in regards to Ule's murder.

A hush fell across the room. Advisers around the table waited for Gorlen to reveal the identity of the prisoner.

"The head clothier," he finally told them. "The gloves used to poison Ule were made by her, and since she won't answer our questions, we've arrested her for not co-operating. For all we know, she may very well be the murderer."

Lyan leaned forward and rapped the table with his knuckles. "Why would Rozafel murder Ule?"

Gorlen shrugged. "During the preparation of the body, Rozafel was very attentive toward the wife. Matters of the heart perhaps. " He ground his jaw. "Love triangles have a way of bringing out the worst in people."

The hairs on Ulmaen's neck and arms stiffened. A whip of anger lashed out, making him feel raw.

Love hadn't anything to do with it, he thought.

Lyan's mood shifted, too. He sat upright and engaged Gorlen with an unfaltering glare. Their contempt for one another was palpable.

Others sensed their growing tension, Mbjard especially, who squirmed in his seat. Ulmaen thought it unlikely for a man affiliated with criminals to be so nervous, and every time he passed Mbjard, he searched for unusual marks on Mbjard's flesh which might identify the criminal circuit he belonged to.

Kerista interrupted the standoff between Lyan and Gorlen by asking, "Is there any other evidence besides the gloves to support Rozafel's involvement with the murder?"

Gorlen shook his head slowly. "Once she sees the gravity of her situation, she'll give us what we want. And if she is the murderer, she can't hurt anyone else as long as she's locked away, can she?"

"And if she's innocent?" Lyan countered.

"We'll let her go," Gorlen assured him. "No harm done."

At the far side of the table, advisers talked over one another, addressing other issues. Lyan only had to say the word and his advisers would obey, but he leaned back, welcoming the discord.

He sat in quiet reflection, and when the sun suddenly broke through a cloud and lit the room in reds, greens, and blues from the stained glass window behind him, he looked otherworldly. Then the sun retreated behind another dark cloud and the Inner Sanctum grew dull again.

Gorlen drank deeply from a goblet filled to the brim, then began reporting on the number of arrests he'd made, mostly farmers setting up markets too close to the rampart walls, which had been an ongoing problem for hundreds of years.

Ulmaen thought about Rozafel, and made a mental note to visit her in the Prison and speak with her. If she was the murderer, he'd find out why she had done it, by any means necessary.

His mind elsewhere, he was instructed to stack ripe red apples on a plate, but as he did so, they slipped from his fingers and toppled over. Apologizing profusely above the curses of a few generals, he chased the apples as they spun across the table and onto the floor.

Back at the serving counter, the other servant cautioned him that he'd be fired or worse if he wasn't more mindful. When Ulmaen asked what could be worse than being fired, the servant mentioned cleaning the Sewers or serving food to the most heinous of prisoners.

He thought about Rozafel, of discreetly acquiring access to her, and what better way than to be the one who delivered her meals. All he needed do was make it so he'd be punished and assigned to the Prison. But what if they assigned him to the Sewers instead? He'd just what? Negotiate?

The idea of negotiation seemed odd. Suggesting an alternative to the punishment given felt a little masochistic. However, if there was a way to avoid depleting his inner reserves through shifting, he'd consider it. Now he just needed to figure out what would assure this kind of reprimand.

Again, because he wasn't paying attention, he knocked a goblet on the floor, spilling what wine remained inside. Advisers complained noisily, and at that moment he knew what to do.

Ulmaen cleaned the spilled wine. The meeting ensued, and as issues segued toward the topic of the upcoming election, he began to make small messes on purpose, apologizing loudly after every spill, annoying nearly everyone in the room. The other servant, out of fear of being associated with Ulmaen, completely ignored him.

Electoral protocol and security procedure were the main topics, which stirred a whirlwind of arguments among the advisers. Ulmaen watched Lyan remain stoic in the face of rising tempers and remembered that Lyan was a pacifist, despite having fought in the war. He had become one on account of having fought since he was a child, but today Ulmaen saw the Magnes a little differently. Lyan embraced the discord, ever a soldier at heart, forever comfortable amid conflict.

Lyan's advisers—all of his people for that matter—were divided within the castle as well as beyond the castle regarding their loyalties to him, not for lack of appreciation for what he had done to bring stability to the shor. He had, after all, been the one to claim and occupy the Chair in a world on the brink of despair and destitution.

Now that the world was less chaotic, instating a reigning family lineage, a new bloodline, had been demanded. People simply wanted their say; they needed to have some control over future Magnisi. The ancient Sondshor law of Protos permitted them that privilege.

Ulmaen rounded the table again, refilling wine glasses, and approached the Magnes and those who sat on either side of him. Ulmaen noted the sharp, hard-edged wisdom of Kerista, and compared her features to those of Mbjard's, which were softer and far more inclined to be deceptive even though nowhere on his hands, wrists, or neck did he show any cryptic marks indicating his criminal family.

Beside Kerista, Gorlen downed a large mouthful of wine and belched. At the sound, Kerista sucked in her breath.

Ulmaen tended to Lyan's empty glass. The angle of the decanter he held tipped wine into the goblet with fine precision. The lack of splash or spill dented Lyan's stoic expression with the slightest of smirks.

"Did I ever mention," Lyan began to speak to no one in particular, "Osblod was the first to kneel before me when I claimed the Chair?"

Gorlen laughed.

Kerista hushed him, annoyed by the outburst.

A subtle confusion settled over the room. Mbjard was the first to break the silence. "I recall your witness was someone you knew from the war." He made a note a ledger, and when he'd finished, he addressed Lyan with keen interest. "You must let me record this story from your past. We can use it—"

"Osblod?!" Gorlen sat forward, leaning in front of Kerista toward the Magnes. "He endorsed you? And now he campaigns against you?" He laughed again.

Lyan shrugged.

Kerista pushed him back into his seat, and he complied, a wide grin on his face.

"I'm surprised you haven't entered Protos," Mbjard said, addressing Gorlen. He pushed his spectacles high onto the bridge of his nose.

Gorlen's smile faded. "Maybe I will."

"You're being rude," Kerista snapped.

Gorlen had always been rude and direct, just like the other advisers. As Ule, she'd had a way of ignoring him that Ulmaen couldn't bring himself to do. As a man, he wanted very much to grind the general's face into the nearby bowl of ripe cherries till he choked on their pits.

Across the tower room, other advisers resumed their discussions, their voices steadily growing louder.

Gorlen leaned across the table. "Your Magnes," he began, "while the squabblers debate their need to be right, and you've done reminiscing, might I update you on relations with Woedshor?"

Ulmaen slowly refilled goblets and stacked plates with biscuits, cheese, and grapes, so he could overhear their conversation. When he wasn't in close proximity to Lyan, he used a bit of inner energy to extend his hearing.

"Yes," Lyan replied. "Please report."

"Our troops have returned from Woedshor intact. The last of the foreign ambassadors and advisers have returned to their homes. There have been no reports of retaliation. Despite the length of time since our shor's last Protos, everyone seems to be aware that foreigners of influence cannot work at the castle during the election."

Lyan seemed pleased by the news. "The last thing we need is another shor manipulating the election to their advantage through their ambassadors."

Ulmaen had known some of these foreign officials. One day, they had attended to their responsibilities, lived their lives, and the next day, they no longer lived in the castle. Their departure had been swift, but he understood the reason for it now. As for other foreigners in less powerful positions, such as himself, he was welcome to stay but wasn't allowed to vote.

"Since we're discussing troops," Lyan said. "I need one assigned to Warfield. I need skilled men to help test a new weapon in development."

Gorlen ruminated on the request, rubbed his cleft chin, and though his expression was unreadable, he finally nodded. "I'll assign some soldiers."

Kerista raised her head. She'd been reading a letter the entire time and finally joined in the conversation. "A word from the arch mystic of Eelsee," she said, lifting the parchment for Lyan to see. "His Magnes wishes you a successful campaign during Protos, hopes you have a long and fruitful lineage, one that surpasses Adinav's and shadows all memory of him."

Mbjard nodded in agreement and ceased recording details of their conversations in his ledger. "We are in exciting times," he said. "It's been six hundred and thirty-two years since an election of this nature has been held."

"That long, eh?" Gorlen stated coldly.

"We're establishing a new family lineage not just a leader," Kerista interjected. "The family must show promise of upholding tradition, by conditioning and teaching the elements which cultivate intelligence, strength, business, even culture."

Lyan winced at the final word.

As far as Ulmaen knew, Lyan hadn't ever openly appreciated culture, especially when it came to works of art. A sword he could appreciate, for its function though, not its aesthetic.

When, on one occasion, he had taken an interest in a landscape painting and was asked what he saw, he spoke of blood soaked fields and broken bodies piled high. When it came to music, he knew only sword song and the dance of war yet saw no celebration in it.

His inability to understand the value of art helped facilitate the erasure of references to Adinav, but at a loss, for Ulmaen saw now that Lyan was cut off from the pleasures these forms of creation provided. He'd only ever known destruction.

* CHAPTER 16 *

Many of the advisers had gone flushed in the face and glassy-eyed from drinking wine. Their reports and advice had deteriorated into bawdy tales, and Ulmaen tried his best not to laugh at their stories as he continued making rounds about the table, refilling empty wine glasses and food plates.

Mbjard showed no interest in recording any of the tales, and set down his glass pen. As he began to gently massage his writing hand, he exposed the insides of his wrists and palms. Ulmaen searched for insignia but Mbjard's flesh was smooth and clear. Not even a scar marked him, which seemed unusual for a criminal.

Mbjard's physical discomfort amused Kerista, giving Ulmaen yet another reason to dislike her. She smirked as she made notes in her journal, then discreetly addressed Lyan.

"If I may speak with you on a minor matter?"

"Of course." Lyan's response was automatic, lifeless, in comparison to the sudden upheaval in the room as advisers called for official dismissal. Lyan complied with a nod.

Chairs and stools scraped the floor, bodies shuffled, and casual discourse swelled. Most of the advisers downed the last bit of wine from their glasses then staggered from the chamber. A few remained behind to discuss minor issues.

Ulmaen struggled to hear through the eruption of noise.

"A chamber in the Catacombs has collapsed," Kerista reported. "General Gorlen and I would like your permission to investigate."

Ulmaen quietly chastised himself as he retrieved an empty food basket from the table. Had he heeded Navalis instead of thoughtlessly harvesting new matter, he wouldn't have had to destroy the gallery to conceal the decimated bodies, and Kerista wouldn't have a need to investigate it.

She peered over her spectacles. The intensity of her eyes, her firm composure demanded only one response from the Magnes.

Lyan contemplated the request.

Ulmaen had never known Lyan to appreciate certain social customs. Death, that too was another kind of culture, a necessary one, but he had never indicated he was a sentimental type. Walking through gore for most of his life must have made him practical about death. Certainly, the issue of a collapsed Catacomb must be trivial in comparison to keeping people fed and protected.

Lyan stirred from his musing. "How long ago were the dead interred?

"Two, maybe three centuries ago," Kerista replied.

"The room was filled beyond capacity," Gorlen added.

"A pity," Mbjard mumbled as he resumed writing and scratched notes about their current topic.

Forget about it, Ulmaen thought, wishing to impress the notion into Lyan's mind. Surely he knew the older galleries in the Catacombs eventually buckled under the weight of others; it was expected, eventual.

"Was it sealed?" Lyan asked.

"No," Kerista replied. "But the tunnels have been altered. No one visits there anymore."

Lyan eyed her suspiciously. "With the air supply gone, how do you expect to investigate?"

"The galleries above have accessible air," Gorlen began to explain. "We can run clay pipes through the tunnels or through drilled holes in the floor. With your permission, of course."

Mbjard raised a hand, to gain everyone's attention. A genuine inquisitiveness overcame him. "Don't the older galleries tend to collapse?"

"It's not *that* old!" She glared at Mbjard, who raised his hands in peace and withdrew from the conversation.

"Galleries dating back five, six hundred years or more, yes, those kind tend to collapse," she admitted. "This one's too current. Even more curious, the room had a reinforced ceiling."

She leaned back in her chair, straightening the front of her teal robe. "Besides, I worry for the galleries above. People still visit them, and we just interred a body there."

Ulmaen knew Kerista referred to Erzo's Gallery, where Ule's body remained intact. Lyan recognized the reference too, for he turned solemn and tapped his empty glass, requesting more wine.

Ulmaen obeyed and retrieved a decanter, growing uneasy by the sudden shift in Lyan's mood, so similar to the regret which had overcome him during his confession in the Mortuary.

Let the matter rest. Let it go. Let Ule go, Ulmaen thought, wishing he could project the message into Lyan's mind.

Lyan drained the glass in one haul, and finally said, "By all means, conduct your investigation."

Her smile was brief. Satisfaction lingered in her eyes. Obviously, the gallery was of great importance to her. "We'll start tomorrow," she told Gorlen.

Ulmaen stumbled, spilling the decanter of wine he carried, this time truly by accident.

Gorlen grumbled and stood abruptly, glaring at the mess. "If there's nothing more, Magnes, I'd like to get away from this walking wreck."

Kerista rose too, her journal pressed against her chest.

Ulmaen bowed, nearly prostrating himself, as he slopped an already wine-soaked cloth at the puddle.

The last of the advisers stood and vacated the room, Kerista and Gorlen at the lead. Mbjard stood and prepared to depart along with a few other scribes, who began stacking parchments and gathering their writing implements.

Lyan stopped him. "There's a personal matter I need to discuss with you."

Mbjard ordered the other scribes to leave without him, then returned to his seat. "Shall I ask the servants to leave?"

Lyan looked at the other servants, who had begun gathering up discarded bits of food. Then, he examined Ulmaen.

"It doesn't matter," Lyan replied. "Looks to me they need the extra time to clean up *his* mess." Then he addressed Ulmaen. "You're new here?"

Ulmaen nodded. "My apologies, Magnes. I come from a merchant family." The back story was coming easier to him now. "My skills don't include handling food. I'll do anything to keep this job, scrub toilets, service the Prison, any—"

Lyan raised his hand.

Ulmaen fell silent.

"We'll discuss this afterward," Lyan said. "In the meantime, clean the Inner Sanctum. Make it spotless, understood?"

The other servants nodded, and worked faster.

"On his own," Lyan told the others. "Take your leave."

The other servants hastily thanked the Magnes and bolted from the room.

Lyan stood and walked toward the stained glass window. There, he peered through a clear bit of glass at something far below.

Now that the room was nearly empty and quiet, Ulmaen heard the faraway sound of men shouting in unison, soldiers being led in late evening drills through the yard below.

"Never again," Lyan muttered to himself. "At least, not in what remains of my lifetime."

In the absence of others, something within Mbjard's slight frame swelled. His presence competed with the light shining through the stained glass window. "Never what again?"

"War."

The cries of soldiers thundered outside.

"And yet I train the soldiers, prepare them to defend our peace, have the smiths and architects develop new weapons in case the shors nearby threaten our stability." He sighed deeply. "To keep the peace. By any means necessary. Even war."

Mbjard folded his hands in front of him, and leaned forward. "Am I here to help you solve the riddle of what it means to be in power?"

Of all the advisers, Mbjard listened well, spoke cautiously. He was the most sought after for providing sound advice. Ulmaen wondered if any of his colleagues knew that their confidence was being undermined by a criminal.

In a moment of clarity, Ulmaen finally grasped the nature of Mbjard's hidden profession. The message on Ule's wrists, his access to a library of information, his private conversations with the Magnes. Mbjard was a spy!

Lyan laughed and shook his head. "No, my friend. My concerns are about... the kind of man I am. And if I can change? Can I be the one to begin a new reigning lineage?"

Of course you can, Ulmaen answered silently.

Mbjard nodded. "Of course—"

Lyan spun around, agitated at first. "I lack certain... traits. I know this. But..." He settled down again. "I'd like to be *that* kind of man. We need to experience peace for a while, and this election smells like a battlefield. My nerves are starting to twitch again. I don't want to fight."

Lyan remained quiet, his thoughts turned suddenly inward. Seeing him this way felt strange, and when the stillness persisted, Ulmaen held his breath so as not to make any noise.

Mbjard finally broke the silence. "What is it you require from me?"

Lyan approached the back of the chair where he had been seated, and leaned on the backrest. "Your knowledge of history."

"Oh!" Mbjard's eyes widened at the mention of his passion. He extended his hands in an open manner. "What is it you wish to know?"

"Tell me about some of the past Magnisi, the ones who established new family legacies here in Sondshor and elsewhere. Nothing about protocols. I want to know what kind of people they were."

Ulmaen thought the request unusual. Lyan had never shown an interest in history. And Mbjard? Lyan couldn't expect his adviser to answer that question without some research. Mbjard's memory was terrible, and with good reason. Despite the number of books he was always reading, his only focus was intelligence that sold well.

"How soon do you think you could gather this information?"

Mbjard smiled. "There are two worthy of mentioning in our recent history," he replied instantly.

Impossible, Ulmaen thought.

He recalled how Mbjard was always reading—scanning statistics, researching facts, muttering under his breath, lost in thought. Had he been truly taking an interest in everything he had been reading after all? What parts of it did he sell, and for how much?

Struck by the revelation, Ulmaen dropped a plate. He lunged down to catch it, but it slipped between his fingers. White shards of ceramic shot across the floor. He sagged at the mess. Normally, he'd hide behind a curtain of hair, maybe even blush with embarrassment; instead, he rubbed his bald head and cringed.

Lyan regarded him with mild amusement. "You're useless as a servant, aren't you?"

Ulmaen laughed. Normally he'd be embarrassed or offended by that kind of comment. Perhaps Ule would have been, but Ulmaen saw its truth. "Seems that way, doesn't it?"

Mbjard leaned across the table. In a hushed voice he asked Lyan, "Perhaps we should discuss this in private?"

"Perhaps," Lyan agreed. He skirted the chair and sat down again, then pointed a finger at Ulmaen. "You!"

"Yes Magnes?"Ulmaen's nerves fired off. Every part of him was willing to obey whatever Lyan commanded. As Lyan pointed toward the open doorway, what hope Ulmaen had for acquiring clues sank into disappointment.

"Stay there out in the hallway until I tell you otherwise.," Lyan ordered.

He nodded vehemently and immediately obeyed. As soon as he made it to the hallway, where two guards stood either side of the doorway, he realized that the Magnes hadn't specified exactly where he should stand, so he picked a spot next to one of the guards. Hugging the edge of the doorway, he peered back into the room and listened in on their conversation.

"As I was saying," Mbjard began, "There are two Magnisi that come to mind: Fehran and Kugilla. Now Fehran's lineage came about through a marriage to a rumored survivor of the preceding lineage which was established by Kugilla, but the rumor proved false. Kugilla was a nasty tyrant who usurped this shor and Woedshor in a violent coup. He and Fehran were very different kinds of men. Kugilla was vulgar and angry and sadistic, and Fehran was kind, humorous, and tenacious, yet both shared a similar trait."

"What trait is that?"

Ulmaen pressed against the door, turned his ear toward the opening, ignoring the strange looks from the guards.

"To win favor with the people," Mbjard replied, "Kugilla invented stories about the previous family's secret atrocities as a way to diminish his own. And when Fehran came into power, he made up stories to discredit the accomplishments of his predecessors to make his own accomplishments seem grander."

Ulmaen was struck by Mbjard's assessment of these two Magnisi. To find a commonality between two such disparate figures was impressive.

"You've nothing to worry about," Mbjard assured Lyan. "You, as well as many other Magnes share this one trait. The ability to bend the truth."

"I have done nothing of the sort!"

"Haven't you?" Mbjard asked, his voice much softer. "What of destroying the very memory of a man's existence?"

"Adinav wasn't a man." Anger laced Lyan's tone. "In ways, he was worse than a demon."

"In the end, perhaps," Mbjard agreed, "but he was a man once, from a distinguished family instated by Fehran. The longest lineage in Sondshor's history to date." Mbjard paused. "It would be a shame if the people forgot that."

Ulmaen leaned closer to the edge of the door. For a moment, there was silence, then Lyan spoke again.

"I asked for insights into their characters. I want to achieve a greater state of nobility, and you tell me their common trait is their ability to make up stories."

Ulmaen failed to understand what Lyan found so incredulous about Revisionism. Revisionists were a dime a dozen in Elish's history, and in any of the histories she encountered in other worlds built by the Xiinisi.

"Did they ever succeed in skewing history?" Lyan asked.

"No." Mbjard's response was quick and candid. "No one has ever been successful at entirely undermining history. Documents and evidence always survive, no matter how hard others try to destroy them. There are always a few who see past illusions, all those attempts to veil their sight."

"And what kind of people are those?"

"Usually... artists."

Ulmaen shifted his stance, listening to Lyan's candid, honest discourse and Mbjard's uncanny insights into Elishian nature.

"As you must know," Mbjard continued, "my profession came about several thousands of years ago as a counter to those in power seeking to diffuse the facts. That's why to this day scribes make it a frequent practice to have several of their number record the same event, so we have more than one viewpoint with which to examine our past."

He paused a moment then asked, "Are you concerned about Ule's work?"

Lyan's answer was swift. "Yes."

Ule had convinced the Magnes that Adinav was best forgotten. People were less likely to follow in the man's footsteps if they didn't know he existed. Eventually he'd fade from everyone's memory, becoming nothing more than a bogey man to scare children.

"I'm reconsidering her request," Lyan admitted. "I know I agreed to it, and I want to honor her memory, but if there's any truth to Kerista's counsel and what she told me in the Infirmary about being mindful of how people see me, then I must reconsider it."

Mbjard sat a moment in silence. Nodding to himself, at some unspoken thought, before he began again.

"Although Ule never spoke of her experiences with Adinav, it is commonly known she was a part of his court. Equally accountable for Adinav's atrocities yet forgivable given his powers of persuasion. Guilt can be a very powerful motivator. It may have been what drove her, but it doesn't have to motivate you."

Ulmaen's stomach clenched at the idea. Guilt was indeed a powerful motivator, he thought, but it wasn't the true reason for wiping Adinav from the memories of people and the world. He intended to prevent Elish from nurturing someone else like Adinav. That's what Sentinels do among the Xiinisi—they protect worlds.

"What do the people think of me?" Lyan asked. "What do I need to do to become the kind of man who is elected?"

"To begin, understand that it isn't *you* that needs changing," Mbjard replied. "It's people's *opinions* of you that do."

Lyan grew pensive and quiet.

After a moment, Mbjard took it upon himself to explain further. "You see, you needn't change into someone with a trait you don't value. Showing that you respect and admire that trait in others creates a... relationship."

"Even with my competitors?"

Mbjard chuckled. "Not so much with them."

Ulmaen wondered what thoughts were spinning in Lyan's mind. Was he raging at the suggestion or taking it to heart? As far as Ulmaen was concerned, Lyan didn't need to change. He was a leader. He'd led campaigns in the war; he claimed the High Chair of Sondshor as his own. Wasn't that enough?

Mbjard sat back in his chair, and pressed the bridge of his spectacles high on his nose. "Are you sure you want to know what others think of you?"

Lyan nodded.

"Very well." Mbjard folded his hands across his chest. "The merchants respect and admire you for rejuvenating our economy. The generals envy your position. They wait for the moment you stumble so they can take the High Chair."

Lyan showed no surprise at this revelation.

"The farmers are divided. They adore you for helping to restore their lands with abundant crops, but aren't happy with their markets being torn down and moved farther away from Southgate. I'm certain once the new rampart wall is finished, they'll go back to ignoring the laws and rebuild their markets directly in front of the new gate."

"Of course," Lyan agreed.

"The artisans and artists are flourishing. But, unfortunately, they despise you."

Lyan laughed. "I'm not sure *their* opinions of me matter."

Ulmaen agreed. Drunk, insane fools, the lot of them, he thought, recalling how they celebrated Ule's death. It was a marvel how any of them managed to create such beautiful work being so afflicted with such impulsive and destructive personalities.

"They should matter," Mbjard urged. "Historically, artists have always been able to influence the common folk in ways political leaders can't. They can memorialize or satirize or... demonize subject matter. At this very moment, every artist hates you."

The softness with which Mbjard conveyed this sentiment prickedled Ulmaen, as it must have Lyan. No ego could withstand the sharp point of that revelation, yet Lyan didn't explode into a tantrum the way men like Gorlen did.

Lyan had never been a coward, as far as Ulmaen could tell. His instincts served him well. Certainly he wouldn't allow himself to be cowed by what others thought of him. He had a wonderful vision for Sondshor, based on what he had told Ule during many private conversations.

Introspection took hold of Lyan again.

Mbjard waited patiently.

When Lyan's focus returned, he called for a guard.

The guard next to Ulmaen barreled into him, anxious yet eager as he rushed toward the doorway. Ulmaen tried to step out of the way, but ended up careening through the doorway and being dragged along by the guard.

Lyan cast him a wary glance before addressing the guard. "Do you know the curio dealer, the one people refer to as The Storyteller?"

The guard nodded.

"Find him. Bring him here, immediately," Lyan commanded.

The guard nodded again and as he turned to make a hasty exit, Ulmaen jumped out of the way.

"And you." Lyan sat back in his chair, leaned his head against the back rest as he stared at Ulmaen. "What to do with you?"

"I-I can do better." Ulmaen stumbled for words, doing his best to be humble about the mess in the room. He wrung his hands then stopped, shoving them behind his back.

What happened next mattered. He wanted to be sent to the Prison. He'd accept being in the Sewers if it meant he still had access to the castle. However, if he was fired, he'd be forced to leave the grounds, and he needed to speak with Rozafel to figure out who had murdered Ule.

"Any chance I could persuade you not to sack me? I'd be willing to work the Sewers or the Prison. Yeah, the Prison! What's the standard time of punishment for the Prison?"

Lyan tilted his head, his face solemn.

Mbjard answered, "A month!" Though he didn't smile, his eyes did, and he buried a laugh in a cough.

Ulmaen reigned in his panic and felt inclined to bargain. Leaning forward slightly, he held up two fingers. "I'll give you two months in the Prison if you don't fire me."

Lyan smirked. "I don't like how you handle dishes, but I do like how you handle yourself. Any other Magnes might have had you beaten or executed." He leaned forward. "You're lucky I like you." Mirth broke through his grim mood.

"You're bold without being obnoxious, and you've got a sense of humor. You'll need it in the Pit."

Ulmaen grinned. "The Pit? That's the Prison, right?"

Lyan laughed. "Part of it."

Ulmaen had done it. He'd maneuvered himself into the Prison, creating an opportunity to question Rozafel about the gloves she had made and her involvement in Ule's murder without having to shape-shift or phase out of the material plain. He'd never negotiated like this before, and was overcome with a tremendous sense of self worth and satisfaction.

"You're not supposed to enjoy the punishment, fool." Lyan slapped the table. "Three months!"

In the past, as Ule, the unyielding strength in Lyan's command always made her quiver. Now, as Ulmaen, hearing the extension of his punishment, Lyan's words struck his nerves in a different way. He couldn't help himself. He laughed.

❋ CHAPTER 17 ❋

The Dining Hall teemed with folk, like a swelled beast at the mercy and command of a hungry, massive brood. All designations of castle staff squeezed in along the tables. Most sat on stools and others brought their own chairs. Tonight, there wasn't enough space for everyone, for some of the soldiers sat on the floor along the walls.

Ulmaen launched himself through the doorway at the serving counter. Spices and steam clung to him as he moved through the crowds, swaggering with new found pride. He stood tall, a plate of food in hand, and begun searching for Navalis or a vacant seat, whichever appeared first.

His smile widened every time someone smiled at him in return. He couldn't help himself. Satisfaction was addictive. He'd negotiated his way into Prison duties, bringing him closer to the one and only person who might help provide him with information about Ule's murder. Figuring out who had killed her was all that mattered, and yet he was consumed with delight, his mind exploring fantasy scenarios in which he negotiated his way toward some other goal.

A gloating overtook him, briefly, until he was struck by an unusual thought. Had he been Ule, she wouldn't think to applaud her wit and gall. She'd never consider that she had affected change. Instead, she'd be relieved about her good luck, with how events had gone in her favor.

She had focused on rules, on whether she was breaking them or stepping out of bounds, on how well she was obeying and fulfilling them, especially since being welcomed back among her people.

She had cared about being a part of their world, and now, well, *he* regarded such a notion as silly, and doing so made him feel free. Marveling at the shift in his attitude, he wondered if it was the result of changing genders or of being in a new position within the castle.

He plodded from table to table. They were all full. As he passed each one, his gut clenched tighter. He searched for a vacant space, but none was to be found. As he drew nearer to *that* table, growing closer in proximity to the place of Ule's death, where she struggled for motor control and breath and witnessed the fear in Bethereel's eyes, his heart skipped a beat. He hoped there was no vacant place to be had there.

And what of Bethereel?

His mind flitted at the mention of her name, locking onto the new subject, desperate to ignore the storm of anxiety brewing within. He hadn't yet seen her since his return to the castle, and he wondered just how he might react being close to her again. How would his arousal feel as a man? He had loved her, and now he wondered if that love persisted or if it had diminished too, like his attitude toward the Xiinisi.

He passed Sabien sitting at the end of a table in the middle of the room. Sullen and grim, Sabien corralled the last few peas together on his plate while deeply absorbed by his thoughts, oblivious to the chattering clothiers who surrounded him.

Ulmaen searched for Bethereel, but she didn't sit among them.

Where is she? he wondered. Certainly, she must be alright, mustn't she? Why else would her only kith and kin leave her alone?

The last of his delight and self-satisfaction oozed from every pore in a cold sweat as he approached the very last table, the one closest to the far wall, the same table where Ule had been poisoned.

Navalis sat where Bethereel had, in the very seat where she had listened to Rozafel tell her humorous stories, except Rozafel had become Boriag, who leaned over his plate telling stories of his own. To the other side of Navalis, a stool remained empty.

Ulmaen shuddered. Surely Navalis remembered this was where Ule had been poisoned. This had to be a sick joke. His knuckles turned white from keeping his plate of food steady.

Navalis waved him over.

Walking away seemed the most apt of actions, certain to ease his anxiety. A short walk to the open main doors and in a minute, he'd be outside, sitting against the cold cobblestone, keeping company with the guards and soldiers. It wasn't an uncommon practice to eat in the courtyard, but tonight was different. Everyone had gathered to hear a special announcement.

His legs obeyed his Master. Weighty and stiff, they moved awkwardly. He squeezed through the narrow passage between occupied stools at the table and the soldiers leaning against the wall. When he slid into the empty seat saved for him, his breath stopped a moment.

He coughed away a tickle at the back of his throat, the tremble in his uvula signaling for some kind of release.

Navalis smacked him on the back. "What's wrong with you, brother?"

Boriag, hearing the comment, leaned toward Ulmaen. "You look like you've been yelled at by the arch mystic. She's a screecher, eh?"

The suggestion of screaming caused his uvula to tremble again. He coughed again, focused on his shallow breath.

"She sure is," he mumbled, unable to relax.

Leaning into him, Navalis lowered his voice. "What's the matter?"

Uncertain at first, Ulmaen finally leaned into him and whispered, "This is where... she was murdered?" He fought against the twitch of his nose and the curl of his lips, but the sneer won in the end. "Is this a test?"

Navalis remained silent.

Ulmaen clenched his fist. "Is this a part of my training? Forcing me to sit in the very place where I died?"

"What's that?!" Boriag cupped a hand around his ear. "Everyone's got to share their stories." He gobbled down a chunk of chicken and smacked his lips. "Wow, it's a bustle in here today," he said. "Wonder what the mighty Magnes has to say?"

Ulmaen whispered in Navalis's ear. "Am I uncomfortable enough for you yet?"

"This isn't... a test," Navalis projected, his words thundering in Ule's chest. "It's not a part of your train—"

The roar of laughter and conversation throughout the hallway diminished all at once. Advisers began to trickle through the archways at the back of the Hall behind the head table. General Gorlen and Kerista, engaged in conversation, led the group and occupied the seats immediately to the right of the Magnes's chair.

"There was nowhere else to sit," Navalis continued.

Although this knowledge eased Ulmaen's distress considerably, it didn't alleviate it. The voice inside his solar plexus which had been calming now mildly irritated him.

"You need to start seeing your opportunities," Navalis suggested.

"How is this an opportunity?" He spoke louder than he intended.

Boriag stopped in mid chew, his eyes bulging, and he asked, "What opportunities?"

Navalis held up his hand, gave his friend a stern look. "This is a private matter. Give us a moment."

"Family stuff. I get it." Boriag shrugged and resumed eating.

Instead of projecting, Navalis spoke normally again, lowering his voice. "Use this as an opportunity."

"For what?! Reliving every moment of being poisoned?!"

"Keep your voice down," Navalis warned, unaffected by the outburst. He speared a chunk of beef with his fork, brought it to his nose, and sniffed at the spiced meat before gulping it down.

"Look around you," he suggested. "Use this as an opportunity to help you figure out what you need."

"How?"

"Use the vantage point as a way to bring back memories of anything you've overlooked. Remember the faces of the people you were sitting with, their expressions. Was someone amused by what was happening to you? Perhaps someone was ignoring you completely."

They were shocked, Ulmaen remembered. And disgusted. Mostly they were scared, not for her though. They had been scared for themselves.

Something stirred the crowd within the Dining Hall. The wall of din settled into hushes. Everyone's attention turned toward the head table.

Lyan and Mbjard appeared through an archway, accompanied by a small group of guards. Lyan immediately settled into his chair, and Mbjard stood next to him, near the empty chair to his right.

"A moment of your attention," Mbjard called out. Though his voice was gentle, it carried through the room with great volume. "On this evening, our Magnes has words of great interest to everyone. Be sure to tell everyone what you hear this evening."

Mbjard sat at the table and rushed to prepare parchment on which to begin transcribing.

Lyan stood before the assembly and began to speak. "Hear this, know this."

Lyan's authoritative tone fired off Ulmaen's nerves again, making his muscles tighten. He wasn't sure why or even how, but if Lyan had asked him to fight in battle, he'd deliver the first punch without thought or need of reason.

"I cannot undo the damage that's been done," Lyan declared.

"What's thaaat?!" Boriag gaped at everyone around him, stunned by the opening of Lyan's speech.

"For two years, countless pieces of artwork have been destroyed. Lost to us and to future generations forever." Lyan cleared his throat. "Let it be known, I am not without appreciation for what our smiths, artisans, and artists are capable of. They have skills and talents of a unique kind. Not the kind that nurture or sustain our bodies. The kind that nurture our minds, our spirits."

At the table, Mbjard deftly recorded every word Lyan spoke.

"For that reason, I would like to honor our artists, by first apologizing for the destruction of their creations. My intention was to protect the citizens of this castle and the world itself from the memory of Adinav's devastating and despicable legacy."

Cries and shouts rose from the soldiers and other supporters of Lyan's. Lyan raised his hands, as did some of the advisers sitting at the table. The signal took effect swiftly, and the room fell silent again.

Ulmaen's flesh dimpled and shivers ran along both arms. Dread of another sort crept through him, as Lyan resumed his speech.

"Starting at this very moment, all art depicting, referencing, or otherwise recording the memory of Adinav will cease being destroyed."

After a moment of stunned silence, a small cheer burst throughout the room, rallied by the tiny Laere. Her arms nearly tangled in the knots of her unruly long hair, she climbed onto her stool and waved a large, dramatic kiss to the Magnes. About her, fellow artists hooted in celebration, knocking the table with their cups.

Again the advisers waved their hands, and although this time it took a little longer, the Dining Hall again fell into a hush. Laere spilled onto her stool, flushed in the cheeks, grinning from ear to ear.

"Our history is precious," Lyan continued. "We must learn from it. Sometimes the lessons are harsh and painful. Regardless of our wounds, we must remember so history doesn't repeat itself. Adinav is a warning, a cautionary tale."

No, no, no, Ulmaen mentally projected.

Two years ago this very idea had been suggested, but Lyan was easy to convince otherwise. Nothing good came of cautionary tales. Over time, their message changed, and what was meant to frighten and deter became a beacon of faith and hope for anyone who desired that kind of power.

At the head table, Kerista suddenly looked up and cast a discerning glare over the room. Ulmaen realized his error and immediately shut down his thoughts, letting Lyan's speech take precedence in his mind.

"I'd like to make amends by hosting a celebration of the arts within the castle grounds."

Excitement bubbled among the many whisperings about the Dining Hall.

"Yes, a celebration," Lyan called out forcefully, "the likes of which no one has ever seen. I admit, I know little of the arts. I've never had the time for it, but now, I look forward to learning. I invite all artists to join in this fest. Smiths, weavers, spinners, and clothiers; engineers, architects, and draftsmen; sculptors, painters, and actors... You're all welcome."

Applause erupted from the middle of the hall, where Laere and her troupe of artists sat. Laere's approval was the most ecstatic of anyone's. Again she smiled, and Ulmaen at one time would have begrudged the artist her day of triumph; instead, he found her radiant.

"Listen everyone," the Magnes said. "Words aren't enough to mend this unfortunate wrongdoing. This festival will come and go. To prove to you my long term commitment to the preservation of our history, its accomplishments and its atrocities, several rooms within Fehran's Hall will be dedicated to a museum of history and oddities of Sondshor Castle."

Whispers filled the room again.

"Sabien the Storyteller has agreed to curate this special collection." Lyan called across the room. "Sabien? Please stand."

As though risen from a slumber, Sabien shook off his dark mood and stood.

"Will you tell everyone something about the project?"

In the tradition of all great performers, Sabien pushed away whatever consumed his thoughts. He stood and projected himself with intensity.

"Only that it will be the greatest museum in the shor."

The statement was met with polite applause.

"And..." He paused until the room fell quiet. "As a way for everyone in the castle to learn more about the project, to ask me questions and offer their suggestions..." He waited a moment, long enough for a seed of anticipation to take root. "I will be opening the celebrations with an intimate show of curios and oddities from my personal collection."

Excitement trickled through the crowd, and the applause that followed thundered with approval.

❋ CHAPTER 18 ❋

Ulmaen hesitated at the edge of a field west of the Sondshor Castle. Morning was well underway, the sun just beginning to climb the sky, leaving peaks of pinks and yellows along the dark canopy of the forest to the west.

He stood where a section of the old rampart wall used to stand. He glimpsed the Infirmary to the south, where the rampart curved toward Old Southgate. Behind him the ruins of the northern Colonnade came to an abrupt end near the Bath House, where construction had been abandoned hundreds of years ago.

The whinny of horses drifted from the stable by the northern wood, which ran along the precipice of a steep hill and down into Warfield.

He strode south along the edge of the field and turned down a narrow dirt path which originated behind the Infirmary. He paused again to shift the wide leather strap of a basket filled with food, which was slung across his bare chest and dug into his flesh.

He stretched his shoulder against the heavy load. Under the circumstances, he'd prefer a shirt but was advised against risking the ruin of his good clothes in a place everyone liked to call the Pit.

The Prison stood in the southern most part of the field. Its rigid silhouette erupted from the ground like some eyeless gray worm.

He did his best to ignore the unsettling atmosphere of the place. The Prison, like the Mortuary and the Catacombs, hadn't been a place Ule had ever needed to visit. Now, Ulmaen had a mission. Rozafel was his only lead to figuring out who had poisoned Ule and why. She was, possibly, the one responsible for murdering Ule.

Built in the shape of a quadrate cross, square watch towers reinforced every exterior corner of the Prison. Its smooth, plain walls looked higher, as the path veered downward, carving into the grassy field, until the ground was well above his head.

Packed earth became a series of wide narrow stone steps. The arch of the entrance, which when seen from a distance seemed to hug the ground, loomed high above him. From this vantage, he scanned the smooth quarried stone all the way up the wall into the peaks of squat towers, where guards peered down and watched him.

He descended the remaining steps and crinkled his nose. The stink of damp earth and old urine made him gag, and he rushed inside for reprieve, brushing past a guard at attention just inside the entrance.

The ceiling was high, the walls tall slabs of gray stone like sheer cliffs all around. In this arm of the building, the hall was narrow and rectangular. The only furniture was a long counter near the wall across from the entrance. Made of wood and stone, it spanned the width of the room, centered between the start of two corridors.

Ulmaen cringed at the sight of General Gorlen standing behind the counter. Other guards stood at the entrances to the corridors and against the wall behind the counter.

Mustering a fake smile, he approached Gorlen who examined a pile of iron shackles and chains strewn across the counter.

"These won't do," he muttered. "Hinges too small. Chain links, too. A dog's breath would snap these."

"Hello?"

Gorlen cocked an eyebrow in his direction. "You again." He laughed. "So this is your punishment then? I had you pegged for cleaning the Sewers."

"I'm delivering food."

"What's that?"

Ulmaen cleared his throat, stood a little taller. "I'm here to hand out food."

"I know that, you idiot." Gorlen glanced down at the shackles, moving them about. Suddenly the chains came alive, rattling, as one of them snaked to the floor. The attached shackle fell with a clang. Somewhere in the Prison, past the stone walls beyond the counter, someone moaned.

"Anyone meant to be fed is in the Core," Gorlen declared, and he pointed to the corridor on the left.

The opening to this corridor mirrored the one on the right—both felt cold and cavernous, for the sheer gray walls rose high until they butted against the ceiling several stories above.

For some reason, he felt drawn to the corridor on the right, where he noticed the far wall angled sharply into another hallway. At the corner, he discerned a gate made of iron bars in a grid pattern, and guessed that the room behind those bars was a holding cell, which currently sat empty.

Directly behind the counter, at the base of the cliff-like wall, was a recess in the architecture.

"What's the Core?" Ulmaen asked, craning over the counter to examine the recess and discovered steps leading down farther into the ground.

"Here," Gorlen said. "Around here. The middle, boy!" He pointed to the left corridor again. "Pay attention!"

Ulmaen backed away from the counter, unsettled by the way Gorlen's lip curled and trembled. He seemed to think twice about what he was about to say, then stopped himself.

"Right," he mumbled. "You're new."

Ulmaen pushed back at his swelling ego.

"The Core's the group of holding cells in the middle back there," Gorlen explained. "They hold the ones not fit for quarry work." He pointed again to the left corridor. "Go that way, feed the prisoners in the cells to your right and work your way 'round till you come back here."

Ulmaen made his way toward the left corridor, which was flanked by attentive guards. As he passed the counter, he stopped a moment fighting with his inquisitive nature.

"What is it now?" Gorlen groaned. "Need your hand held?"

"No, that would just make my palms sweaty." The words slipped out before Ulmaen could censor himself, and he winced at his mistake.

Nearby, a guard snickered.

"I didn't mean anything by it." Ulmaen laughed, hoping to prove his humorous intention. "Honestly, you're not my type." He laughed again.

Gorlen wasn't impressed. "A jokester, eh?" He rubbed his chin. "Seems you're in the wrong profession. Sure you're not an actor? Liars, the lot of them." He grew more pensive at his last comment.

"What about the other prisoners," Ulmaen blurted, taking advantage of Gorlen's sudden quiet mood. "How do they get fed?"

"No one's explained the protocols to you, eh?"

Ulmaen shook his head. "A grease fire in the Kitchen this morning kept everyone hopping. Senaga said take this and go." He patted the basket.

Gorlen grunted. He relaxed a little, placing a hand on the hilt of his sword fully sheathed at his hip. "The petty criminals, they get sent to the quarries," he explained. "They get fed there. Those who aren't capable, stay behind. They're kept in the Core. It's safer that way. Stops visitors like you from wandering off and snooping about, getting yourselves hurt or killed."

"And down there?" Ulmaen pointed to the recess in the wall beyond the desk, where the stairs descended farther below ground.

"The Pit? That's the old Prison." And Gorlen gave the hilt of his sword a squeeze.

Ulmaen didn't need to know the language of soldiers to understand what the gesture meant. He'd exceeded his question quotient for the day. Though it made him nauseous to do so, he respectfully nodded at Gorlen and turned toward the hallway, his eyes lingering on the stairwell until it was out of sight.

Immediately to his right he saw a row of holding cells at the base of the granite walls. Inside each cell, the ceiling hung only a few inches above him and was lined with thick wooden beams. In the floor was a small hole, and along the back wall was an exposed gully that contained clean flowing water.

The first cell was empty. The second one, too. In the third cell, he discovered an obese man laying on the floor snoring loudly, yellow bits of foam and matter caked to his lips. The room was large enough to hold three or four people if needed, but he was the only one. The smell indicated the room had been recently cleaned and almost hid the stench of vomit.

The pristine cell created an odd contrast with the mess of the man.

Ulmaen called to the man several times, and even reached between the narrow bars of the gate to see if he could jostle him awake, but he was immediately stormed by a guard and told to slip food through the gap between the bottom of the gate and the floor.

His ego railed against the authority of the soldier, but he calmed it. He apologized, a smile on his face, and the guard relaxed a little, looking a little less austere when he resumed his post. Ulmaen resumed his task and placed an apple, bits of cheese, and a chunk of bread into a filthy dish on the ground.

In the next cell, two older men had collapsed against opposite walls, both dozing. Both were bruised and bloody, one missing most of his front teeth. Upon hearing the rattle of the gate as Ulmaen slipped food beneath it, they both perked up, scrambled across the floor, snatched their portions, and resumed their respective positions.

Ulmaen continued down to the end of the first corridor, noting that he passed a hallway to his right, each side containing seven or eight cells. And based on the dimensions of the hallway, he realized this was the western arm of the quadrate cross.

His footsteps echoed as he passed by the hallway, and he heard another persistent sound—the trickle of running water, which he assumed had been piped into the walls.

Keeping to the right, he turned at the end of the corridor and passed another exit. He peered into the hall beyond and saw the southern arm of the Prison was heavily guarded and less well kept.

Crates were stacked in the corners and the walls covered in weapons and shackles. Remnants of hay and horse dung sullied the floor, and beyond the open doors, he saw a horse hitched to a wagon that was being unloaded of small barrels. This was where prisoners were herded into horse drawn wagons and taken to the new quarry northeast of the castle.

He plodded on, the cells to his left empty, but the cells on his right occupied. Not a single one caged Rozafel, the only person he had a need to speak with.

He turned the corner and proceeded along the east side of the Prison. The farther along he went, the more prisoners he served and the lighter the basket's load became. After several cells, he began to doubt Rozafel was there.

He hadn't considered the possibility of her working in the quarry. She was more than capable. When he had been Ule, he had witnessed her lift heavy bolts of fabric, and once, a sewing needle punched clear through her thumb and she didn't even bat an eyelash.

Immediately, he thought of reasons for visiting her in the evening, after she had returned from the quarry. With no need to linger, he quickened his pace.

He saw the same layout he had seen on the other side of the Core. Another arm of the cross—a hallway filled with more cells, except on this side, the hallway didn't come to an abrupt end. Instead of a wall, he saw a doorway cast in shadow and assumed it had to lead either up or down to another level.

He continued along, but at the second to last cell of the Core, he halted.

Crouched on the floor alongside the gully of water, Rozafel rocked slightly, her focus dedicated to a single dreaded lock of her dark hair. Her dress was soiled along the hem, and a smudge marked her cheek.

"Rozafel," he whispered out of concern at first, until he considered that she might have murdered his former self. Anger quickly buzzed through him.

Slightly dazed, Rozafel looked at him. "What's that?"

Remembering she wouldn't know him, Ulmaen reigned in his bitter mood, knowing that he needed to pretend to be nice to her. He attempted a smile.

Rozafel stood. Cautiously she stepped forward then stopped just beyond reach of the barred gate. "Do you know me?"

"Only what I've heard from rumors," he replied. "About Ule's murder."

Rozafel's lower lip quivered. "What are they saying now? I'm some monster? There's no proof." She grew sullen. "Not yet."

He wasn't sure what to make of Rozafel. He reached into the basket and pulled out a chunk of bread. Hesitant to give it to her at first, he finally knelt down, snaked his hand through the gap, and held the bread out toward her.

Like a cautious cat, she took interest in the food, staying at a distance to assess the danger.

"You new?"

"Yeah," he replied. "My name's Ulmaen." In the briefest of moments, a rage seized him. He envisioned himself snapping her neck. He shuddered at the graphic and unexpected image, and felt sick afterward, as though he had actually killed her.

She took a step closer. "What'd you do to get sent here?"

He managed to laugh, that good-natured joking laugh that seemed to appease others, including Lyan. "I spilled a bunch of wine during a Council meeting."

Her face paled.

Laughing again, he shook his head, the smile on his face widening. "No more than any of the drunken generals spill."

She remained sullen. Her fingers climbed the long dread, pulling at bumps and snags, as though she were trying to untangle it.

"Have you met Laere?" she asked him.

"The artist?"

Rozafel nodded. "You've met her. Good. She's alright then?"

"There's going to be a celebration of the arts," he told her, wondering why she cared about Laere. "She's a happy girl right now, I suppose."

"She's better, is she?"

Ulmaen waved the bread about, and after a few moments Rozafel lunged toward the ground and snatched it from his hand.

"Better than what?"

Rozafel nibbled a bit of the brown crust, and she closed her eyes and savored the small morsel. Regaining herself, she spoke again. "She was a mess when she was in here," she began. "A little drunk I think. Mentioned something about playing Rant."

"What's that?"

"Mmm, a drinking game. You know?"

He shook his head.

"You take turns ranting about something. When you fumble your words, you drink." Rozafel picked at the bread. "She'd been going on about Ule, by the sounds of it. The party shifted to the Mortuary and got out of control."

"It sure did," he agreed.

"Were you there? I don't remember seeing you put in a cell."

He winced at his error and shook his head. "No, I... just heard about it. Word gets around."

Rozafel's face grew slack. "Oh," she said sadly. "Yeah, words do that, don't they?"

He shifted the contents of the basket, looking for bits of cheese wrapped in paper. He pulled them out and placed a couple on the ground.

"She had quite the swollen lip," Rozafel continued. "Guess that happened during the brawl."

He remembered Laere being carried on a soldier's shoulder after Gorlen disbanded the artists, but knew nothing of what had happened to her on the way to Prison.

"You know, she was kind enough to ask me how I was. No one's really asked since they locked me away in here."

Until then, Ulmaen hadn't much cared how Rozafel felt. Ule would have cared. Knowing that made him feel bad for being so thoughtless. After he recognized his selfishness, his focus shifted onto Rozafel. Until he knew how she might be involved in the murder, he promised himself to work harder at remaining emotionally impartial.

He asked, "How are you doing?"

Rozafel's lips twitched. Her smile was brief. "Mmm, okay," she said in a diminished tone. "I'd like to get out of here."

Fishing around for apples, he cradled two in the palm of his hand. "Well you killed someone, didn't you?"

Frantic, she shook her head. "No, no. I just made gloves." Her face saddened. "A real long time ago."

The anger that had been coursing through him cooled. He considered the possibility that Rozafel hadn't been the one to poison Ule. The idea relieved him, briefly, and then he grew annoyed at having to search again for the identity of the murderer. He thought of other possibilities. "Did you make them for someone?"

She rushed toward the gate and knelt down. Up close, her dress smelled of musk mixed with urine. Her teeth were yellowed. Her eyes bulged.

"I did!" She grasped the gate tightly, her pudgy fingers spread out over two squares of iron bars. "I sold them." Her face grew sullen again.

Ulmaen placed the apples on the ground in front of her. A feeling of doubt overcame him. Rozafel didn't seem the kind to have the constitution to murder someone, but then most women didn't. That's why, when they did succumb to their murderous urges, their methods of execution were of a passive nature, like poisoning food or wine.

Searching for some way to pry open Rozafel's memory, he asked, "Was it to someone in the castle?"

"Mmm, no, don't think so." She thought a moment. Her eyes danced about, looking at nothing yet searching. Suddenly, she grew excited by a surfacing memory. "I sold them to a merchant."

If Rozafel was telling the truth, her murderer could be anyone, and the death of Ule could have been for any reason.

"And you don't remember who?"

She shook her head, squeezing her eyes tight. Her lips twisted as though she were in pain.

He nodded, not quite sure what to say. Nearby, a guard cautioned him, told him to get on with his duties. Reluctant at first, Ulmaen obeyed and stepped back from the cell. He fidgeted with his basket, hoping to find a way to extend his time with Rozafel.

She returned to the far wall of her cell, sat down, placed the bread in the folds of her skirt, and began picking at her scalp. The dread lock she had been fussing with suddenly came free from the mess of her hair.

Rozafel seemed unlikely to have killed a fly, he realized. Unfortunately, she was his only lead, and he'd need to speak with her again.

He served the final cell, then returned to the south entrance, back to the beginning of his journey. The counter was on his right side now, and he still had food remaining, so he walked behind the counter toward the recess in the wall, aiming for the stairs.

"Whoa! You've no business there." Gorlen blocked Ulmaen.

Appreciating being taller now, Ulmaen easily saw the steps lead down to a dimly lit tunnel. Though he couldn't see beyond that, he heard shuffling and the occasional grunt or cough. Someone lingered there, just beyond sight; another guard, perhaps.

"I have a little food left, some bread and apples, a few bits of cheese. Surely someone down there must be hungry." He stared down at Gorlen, enjoying the certainty that no matter what skill the soldier possessed, Ulmaen could overpower him.

Gorlen smirked. "There isn't anything in that basket those kind will eat." He reached into the basket and pulled out a couple of apples then threw one to each of the guards on either side of the stairs.

"Just wait," he said, retrieving the last chunk of bread for himself. "*Their* feeding day's coming, you'll see. Have to wonder though, if you'll be able to handle it."

* CHAPTER 19 *

On the mornings Ulmaen distributed food at the Prison, he made the effort to speak to Rozafel. Most of the time, she was quiet and withdrawn, either playing with the dread lock she had worked free from her hair or picking away at others still rooted in her head. On a couple of occasions, the guards prevented him from speaking with her. By the end of the first week of fulfilling his disciplinary duties, Ulmaen hadn't learned anything else from her.

As for the Pit, he had yet to bring food to the felons detained below ground, but he repeatedly reminded himself of the importance of his purpose—to find out who had killed Ule and why. In the meantime, he listened.

He listened in on many private conversations while stocking the pantries, prepping vegetables, or dishing out food. The cooks, the cutters, the bakers and butchers, unfortunately seldom spoke about matters within the castle. Their concerns were of a personal nature—relationships and sex. Senaga, with her fiery tongue and determination to stay on schedule, barked at anyone who spoke too long about anything.

"And you!" Senaga had pointed an accusatory finger at him one morning. "You're to tend the reception for the art festival, do you hear?" She poked him in the chest and left behind a light dusting of flour on his shirt, daring him to defy her. When she was satisfied that he understood, she tucked a fine white hair beneath her red kerchief.

The day was a long one and began with him serving breakfast at the Prison, then tending to the day long reception for the upcoming festival. Mostly he stood about holding a decanter, serving wine to the gathering crowd in Fehran's Great Hall.

Fluted pink marble columns supported a vaulted ceiling. Stones set in mortar made simple patterns above the peaks of every window and door. Mezzanines lined the north and south sides of the hall, and fastened to their banisters were finely woven tapestries which hung down and hid doors to various chambers below.

Murals in bas relief adorned every wall, and at the back of the hall, where the Magnes greeted and entertained foreign dignitaries, the area had been stripped of its high back chairs, revealing an elaborate depiction of Mxalem and the beasts that skulked about there. Not even the long row of tables draped in red cloth and laden with food detracted from the meticulous skill with which the stone had been carved.

Ulmaen struggled to listen to nearby conversations. Upon hearing the name Ule, he listened to two clothiers ask one another if they'd heard anything new about Ule's death. Both of them shook their heads and proceeded to discuss an elaborate theory of conspiracy.

Disappointed, Ulmaen retreated from the nonsensical discourse, and watched as the gathering grew in size, becoming more boisterous as the day progressed. Listening in on conversations became increasingly more difficult, requiring him to push his hearing ability beyond its normal capacity.

A tap-tap on the back of his shoulder jolted him from his eavesdropping. He flinched, clutching the large decanter of red wine he held. Before turning fully about to tend to the guest, he recognized the soft, sombre voice of Sabien addressing someone at his side.

"A little wine?"

Hope wrenched every muscle in Ulmaen's body and stilled his breath. Familiar lavender perfume drifted over him. He spun around, nearly spilling the wine, a wide smile on his face. And there she was, Bethereel, his love.

He glimpsed her pale, gaunt face, and his smile waned. She was looking elsewhere, at other patrons, all the while shaking her head. Cosmetic powder failed to cover the dark circles around her eyes. She squeezed Sabien's arm and with a weary sigh, she glanced up.

Ulmaen mapped the sharpness of Bethereel's cheekbones, every pale freckle, the dimness in her eyes.

He froze.

Bethereel flinched, like she had been splashed with cold water, yet remained fixated on Ulmaen.

"Wine for me, then." Sabien held out his glass.

Whatever sadness haunted Bethereel receded as she searched Ulmaen's eyes. He savored every moment, his heart quickening and his upper lip moistening with perspiration.

Yes, yes, he thought. See me. Come on. It's me, Ule. I miss you.

"Hello?"

Ulmaen unwillingly broke his gaze and noticed Sabien waggling an empty glass in front of him. Forgetting he had a reputation for being clumsy, he deftly filled the glass.

"I half expected a puddle on the floor. Well done," Sabien applauded.

Ulmaen's thoughts were elsewhere. He had expected his body to yearn for Bethereel, for his flesh to buzz with energy at their close proximity. They had been lovers, so it seemed a natural response. What he discovered was his body only yearned to return to his previous form, the body and molecular array Bethereel had imprinted herself upon.

What arousal trickled through Ulmaen's new flesh was void of love, trust, and desire. Instead, his flesh felt raw and uncertain and lustful, as though it had no experience and waited for those first carnal impressions to sate its curiosity.

Although Ulmaen's mind and heart retained the memory of his love for Bethereel, his body didn't, and the yearning in his heart and mind clashed with his virgin flesh.

"I know you!" Bethereel blurted, nearly stumbling backward from the outburst. She squeezed Sabien's arm tighter to steady herself.

"I think he's new to Sondshor," Sabien told her, then he nodded at Ulmaen. "Aren't you related to Nav somehow?"

Ulmaen nodded.

"You..." Bethereel frowned. The single word sounded almost accusatory.

"What is it?" Sabien asked her.

"You," she began again, focused on Ulmaen. "I'm not supposed to know you." She shook her head, confused. "I don't... know you." She tilted her head, her eyes welling with tears.

Ulmaen waved toward the table. "Some food might make you feel better. You could certainly eat something. Let me get you something."

"I can't—" She shut her eyes. Her lips paled. "He," she began, speaking to Sabien, but she couldn't finish the sentence. Mustering strength, she opened her eyes. Again, she winced at the sight of Ulmaen. She leaned in to Sabien and spoke again. "He reminds me of *her*."

Sabien choked on a mouthful of wine. "Hardly," he whispered back. "He's too tall," he told her, then laughed.

Bethereel sagged.

"Just a little jest to ease your mood. I meant nothing by it. I guess there is something familiar about him, in his eyes," he assured her.

Letting out a long sigh, Bethereel leaned against Sabien. "I can't do this. I'm... I'm going back to my room."

"I must work the crowds, get them excited about the first show," he told her. "You're going to miss it."

Bethereel stood on her own again. She forced a smile and said, "All the best cousin." After she glanced at Ulmaen a second time, she shook her head again. Tears welled up in her eyes as she slipped through the crowds.

"Make sure to see the show if you can," Sabien told Ulmaen. "I bet you there's nothing like it where you come from."

He downed his wine in a long single haul and handed Ulmaen the empty glass. He straightened his vest then eased himself into the nearest cluster of people, joining in their conversation. Eventually, he'd steer their discussion onto a new topic and whet their appetites with tidbits about the show.

Dazed by Bethereel's distress, Ulmaen automatically gripped the warm glass in his free hand. The urge to go after her, to hold her and soothe her, consumed him. He fought the compulsion, the excess energy channeling into his muscles. They tensed. Ulmaen flexed, and the bowl of the wine glass caved in.

He grew aware of those nearby watching him. Kerista scowled, and next to her Boriag snorted. Navalis, who was a part of their company, spoke loudly. "My brother in law still can't sort out how to serve wine!"

Then Navalis was close by, pulling Ulmaen with him toward the food tables. Still dazed by the encounter with Bethereel, the most Ulmaen was aware of was Boriag's snort-like laughter.

Navalis picked up a sweet delicacy made of fine pastry and fig paste. He popped it in his mouth and approved of the flavor. "What's wrong with you now?"

Ulmaen trembled. "This is the first I've seen Bethee since my funeral."

"Watch it now," Navalis warned. "You need to exercise some discretion."

Ulmaen hunched to whisper to his Master. "It's just... she's so close. I want to squeeze her in my arms, make her happy again. Taste her lips. She has this dry spot on her lower lip. We've tried every balm to try to fix it. When she kissed me in the right spots, it tickled—"

"Stop doing this to yourself."

The intensity in Navalis's eyes, the sharpness of his tone—he was serious. His earlier humor had evaporated in an instant.

"It's never going back the way it was," he urged. "Don't try to re-initiate that level of intimacy with her."

"Why?"

"You might do or say something to remind her about Ule," Navalis explained. "Eventually Bethereel will start to see beyond this surface." He pinched the flesh on Ulmaen's forearm for emphasis. "She won't know how or why, but she'll suspect something's different about you. Some of these Elishians have uncanny perception. They may see more of us than we'd like them to."

Ulmaen hadn't thought much about why Navalis kept his distance from others, why he never got involved with anyone romantically, especially after Sabien. Even after Navalis returned to Elish in a different form and identity, and Sabien regarded him as someone new, there remained a familiarity between them. Somehow, something between them had soured.

"Is that why you avoid Sabien?" he asked. "So he won't see that you and Avn are the same person?"

"Yes." Navalis looked out across the Hall, reluctant to elaborate on the topic.

Ulmaen leaned in a little closer. "What aren't you telling me?"

"It's complicated. You'll see."

Unable to shake the feeling that his question had been skillfully deflected, Ulmaen wanted to force answers from Navalis, but he was interrupted.

"How is she?" Laere's plaintive voice sounded childlike. "Bethereel, how is she?"

Ulmaen sniffed. "She could stand to put on a few pounds." He cringed as the words spilled off his tongue, not intending to be hurtful or spiteful, just a comment. Had Ule said the same thing, she might have been shamed for it.

Laere gently laughed.

How odd, Ulmaen thought. Usually tht kind of comment incurred anger, not mirth.

"She's been through a lot," Laere tried to explain Bethereel's condition. She paused a moment, then drank the last bit of wine in her glass while holding her mop of hair off her face. When she was done, she smacked her lips.

"You're that new fellow, aren't you?" She grinned, her cheeks growing flushed. She held out her empty wine glass and waggled it before him.

Ulmaen emptied the decanter into the glass, nearly filling it to the brim. He suddenly found it strange pretending to be a stranger to all these people he knew.

"Oh, that's a lot." She sipped at the wine to prevent it from spilling down the sides of the glass. When she was satisfied, she flicked back her hair again.

The way Laere's eyes and mouth opened made her quite pretty. In the past, when he had been Ule, Laere was prone to glaring a lot, looking about as pinched as a raisin yet certainly not as sweet.

"I've seen you around the Kitchen," Laere claimed.

He nodded.

"Heard you made a mess of the Council Room." She laughed through her nose, her eyes becoming glassy.

Ulmaen really didn't want to converse with her. He needed to keep tending to others, listening in on as many conversations as he could. More importantly, he needed to know if Bethereel was feeling better.

She laughed through her nose again, but she didn't care. "I'm Laere," she told him. "I'm an artist."

At the mention of her profession, her mood turned passionate. "I cannot wait until the festival starts tomorrow. I have an amazing project. Do you wanna hear about it?"

Before he could say no, she began rambling again.

"I'm going to do a life size portrait of Ule."

At the sound of his old name, Ulmaen froze in confusion. So certain Laere hated Ule, why would she do such a thing?

"You wouldn't have known her. She died before you came, and we never got along." Laere rolled her eyes. "Who am I kidding? I hated her, but I need to do right by Bethee."

Although Laere's admission of hatred resonated with her recent actions of celebrating Ule's death, Ulmaen had a difficult time correlating her hatred with the desire to paint Ule's portrait. Why would she devote her talent, energy, and time to a subject she detested?

Laere detected Ulmaen's confusion yet misunderstood it when she said, "Bethee? It's short for Bethereel."

When he didn't respond, she shrugged and her smile waned. "To make a long story short, I'm doing the portrait for her."

Ulmaen's confusion subsided. Laere's giving gesture, the meaningful sentiment behind it, pleased him in a way he didn't think possible.

In a flash, her passion resumed. "I found a couple of models who kind of look like Ule, but I haven't decided which one to use yet. And I've been researching. A few sketches, some descriptions, her favorite objects and clothes, then there's drawing from memory. I'll be set up by the Starry Rise. You know where that is, right?"

Ulmaen knew exactly where the Starry Rise was. "Nope," he replied, knowing he needed to lie.

"It's the fountain by the Temple, on the west side of the grounds, where the walkways merge—"

A bell rang throughout the hall.

Her gaze locked onto him. Eyes wide, lips parted, she waved her free hand frantically while downing the rest of her wine. Setting the empty glass on one of the food tables nearby, she smacked her lips and shouted, "It's him! That's him isn't it?"

"Who?" Ulmaen scanned the people nearby.

He saw Mbjard on the outskirts of the crowd speaking with a strange fellow. Mbjard was an impressive man, but not the kind that evoked a fanatical response.

Perhaps Laere referred to the fellow with whom Mbjard spoke, whose hands were heavily scarred, his head covered by a cowl. He wore a belted sword, a whip at his hip, and slung across his back were a pair of shackles. He wasn't dressed in any kind of uniform and looked like neither a guard nor a soldier.

Ulmaen remembered the message written on Ule's wrist, written in the language of criminals, and his imagination ran wild thinking of who the cowled man could be. Thieves were a dime a dozen. Perhaps, he was a murderer. Or... a bounty hunter?

"Hallo!"

Ulmaen flinched at the greeting. He'd been so caught up in his speculations, he'd failed to notice the cowled man had approached him. The man extended his hand.

"Mbjard tells me you're new to Sondshor," he said in a gruff voice. "Welcome, welcome."

Reluctantly, Ulmaen shook his hand and found his grip was firm and strong.

"*Frld*," Ulmaen responded in the language of the abjad that Mbjard had written on Ule's wrist. He hoped the salutation might help bridge the gap between him and the criminals Mbjard worked for.

The man in the cowl shook his head. "What's that?"

"*Frld*," Ulmaen repeated himself. "Surely you know that?"

The man in the cowl shook his head and laughed. "Sounds like someone punched you too many times." He laughed again. "A pleasure to meet you. Now, I'd stay but it's back to the quarry for me."

"Q-quarry?" Ulmaen stammered. "A-are you a Prison guard?"

"Nah," he replied. "I'm the executioner, but there aren't a lot of heads to chop anymore, so I keep an eye on the crew at the quarry, make sure they stay in line." He shook Ulmaen's hand again. "*Frld* to you, too, whatever that means."

Ulmaen laughed at himself. He'd been so caught up in seeing shadows in every corner, it never occurred to him the cowled man could have been anyone really. He felt embarrassed by the suspicious assumption, and promised himself to be more careful in the future.

"Oh, it must be time!" The shrillness of Laere's voice and her wide eyes made her look maniacal.

"Time for what?" he asked, trying to keep up with her.

The bell rang again. The myriad of conversations settled into hushes and whispers, while Laere danced on the spot, grinning from ear to ear.

✳ CHAPTER 20 ✳

Laere craned to see above the crowd. Everyone's gaze was directed at the mezzanine on the north side of the room, where in front of a pale pink tapestry covered in geometric depictions of eyes, the man with a reputation for telling stories climbed onto a chair and addressed everyone.

"Isn't he handsome?" Laere sighed. "I just love listening to his voice."

Ulmaen snorted. "Oh, that's who you mean."

He expected his response to Sabien's deep intonations and earthy voice to be different now that he was a man, but as he listened to Sabien encourage everyone to step a little closer, he discovered he still enjoyed listening to him speak.

"He's doing three shows today." Laere nodded her head. "Have you ever been to one?"

He was about to answer when she cut him off.

"Of course you haven't. You're from the North."

She grabbed his hand in hers and pulled hard at his arm, intending to drag him toward the mezzanine where Sabien beckoned to them, but Ulmaen remained rooted to the floor. She flung back, careening into him, bracing her hand against his stomach, and although his body didn't mind the contact, his heart and mind preferred Bethereel's touch.

"Need to keep an eye on the food," he told her.

Her smile failed to falter as her eyes narrowed on him, sparkling at the prospect of possible mischief.

"Oh come on," she urged, peeking out from behind the mess of her hair. "You won't get into trouble. No one'll even know you're gone."

"I'm already in trouble."

She stomped the floor, tugging at his arm. "We'll be gone and back before anyone gets low on wine. Besides, there's two others serving wine, and everyone's too drunk to remember their names." Finally, she gave up on moving him with what little strength she had and tried with words instead.

"The fumes in here are as thick as monkey's breath. If anyone were to ask where you'd gone, you could tell them you sprouted wings and flew to the moon and they'd believe you."

He found his body wanting to yield to her as she resumed tugging at his arm.

He backed off, cast her a brief smile, then retreated to one of the wine stations near a section of the bas relief mural depicting a giant bird man surrounded by a series of spirals that could either be suns or galaxies; he couldn't decide.

He set the broken glass in a bucket filled with other broken dishes. Tipping the decanter beneath a keg spout, he began refilling it. As the thick red wine neared the top, he shut the valve and turned back toward the crowds.

Nearby, Mbjard stood alone. He raised an empty glass and waggled it about, signaling for more wine. Ulmaen approached him, and Mbjard was kind enough to meet him halfway. He filled the glass, Mbjard nodded in appreciation, and as Ulmaen turned about to search for others in need of wine, Laere stood in his way.

Ulmaen flinched. The decanter slipped through his fingers and hit the pink marble floor with a loud wet explosion. A cheer erupted throughout the Hall, and as the outcry came to a stop, he heard Senaga on the far side of the Hall call out.

"That's another two weeks serving The Pit for you!"

A second cheer resounded, followed by laughter. Their mirth toward him for being clumsy had never bothered him until now. This time he hadn't been pretending. As Ule, this kind of repeated accidental behavior was charming and quirky. Now, as a man, he felt embarrassed by it. What made him even more self-conscience was the sympathetic way Mbjard regarded him.

"I didn't mean to scare you," Laere told him.

"Startle," he corrected her. "You *startled* me." He squatted over the mess and began picking out shards of glass from the puddle of wine. A young girl with a rag mop and a bucket of water helped clean the spill.

"Sorry." Laere squatted down with him. She smiled weakly. "I didn't mean to *startle* you."

"Something tells me you don't mean to do a lot of things."

He expected her to pout at the comment. Instead, she laughed.

A third person joined them, and beneath their shadow, Ulmaen heard, "*Mdsi al.*"

The words were unexpected and foreign. Diminished Eelsee to be exact. A command to others to take what was being offered to them. Ulmaen stood and accepted the broken arm of the decanter from Mbjard, curious as to why he spoke to him in a different language.

"It traveled far," Mbjard said. "Like you."

"*Agya,*" Ulmaen replied without thinking. *Thank you* seemed the appropriate response. And he hoped the indication of keeping their conversation private might help him gain Mbjard's confidence, especially if he was the criminal he thought he was.

"I assumed you were from the D'Achta Clan." Mbjard crinkled his eyes, scrutinized Ulmaen. "Because you were familiar with their unique dance custom for serving wine. It isn't common knowledge. Are you now going to tell me you're from Eelsee?"

Ulmaen coughed, inwardly cringing at his mistake. "Ah no. I know some dialects other than D'Achtan. I recognized yours and just... spoke the same."

Mbjard smiled. "*Frld?*"

Ulmaen's eyes grew wide. He froze, unsure of what he was getting himself into. "It's... It's—"

"That's the greeting you gave my friend," Mbjard insisted excitedly. "Not too many know Attalag. It's a very old sea language, recorded as an abjad by pirates. Do you know any other words in the language?"

Ulmaen shook himself from his panic. "Just a few," he replied. "What my uncle told me," he lied, then quickly added, "He was a sailor."

"That makes sense," Mbjard said. "Some of the words have survived and continue to be used by sailors." He folded his hands behind his back and nodded. "I have—" He caught himself, then started again. "I *had* an apprentice who helped me solve puzzles written in Attalag. The absence of vowels made some of the solutions sound quite amusing."

The memory struck Ulmaen hard. Both Ule and Mbjard had spent hours together coming up with the absurdest sounds as interpretations for the mysterious missing vowels in old abjad puzzles they had discovered in the Library.

Why hadn't he remembered that? It explained why Mbjard had written in abjad on Ule's wrist—he simply meant to honour a memory they had shared. Though the message he inscribed remained a puzzle in itself, he suspected it was harmless.

"Seems you might have other talents going unused," Mbjard said, then retreated into the crowd.

Why had he needed Mbjard to be a spy instead? He had been, if nothing else, forthright and honest in their past relationship.

Ulmaen returned to the mess on the floor, any doubts he had about Mbjard fading quickly. He was a man of languages and nothing more. The message he inscribed on Ule's wrist must have been a farewell message, albeit a cryptic one.

Satisfied he'd found every bit of glass on the floor, he let the young girl mop up the wine and retreated to discard the broken decanter. Task completed, he turned about and flinched yet again at the sight of Laere.

He laughed. He wasn't sure what to make of her but he did appreciate her tenacity.

"Come on," she resumed her coaxing. "Before Senaga reassigns you to the Sewers."

This time when Laere pulled on his arm, he yielded. She cut through clusters of people without apology or any thought to their well-being. She'd always been headstrong that way, and Ule had always found that trait to be. Now, as Ulmaen, he found it amusing.

Unable to penetrate certain crowds, they snaked their way toward the front of the hall, where people ducked behind a tapestry depicting a lion-like creature with serpents for a mane. Behind the tapestry, they emerged beneath a narrow portico where an open door awaited them.

"Hurry," Laere insisted. "We've already missed too much of the show." She released his hand and bolted through the door.

The room beyond had been neglected over the years yet accommodated the show nicely. Given the heavily plastered walls covered with strings of cobweb and the dusty shelves and small tables, Sabien must have poured his energy into the presentation of artifacts instead of cleaning.

Laere lingered near a table, in proximity to Sabien. Ulmaen preferred to stay far away, across the room where he examined ethereal-like deep sea creatures bottled in amber solutions.

Sabien began to tell a familiar tale, one Ulmaen had heard many times over the past couple of years—the story of a demon who fell in love with an Elishian and how all that remained of this demon was the rock on display.

At the mention of how deeply this demon loved, a rage flooded the room. Istok must have heard the account thousands of times by now, and still he succumbed to a fit of rage at the exact same point in the story.

Those nearest the stone recoiled in shock at the intensity of the emotion. Some laughed. Over the years, responses seldom varied: *Did you feel that? Was that for real? How do you do that?*

Even Laere ceased gazing at the strange deformations in the articulated skeletons of animals on the table next to her. She stood on tip toe to see the rock. Ulmaen expected her to push through the crowd, but she restrained herself.

"You!" Istok's disembodied voice boomed throughout the room.

Ulmaen glanced around nervously. No one else had recognized him as Ule. He hadn't expected Istok to either, but as a disembodied essence, perhaps Istok perceived differently now. Ulmaen began to project, "What do you—"

"All of you! Sheep," Istok projected furiously. "Fucking useless sheep."

Istok hadn't been talking to Ulmaen at all. In a panic, he pulled back his thoughts. In the silence that followed, he scanned the crowd. Nothing had changed. No one had noticed, except...

Laere's intense enthusiasm had faded. Her face was pale and her eyes darted about the room.

"Who's there?" Istok grumbled. "I can sense your thoughts. Ule?"

Laere's lips parted, her eyes resuming a frenzied search of the room.

Ulmaen thought her behavior peculiar, but then there was a lot about her that was peculiar, and there were plenty of intriguing specimens in the collection to be disturbed by.

"It's me." Ulmaen finally said, reluctant to engage in conversation with the demon

"Huh, you sound different." The demon's rage subsided a little. Based on the reactions of some of the crowd, the reprieve from the demon's emotional intensity was welcomed.

Laere brushed by Ulmaen, searching under and behind the tables.

"There you are! You look different, too," Istok mused. "That's right, your kind don't die, do they?"

"We can," Ulmaen corrected him. "We die, just like your kind. I have a new form, that's all."

"Doesn't matter," Istok growled. "You're still a fucking cockwart no matter what you look like."

Ulmaen snorted out loud, surprised he wasn't offended by the remark. A few patrons nearby glanced at him, including Laere, and for an instant, he considered the possibility that Laere had heard something other than his snort.

Istok boomed inside Ulmaen, and he asked, "With your talents, little cow, what makes you stick around this hole?"

"Searching the castle, that's all." Ulmaen feigned boredom, determined to end their conversation once and for all.

"Looking for what?"

"None of your business."

Pleased by the demon's silence, Ulmaen assumed their conversation had ended until Istok spoke again, his mood determined and menacing.

"You're looking for *it*, aren't you?"

"Looking for what?"

"Don't play games," Istok grumbled. Another wave of anger flooded the room, causing a woman to swoon. "Have you found the treasure then?"

Ulmaen laughed, and for a moment was distracted by more people turning to look at him.

Even Sabien paused in his telling. "I've told this story many times," he said. "Many have cried but none have laughed." He gestured toward Ulmaen. "Does the story amuse you?"

"Sorry!" Ulmaen rubbed the back of his neck again and bashfully shook his head. "Go on, it's a great story."

Sabien nodded with gratitude and resumed speaking to the crowd.

Ulmaen returned his attention to Istok. "I know the treasure you talk about. Whatever it is, it's a myth."

"There's always some truth to the old stories." Istok laughed. "Just ask me, I was there for many of them. Better still, ask Mithreel."

Ulmaen recognized the familiar use of the -eel suffix which indicated the name's ancient origin.

"Who's Mithreel?"

"Ah, so you haven't searched the castle very hard then if you haven't met *him* yet. He used to guard it, a very long time ago, hiding it here and there. Then he was caught, and no one's found it since."

A rustle at the door broke Ulmaen's concentration. Nearby, Laere stood stiffly, staring directly at him. Her face was flushed and her chest rose sharply as though she were out of breath.

"Are you alright?" he asked her.

The sudden presence of the arch mystic in the doorway silenced the buzz of excitement in the room.

"Keep quiet for now," Ulmaen projected toward Istok.

A group of patrons stepped back to give Kerista space and others quickly exited the room as she moved toward the feature display.

"Don't tell me to shut up!" Istok's anger flared. "Ugh, it's her again."

Kerista hesitated in mid-stride, tilting her head as though listening for the subtlest of thoughts. Laere fell in behind the arch mystic, nearly clinging to her.

Ulmaen expected Istok to continue his rantings, but he remained quiet.

Eventually Kerista drew closer to the table where the kornerupine was being displayed. For several moments, she gazed at the object.

"This is it? The stone everyone's been talking about?"

Sabien nodded in response.

"It does what the stories say," Laere told Kerista. "I felt it."

"It only responds while I tell the story," Sabien explained. He bowed respectfully. "If you return in about an hour, I can demonstrate during a retelling." He coughed. "My voice needs a rest."

"There are trigger words you speak that cause it to respond?" she asked.

Sabien shrugged. "When you say it like that, sure."

"May I?" Mesmerized, Kerista reached out to touch the stone.

As though accustomed to this behavior, Sabien calmly grabbed the stone, placed it back in its iron box, and closed the lid.

"It's... a family heirloom," he lied to her. "My apologies, but I'd rather not. If you come back..." He never finished his sentence.

Determined to save Sabien from lying further, Ulmaen strode the length of the room and asked Kerista, "So what'd you think of that tale?" Then as an aside to Sabien, he added, "Nice research there. You've been to the Archive in Woedshor, I can tell."

Sabien balked at first, then admitted to the observation with a nod. Recognizing the interruption as an opportunity to escape, Sabien withdrew from the podium to mingle with other patrons and answer their questions about the articulated skeleton of a rat demon.

"To answer your question," Kerista eventually replied, unable to pry her eyes away from the iron box, "the story sounds contrived, no matter how well researched. As for the feeling emanating from the stone, that's undoubtedly genuine. And strong. I felt its presence out in the Hall."

"And how 'bout you?" He leaned forward to pinch Laere, but she cringed.

How odd, he thought. Less than half an hour ago, she couldn't keep her hands off me.

"I felt rage pure as fire," Laere told him, her eyes dancing all over his face. "I almost expected the stone to start *talking*."

Her comment was unusual and he wasn't sure what she meant.

"Did you feel anything?" Laere asked Kerista tentatively.

"Yes," Kerista replied, her thoughts elsewhere.

"Do you think it's a trick?"

"No, it's genuine." Kerista fixated on the iron box. "And unfortunately sentient."

"Unfortunate for the one whose spirit is trapped," Laere speculated.

Kerista grunted. "And unfortunate for The Storyteller. Buying and selling of objects that have been bound with a sentient being are illegal in Sondshor."

"But he said it's an heirloom," Ulmaen argued, feeling the need to protect his friend. "It's not been sold, it's been passed down in his family."

Kerista crinkled her nose in disgust at first, then narrowed her eyes. "He may have to prove that."

✳ CHAPTER 21 ✳

Ulmaen lay stretched out on a cot too short for his stature, in a cellar room far too small to accommodate the additional half dozen cots. Around him, fellow servants from the day shift slept fitfully as the night churned and thundered outside Kugilla Hall.

He usually spent this time fantasizing about reuniting with Bethereel. Some of his scenarios were more vivid and satisfying than others, but his favorite involved Bethereel finally recognizing him, looking past his body and truly seeing the essence of Ule.

Ulmaen struggled to think about her, but Laere kept invading his thoughts like a mischievous cat looking for attention. Yet, there was something beyond her personality that kept bothering him.

Laere had befriended him at the opening reception, eager and precocious, a little flirty too. Then, during Sabien's show, she'd grown fearful, perhaps of the strange artifacts, which seemed odd since she had seen his show before.

What was it about her that had been so peculiar? She'd started searching the displays, that's what. During the story of Istok, she'd looked all over the room, behind tapestries and beneath tables. After the story had finished, she kept her distance from Ulmaen, and after she spoke with Kerista, she'd calmed down again.

Then there was what she had said to him afterward. What had she meant when she said she expected the stone to start talking?

Ulmaen turned onto his side. One of the other servants called out in the dark and told him to settle down. Curling tighter, Ulmaen focused on the aches in his body. The solidity and bulk of his muscles were unsettling at first; now he appreciated how they pulled his body into alignment no matter how he laid.

The other servant called out again, a disembodied voice in the dark. He repeated himself, requiring acknowledgment that he had been heard.

"Yeah, I'm sleeping now," Ulmaen said, and was hushed by others nearby.

Voices. In the dark.

Ulmaen bolted upright and was bombarded by groggy curses and moans as he rolled out of the cot and shuffled across the floor toward the exit.

She'd heard.

Outside the room, he paced the length of the short corridor. Laere had heard him project. How was this possible? Had she been related to someone with powerful perception?

Adinav came to mind first. Perhaps Laere was a distant relative or descendant of his, which would explain her need to preserve his image.

She could be related to anyone, like a powerful mystic. Was she descended from Goyas?

Ulmaen recalled his experience within the Catacomb, the partially ingested body of Goyas, some of whose molecules made up Ulmaen's current molecular array. Perhaps Laere didn't need to be a descendant? Perhaps the ingestion of Goyas combined with a ritual...

She was an artist, he reminded himself, reining in his wild theory. She wasn't dabbling in the mystic arts? Or was she?

The desire to protect Elish surged through his muscles. He'd made a promise to his kind to destroy anyone who dared threaten the world or his home realm, but Laere? Tiny, annoying, pretty little Laere, who liked to drink too much and shoot off her mouth whenever she felt impassioned or indignant?

He needed to find out the truth about her, for he wouldn't let another like Adinav rise to power again.

Sweat rolled down Ulmaen's head and back, making his shirt cling to his muscles. He skirted a wagon led by a horse along the eastern Colonnade. On the outskirts of the castle grounds, mostly fluted pillars remained of the old walkway, but toward the middle of the grounds, where the three walkways converged, the original pink marble covering stood fully intact and he welcomed its shade.

He slowed his pace, stopping every now and again to peer at painting of landscapes and portraits in progress. Occasionally there were other images which incorporated distortions into their rendering—caricatures, cartoons even. The vivid fluidity of these forms often depicted unrecognizable creatures, and the longer he stared at them, the more he felt like he was in a dream about birdmen, lions with snakes for manes, giant white wolves, and a mysterious figure made of eyes—unnerving reminders of his own kind, the primaries of the Xiinisi Council.

Near the Temple, there was a bend in the eastern Colonnade before it curved southward, which obstructed the view, but once he rounded the corner of the Temple, he was struck by the dull roar and smell of fresh fountain water.

The covering of pink marble opened up to the sky in a wide circle and beneath it was a fountain in the heart of a flower garden. Sprays of water sparkled and frothed as they shot into the air and crashed back down into a wide circular pink marble basin.

The Starry Rise looked resplendent this morning, and Ulmaen enjoyed the play of light in the moving water. He spied the occasional shadow, and when he looked up, every now and again someone leaned on the railing around the opening and peered down.

Ulmaen wondered if some of the artists had hiked their gear across the bridge from Old Slate Tower and were set up on the roof of the Colonnade—there was so much to see. What surprised him most was that none of the artists bothered to render the beauty of the Starry Rise, as it gushed and gurgled.

Recently trimmed footpaths wound through a sea of red roses and purple catmint which swelled and cascaded over the remnant of a crenelated parapet made of white stone and mortar. It had been dug up when the fountain was built and belonged to the original castle buried below.

Ulmaen knew about the castle below, based on what he had read in the Archive, but he wasn't sure who else did. Beneath the fountain, parts of the original castle remained intact and some of the towers were still in use.

Beneath that castle existed the remnants of a town. And beneath that town, a village had once revered the sanctity of a natural spring. Now, they revered the Starry Rise, even if they didn't remember why.

A large concentration of artists had set up work near the garden. Some were by the fountain beneath direct sunlight, but most preferred the shade of the covered Colonnade.

He spotted Laere in a shaded spot in front of the Temple, where the Colonnade veered south. She sat on a rickety stool, the wobbly legs of little concern to her as she remained deeply engrossed in brushing bright cadmium red into the corners of a giant canvas.

In the middle of the canvas, Ulmaen stared at his reflection in female form. The clothes and hands were roughly sketched. There was an absence of detail except for what Laere had captured in the eyes—the very essence of Ule.

This piece promised to come alive like her other finished works. Laere undoubtedly was a skilled artist. What had always been questionable were her choices in subject matter. Ulmaen never regretted destroying images of Adinav, but he had felt some misgivings when those works expressed great talent.

"You came." Laere strained to look over her shoulder, her arm raised high, her hand gripping a large red stained brush.

"Don't stop on my account," he urged. When he glimpsed the model, he stopped and stared at what she wore: a lavender jacket with tapered pants of the same color and brown suede boots which laced up to the knee. At first glance, the outfit looked identical to what Ule had last been seen wearing, but the cut of the collar and the waistline were different.

"Oh, not a bother." Laere rose from her stool and instructed the model to rest awhile. Slowly, cautiously, she approached him.

He expected her to act oddly again. If she had heard his projected thoughts, she should be frightened beyond her wits. Instead, she regarded him with cautious fascination, her eyes darting all over him, making note of what, he didn't know.

"What do you think of the portrait so far?" She invited him to look at the canvas more closely.

He found it odd scrutinizing his previous form. She, Ule that is, had been too skinny, her hands too large, her nose too wide, her breasts too small, and none of these attributes were the result of Laere's inaccurate rendering. He stopped himself and wondered when exactly he had become so critical. He, at one time, had loved *that* particular female form.

In the developed areas of the portrait, Laere had captured the likeness of Ule as well as some of her qualities he had difficulty identifying with anymore--her vulnerability, her defiance, and what came across as snootiness.

"I like to always do an under sketch," Laere began to explain. "With every layer, the image gets refined, and the top most layers are for details. I always make sure to capture something significant about the subject, the way they stand or the way they look, especially around the eyes." She paused a moment. "Details unique to that person. You know, to reflect what makes them *special*."

He detected the extra emphasis on the final word she spoke and wondered what she meant by it.

"What makes you special?" Laere smiled.

There was an underhandedness about the question he couldn't quite grasp. A neediness, too.

Be careful, he told himself.

"I spill wine," he replied.

A tense, nervous kind of laugh shook Laere. She was, for lack of a better word, fishing—casting her charm like a line and hook.

"Do you think some people can see more than others?" she asked, scanning his face for an answer. "Do you think there are layers to the world, just like a painting, and some can see the under layers?"

He wondered what she meant by the question

"Maybe even *hear* more than others?"

Uneasiness took hold of him, and he shivered. She had heard his projections after all. Not quite sure how to hide his panic, he resorted to deflecting her inquiries.

"You're full of questions today. Best cut back or you'll bloat," he told her, hoping to deflect her with humor.

She laughed again, covering her mouth, this time her mirth genuine. "You're so funny. Did you know that?"

Usually his comments were met with odd stares and uncomfortable silences, at least when he had been Ule. Now, he felt a divide within himself, an unusual distance again, a part of him unsettled and concerned, and the other, a facade of good humor. As Ule, these two parts had been intertwined and inseparable.

Laere returned to her stool and nodded at the model. The model resumed her pose, and Laere picked up her brush and palette.

"Do you think it's possible for anyone who isn't a mystic to start hearing the thoughts of others?" she asked.

The only Elishians he knew who possessed the ability to sense others' feelings and thoughts were potentially dangerous. Suddenly awakening to a skill was very rare, but he knew of two Elishians with that gift. One had been a tenacious yet kind mystic name Goyas, and the other, Adinav.

He shrugged. "I don't know—"

A shrill, forceful voice cried out and interrupted their conversation. "What is this?!"

Ulmaen spun around. Bethereel teetered next to her cousin, Sabien. She lurched forward, unhooking her arm from his, and lost her balance slightly. When Sabien offered to help her, she smacked his arm away.

She was strikingly paler and thinner since Ulmaen had last seen her, and she inched toward the painting of Ule. Her dull eyes honed in on the model, she curled her fingers into fists, and shook.

"Where did you get those clothes?!"

Her words reverberated along the portico. Her lower lip quivered.

Sabien called out to her softly, on the verge of losing his patience. "They're not anything like Ule's clothes," he told her. "They look similar, but what she wore was destroyed. Remember what Osblod said when you asked him to return them?"

His words sank in, but they only fueled Bethereel's emotions. "Is that it? Did you steal them from the Infirmary and patch them back together again?"

Ulmaen instinctively reached out to calm Bethereel, but she ignored his gesture. She uncurled a hand and brought it to her mouth. Tears sprung from her eyes.

"Bethee, please," Laere implored as she clumsily rose to her feet. The palette spilled from her lap and splattered the walkway.

"I-Is this a... a joke?"

Laere shook her head. "N-no," she sputtered, clutching the red brush. She stepped a little closer to Bethereel. "Let me explain. This? It's a gift. For you. A reminder—"

Bethereel's face distorted with fury. "I don't want to be reminded of what she died in."

Laere's face dropped. She swiveled back toward the model. "I... I didn't—"

"That's what she wore," Bethereel shouted, her lips whitened, "when she died."

Laere gasped. "I'd seen her wear it before, many times. It was pretty. I didn't, I didn't... think."

Bethereel screeched a loud, distorted cry, and Ulmaen's heart sank at the sound of his lover's anguish. She cried out again. Her raised arm snapped forward, hard. She snatched the brush from Laere and flung it at her. Red paint smeared the skirt of Laere's dress. Then she struck Laere across the cheek with the heel of her hand.

Laere fell backward like a heavy sack. Sprawled across the ground, she cradled the side of her face as she sat upright.

Bethereel was a passionate woman. Willful and opinionated, too. She was also kind and gracious but had never been violent. Yet, twice now, Ulmaen had witnessed her lash out and inflict pain on Laere.

He took a deep breath, trying hard not to interfere, realizing he was losing Bethereel—in body, mind, and spirit.

She's grieving, he reminded himself.

He understood her helplessness, her lack of control. As a child, he had nurtured a world containing two beautiful races, the Gypsums and the Granites. After they annihilated one another, he struggled with rage regarding his lack of control over their fates. So he destroyed the world and was later incarcerated for its destruction.

Ulmaen needed to find some way to ease Bethereel's suffering, either with answers about Ule's murder or through re-connecting with her, before all of her beauty vanished.

Bethereel screamed again. The garbled, indecipherable wail was deafening this time. An uneasy quiet crept along the Colonnade and around the Starry Rise.

Ulmaen couldn't stand by and do nothing. As he offered to help Sabien with Bethereel, Navalis appeared from around the bend in the walkway.

* CHAPTER 22 *

Boriag buzzed around Navalis like a dazed bee. "You know, it's good to get out once in a while. Some fresh air. I'll tell ya, what we breathe down there isn't the same. Oh, look at that!"

Navalis glanced in the general direction Boriag pointed. In front of the Games Hall, he saw a partially nude model posed on the Colonnade.

"Taking a break from you know what is truly the best," Boriag mumbled, as he ogled her. "Gain some perspective."

Navalis yawned, mindful of not bumping into anyone who loitered there.

"Hey, I can teach you a little bit about art," Boriag suggested. "Broaden your horizons. The best part, we get to gaze at wondrous naked bodies and draw them."

Navalis lacked Boriag's awe-inspired fervor for the festival. His mind chose to mull over demons instead, but he knew he needed to at least feign interest in his surroundings. He nodded and smiled, but Boriag wasn't convinced.

"Whaaat? You're not enjoying the view?"

Navalis had seen forms of wonder and great beauty for several millenia, and they seldom moved him anymore, not in the way they did when he was younger. He appreciated their proximity to perfection and was simultaneously bored by their symmetry. If given the chance to gaze at a cut and polished stone or one that had just been mined, he'd prefer the mined one with its many rough edges.

"It's a fine view," he lied.

As they passed another nude model on the other side of the Colonnade near the Studio and the Temple, the model rolled her eyes at the sight of Boriag, preferring to fixate on Navalis. A smile curled her plump lips until an artist scolded her for changing her expression.

"I love art!" Boriag was nearly beside himself with joy. "Ah, look at that brush stroke, so thick with emotion, a swell of sensuality." He nudged Navalis. "Thanks for coming along. I won't be so nervous when we find Laere."

Navalis shook his head. "Who's Laere?"

"An artist. Does portraits, I think. I want to see her work." Boriag craned his head to search the crowds.

They followed the bend in the Colonnade, guiding them toward the Starry Rise. All about them onlookers watched artists displaying their skills. The chatter was serene until a screech pierced the air.

Wide-eyed and stunned, Boriag gulped several times before he found his voice again. "W-what was that?"

At the outcry, patrons stopped talking and turned to one another in confusion. Painters froze in mid dab, and sculptors rested their hands against blocks of clay or wood. Nearly everyone looked in the direction of the Temple for the source of the distress.

Navalis hurried around the bend and collided with a familiar man. Memories of intimacy prickled his flesh, and he immediately dreaded the physical contact with Sabien.

Sabien flashed a scowl, the veins in his neck bulging. He turned to speak his mind but upon recognizing Navalis, he relaxed a little. His anger persevered as he waved at onlookers, urging them to move on or, at the least, move back.

Next to him, Bethereel stood vibrating with fury. Her fingers curled and uncurled. Rage chiseled her thin face. Sprawled on the ground before her was an artist with a red streak across her dress and cradled another on her cheek.

Nearby, Ulmaen stood. He seemed frozen, as though he had been caught doing something he shouldn't. Even stranger was the model, who bore an uncanny resemblance to Ule.

"What the..." Boriag gaped at the scene before him.

Navalis didn't share his friend's confusion. He'd gleaned enough from what he saw to understand Bethereel had been upset by the painting of Ule. And given the intensity of her rage, he wasn't as shocked as everyone else when she began to collapse.

Ulmaen was expectedly frantic over her deteriorating condition, but his behavior was worrisome. His emotional reaction toward her didn't accurately convey their current relationship. He and Bethereel were strangers, nothing more. Yet the way he fretted, anyone might think otherwise if he rushed to help her.

Navalis lunged forward and grabbed Bethereel beneath the arms before Ulmaen could. Sabien secured her about the waist. Together they helped her regain her balance.

Discouraged, Ulmaen backed away.

Sobs wracked Bethereel. No longer able to stand on her own, Sabien pulled her arm about his neck. He stumbled, righted himself, and looked to Navalis for assistance.

"Will you help me take her to her room?"

"Oh gosh!" Boriag shuffled back and forth, not sure what to do. "Is she alright?"

"I'm fine," the artist sniffed. She shakily pushed herself from the ground and stood as tall as her slight frame would allow.

Boriag seemed startled by her response. "Oh! Hey, Laere. No, I meant Bethee." He turned toward Sabien and asked again. "Is she alright?"

The question infuriated Laere. She spun around, cradling her bruised cheek, and hurled orders at the model. "Clean the brushes. Scrape what you can from the ground. Pack everything!" She stepped over the spilled paints and let out a sharp huff. "I've got to get this paint out of my skirt before it stains." Then she pushed her way through the onlooking crowd and disappeared.

Forceful words plowed into Navalis's mind.

"Let me help her," Ulmaen projected. "She needs me. Only I can comfort her."

Navalis ignored the plea. He wrapped Bethereel's arm about his neck, and addressed Boriag.

"Fetch Osblod. Have him meet us at Kugilla Hall."

Boriag nodded, turned toward the southern Colonnade, and disappeared into the crowds near the Armory.

A bubbly mood returned to the art festival around them as onlookers disengaged from the drama and returned to admiring artwork.

Ulmaen remained, his rage jetting fiercely. He stepped forward and reached for Bethereel.

"Why don't you help pack Laere's equipment?" Navalis suggested.

He understood Ulmaen's frustration with not being able to help Bethereel. Emotions played out a little differently in men than in women, and that was something Ulmaen needed to figure out.

About to protest, Ulmaen stopped and heeded the instruction. He grabbed a rag and began cleaning the mess made by the fallen palette.

Navalis helped Sabien carry Bethereel around the Temple and back along the eastern Colonnade. Even though she was lighter than expected, she remained limp for most of the journey, and he warmed quickly from the exertion. Up close, he saw dark circles around her eyes, the sharpness of her cheekbones, and he discerned she hadn't been eating properly.

Past the library, the covering above them turned to ruin. Broken slabs jutted out from several pillars and then only pillars remained. The sun blazed down, making him sticky with sweat. Sabien wasn't faring any better, for his turquoise shirt had darkened across his chest and beneath his arms.

Off the Colonnade, near the entrance to Kugilla Hall, they stopped and rested a moment to catch their breaths. Half-unconscious, Bethereel swayed forward, let out a plaintive cry, then vomited bile upon the steps.

Navalis searched the Colonnade, hoping for any glimpse of Boriag or Osblod. At this point, either one would do. He needed to put some distance between him and Sabien. Somehow their discourse, no matter the circumstances, returned to the mysterious familiarity they had with one another, and he didn't want Sabien to become more agitated than he already was.

"Ready then?" Sabien asked.

"You sure?" Navalis leaned forward, averting his gaze.

Sabien nodded.

Bethereel clung to them, and when they hooked their free arms behind her knees to carry her, she struggled at first. By the time they carried her the three flights of stairs, and laid her to rest in bed beneath a white and violet blanket, she'd fallen unconscious.

Soaked by sweat and out of breath, Navalis was struck by Sabien's scent—a heavy mix of musk and sweat and sweet tobacco smoke, reminding him of the many nights they had laid together, of the comfort Sabien had provided when Navalis believed he would be trapped in this world forever.

"Is there water? We need water." Sabien burst through the chamber door and yelled down the corridor. "We need water in here!"

Navalis tended the night table beside the bed and raised a jug. Very little water sloshed around inside. He poured the water into a basin, then searched for a small cloth on a shelf in the open wardrobe. He found a thick kerchief, soaked it in the water, wrung it out a little, and placed it on Bethereel's face, hoping to revive her a little.

When he touched her forehead, he expected her to feel warm. Instead, she felt clammy and cold. She moaned, and curled onto her side, stray strands of black hair sticking to her cheeks. She clutched her belly and moaned again.

His mind invoked a similar image of Sabien lying there, doubled in pain, wracked with shakes, sweating till his clothes were soaked, calling out...

For Avn.

Navalis shuddered, knowing the torture Sabien might have endured if he hadn't believed Avn was still alive back in his home land.

"Do you think she's been poisoned, like Ule?" Sabien folded his arms across his chest. He always did that when he was upset.

Navalis shook his head. "She's grieving," he tried to assure him.

"This—" Sabien pointed at Bethereel. "This isn't grieving. I've seen grief, experienced it myself—"

"Everyone grieves in their own way." Navalis removed the cloth, rinsed it in the water again, and placed it back on Bethereel's forehead. She moaned again.

"I'd like to talk with you, since we have a moment," Sabien said. "They're rare to come by. You're always running away."

Come on, Boriag, Navalis thought. Interrupt anytime now.

"When we first met, a couple years back, we got along well, didn't we?"

Navalis remembered. They had got along well, until Sabien started showing signs of confusion and began commenting on how similar Navalis was to a blacksmith he had known. Their relationship had to end. The risk of being discovered as something other than an Elishian might force him to silence Sabien in some way.

"You won't answer, will you?" Sabien accepted defeat with a gracious nod. "I don't know why you avoid me, but I'm glad you stuck around today. Thanks for your help."

"You're welcome," Navalis replied.

Sabien leaned against the wardrobe. Though Navalis could see him in his peripheral vision, he remained fixated on Bethereel.

"Will you stay until Osblod arrives?"

Navalis sighed. "I can't."

"I'm sure he won't be much longer," Sabien nearly pleaded. "In case—"

"There's a time-sensitive experiment waiting for me." He wasn't lying. Back in his lab, another snake demon had been acquired. An older one this time, with a nearly fully formed humanoid head. Every moment that passed, the corpse degraded.

A knock at the door revitalized Sabien. He rushed to greet Osblod and explained to him what had happened near the Starry Rise.

Fully focused on Bethereel, Osblod ducked through the door and lumbered toward the bed in a few even strides. He lifted Bethereel's arm. It hung limply as he pressed his fingers across the underside of her wrist.

"Her pulse is rapid," he announced.

"She went feral at the sight of a model who looked like Ule." Sabien shook his head. "I've never seen her so... violent."

Bethereel stirred, her breath quickened, her face beaded with sweat.

"Let me examine her." Osblod glanced toward the door, indicating he needed privacy.

Navalis bolted for the open door, but Sabien leaned in and stopped him in his tracks. In a low whisper he asked, "Can he be trusted?"

Navalis hesitated. He regarded Osblod and knew for certain that when it came to healing wounds, Osblod could be relied upon.

"Absolutely," he replied.

The answer eased Sabien. He uncrossed his arms and together they left the room. As Navalis made to leave, Sabien blocked the hallway.

"It's not the right time, I know this," he said. "But I can't shake this feeling that we've met before. I know it."

Navalis shook his head. "No, I don't think so. Sondshor Market, that was the first time we met," he told him. "You keep saying this." He shrugged. "I don't know what to tell you."

Dissatisfied by the response, Sabien sneered. "Will you stay—"

The bedroom door swung open. Osblod exited the room and pulled the door partially closed. "I'm no where near done examining her," he told them. "But it's clear she's going through more than an emotional breakdown. She's all the classic symptoms of withdrawal."

"I knew it," Sabien whispered.

"There's no judgment between us, eh?" Osblod raised a hand toward both of them, the gesture urging a reply. Sabien nodded in agreement first, then Navalis.

"I need to know what euphoria substances she indulges in."

"I wouldn't know," Sabien responded. "I've only ever seen her drink wine." He closed his eyes and shook his head. "I've never seen her do anything else. I don't know."

"This is grim," Osblod replied. "I need to know what she's been getting into."

Sabien turned toward Navalis. "If you know something—"

"Wouldn't it be better to ask her friends?" Navalis countered immediately.

Irritated by his questions going unanswered, Sabien grimaced, then said, "If her friends are using an unregulated substance, they'll just lie to cover their own arses." His tone turned acidic. "Besides, you're a mystic. Your kind use strange substances all the time. You'd know if they were stealing or buying from your stock. For once, put those perceptive abilities of yours to good use instead of listening in on the banal thoughts of the servants."

Navalis withheld a laugh at the intended insult. He promised himself this time would be the last time he'd give into Sabien's demands.

"No," he told them. "I've never seen Bethereel partake in any kind of substance. Alcohol and dancing were her and Ule's preferred forms of relaxation, as far as I know."

Osblod nodded. "I'd like to take a little blood, have a look." He pushed the chamber door open, and returned back inside. "Can't promise... What have you done, girl?!"

Alarmed, Sabien rushed into the room and Navalis followed.

There, kneeling on the bed, Bethereel leaned back against the headboard, her legs curled beneath her, the corner of the white and violet blanket pulled around her shoulders. In one hand she held a pair of sheers and in the other a fist full of her long hair she had cut off.

Sabien fell to his knees on the chamber floor at the bedside. The drawer to the nightstand was open and inside, a sewing kit had been unraveled.

Sabien gathered up a handful of long hair that had fallen onto the bed. "Your beautiful hair!"

Bethereel breathed heavily, as though it took most of her energy to speak. "I don't need it anymore."

Sabien sat next to her on the bed, wrapped his arm around her. "So you want to be bald?"

His mood shifted; his personality, too. In stressful situations, he turned to his storyteller persona to anchor himself. His assuredness in times of uncertainty was the most attractive part of him. When Navalis had been struggling with his own stability, that trait was what had drawn him toward Sabien.

"Unless you're very, very young or very, very old," Sabien told her, "this new look isn't going to be attractive for you. Even babes and wrinklies have some fuzz on them."

She ran a trembling hand up her forehead and along the side of her pale head, where an oblong cherry mark just above her temple peeked out from beneath her shorn hair.

"I-I miss her." Bethee looked from beneath heavy lids. "You know how it feels. You felt like this after Avn left."

Navalis's desire to leave suddenly subsided. His reason for distancing himself from Sabien was to spare him this kind of pain, but it seemed he had suffered anyway.

"It's not the same." Frowning, Sabien waited until she settled against his shoulder. "Avn left because he needed to go home, but he isn't gone. He can always come back. Ule can't."

Bethereel cried again. This time, only tears fell, as though nothing of her remained.

✳ CHAPTER 23 ✳

Ulmaen trudged toward the Prison, preoccupied with thoughts of Bethereel and schemes of how to see her again.

He had tried visiting her the day of her breakdown, but when he climbed the servant stairs in Kugilla Hall, he discovered Navalis and Sabien in the hallway, blocking the way. For a time, Osblod was there, too.

Ulmaen hid in the shadows listening a while, before a guard found him and escorted him down to the main floor. Later, when he returned upstairs, guards blocked the door to the room. They refused to let him enter no matter what stories he told them.

When he asked Navalis about her, he said to let her be, that she'd be fine eventually. But he couldn't. He had to know how she was feeling.

He descended the steps into the Prison. Upon passing Gorlen, he straightened himself, preparing to deflect some slight or vitriolic comment, but Gorlen was quiet today, and the prisoners in the Core behaved the same as every other morning.

At Rozafel's cell, he found her nesting on the floor, her thick legs tucked beneath her as she hummed. She held onto a dread lock. Several more spilled down her lap onto the floor. She dunked the one she held into the gully, wetting it in the water, then picked at it.

"Breakfast," he called to her.

She looked up, still humming, not at all interested in the piece of bread offered to her beneath the gate.

Ulmaen waggled the bread again. "Come on, Rozafel." When she still ignored him, he placed it on the floor.

He recalled what he had overheard in the corridor outside Bethereel's room, when Osblod had mentioned Bethereel was suffering from withdrawal. From what, he wondered? Bethereel had never shown an interest in euphorias other than alcohol.

Rozafel sneezed.

"How about some sweets then? They're from the reception."

He reached into the basket and pulled out a folded napkin.

"Lots of folk traveled in from all around. The artists are sure to be inundated with new commissions now. Nothing like a little money thrown their way to settle their hostility toward the Magnes, eh?"

Rozafel watched him, her eyes on the small package he placed on the floor. He unfolded the edges to reveal almond pastries and a few bits of chocolate bark. She sat still, fixated on the sweets. Then she gently laid the dread lock down next to the others, rose to her feet, and wobbled toward the gate.

She knelt down, picked up a piece of chocolate bark and began sucking on it.

"When I was a kid," she mumbled. "I used to climb trees. No branches, no ropes, no belts." She shook her head to emphasize her claim, her mouth busy at work melting the sweet morsel.

"I'd just climb up nimble and quick-like, fetch the ripe apples, and never gave a thought to falling. I was fearless when I was young." Her large, sad eyes locked onto his. "Now, I'm afraid of everything."

She smacked her lips.

"I miss 'em. My parents," she continued rambling. "They loved me no matter what. No conditions, no punishment for having a talent. I was lucky. I grew up with plenty of kids whose parents were nasty." She sighed. "You know, out there, I've never really found that kind of love again. Do you think it exists?"

Yes, he wanted to tell her that kind of love does exist and when it's gone you'd rather have every limb broken than feel the pain of its absence.

Ulmaen fumbled about in the basket, pretended to search for other portions of breakfast.

"I remember some stuff," she said. "About the gloves."

As he was about to ask her what she remembered, she spoke again.

"He was handsome. A tall fountain of confidence, he was."

Did Bethereel possess information about Ule's murderer after all? He leaned into the bars of the cage.

"Who was handsome?" he asked. "The one you sold the gloves to? Do you remember who it was?"

Rozafel shrugged. She closed her eyes. The darkness seemed to help her remember.

"He was well dressed, like most merchants. He wore this black hat, the kind with a wide brim. It made him rather mysterious. I'd asked him where he got it and he said, 'Next door.' But I thought he said Nexdor, like it was an exotic place, and he laughed. Not at me for not listening right, no. He made it so he was the one needing his mouth fixed, and he said maybe it was time he laid off the whiskey." A huff of a laugh escaped her lips. "Who'd give up whiskey?"

She grabbed a second piece of chocolate and rolled it over and over until it started to melt. She popped it in her mouth and licked her fingers.

"So he was a merchant in Sondshor Market, one who worked next door to a hat shop?" He waited for confirmation of his summarization of her narrative.

Savoring the sweet, she nodded again.

"Was he young? Was he old?" He fetched a couple apples from the basket and placed them on the floor next to the bread.

Rozafel's eyes glossed over. "Older." She didn't sound quite sure.

Her eyes widened. "I remember something."

"What?" He knelt forward, nearly pressing his face against the gate. "What is it?"

"There was another fellow with him." She started to nod, smiling. She licked her lips again. "Yeah, a young guy. Shorter. Couldn't look me in the eyes. Had this mess of dark blue hair."

Ulmaen froze at the familiarity of the description, thought of anyone else who might fit it, but no one came to mind.

No, not *him*, Ulmaen thought.

He needed more information to be sure, and asked, "The merchant, the one you sold the gloves to, did he sell fabric?"

She scrunched up her face and nodded. "Do you know him?"

"I—" He stood abruptly and backed away from the gate. "I don't know." There was no doubt in his mind who Rozafel had described. The men she referred to were Elusis, a textile merchant, and his assistant, Milos.

The sale of the gloves had to have occurred well over two years ago, before Elusis had disappeared. Had Ulmaen not interrupted that fateful day, when Elusis had been passed out in the desert soused on whiskey, he would have died. Instead, Ulmaen brought him to a sacred grove ruled by a cat demon, where as far as Ulmaen knew, he still lived there.

As for the assistant, Milos, he'd moved to Eastgate after Elusis's disappearance, where now and again he was seen carousing in seedy taverns near run down playhouses.

"How long ago did you sell the gloves?"

Rozafel shrugged. She counted on her fingers. When she was done she shook her head, still not sure. "During the war?"

Ulmaen thought anyone who had ever worked in the castle under Adinav's rule had been killed or found somewhere to hide for the rest of their lives.

"You worked here?" he asked.

Rozafel shook her head. "In Eastgate. Mended garments mostly. Sold accessories, too."

In the next cell over, the last in the row, a man called out and told him to hurry along with the food.

"Tell the general what you remember," he urged.

She pouted, and her lower lip trembled. "But I have. He doesn't believe me."

Whatever uncertainty he felt about the woman dissipated in a rush. Her mental state, her withdrawal, and her personality revealed a fragile constitution. A deep breath chased away his suspicion toward her. She couldn't have been the one to poison those gloves. Someone else had. He was sure of that now.

"I'll talk to him," he assured her, imagining those white satin gloves on

a journey, passing from Rozafel to Elusis and onto someone else—
the murderer, perhaps?

"I like you," Rozafel said to him. "You've got a kind face."

Ulmaen knelt again, pulled out a second chunk of cheddar, and slid it
beneath the gate. With a nod, he continued to the next cell and fed the
prisoner there, ignoring the snide comments about the long wait.

Returning to the front of the building, Ulmaen glanced down the
stairwell behind the counter and came to a halt when Gorlen blocked his
way.

"Now, how is it you got her talking, I wonder?"

Not wanting to cause any trouble, Ulmaen chose to tell the truth.
"A little bribe. A couple of sweets. A smile or two."

"You're a thief now?"

Ulmaen winced at the accusation. "Not really." He considered how he
obtained the sweets and shook his head. "No, technically I'm not a thief."

Gorlen didn't believe him.

"It's like this, see," Ulmaen continued, hoping an explanation might
convince him. "I took them for myself, but then I wasn't as hungry as
I thought, so I put them away. Later, I thought, hey, maybe Rozafel might
like them."

"We'll see what Senaga has to say about it."

Ulmaen laughed. "I'm sure she'll have plenty to say about me. As for the
sweets, she always lets the servants have first go at leftovers so food
doesn't go to waste."

Gorlen curled his lip in annoyance. "So, are you going to tell me what
Rozafel said?"

"Should I?"

Gorlen tilted his head. "If you know what's good for you, you will."

Had he been Ule, he would've caved into the demand unwillingly.
As Ulmaen, he laughed instead. Though he didn't feel threatened by
Gorlen, he answered him in the spirit of co-operation. "She sold the gloves
to a merchant in Sondshor."

Gorlen glanced down the hallway in the direction of her cell. "Anything
else?"

"Only that she already told you what she knows."

Gorlen grunted and turned back toward the counter.

Worried for Rozafel's well-being when no one else seemed to be,
he asked, "Why is she still in here then?"

Gorlen picked up a soft cotton rag, dipped a portion of it in oil, and
began rubbing it along the blade of a sword laid out on the counter. The
blade was beveled in the middle, both edges sharpened; the grip was
ribbed and the hilt a single, graceful arc of metal that wrapped halfway
around.

"Until we have evidence to support her story," he answered, "we've got to hold onto her."

"She can't very well search for evidence locked in a cell!"

"Mind yourself!" Gorlen's eruption simmered quickly as he continued rubbing the cloth in small circles over the blade. "If there's proof to be found, it'll show itself." To ensure no more would be said on the matter, he added, "She's none of your concern. The truth will be found."

Not in this place, Ulmaen realized.

Truth seldom poked through the layers of lies. If Rozafel was to have a chance at freedom again, if Bethereel was to feel peace again, someone needed to find proof for both of them, anything that provided answers about Ule's murder.

"Alright. Very good," he conceded. "If I discover anything new, I'll let you know."

A strange smile came over the general. "You do that!"

Ulmaen regarded the sword again. The blade gleamed beneath the gaslights. "That's a beauty," he said.

"Keep your sticky fingers to yourself," Gorlen warned. "Her song is spoken for. Go on now."

Ulmaen chose to ignore him. He didn't desire the weapon for himself. He'd meant to make a compliment, and as he lingered, he found himself drawn toward the recess in the wall, where the stairwell led down below ground. Whoever was kept down there hadn't eaten in a very long time.

"You know, I still haven't brought food for whoever's down in The Pit."

Gorlen grunted, indicating he'd heard Ulmaen.

"Senaga says I'd be lucky if I was reassigned before then. That way I won't have to worry about going down there."

"I'll say!" Gorlen grinned, then nodded toward the stairwell. "They're getting very hungry."

"Who eats only once a month?" Ulmaen wondered if perhaps he should have asked, *what* eats only once a month?

"You're fucking gullible, boy!"

Gorlen laughed loud and hard. His laughter was an obnoxious sound that resounded throughout the Prison. Someone from one of the Core cells whooped and joined in.

Gorlen caught his breath and explained, "There's nothing down there. As long as none of the prisoners act up and need a good reprimand, you won't have to go down there at all."

A woeful howl rose up the stairwell.

All mirth vanished from Gorlen as he peered in disgust over his shoulder toward the steps. Something was being kept down there, and it howled again to prove him wrong.

"Once in a while the beasts get riled up," he said. "That's for us to handle."

Ulmaen wanted to ask what kind of beasts until Gorlen threw himself toward the stairwell, stomped down the steps, and somewhere below he cursed at *whatever* had howled. Appreciating the opportunity to make a hasty retreat, Ulmaen bolted for the main door. Outside, he scrambled up the steps and stopped at the top to inhale the fresh air.

Questions buzzed about in his mind, some dazed, others agitated. He thought of gloves and beasts, and every once in a while an image of Bethereel wracked in anguish overcame him until he shook it away.

He climbed the inclined path, and his head emerged above the grass. As he cut across the field toward what remained of the old rampart wall, his mind trapped him in a maze of questions till he found his way to a focused universal law.

Energy feeds energy.

All living creatures required sustenance of some kind. If Bethereel didn't eat, she'd die. Without the sun, the grass around him would die. Sustenance was necessary.

Ulmaen suck in a breath of fresh air and mumbled to himself, "What the Mneos is hidden away in the old Prison?"

❋ CHAPTER 24 ❋

"It'll take some getting used to," Senaga had told Ulmaen early one morning, as she prepared small pails of days old food. "Sometimes the prisoners act up, but they've got to be punished when they do. And how do you punish someone who's already being punished, eh? Just remember: Don't linger. Don't poke your hands anywhere. Stay toward the middle of the tunnels, and you'll be fine."

He hadn't expected to visit the Pit so soon after beginning his service in the Prison. He'd been curious, of course, about *what* was being kept there, but as he teetered on the top step of the stairs leading down below the ground, he hesitated.

"Need a little push to get going?" Gorlen laughed, and the guards who stood at either side of the stairwell joined in.

Ulmaen decided to join in their laughter, and as he did, he descended the quarried stone steps in a buoyant, playful manner, enjoying the way their derision deteriorated into silence.

The doorway to the Pit was shorter than he thought. He ducked through the opening and paused on a landing, waiting for his eyes to adjust to the dim light of old oil lanterns hanging from hooks along the plaster walls. Why they hadn't used crystal lanterns instead baffled him.

The landing sloped toward what remained of a stone and mortar stairwell that had later been reinforced with rotting wood. Along the walls, patches of plaster poked out from beneath the dirt, yet near the bottom of the stairs, he saw a mess of terra cotta bricks kept in place by beams of wood.

Each layer of material indicated a past incarnation of the Prison, now hidden by the building above, and he likened it to his future as a Sentinel. With every new identity, he'd hide the ruins of his previous ones.

The first cell he approached was a dug cave with a grate over the entrance. Inside, a pile of stone and rubble filled one end. He leaned toward it until he remembered what Senaga had told him. Quickly, he backed away.

No one bothered to explain to him about what to expect. Senaga had told him to place a pail outside certain cells, and then clarified further by saying, "Mind the cells with men. Ignore the rest... if you can."

Gorlen, also, offered little guidance, preferring to mock his misery. "Guess you're going to find out what's down there after all, thanks to Ilgaud and his cronies trying to escape from the quarry. They'll be rotting in the Pit a while. Hope your stomach can take it."

Ulmaen had been imprisoned himself once, long ago as a child, in a place where practically nothing existed until he remembered he could create.

He had created this world, and since being in it he'd been nearly beaten to death by sticks and stones, changed into a gemstone, poisoned by a cactus pup, and poisoned again very recently. He was pretty sure he could handle whatever was kept down here.

Beyond the curve in the passageway he encountered a set of cells, one on each side of him. Although the lantern light failed to penetrate the darkness of any of them, he sensed creatures dwelt within. The cell to his right was closest, and a man's face suddenly pressed against the gate.

Ulmaen recognized Ilgaud, recalling his gruesome crime in Eastgate from well over a year ago; one that had shook everyone to the core. During the trial, Ilgaud's psychopathy had become evident, graphic details forever seared into everyone's mind. Anyone with a conscience might have understood the account as a confession, but he had been candid, exact, and had seen nothing wrong in any of the brutality he inflicted on his victim.

Psychopathy wasn't an uncommon phenomenon among the creatures the Xiinisi created. They consistently made up a small fraction of any population. Psychopathy served a very narrow function and was a particularly sensitive personality type. Nurtured in hostile and abusive environments, psychopaths were more easily prone to becoming destructive toward others, causing great suffering.

"I don't deserve to be here," Ilgaud said.

Overcome by an overwhelming urge to beat Ilgaud's head against the stone floor, Ulmaen shuddered. When he had been Ule, she had struggled to find compassion for Ilgaud. Now, Ulmaen struggled with a dark violent compulsion no different from Ilgaud's.

"I don't know," Ulmaen said. "You tortured a man and flayed him alive 'cause he called you a pug."

In the dim light, he noted Ilgaud's round wrinkled cheeks, small pinched nose, and woeful eyes hadn't changed much. He still resembled a dog.

Ilgaud scrunched up his nose. "You'd do the same."

"Maybe." Ulmaen shrugged, unwilling to admit what he had thought of doing to Ilgaud only a few seconds ago. "Doubtful. Someone died 'cause you couldn't just laugh it off. Don't you know how to push your ego out of the way?"

Ilgaud lunged toward him, both arms extended straight between the bars of the gate, but Ulmaen deftly dodged his grasping hands.

"No matter." Ilgaud grimaced. He tilted his head and cracked his neck. "I still don't deserve *this*." With his jaw, he gestured to the cell across the narrow tunnel. "It's at it again."

Ulmaen looked into the dark cell and saw something move.

"Can't stand looking at that *shiiit!*" Ilgaud pushed his face against the bars and spit toward the cell opposite him.

Ulmaen's eyes adjusted to the dark and he saw a figure in the corner sitting on a cot. Bloated flesh swelled into a naked androgynous humanoid with a square torso and long, narrow arms. Shadows of veins snaked beneath the quivering flesh. The body pulsed and spasmed. Gelatinous legs and arms bounced into the air and slapped back down like a rag doll.

The figure shuddered all at once, as something inky and mercurial bubbled from the top of a head that stopped at the base of the nose. Each sphere that formed darted back and forth like eyes.

A long, slow exhale issued from the creature, mournful and raspy. Then it convulsed uncontrollably, arms and legs and torso twitching. A woeful howl rose from deep within its body, and Ulmaen recognized the sound Gorlen had warned him about.

"What do you see?" he asked Ilgaud.

Ilgaud trembled. "Him! Bleeding and twitching, after what I did to him. Every. Fucking. Day. I got to look at the face of my idiot da, sitting right across from me, calling me that name day after day, when I know I killed him."

Ulmaen realized he saw something different from what Ilgaud did. The beast seemed to manifest and mimic the worst memories of others. His current worst memory was of Ule, of being wracked with pain during her final moments, convulsing, writhing in the remains of her dinner on the floor.

He shivered at the memory more than the *beast*.

The creature's blue lips parted and a long pale pink tongue slopped down the folds of its white chest and belly. He didn't want to be reminded of his death, the nightmare it had created, and he looked away.

"Stop looking at me!" Ilgaud cried.

The whites of Ilgaud's eyes glowed in the darkness of his cell. The earthen walls deadened the intensity of his desperate plea. He clutched the bars, staring at that thing. The muscles in his neck strained. A vein popped across his forehead.

"But it's not my da. Do you see? It's changing again. Why does it have so many eyes?" Ilgaud whined, his voice cracking. "Can't you see its eyes?"

Ulmaen looked. The beast hadn't changed. Indeed, what he and Ilgaud saw were very different imaginings.

A chill coursed through Ulmaen as he considered that this demon approximated the ability of the Xiinisi by being able to shift its form. It formed and reformed at will, except what he saw and what Ilgaud saw were very different, and he wasn't sure what to make of that just yet.

He had met demons who had represented fears of cactuses and cats. These were concrete objects they easily mimicked in form. But what about less tangible fears, like fear of the dark or the unknown? These were abstract in nature. Without a basis of form, what shape would these kinds of demons take?

And what should he call a demon that guaranteed to give him nightmares come nightfall? A nightmare demon. The label felt too dramatic. So he settled on mare demon instead, and as if the demon could read his thoughts, it shifted and convulsed in approval.

Simultaneously delighted by the discovery and sickened by the encounter, Ulmaen placed a pail by the gate of Ilgaud's cell. He treaded lightly along the hall past the mare demon's cell.

The demon's skin began to peel. The viscera beneath glistened pink and pulsed, changing again, falling apart in pieces and coming back together again, reminding him of his recent deathmorphing.

Once he passed the cell, he relaxed a bit and looked back toward Ilgaud's cell.,. Had he been Ule, he'd feel empathy for the man with his pale pudgy faced pressed against the grate, regardless of what he had done. Now, he only felt contempt. Ilgaud deserved to be here.

"Try not to let the mare demon bother you," he told Ilgaud. "They'll show you your worst dreams."

Ilgaud snarled. "They're the only kind I have."

A growl rose from the cell of the mare demon. It swelled and ebbed. After a moment of silence, an earthy, perverse laughter rolled along the hallway, and Ulmaen let it wash over him.

At the next cell, an eerie stillness made him stop. From within the darkness he heard a low rustle, like a breeze rushing through the leaves of a tree. He stopped and peered into the cell, glimpsing the outline of a demon rooted in the far corner. The demon leaned forward into the light, and he admired her proportionate form and deeply ridged flesh.

Chorded knots crested her shoulders, elbows and knees, and marked the nipples of her small breasts. The demon was perfectly humanoid in shape from the tips of her toes and fingers to the top of a leaf-adorned head. Her beady, dark green eyes were skewed, not quite level, and there was a knot settled in the middle of her face where a nose should be.

The tree demon smiled at him with raw wood lips glossed in sap.

In the next cell, he found a regular man. As he set down another pail by the gate, he wondered how many other prisoners there were and why they had been imprisoned.

He saw snake demons and cat demons, even a dog demon. Occasionally, he'd pass a cell and glimpse something less recognizable and he'd have to stop and look to figure out the idea of it. One was a black cloud in the shape of a man, and when he stared at him, Ulmaen felt like he was falling.

He shook his head and surmised the creature must be a vertigo demon. Another abstract fear. Another with the ability to affect his... what? He began to dwell on his recent observations.

What if, he thought, instead of a demon having the ability to change its form, it changed how others saw it? That's it! The vertigo demon affected my perception.

He considered how similar it was to the mare demon's ability, and understood now why he and Ilgaud saw something different. The revelation caused the hairs on his arms to prickle.

If these Abstracts, as he started to call them, could alter perception, then they shared a similar power with the Xiinisi, an ability for projecting thoughts into the minds of others. He shivered at the very notion that his perception had been altered without his consent.

Thankfully, they don't possess control over matter and energy, he thought at first. As soon as he considered the notion, he realized demons *had* demonstrated the ability to affect the shape of their bodies over long periods of time. In very subtle ways, they seemed to be very much like the Xiinisi.

He past another empty cell. Beyond the gate was a door in the far wall. Across from that cell was another demon.

Something blue and decimated sat on the floor. Legs curled up to its chest, its bald head was turned to one side and rested a cheek on its knees. Black eyes stared through torn eyelids. Rows of tiny lines marked the flesh, the shape of the scars reminding him of cross stitching.

He saw no movement, heard no breath, and the stillness unsettled him.

He called to it. "Hello?"

The head jerked, as though trying to pry itself from the knees. The neck cracked and popped, snapping with every degree of movement.

By reflex, Ulmaen stepped back from the cell as the creature stiffly rose to its feet, bones cracking, flesh tearing and stitching together again. The scars were the result of black thread pulling flesh back together again, keeping the body sealed, which had been a long standing practice for the dead in many cultures of Elish.

As the demon approached the gate, emaciated bone arms uncurled from across its chest, revealing shriveled flaps of flesh that had once been breasts, and she rested a skeletal hand on the gate.

Despite the decay, Ulmaen saw a symmetry in the well-formed demon the others hadn't possessed. This one moved and looked and smelled... ancient. He suspected this one wasn't the only manifestation of this kind of fear, but it certainly embodied the primary fear known to every living thing.

The death demon tilted her head. Something snapped inside her neck. Black eyes flickered across Ulmaen, and when she spoke, her breath was sweet and rancid.

"You've grown," she moaned.

Unsure of what she meant, he decided not to engage and walked farther along the passage. Her words followed him, needful creatures demanding sustenance, and then a whisper overtook them.

"Uuuuleee!"

He froze. He looked back over his shoulder. The cell was dark. He shook off the goosebumps, the rising panic, and the urge to run. Pushing forward down the corridor, he let out a long, slow exhale, and though he was tempted to wonder about how the demon knew his true name, he chose to focus on his task.

To the right, he found another corridor and had a choice: continue straight or turn. He continued straight, seeing more cells. There, he found more demons and a third Elishian, and he set another pail of food on the ground before moving on.

He descended another set of steps, stone ones this time, well-worn and cracked. They were few, and at the bottom, the corridor narrowed. Along both sides, cells had either collapsed or were being used to store old weapons. At a stone archway, the corridor forked. To the left, the way was blocked by beams, boulders, and earth, and to the right, the passageway continued.

He ducked to fit into the tunnel and discovered darkness. The air had grown stale, too, so he retreated, returning back up the stairs.

He turned down the newer corridor, climbing small sets of wooden steps. Farther down, he found an adjacent corridor that veered to the right, but ahead of him, a wide iron door at the very end incited his curiosity.

As he approached the iron door, he saw there was a small window covered with a grate. A faint brassy glow from within lit the window. He ducked to peek inside.

His eyes adjusted quickly to the dim light, and there, in the middle of the chamber, so much bigger than the others, sat a man on the edge of a cot.

He was bare chested with bronzed flesh. Well developed shoulder and chest muscles made him look top heavy. His hair was short and light colored, and his eyes... Ulmaen couldn't make out his eyes, for the man's head was bowed.

"I've got food for you," Ulmaen said. He looked down at a pail and then at the door, but there wasn't any slot for the prisoner to access the food.

The man stirred, lifted his head.

Ulmaen regarded the prisoner again, and though he wanted to speak, words failed him. Black eyes on the verge of being dark blue stared at him. Beneath those eyes, along either side of the man's angular face were clusters of black spots.

"Never mind," Ulmaen muttered to himself, not wanting to disturb the demon.

But the demon was a man. Two arms. Two legs. A torso. A head. Well proportioned. He even had flesh. If not for the marks on his face,

Ulmaen wouldn't have thought him a demon, for his eyes were well spaced and aligned.

The demon stood, and as he did, something massive moved with him. Metal scraped the floor. His feet were shackled and strung with rusted chains that hung down from bolts in the walls. His wrists were shackled, too, and his hands cupped in metal.

He dragged the chains, tightening their slack as he shuffled from the shadows toward the door until they were extended to their limit. Flakes of rust drifted to the floor as they groaned under the pressure.

Ulmaen blinked, eyes riveted to not just one pair of shackled arms but three, each pair of hands cupped in metal, each fastened by a chain. The extra arms were the same length and size, proportionate and humanoid, each erupting from the ribcage one below the other.

Up close, Ulmaen saw the demon's facial spots were lumps. Their cluster pattern and the multiple limbs reminded him of a familiar creature.

"You're a spider demon."

The demon nodded and smiled. The demon had bone white teeth instead of black ones, and roughly chopped hair.

The spider demon examined Ulmaen, tilting his head in different ways, and then he gasped. "There you are," he said. His square jaw softened. "Hello again."

Ulmaen's torso stiffened. His biceps contracted as his hands fisted about the handle of the pail. He didn't care for the knot of fear tightening in his stomach. He'd prefer to flee The Pit, yet his body was gearing up to fight.

"Who are you?"

The demon strained against the chains, his neck muscles thickening. "I am Mithreel."

The demon's name triggered a memory. Ulmaen searched his thoughts. And there! He recalled a recent conversation and reviewed its context— Istok seething and ranting, then a few words about a treasure. *Better still, ask Mithreel,* Istok had said.

Ulmaen didn't care about any treasure. He wanted more clarity about Ule's murder. He wanted to know why a death demon and a spider demon talked to him as though they knew him. He also wanted to know why the name Mithreel crawled through his mind, as though it were linked to other memories.

"Am I supposed to know you?"

"You look... different." Mithreel stepped back, relaxing the chains. "Bigger. But your eyes..."

"What about my eyes?"

"They are the same. I can see you, Ule."

They stood face to face, eye to eye. Ulmaen examined the demon's realistic flesh and proportionate muscular and skeletal form. Mithreel examined him in return.

Images invaded Ulmaen's thoughts. They wove together and he watched an old memory take shape—a very old memory dating back to the earliest stage of world building, when Elish was thick with vegetation vying for space and Ule was just shy of one eon in age.

She hadn't meant to fall into the nest of prehistoric spiders. She'd lost her footing on a rock and slipped. She could've stopped herself, but for the briefest of moments she was preoccupied with patterning crystals and forgot to levitate to safety. Instead she found herself sprawled in the heart of the nest, her body straddled and pinned by one of the creatures, its five-eyed head larger than hers.

The threat of being physically overcome by the large beast hollowed her mind, and she forget she was Xiinisi, that she had power the spider hadn't. In that moment, her existence felt small and the profoundness of that idea overwhelmed her.

Repulsed by her vulnerability, she panicked. It was a genuine reaction. By the time she regained herself, her emotions had been absorbed into the An Energy, adding to a growing collective fear toward these beasts. Later, the An Energy spat out a vapor that crawled through the grass.

As the world evolved and more vapors emerged, this one always stood out from the others, the way its smoky tendril legs shot out from its amorphous body and pulled itself along in a slippery way. She hadn't given much thought to why it resembled a spider, for she had been preoccupied with the world. Had she been more attentive, she'd have known a spider demon had been born, the very first of its kind.

Unlike the other demons, this one eventually developed a rudimentary language that it projected into her mind. It even named itself—Mithreel.

Ulmaen gasped at the recollection. He'd forgotten the incident with the spider nest, the birth of the demon, and the strange conversations they had shared so long ago. Then a thought wiggled inside his mind.

He stared down at his hands, imagined his fingers long, sleek, and pale. Then he imagined them tainted with black stains caused by venom. Spider venom.

What kind of spider venom could cause such fatal toxicity? Or cause Kerista to keel over in pain when she looked at it through a scope?

Perhaps, a demon's.

✳ CHAPTER 25 ✳

"Anything yet?" Boriag asked, his voice carrying along the stone walls from the far side of the laboratory, where he sat on a stool hunched over a table. His tone was distorted by the paper plugs he used to block his nostrils from the magic scent of the new demon specimen, which reeked of rancid milk.

"Ugh, I can still smell it!" Boriag complained. "How can you stand it?"

Navalis sniffed at the snake demon stretched across the length of the table. His nostrils still picked up the creature's benign signature magic scent, but he had blocked the signal to his brain, dulling his sense of smell and taste.

"It won't kill me," he mumbled.

"You don't know that!" Boriag shifted on the stool, making it creak. "Remember what happened to your hand last time?"

Given how long Navalis's hand had taken to heal, and that matter had vanished from his molecular array as a result of encountering what lay inside a demon's body, he wasn't willing to take that same risk again.

He wore gloves this time. They were made of leather, the kind Osblod had worn when he had examined Ule's body. He wasn't sure if they'd protect him or not, and their thickness diminished any tactile sensation as he folded back the snake demon's flesh. They were still better than nothing at all.

He slipped a metal clamp over the folded flesh along an incision. After screwing the clamp in place, he aligned it with others along the cut that began beneath the snake demon's humanoid jaw and ended where a belly button might have been, just above a pair of well-developed hips.

"I'm farther in this time," he reported.

He glanced up and discovered Boriag had found the courage to stand closer to the examination table. Positioned halfway across the room, Boriag craned his neck to observe, muscles straining, his arms clenched tightly to his sides. One held a block of paper in the crook of his elbow and a pot of ink in his palm. With his free hand he grasped an owl feather quill.

"Where's your glass pen?"

Boriag grew sullen. "It broke. It'll take a week's worth of wages to buy another."

Navalis resumed the dissection and stared into the gaping cut. Although the flesh at the top was folded back, the lower layers of the dermis engulfed a ribcage and descended just beyond, obscuring his view of what lay beneath oddly formed bones.

"The outer dermis is thicker in this specimen." Navalis grunted as he carefully worked his fingers around the ribs and yanked upward and to the sides. The bones were stronger than he first assumed, so he extended his strength beyond Elishian capacity, draining a fraction of time from his current generation. The ribs cracked and gave.

Boriag whistled. "That's some strength you've got there!"

"It's really all about leverage," he lied, and reminded himself that in the future, he needed to be more careful about displaying his Xiinisi abilities around Boriag.

Navalis heard Boriag's quill tap against the opening of the inkwell and return to scratching on the parchment.

"The ribs are a little stronger than regular bone," he continued reporting. "They're gray in color and too smooth for anything to attach to. There are no tendons, no muscles, no capillaries or veins of any sort."

The rhythmic pattern of sharp scratches on paper turned to long ones.

Navalis glanced up. "What are you doing?"

"I'm sketching," Boriag replied, focused intently on the demon. "The features, they're so like us. Except for the eyes, they're not quite even enough, like the two sides of the face are slightly shifted. I hadn't noticed before. Eerie, eh?"

"Didn't know you could draw." Navalis examined the security of the clamps and retrieved a scalpel from a nearby table.

"I used to draw a lot when I was little. Loved it. Still do. According to my folk, following behind a cow's butt all day was more important than drawing on my ma's cupboards."

"Cow's butt? Is that what you said?"

Boriag laughed. "Yeah. I grew up on a farm." He shrugged. "After talking to Laere, I got to wondering if I still had it in me to draw. She showed me a few tricks of hers. Real spitfire that one. Pleasant on the eyes too." He drew more long scratches on the paper, then sighed. "Need a bit more practice, but it's mostly coming back." He held up what he had drawn so far of the demon specimen.

His rendering was realistic and detailed. In places the forms were roughed in but the shading captured the contours of the body nicely. Boriag certainly had talent.

"It's a shame you can't show her those," Navalis cautioned him.

"No, I wouldn't!" Boriag's insistence bordered on panic.

The reminder was necessary. Their activities in the laboratory needed to remain relatively covert, at least when it came to the general public— a secret between Boriag, Kerista, Magnes Lyan, and himself.

"I can always draw Laere a..." Boriag struggled to find a subject. "A... a fish or something. I could show her that instead if she asks. Do you think she'd like a fish?"

Faint footsteps sounded on the stairwell beyond the open door to the laboratory. Navalis froze. Boriag clamped his mouth shut. Eyes bulging, a wad of paper flew from one of his nostrils, clearing a path for air.

"Maybe it's Kerista," Boriag suggested.

Navalis raised a gloved finger in the proximity of his mouth and hushed him.

The footfalls grew louder, slow plodding steps. They stopped a moment at the landing outside the door then continued on, descending farther down along the stairwell.

"That was weird," Boriag whispered.

The footsteps grew faint again, slow, plodding.

Boriag frowned, the crease between his brows making his nose look more bulbous and prominent.

Navalis held his hands poised above the open cavity of the demon. He stared at the door and waited a moment. Stillness and silence returned to the stairwell.

"Is the door shut properly?" he asked.

Boriag glanced at the door briefly. "Mostly," he replied.

"What's that mean?"

"It's open just a bit," Boriag explained. "To let out the smell."

"Shut it!"

Boriag reluctantly obeyed, and after easing the door closed with a gentle touch, he took up a new position only several feet away from the dissection table this time. His face paled and his eyes grew vacant as he stared at the spread ribs of the demon and what lay beneath.

"What do you see?" Navalis asked him.

Boriag pinched his nose. The nib of the quill he held grazed his cheek and left behind a smudge of brown ink. "Don't know," he mumbled. "Feel queasy when I look at it." He shook his head to regain his senses. "What's new, eh?"

Navalis chuckled, resuming a closer examination of the tissue that lay just beyond the ribcage. There were gaps in the incision, where the tissue had parted and receded into darkness.

"You're the one dissecting, what do you see?" Boriag asked.

Using his Xiinisi perception, Navalis peered through the gaps into the darkness, projecting his mind past the confines of his body's dimension and into the demon's.

"Nothing."

The knife remained poised between thumb and forefinger, ready to cut down into that darkness. After a moment, he steadied himself and pushed the blade downward, burying it into the lower layers, slipping past the outer shell. Nothing resisted the blade, and it felt as though it slid through air. Then, the weight of the scalpel lightened.

He pulled the scalpel free and held it before him, carefully examining a fraying of black filaments where the blade had been. Beyond the demon's body, the black filaments whipped back into a form, a chunk of amorphous metal at the base of the scalpel's grip. The rest of the blade was missing.

He placed what remained of the tool on the instrument table. Very carefully, with both hands, he pushed the flesh on either side of the incision, his fingertips near the edge where the tissue seemed to end. He wrenched the incision wide apart and peered into a chasm.

His head spun. His stomach lurched as though he were peering over a cliff at a vista far below yet he couldn't see anything. His perception found nothing to anchor itself to and it reeled. His knees wobbled. He wanted to fall. Was he falling? Falling into the chasm? The darkness was nothing, yet it was everything pressing in around him.

He fell...

Backward. Against the wall of the laboratory. The hardness of the stone woke him from his stupor. The harsh white light of a crystal fueled lantern nearby stung his eyes. He rubbed his face as his senses came back to him, including his sense of smell.

He was struck with the heavy scent of roasted meat cutting through the magic scent of rancid milk. The disconnect between his nose and brain had been undermined. A few seconds later, he sat upright on the floor.

Boriag towered over him, partially blocking some of the light. His eyes were bright caverns welcoming Navalis back to a world with definition and detail.

"Your gloves!" Boriag pointed at him.

Navalis squinted at the tips of his fingers where the leather had melted and solidified. He wrenched them free from his hands and examined his fingers. The very tips had been grazed by something. A few layers of flesh on the middle and forefingers on both hands bled.

"What happened?" Boriag asked.

Navalis shrugged as he stood.

Boriag cradled the block of parchment against his chest. "Looked like you were about to do a nose dive." He craned his head toward the demon. "Pushed you back before you hurt yourself—"

"You alright?" a strange voice asked.

Boriag flinched and froze.

Navalis scrambled to his feet, his focus fully on the intruder at the door. On the verge of telling whoever had entered the lab to leave, he stopped himself as Sabien inched into the room. His eyes darted all about the dissection table.

"Are you alright?" he asked again, his attention fully absorbed by the demon.

Navalis's tone turned dark. Panic pressed against his lungs. "You can't be in here."

And if you see too much my old friend, he thought, I may be forced to do something to ensure you won't tell anyone.

Sabien snapped out of his daze. "I didn't mean to intrude. I've gotten turned around somehow. I heard voices."

Navalis blocked the view of the table with his body, heading toward the door. "Take notes," he commanded of Boriag, who nodded quietly and returned to the stool at the table.

"What are you—"

Before Sabien could finish his question, Navalis walked him back through the doorway and out onto the landing. Stairs rose upward and downward from the landing lit by more crystal-fueled lanterns which hung from the walls.

Navalis motioned upward. "This way."

"You're bleeding." Sabien pulled at Navalis's arm to better look at his injured hand.

Navalis snapped his arm away, and pushed Sabien toward the ascending stairs before he could notice any more details.

Annoyed, Sabien began to climb. "If I need to stop," he said, "it's to catch my breath. No need to shove, understood?"

Navalis grunted in reply, following close behind. "What brings you down here?" he asked, hoping his stern tone conveyed the gravity of being caught roaming around the old castle. "No one comes this way anymore."

Sabien glanced over his shoulder and nodded slightly, his damp from perspiration.

"I'm searching the castle for artifacts," he said. "I've the Magnes's permission to explore anywhere. At my own peril, of course." His breath became ragged, his words more clipped. "I'm not sure how... got to here... Climbed to the top... No way out."

He began to shake and stopped. He clung to the stone wall and when he caught his breath, he turned around to face Navalis. Somehow the sight of him and the stairwell horrified him, and he closed his eyes. "Where are we exactly, according to what's on the surface?"

"Will it calm you to know?"

Sabien nodded many times. "Absolutely."

"We're just beneath the Starry Rise."

"Ah!" Sabien's breath grew shallow. "I shouldn't have agreed to this," he muttered to himself. "Being underground... People aren't supposed to be *under the ground*..."

Navalis joined him on the step. His instinct was to calm Sabien before he succumbed to claustrophobia, and he reacted by grasping Sabien by the shoulder. Immediately he dreaded the touch—a reminder of the connection they had once had. He'd willed his body to forget many times before, even swapped his molecular array for another, but some bond persisted between them.

Releasing his hold, Navalis pointed up the tower stairs. "I'll show you the way out. You mustn't come back this way. There are far more interesting places to explore than this old castle."

Sabien opened his eyes and nodded briefly. "Oh, I don't know about that," he said. He reached inside his vest and pulled out a small, egg-shaped object. His fingers trembled as he held it out. "Do you know what this is?"

At the moment, Navalis didn't care about the tarnished oval of silver. His only concern was helping Sabien along before he began sensing their former bond to one another.

"It's an urn," Sabien told him.

Unexpectedly, their eyes met briefly. "For what?"

"A mouse."

He averted his gaze, urging Sabien to climb.

"Cremation's never been a tradition in this shor," Sabien explained, climbing a few steps to the next landing, where he paused a moment. "Except for a brief time, a long time ago, it was common for people of wealth and position to cremate their beloved pets."

Sabien extended his arm, displayed the side of the urn and brushed his thumb over an impression there. "Under better light, if I were to do a gentle rubbing of this mark, I bet you it's the crest of the ancient Magnes Mareel. There are old portraits of her with a pet mouse." He stopped to tuck the tiny urn back inside his vest.

Navalis nodded, keeping his eyes cast down toward the steps. "Come on, it's the next landing you want."

Sabien resumed ascending the stairwell. "It's alright to have secrets."

Navalis smiled. Sabien hadn't lost his gift for reading people, for asking questions and acquiring information. He had a certain charm, the kind that lulled people into a false sense of security. Sabien never meant to hurt anyone with it, he mostly just wanted information.

"Everyone has secrets," Navalis told him.

"Mmm, I don't." Sabien laughed over his shoulder. "I tell everyone everything. Still, no one believes me. It's a curse."

"Sounds like a blessing."

After a few more steps, Sabien paused again. He leaned back against the wall to catch his breath and stared at Navalis who waited a few steps behind him.

"Nobody's supposed to know you're experimenting on demons, are they?"

What little levity Navalis possessed shifted into a dark mood. Putting caution aside, he glared at Sabien, dreading what he might have to do to silence him. "We aren't having this conversation."

Sabien smiled weakly. "No need to get aggressive," he said. "Secrets. I am capable of keeping them for others when it matters."

Navalis remembered how well Sabien could keep secrets. Could he still trust him to do that, even though they were no longer lovers?

Sabien grew silent. He began climbing again. "What could you possibly learn from dissecting a demon?"

"That's none of your concern."

Sabien suddenly turned about on the step. Navalis stumbled back to avoid physical contact. Once had been enough.

"I could help," Sabien offered.

"You'll only get yourself in trouble." Navalis stared at the wall. "These are political times. You don't want to be called a demon ally or some other nonsense, do you?"

Sabien resumed his climb. "Are you sure the way out is up? It seems more sensible to go down. There was a tunnel—"

"There's a passageway that leads beneath Fehran's Hall," Navalis informed him. "It'll take you to the cellar beneath the building."

"I know interesting things," Sabien persisted. "Have interesting tales."

Navalis had found very little in the way of anecdotes and stories in the Archive about demons so far, but he hadn't much time to do a thorough search discreetly—Kerista would've disapproved—yet here was Sabien, both a threat and an opportunity.

"Unless you know any origin tales about demons, can't say you'll be of any use."

They came to a small landing off the side of the stairwell. Beneath an awning, the shadows hid a break in the wall which led into a dug tunnel braced with wooden beams.

"Oh, now I see it!" Sabien pulled a handkerchief from the pocket of his vest and wiped his brow. He stood there, catching his breath, lost in thought.

"There's an old story," he began once his breath came easier to him. "It's often been confused for being an origin story for the desert. It's about a valley that catches fire and a girl who, and I quote from a recent translation: *reaped the air, catching fumes with a net woven from spider web and fed them to a giant flower.* In the end, she stops the fire from spreading and that's why the desert ends so abruptly along Sondshor and Woedshor."

Navalis reclined against the wall beneath the awning, sinking into the shadows. He knew the true reason why the desert abruptly ended. It marked the span of roots belonging to Elishevera, the giant flower mentioned in the story.

When Elishevera had been alive, her roots simultaneously suppressed and fed from an underground salt sea while trapping fresh water above in the topsoil. The desert had at one time been a veldt lush with plants and groves. Now that Elishevera was dead, the water above ground evaporated and the underground sea rose and dried up, too, making the land barren.

The story intrigued him. Desperate for an infusion of new information, he risked prolonging his encounter with Sabien, hoping to mine more clues about how demons came into existence.

Sabien settled against the wall, growing more comfortable. "My feeling is these are two separate stories that have fused together over time. That happens a lot. Back then, meanings were interchangeable. The imagery is interesting, because the glyph for *demon* was the same as *smoke*. Given the actual strength of woven spider silk, these fumes had to have been quite powerful."

"I'm more interested in when and how demons became like us." Navalis sighed. "Solid. Corporeal."

Sabien shrugged. "If anything comes to mind, I'll tell you, perhaps over a drink."

Navalis abruptly propelled himself away from the wall. He jumped from the landing and down the stairwell at the suggestion, trying hard not to smile at Sabien's persistence.

"Wait!" Sabien called out.

Navalis slowed to a stop and listened.

"There's an old farmer in Eastgate, at The Black Horse." Sabien forced the words out, then gave in bitterly. "Once he told me, and I've never forgotten it on account of it being so odd, he told me, *Tilling and turning the soil at night made the baby demon babe's bones grow bright.*"

Navalis repeated the line in his mind, imprinting it there permanently. Tilling and turning the soil at night made the demon babe's bones grow bright.

"He's soused most of the time," Sabien confessed. "Could be nothing more than drunken ramblings, don't you think?"

Navalis shrugged. "Could be," he said. "I'll have to find out, won't I?" He resumed his descent toward the lab.

"I can take you to him, if you'd like?"

He ignored Sabien's offer.

"He goes by the name of Rolen," Sabien added.

Navalis turned the corner of the stairwell, and Sabien raised his voice to be heard.

"You'll at least tell me what you find out, right?"

By the time Navalis had returned to the landing of the laboratory, he figured the least he could do was thank him. "Your help is much appreciated." His voice floated up the stairwell, echoing lightly. He waited a moment, but there wasn't any response.

✳ CHAPTER 26 ✳

Ulmaen rounded the corner to the corridor with the iron door at the far end. The food pail he carried swung about and knocked against his thigh. On his first step toward the adjacent corridor a little farther down, the spider demon's earthy, dulcet tones drifted along the walls.

"Hello again."

He stood there, staring at the door with the grate across its small window looking like the maw of a beast. Accustomed to seeing a dim glow there, he was surprised by the darkness. He passed the turn where he had intended to go and pushed onward, toward that door.

He ducked down to peek inside the chamber. His sight adjusted, and when he made out details, he nearly jumped out of his skin.

Mithreel stood near the iron door, as near as the chains allowed, where he peered back through the window. His eyes flickered as he smiled.

"I knew if I waited long enough, you'd return."

Ulmaen settled his nerves with a long, deep breath. He lifted the food pail, designated for the last of Ilgaud's friends.

"As long as Ilgaud and his buddies are down here, you won't need to wait more than a day, which must feel like a second for someone who's been around as long as you have."

Mithreel laughed, spurring the chains to rattle and chink. The strange chorus faded into silence.

"You're sweet. I *love* that about you."

He pushed himself toward the door. His shoulders, all of them, rolled backward along his torso as the chains pulled at his arms. His arms spread wide and he looked more a spider than a man.

"For thousands of years," he began. "I've seen prisoners come and go, except for the demons. They stay. Those who have been imprisoned the longest, they are from Kugilla's time. The others, they couldn't be influenced by Adinav. Uncontrollable, the lot of them, yet too rare and powerful to be destroyed. Especially the ones that affect your mind. Adinav studied them all." He swung back a bit, then leaned forward again. "We're still being studied."

"Because you're uncontrollable? Is that why?"

When Ulmaen asked the question, he felt safe, but as the words spilled from his tongue, his mouth went dry for he saw the chains that held the spider demon were old and rusty, some of them stretched. If they gave, all that protected him was the wooden door.

Mithreel smiled again, baring his perfect humanoid teeth. "Ever the na." His head fell forward again, his eyes locking onto Ulmaen. "What is it they say now? Never? The world has changed. Words, too. But I hear the changes, I learn, and that's why I persist.

"Since the dawn of time, every beast and creature in this world has fed me their fear. It keeps me alive. And there are other spider demons out there doing my work. Younger ones. I can sense them." He backed away from the door, each chain sagging and chinking. "They grow, as I do, yearning to be recognizable, familiar."

"Why bother?" Ulmaen shook his head. "You'll always be a demon, and it'll take forever."

"We *will* be embraced *when* we return home, one way or another."

Ulmaen wanted to ask what Mithreel meant by home, but Mithreel rambled on.

"I'm the first. I'm the most familiar with time. I've seen so much of it pass by. You can't know how long I've been kept locked in here, or how long I existed before I took this form, back when I was something less... substantial."

He regarded his cell. "Long ago, there was a tower built to imprison me. I lived there a long while, even after the first flood. When the second flood came and buried most of it, they moved me here. I nearly got away after a third flood. By then, the mystics figured out how to leash me."

He raised one of his arms and brandished the tarnished cup covering his hand, making all the chains rattle.

Ulmaen glanced at the tempered metal carved with intricate symbols. They were old, and from what he discerned of the visible inscription, they were incantations intended to contain whatever was stored inside the cup.

And with Mithreel bound, anyone could milk him of his venom if they wanted.

"You've questions," Mithreel said. "I can tell when you're... curious. Come now, ask me."

"Do the cups ever come off?"

Mithreel slowly shook his head from side to side.

Ulmaen bit his lower lip. "Anyone ever try to milk you for your venom?"

Mithreel shook his head again and dragged his tonge over one of his large incisors. "Ever the na!"

Ulmaen wasn't sure if he believed him.

"What are your powers then?" he asked. "Why's everyone so afraid of you that they have to keep your hands and arms bound?"

Mithreel stared a moment, then answered. "I make things... disappear."

The answer was cryptic, no doubt intended to confound and distract him. Although he distrusted Mithreel, he couldn't ignore the possibility that he might be an accomplice in Ule's murder.

"Ask me what you truly want to know," Mithreel insisted.

Ulmaen only wanted to know who killed Ule and why, give Bethereel some peace of mind and set Rozafel free.

"Ask you what?"

"Where it is, of course."

Down the other corridor, the last of Ilgaud's men called out, begging for his food. Ulmaen backed away from the door, grasping the food pail handle tighter.

"Where's what?" he asked.

"What you lost so long ago," Mithreel answered. "So long ago, when you and I were young. Your... treasure."

Back when the world was young, Ulmaen had been incarcerated for destroying another world he had created. Part of his punishment included the suppression of his memories. For that reason, his youth wasn't a time that offered many fond remembrances.

"I need to go," he said, growing uncomfortable.

Hastily, he backtracked and turned down the adjacent corridor before Mithreel could persuade him to stay. At the only inhabited cell, he deposited the last food pail. Instead of turning back the way he had come, he hurried along the tunnel to see where it ended.

The tunnel sloped upward, then curved sharply to the left. He climbed several steep steps made of wood planks then came across a long stairwell fashioned from quarried stone. It led up to the main floor in the east arm of the Prison.

He stayed on the landing a moment. From this vantage point, hidden in the shadow of the doorway, he scanned the empty row of cells. At the far end, he saw Rozafel huddled against the wall in her cell, picking through her dread locks which were piled on the floor. He cringed at the increasing gaps on her head. If he didn't find out something to support her story, she'd be bald in another few weeks.

He stepped out into the east arm of the Prison and stretched. The sound of footfalls surrounded him all at once, and he hunched over, preparing to be ambushed by guards. When he realized none were coming, he skulked along the east arm, ignoring the way the guards regarded him with raised eyebrows.

Back in the Core, he tiptoed along the inhabited cells toward the entrance. When he neared the mouth of the corridor, he glimpsed someone other than Gorlen standing at the counter. He stopped and pressed back against the wall, just before the edge of the corner, where he could observe and listen.

Osblod clutched his side. He sucked air through his nose as he desperately tried to catch his breath. If he had run into the Prison, it explained the footfalls Ulmaen had heard.

Gorlen was there, too, deeply engrossed in a drawing of a building and the rooms it contained. Some of the rooms were marked with x's. Others showed arrows through gaps that must have indicated doors or windows.

Ulmaen recognized the layout of the Inner Sanctum and surmised that Gorlen was devising security protocols.

Osblod began to relax. His breath evened. "We've got a problem," he whispered.

Gorlen marked a large circle around the Chair Room, then rolled the parchment into a scroll and set it beneath the counter.

"What?" Gorlen asked, finally addressing Osblod. "Did that silly mystic finally get flattened by a horse?"

Osblod leaned in closer, hovering above the counter. "There's been another murder."

Who? Why? Ulmaen mentally blurted, no longer interested in Gorlen's security procedures. He remained still, listening to a conversation not intended for his ears.

"I haven't told anyone," Osblod said. "Came to you first. If word of this gets around, Lyan's campaign will have a tough time recovering. And after such a successful festival, too."

"Why do you care? Aren't you running against him?"

Osblod nodded once, brows furrowed. "I'm for a fair fight, when it comes to politics. But murder is suspect. I hope it has nothing to do with Protos."

"Murder is always about politics," Gorlen declared.

"I'll have to tell the cousin," Osblod continued. "That'll be unpleasant. He's an intense man."

Trembling shook Ulmaen's body at the mention of a cousin. His heart began to thunder and his throat constricted, as he struggled to hear them. He tried to focus on the facts instead of succumbing to presumptions.

"He's been asking questions," Osblod continued. "Why I won't let him see her." He wiped perspiration from his face. His long fingers rested on his brow a moment. "I bet the servants at Kugilla Hall have already started with their gossip."

"Who's been murdered then?"

"The wife," Osblod said.

Ulmaen held his breath. Who's wife? Plenty of people had wives—

"Ule's wife," Osblod elaborated. "Bethee... Bethereel. That's her proper name."

Osblod had to be mistaken, Ule thought. He spoke of someone else. Anyone else. Bethereel couldn't be gone. She couldn't be... dead.

Osblod covered his mouth a moment, patted his lips a few times, and said, "She was smothered. There's bruising on her lips, around her nostrils. I've seen it before. It's caused by a hand pressing down over the mouth and pushing up against the nose."

Gorlen stepped away from the counter. "Where is she and who found her?"

"In her room," Osblod replied. "I found her." He shook his head. "I went to check in on her. A few days back she suffered a breakdown."

"You mentioned a cousin?"

Osblod nodded. "That storyteller, the one with the collection of oddities."

Gorlen stepped out from behind the counter. "Tell me more about this breakdown. And the cousin."

Ulmaen heard them well enough as they made their way toward the main door. He wanted to follow them at a distance, to be certain what he had heard was true. He wouldn't mourn for Bethereel, not yet, not until he was sure.

An anguished cry floated along the wall.

The wail crept up behind him, not from the stairwell to the Pit around the corner, otherwise he'd assume the mare demon was having another go at Ilgaud. No, the cry came from behind him.

He returned the way he had come, determined to go cell to cell until he found the source. He hadn't far to go, for he found Rozafel kneeling on the floor, her hands pressed against her mouth, trying to stifle her sobs. Struggling for breath, she shook her head. As to why she cried, he could only guess that the stress of being locked away had finally taken its toll.

"Rozafel, I'll find that evidence for you. You need to hold on." He turned back to follow Osblod and Gorlen, to make sure he hadn't misunderstood them about Bethereel.

Rozafel sniffed, sucking back spittle. She rocked back and forth, wiping her mouth. "Poor Bethee." Her grief-stricken cry elongated the name.

The heartbreak contained in that name struck Ulmaen hard. Rozafel had heard what he had, no doubt as whispers floating over the walls and the floors, along the water piped into the cell in the floor behind her. Sound traveled well within the Prison.

Ulmaen crouched at the cell gate, struggling to contain a swell of grief. He reached through the bars, extending his hand toward her. She stared at it a moment and sniffed.

"I'll get you out of here," he told her. "I promise."

Overcome by the promise, Rozafel clutched his hand and held on tightly.

Ulmaen had to know, he had to see for himself. After Rozafel cried herself to sleep and released his hand, he ran.

He ran through the Core, past the counter, and up the stairs. Beyond the Prison, he rushed along the path and stopped halfway toward the Infirmary. There were many soldiers there, milling about the building, dipping in and out of Soldier Alley.

He didn't want to navigate them to get to the Colonnade. He needed to see Bethereel, alive in their old room, where she had to be. He turned north and waded through the tall grass toward the northern stables. Where the old rampart wall fell into ruin, so too did the northern Colonnade

Piles of broken quarried stone that had once made up the walkway and the wall spilled over into the field. Ulmaen avoided tripping over slabs, as he darted among the granite and marble. Once the path grew more level and shaded, he raced along the Colonnade toward the Starry Rise.

The buildings, the courtyards, the fountain, were all a blur as he rushed toward the eastern Colonnade. He skirted the small crowds outside the Games Hall and was grateful how very few were gathered before the Inner Sanctum or Library. At the entrance of Kugilla Hall, he bolted through the main door.

Inside the air was cool yet stale, and he stood a moment to catch his breath. He half expected to see Gorlen's guards standing watch at the bottom step, but the stairwell was empty.

He climbed three flights of stairs and rushed toward the chamber that he had once shared with Bethereel. Nearing the open door, he slowed and shuddered at the possibility of what awaited him inside the room.

Sunlight streamed through the open window. The room felt warm and alive, reminding him of a dream. Bethereel was alive. She had to be.

The room was how he remembered it. The same bed and bookshelf, the same wardrobe and table... except their white and violet blanket was on the bed now instead of the wall. Still, the rest of it remained the same... except for the stillness and the quiet, except for the presence of a man sitting on the far side of the bed, his back to the door, head hung low.

Ulmaen's mood plummeted.

"Is she..." he began. He couldn't bring himself to finish the question. He began trembling again.

Sabien sluggishly looked over his shoulder, then returned his gaze toward the floor. "I don't know anything," he said.

"She's gone then?"

Sabien waved his arm. "They've taken her body to the Infirmary to be properly examined." With great effort, he stood.

No, Ulmaen thought, I would've seen her...

He recalled the crowd at the Infirmary. The urge to run there caused him to turn back toward the door. His muscles tensed. Given the grim countenance of Sabien, his red-rimmed eyes, the way his body sagged, the last bit of Ulmaen's hope began slipping away, and in its place a profound awareness of his denial lingered.

"If there is any way I can help," Ulmaen offered. "If you need a hand with preparing her." His stomach lurched. "The bathing, the dressing—"

"What's this?" Sabien sparked to life, his mood turning volatile. His arms clutched his ribs. "Do you know Bethee from somewhere?"

"I'm sorry—"

"You've spoken to her one time that I know of, and it upset her."

Sabien strode toward him, his body straightening. He curled a hand and popped his knuckles. "She said you reminded her of someone? Did you..." He narrowed his eyes. "Did she see you do something? Something you weren't supposed to do?" His thought trailed off. "Did you do this?"

Ulmaen strained against the tide of grief and panic. How could Sabien believe he was capable of murdering his lover?

"Where were you while everyone ate their breakfasts?" Sabien seethed. Spittle formed at the edge of his mouth.

A revelation struck Ulmaen. He wasn't Ule. He was Ulmaen. A new stranger among them. Someone capable of anything. Someone who wasn't supposed to know Bethereel at all.

"I was delivering food to prisoners," he said. "First the Core, then the ones in the Pit, like I've been doing every day now since forever. You can ask Gorlen."

Sabien's anger melted into confusion. He shook his head, returned to the bed, and sat.

The tide of panic inside Ulmaen crashed. Profound sadness persisted, and worse, he realized that as Ulmaen, as someone else entirely, he had lost the privilege to openly express his grief for Bethereel, the woman he still loved.

❋

Bethereel's death was the recurring topic of conversation for the next several days. Osblod had examined her, reaffirming his initial observations, and when her body had been taken to the Mortuary, Sabien bathed, sealed, and dressed her.

When it came time for confession, Ulmaen understood why the living had such a need for speaking to the dead. There was plenty he wanted to tell Bethereel, but he couldn't. According to his new identity and his position in the castle, he'd only ever interacted directly with her once—a strange man who had previously upset her in public. If he visited her in the Mortuary, he risked—how did Navalis always say it?—causing suspicion.

Now, at her funeral, he did his best to show interest in the march of the beasts toward the soldiers who gathered around her body, but the ritual had no meaning for him. The beasts only reminded him of his kind back home, making him feel alone.

His gaze wandered along the wide steps carved into the sloping hill that arced about until the steps merged into paths that snaked and climbed up to mausoleums, tombs, and entrances to the upper galleries of the Catacombs.

He'd tried to find a place in the front, closest to the altar near the fire pits, but he was tall and many complained they couldn't see. So he moved to the back of the crowd.

He tried not to let the sight of Bethereel affect him. He still felt raw and angry despite the care with which her body had been tightly wrapped in burlap.

The dirge began, a brief, ethereal song that wrenched open a valve in his heart, pouring out a longing for Bethereel to be restored, to be untainted by this heinous crime. Disgust stuck to his flesh, encrusting him with a sickness—the uneasiness that comes with feeling empty.

Those around him cried openly when he knew he shouldn't. They cried when the dirge ended and when Bethereel was lifted by a handful of mystics destined for the Catacombs. He fought the urge to weep himself, the muscles in his face and neck straining to resist.

As the mystics rounded the altar, Bethereel raised high in the air, her head shifted to one side and remained there, her cheek nestled against a pillow of crimson roses and marigolds. Ulmaen breathed in the final image of her: black thread laced eyes and mouth, an assault against her pale beauty; her chiselled, sunken cheeks suggestive of poor health, and he sat down hard on a step.

With the back of his hand, he patted at the burn in his cheek and discovered his face was wet. Tears gathered in the crevice between his cheeks and nose. He had been crying after all.

Fierce determination came over him like a punch in the chest. None of this would have happened to her, if he—if Ule hadn't been murdered. He needed to know for certain who had started this chain of tragic events, and he needed another approach that didn't involve listening in on conversations between sex-starved wives and their cheating husbands.

His only lead were the gloves that had been sold, according to Rozafel. If only he could prove it, but merchant ledgers were only accessible to financiers and scribes.

A hand touched his shoulder. Lightweight and small, it gently squeezed his bicep. He glanced up, blinking into the bright morning light to discover Laere's face peering at him from behind a curtain of her hair.

"I didn't think you knew her that well," she said sadly.

Ulmaen stood abruptly, dwarfing Laere with his stature. He sniffed and shook his head.

"I didn't," he lied, fighting the urge to yell at everyone that he knew and loved Bethereel with every molecule of his being. "Everyone's just so... sad. She must've been a beautiful woman."

Mourners nearby must have heard what he had said, for they nodded in agreement.

Laere tilted her head. "You're sensitive, aren't you?"

"I don't know about that," he lied again. He noticed how lying was starting to feel a little easier to do, how it created a position of leverage, of power. It created a barrier, too, simultaneously distancing him from her, yet protecting him.

Once the crowd began dispersing, those nearby who had heard what he had said patted him on the shoulder or the back. Others used his stature to steady themselves as they stepped down from the upper steps.

Laere smiled. It was subtle, but he noticed. When those nearest had gone, she brushed up against him. What earlier apprehensions she'd had toward him had disappeared. Her eyes were glazed with sadness and something else. Curiosity? Interest?

The soft flesh of her arm rubbed against his as she stood on her tip toes, digging her fingers into his forearm. He thought of Bethereel touching him, imagined inhaling her lavender perfume instead of the linseed oil that clung to Laere as she brushed her small hand across his thick cheek.

He was simultaneously sickened and aroused by the way the gesture soothed him.

"I've got a bottle of whiskey stashed away," she told him. "Perfect for forgetting."

* CHAPTER 27 *

The sombre din of the Dining Hall offered a perfect lull of white noise for meditation. Navalis focused on the sound, immersed himself in it, and let his thoughts scatter. The absence of thought increased his awareness, and his surroundings intensified as though everything were suddenly ablaze.

Mystics tended to gravitate toward their own kind, usually gathering at the end of the central table closest to the main door, and he sat among them, watching their faces shimmer as they ate and drank. Their words and laughter filtered into his mind, and he acknowledged the mass of information, then let it pass out of his consciousness with ease.

To his right, Boriag leaned over the table, spouting off about the success he'd had imbuing objects with more tensile strength. The others showed greater interest in their food and wine than in Boriag's boasts.

Conversations spilled over one another, from one table to the next. Saddened tones and angry outbursts broke the surface of white noise, as Navalis detected distress amid the clothiers behind him.

They reasoned that Bethereel's death must surely have cleared Rozafel of being Ule's murder, since Rozafel was locked away while it happened. They also made the assumption that whoever had killed Ule must have murdered Bethereel, too. Since Rozafel was in jail at the time of Bethereel's death, then Rozafel was undoubtedly innocent. They prattled on among themselves, demanding their Mistress be released. Had any of them the nerve, they might have dared to stand and address the Magnes.

Lyan sat at the head table, head bowed, not a morsel of food touched on the plate before him. Accompanying him this evening were his top generals, including Gorlen. Kerista joined him as well, sitting at his right hand. Beside her, Mbjard was poised to record points on any issues of importance discussed during dinner.

Outside the Dining Hall, a bell chimed once, indicating the beginning of open discourse between the Magnes, his advisers, and whoever wished to converse with them.

A slow, plodding clap arose from somewhere in the hall. The white noise began to diminish. Navalis's thoughts whipped back into focus with great force and pained him. The brilliance of the room diminished as he reached for his wine, drained the glass, and wiped his mouth.

The hall quieted. Then, like the others around him, Navalis turned toward the source. Beyond the table of the clothiers, close to the head table, Osblod stood. He held everyone's attention, including the pensive Magnes.

"What do you wish to discuss?" Lyan asked.

"First, I'd like to congratulate you," Osblod replied. He clapped some more then stopped when no one joined in. "The celebration of the arts is coming to an end soon, and it remains quite the affair. You've certainly recovered loyalty from the artists."

He encouraged the others in the hall to clap again, and although some did, their effort was weak and the applause subsided quickly as though no one wanted to support anything Osblod had to say to the Magnes.

"What?" Osblod complained. "No love for the Magnes's obvious attempt to soothe the unsettled feathers of our under-appreciated artists?"

At the head table, Kerista scowled with such intensity she began to shake. Her fingers fisted around her fork, and she slammed it against the table.

"Your attempts to mock the Magnes are disgraceful, now of all times," she shouted. "Have you no shame?!"

Lyan rested a hand on her shoulder. At the touch, she withdrew with a smoldering glare and resigned herself to silence.

Mbjard raised his hand to quiet the hall. A gentle smile parted his lips. With an aplomb surpassed by no one else, including the Magnes, he addressed Osblod.

"Perhaps, everyone's tired of what you have to say," Mbjard proposed. "Casting doubt over Lyan's ability at every available opportunity won't win you votes. *Your* intentions are rather obvious."

Osblod laughed in defeat. He bowed toward Mbjard, then addressed Lyan. "My apologies. The pursuit of the Chair is only as interesting as the way we candidates play fight."

Lyan snorted. "Offer a conflict worth fighting over, then perhaps I'll play."

"Fair enough." Osblod's mirth subsided. "Then I speak to you, my Magnes, as a distraught physician and a concerned citizen of the Sondshor district and this castle."

Convinced Osblod was still playing some campaign game, Navalis leaned back and mumbled to no one in particular, "His only concern is getting elected."

"No doubt about that," Boriag agreed, his mouth full of potato. "That's a true cock battle there."

Navalis wasn't sure he agreed. He couldn't quite put his finger on why Osblod persisted more than other candidates in challenging and engaging Lyan in public as often as he did. The most he ever accomplished was angering or exhausting Lyan.

Osblod scanned the hall. "For many of us, this castle's our home," he declared. "We've no want of being elsewhere."

"That's pleasing to know," Lyan acknowledged, visibly wary of Osblod luring him into another public argument.

Mbjard frowned, as he exchanged his fork for a glass nib pen and began to write on the block of parchment next to him.

Navalis drained a nearby bottle into his glass and drank deeply of the wine. He detected a theatrical quality in the delivery of Osblod's address, but he had also sensed sincerity in his tone.

Lyan must have sensed it too for he asked, "What's your concern, friend?"

"The same as anyone's. Another of our own has died in an unusual way."

At this, the assembly responded, calling out Bethereel's name, offering toasts to her memory. When the hall settled again, Osblod continued.

"I examined Bethereel before she died. She suffered up here." He touched his forehead. "Some kind of withdrawal." He shook his head. "I couldn't determine the cause. So soon after Ule's poisoning, too. They were connected in the most intimate of ways. It's suspicious, eh? Am I the only who to see this?"

Around the hall, people answered in agreement.

"We've more pressing concerns at the moment," Kerista began.

Boos and hisses rose above the din, and quickly faded as Lyan stood up from his chair, and asked Osblod, "Why haven't you mentioned your concern during counsel?"

"I have. Security, electoral protocol, the safety of candidates pushes everything else aside." Osblod waved his hand over the table where he sat. "I care about the affairs of our shor, but I also have personal concerns. We all do. Are we safe? Will something strange happen to someone else?"

Gasps erupted around the hallway.

"Hush," Osblod insisted. "I've no want of worrying everyone. I, like all of you, need to know something of what's being done to find answers."

At the table where the clothiers sat, their faces flushed with wine and anger, each in turn found their voices and called out: *And what of Rozafel? She couldn't murder a fly! Set her free.*

Others began to offer possible answers to both Osblod and the Magnes, expressing their concerns and opinions:

Bethee died of a broken heart. Don't make it out to be anything worse.

It's to do with the election. Someone wants to unsettle the Magnes, weaken him, I'm sure.

Ilgaud's escaped, hasn't he?

Ilgaud?

Ilgaud!

Gorlen stood next. His chair scraped against the floor, and the sharp squeal made everyone cringe. He scanned the room, scowling as he chewed the last of a mouthful of food.

"Enough!" he howled, and when silence returned, he addressed everyone. "We're still investigating Rozafel's story. We've got very little to go on here. Till someone has undeniable information, we're fishing for a tadpole in a sea of frogs. Understand?" He paused a moment then added testily, "And cease this nonsense about Ilgaud. He's locked away for life, I assure you of that."

Gorlen glared indiscriminately at randomly selected individuals nearby before he sat back down.

Kerista pushed her chair back and stood, taking a turn at addressing the hall. The growing buzz of conversation ceased again. She scanned the room with austere severity.

"Justice will come swiftly," she promised. "First, we must understand with certainty what has befallen both Ule and Bethereel. We, like some of you, suspect their deaths may be politically motivated, but we're considering other possibilities as well."

Whispers drifted along each table.

"For example," Kerista continued, "I am personally investigating a collapse in the Catacombs, one located beneath the gallery where Ule was interred, to determine if the destruction was done intentionally as a way to... hide something."

Navalis frowned at her final remark. Despite the wine, he felt as if a trail of ants crawled along the back of his neck. Until now, he regarded her interest in the gallery as having to do with Ule's murder, but now he considered another possibility—Goyas's body. Perhaps she was searching for the old mystic's corpse. Had she been the one who moved it there and extracted pieces of its flesh?

"Hide what exactly?" Osblod asked.

"Perhaps evidence on her body," Kerista offered. She smiled coolly. "The kind that takes time to show up after someone has died." She pointed at him. "When Erzo's Gallery is safe to visit again, perhaps you'll conduct another examination, won't you?"

"But she's sealed," Osblod blurted. "Any way I can help, I will, but I won't defy the seal."

Innate to Osblod was a boldness Navalis admired. Many years ago, he'd witnessed that fortitude first hand as Osblod navigated battles and skirmishes, reasoning with soldiers armed to the teeth to tend to the wounded. The soldiers could have easily slaughtered Osblod for his requests, but they always reconsidered, as though Osblod somehow reconnected them back to the decent, honorable parts of themselves.

"Still Magnes, given the close connection between Ule and Bethereel and you," Osblod continued, "some would say very close—"

"Mind your mouth!" Kerista began to tremble with rage again. She silenced herself this time, and sat again.

"If you have a point, get on with it," Lyan said. Annoyance failed to return any of his color or vim.

"Is it possible Ule and Bethereel discovered or knew something they shouldn't, about one of the candidates?"

A murmur rushed through the hall, whispers about conspiracy catching like wildfire.

"Perhaps something about you?" Osblod added.

The murmur rose in volume, grew more frenzied.

Several advisers sitting at the head table turned to regard their Magnes as though they were seeing something about him they hadn't seen before—Gorlen, especially.

Gorlen locked eyes on Lyan like he had spotted prey on a hunt. He reached for the hilt of his sword. He nodded at Kerista, waited for some kind of response. She sat in silence a moment, then shook her head. He released his sword and sneered.

Lyan remained silent. Growing more tired by the minute, he asked, "Are you accusing me of something?"

"No, of course not, old friend." The suggestion of this idea seemed to genuinely wound Osblod. "I hadn't meant... No, never."

"If anyone here knows anything about me, it would be you." Lyan narrowed his eyes briefly, then his expression softened. "That's what you're getting at, isn't it? All these public challenges, they weren't about the election. There's some secret you think you know about me, something that you believe everyone should know."

Osblod shook his head again. "No. No, I've no intention of that," he insisted. "I'm speaking of Ule and Bethereel."

The last of Lyan's strength was directed into the point of his finger, which he drove into the top of the head table, causing the cutlery resting against his plate to rattle. When he shouted, his voice trembled.

"I earned that Chair! "

Navalis nodded, remembering.

Lyan had been a mess of cuts and bruises and covered in gore when he had sat in the Chair. Earlier in the day, Lyan had been pinned between animated corpses. Lyan succumbed to panic, lashing out frantically with his sword and pummeling with his fist, driving both weapons deep into the slick of petrified flesh and entrails until each corpse he encountered collapsed.

Navalis had always wondered if what had caused Lyan to turn maniacal had been the number of undead soldiers or perhaps the emptiness that stared back from the living soldiers, who had no control over their minds or bodies.

He, along with others, had fought Adinav's legions over and over again, the same soldiers risen from the dead. Lyan had screamed with such anguish, a deep and desperate wail as he relinquished his sanity and brilliant mind, forcing himself to become a machine fighting one skirmish after another in the courtyards of the castle.

But that was all Navalis had known of Lyan before Adinav's fall. That much he had witnessed, for he had abandoned the courtyard in search of Adinav himself. Along the way he joined forces with Kaleel the Rex. Together they fought undead soldiers in the Chair Room, up the stairwell toward the tower of the Inner Sanctum, where Navalis drove a disarming thought into the mind of Adinav, one that made him blind. The cat demon struck hard, too, destroying Adinav and the scepter he wielded.

When they went to the courtyard, where Adinav's body had fallen from the tower, and discovered his hold on the possessed soldiers, both alive and dead, had been relinquished. There, they beheaded the fallen Magnes and parted ways.

Navalis mended his ribs as he kept watch over Ule, who had been trapped in the scepter as a gemstone, the pieces of her strewn throughout the courtyard. They buzzed to life and returned her to a humanoid form, but when he saw she had lost her memory, there was little he could do for her. He let her wonder off, knowing she stood a better chance at regaining her own memory, and he returned to the Inner Sanctum, determined to destroy anything that might resurrect Adinav.

At that time, he was on the verge of meeting Lyan and Osblod for the first time. Since then, he had come to know them as purposeful men who had both contributed to the well-being of the shor in ways no one could possibly fathom. Neither were strangers to sacrifice or to each other.

"I know how you earned your position," Osblod said.

What anger had animated Lyan began to dissipate. Fatigue overtook him.

"I was there," Osblod reminded him. "The question is, do you believe you *deserve* the Chair?"

Again, Navalis found it intriguing the way the past invaded the present. The memory persisted.

He knew little about Lyan's activities as Navalis retraced his steps down the stairwell. At the doorway to the Chair Room, he had froze, for Lyan had sat on the only available object that hadn't been incinerated by a Clear Fire grenade—a plain block of blue marble stone sculpted into a high back chair.

By law, Lyan only had to sit on the Chair to acquire the position of Magnes, and it was clear by his fading strength and the blood soaked cloth bound tightly about his throat, regardless of whether or not he intended to rule the shor, he had needed to rest his battle beaten body.

Suddenly, another man had stood in the main door to the courtyard, sword raised. Osblod had glanced around the room, noticing every detail-- Lyan in the chair, Navalis's former self, a blacksmith, who had stood in the shadows of the door to the stairwell, and who had carried an arsenal of explosives in a black leather apron and wielded a sword.

Lyan, with what remained of his adrenalin pushed himself upright and wielded his sword with a grunt. His eyes darted fiercely back and forth to both sides of the room. A feral sort of madness possessed him. His grip failed him, his muscles too, and he collapsed back against the polished marble of the Chair.

"Don't come near," he rasped. "I warn you." Perhaps Lyan intended to raise his sword, but the weight of it seemed too heavy. The sword scuttled down the side of the Chair and hung there, the hilt trapped in the grip of his fingers. Lyan's head lolled once maybe twice before he lost consciousness.

Osblod's glance returned to the blacksmith. "Do I fight you for the Chair then?"

Navalis had stepped inside the room. "I've no desire for power."

Osblod's face softened in disbelief. "None whatsoever?"

"None." Navalis had raised his sword toward Osblod, even though he was grateful for the many times Osblod had tended to his wounds in the past. Unfortunately, the promise of power had a way of undermining empathy and compassion in some, and Osblod had seemed no different.

Navalis braced himself for battle. "I won't let you kill a man who can't defend himself. If you want the Chair, you'll need to get past me to take it."

Osblod lowered his sword and regarded Lyan. Perhaps he had grappled with his temptation, perhaps he tried to predict the future, imagining himself ruling the shor. In the end, he lowered his sword.

"He got there first," he said. "Fair's fair. There are others coming who won't care about fairness. We protect Lyan together, eh? We'll be witnesses. Make sure he's instated."

Navalis hadn't given much thought to why Osblod had stepped back from the power and glory of becoming Magnes. Now, however, his actions and public conversations with the Magnes indicated he had had a change of mind.

✳ CHAPTER 28 ✳

Ulmaen dreamed of the Starry Rise, the spray and tumble of water twinkling in moonlight. Sitting on the edge of the fountain, Bethereel reached for him.

Her straight hair was wavier than usual, like she hadn't brushed it in days, and she wore white, which was odd. She hated wearing white. According to her, the color dirtied easily and made her pale skin look sickly. The color did neither of these things, for she glowed, vibrant and healthy.

He sat next to her. He kissed her, his lips unwilling to let hers go for the longest time. His eyes searched hers, watched her pupils dilate, growing larger with desire. His body responded, very differently than what he had experienced when he had been a woman.

The urge was instant and fierce. He didn't need the slow build up of arousal he drew satisfaction from when they caressed or danced, when they teased one another. Their usual foreplay wasn't necessary. He was ready. When he finally pulled away, he called her name.

"Bethee."

Her pupils grew larger or perhaps her eyes became brown, he couldn't tell. He jumped to his feet, for the woman who sat before him was someone else—

Ulmaen woke with a jolt. He licked his dry lips and fell back against the bed. He shook his head, heard his name called out, and he responded.

"What?"

A hoarse voice shushed him. Around him, his fellow servants turned in their sleep and settled back into slumber.

His head was still groggy from another evening of drinking with Laere, a bottle of gin this time. She had modeled for him, partially nude. Despite the growing numbness of the alcohol, he had become mindful of how much fuller in the breast she was compared to Bethereel. If only Laere had been a little taller.

Eventually, the gin made those differences disappear, and he might have accepted what she had offered. He nearly had.

Laere's chamber had become overrun with her artist mates, and none were shy about their sexual activities. The room had heated quickly, making Ulmaen's flesh sticky. His nerves had begun to buzz. He had wanted to join them, to wallow in release, to just let go... of everything.

Still enraptured by the hazy dream, Ulmaen recalled the collage of entwined arms, the mounds of breasts and buttocks, the moans of pleasure, the sweet tobacco pipe mixed with musk. This time, in his waking version of the dream, he succumbed to the oasis of sex. Laere was completely nude now, but he didn't want Laere, so he changed her to Bethereel, and he stripped off his shirt, his pants—

Ulmaen heard his name again, deep within his solar plexus. Navalis's voice resonated there, forceful and consuming. Ulmaen blinked himself fully awake, disgusted by the lingering lust he felt for Laere when in his heart he desired Bethereel. He was grateful this time for being unable to respond to his Master; he could only listen.

"Meet me by the Prison."

Ulmaen obeyed, making his way silently from his room on the ground floor of Kugilla Hall. Outside, instead of following the Colonnade toward Soldier Alley and risk being seen by soldiers rising for their morning assignments, he crossed the walkway and moved from courtyard to courtyard.

Eventually he slipped through a hole in the old rampart wall into what was once again just a field. In the recent past, there had been shanties and markets. Before that, during the final days of the war, the area had been a field of bodies, soldiers and demons left behind to rot and be plucked clean by the living.

He moved southwest across trampled grass, being sure to stay at a distance from Soldier Alley. He followed a row of large stones marking the base for the new rampart wall, and once past Soldier Alley and the Infirmary, where the field merged with another, he spied the Prison squatting like a dark beast. Despite the lit entrance and towers, the building was a shadow against the night.

Ulmaen trekked west through high grass till he found a path and followed it beyond the far side of the Prison, where the land dipped down toward a woodlot.

"Here, this way." Navalis's projected voice rumbled in his chest again.

Farther along the path, Navalis stood where some of the trees had been felled, and once Ulmaen joined him, Navalis guided them deeper into the woods, well out of view of the castle, where he stopped and announced the nature of their training.

"Tonight, I'll show you how to project your thoughts covertly."

Ulmaen yawned.

Navalis leaned against a tree and stared at the ground a moment. He avoided eye contact and his left foot fidgeted.

"You alright?" Ulmaen asked.

Navalis regarded him. "Yes."

The word was more like a punch than a reply. Their eyes met, and Ulmaen saw a fierce anger in his Master he hadn't seen since his childhood, during the final days before his incarceration.

"You alright about Bethereel?" Navalis asked.

A lance speared Ulmaen's heart for the hundredth time since the funeral. "No," he replied honestly, "but I guess I don't have much choice, do I?"

"No, you don't." Navalis stepped forward and placed the heel of his hand on Ulmaen's solar plexus. "I expect you've got a lot of tension here." He pressed down firmly once, then removed his hand.

Ulmaen felt a knot of high-strung energy in his chest give a little under the pressure, then rush back together, tighter than before.

"Your emotional state will make tonight's lesson difficult," Navalis complained.

Ulmaen didn't care. "Let's get on with it." He rolled his head to loosen his neck muscles and shook out his arms.

Navalis snorted.

"What then?"

"We start here." He pointed to his head. "In our minds, when we talk to the collective, we create an opening there," Navalis began. "It's instinctual. Because our minds are non-material, it's natural to expect it to flex and flow. We relax and we push our thoughts. So much of our nature is based on pushing and pulling. That's why we have so many laws to determine how and to what extent we can push one another."

Navalis glanced away again. "Without those kinds of boundaries, the stronger of us would dominate the weak." With a deep breath, he squared himself. "It used to be like that, a long time ago. Possession was rampant. Ousting a Xiines from a world was like sport, often with disastrous results, sometimes even fatal."

Ulmaen's interest in the lecture began to wane. Other concerns pushed their way to the forefront of his mind, and he laughed at how some thoughts were stronger and pushed others out of the way, a practical example of the very lesson he was being taught.

"Is something funny?"

Ulmaen shook his head. "No. Just observing the push and pull of my thoughts."

"Fine," Navalis said, though he didn't look happy about the revelation. "Pushing our thoughts on their own, projecting them, comes easily. Doing so through a conduit in our body doesn't, but sometimes the effort is worth it, because communicating this way hides our thoughts from the collective..."

Ulmaen nodded slowly, still trying hard to care. At the moment, he'd rather concentrate his effort on searching sales ledgers and whatever materials might help him figure out who had acquired those gloves and lead him to the identity of the murderer.

"...for the effort comes from creating an opening in the presence of energy bonds and molecules..."

Ulmaen had wanted that knowledge mostly to ease Bethereel's grief.

Now that she was gone, he only wanted to ease his own—

Thumph!

Ulmaen stumbled backward. He clutched his chest and gasped at the sudden loss of breath. The tightness in his solar plexus throbbed. "What the—"

Navalis recoiled his fist. Then he closed in again, nearly nose to nose, pressing his fist against Ulmaen's chest.

"Focus!"

Ule might have been patient in this moment, perhaps compassionate, accepting Navalis's behavior as a result of something she had done or said, but Ulmaen wasn't Ule anymore, and he shoved Navalis's arm away.

"Don't do that!"

Navalis's green eyes darkened. He cocked his head slightly. With both hands, he shoved Ulmaen in the chest.

Ulmaen fell back against a tree trunk. His reflexes were swift. He lunged forward and threw a side punch. It sliced through air, missing its intended point of contact on Navalis's jaw and instead stopped against his elbow. He tried again. With his other arm, he struck upwards. Navalis blocked this punch as well. They held onto one another, locked in a battle of strength and will.

"I'm considerably bigger and stronger than you," Ulmaen warned. And he was. He stood a foot taller than Navalis. The girth of his muscles was larger, too.

"Only in form." Navalis strained against Ulmaen's weight. "Besides, leverage is more important."

In an instant, Ulmaen's arm wrenched sideways, and the odd angle restricted the mechanics of his movement. His fingers unclenched, and he lost hold off Navalis.

Navalis's free arm pushed against the front of Ulmaen's neck and barreled him backward into the tree again. Pinned there by a strength exceeding the ability of his body, Ulmaen struggled.

"You've got to get that head of yours on straight," Navalis shouted. "Do you understand?"

His force unsettled Ulmaen at first. As they continued to struggle, the constriction around his neck remained constant, and he felt like a dog being disciplined. Annoyed by the assault, he no longer wanted to be subjected to his Master's fiery mood or heavy handedness.

Ulmaen stopped struggling against him, and simply stared—long and hard and unyielding, until it felt like his gaze burned straight through his Master. "Get off me!"

Immediately, Navalis released his grip and stepped back, his mood returning to a neutral state. The switch felt mechanical, the anger dissipating quickly as though it hadn't been genuine to begin with.

Ulmaen's anger remained a true steady burn. "Don't ever touch me like that again." The warning shot from his mouth, stinging his tongue.

Navalis wiped spittle from his mouth. "Good for you," he muttered.

"I mean it. You won't do that again. Ever!"

Navalis raised his hands in surrender and nodded again. "It's about time."

Tired of Navalis's cryptic nonsense, Ulmaen stood his ground and asked, "It's about time what?"

"That you stood up to me."

"I shouldn't have to, you're my Master."

"You must," Navalis insisted, "because I am your Master. How else are you to learn? How am I to teach you?" He breathed heavily while walking in a wide circle. "Did you know our kind has a long early history of violence and abuse toward one another because we lacked the willingness to respect our differences? Expressing and honoring boundaries became necessary, but we couldn't do that until we learned to defend them first. We have laws and rules now, to remind us not to usurp or destroy one another as we did in the past."

Ulmaen shook his head. "I thought tonight's lesson was about covert communication?"

"You weren't paying attention," Navalis stated. "And that created an opportunity to teach you something else. I'm here to teach you everything I can when it's necessary?"

Ulmaen tried not to show his anger or confusion.

"Consider this a warm-up lesson," Navalis suggested.

Ulmaen nodded slowly, wary of what lessons awaited him, his trust in his Master cut down like some of the trees around them.

"Come." Navalis motioned for Ulmaen to follow him deeper into the woods. "I'll show you how to project your thoughts through the solar plexus, so we can communicate with one another without being detected. With all that's happening within the castle, I can't wait for you to become a Master to teach this."

Being taught a skill used only by Masters seemed suspicious. Ulmaen rubbed the bruised flesh around his neck. He didn't want to go farther into the woods, but he obeyed, falling in step behind Navalis.

"And before you start thinking that learning this will make you a Master, it won't. It'll make you a more skilled Sentinel," Navalis explained. "It'll take you a while to learn. If you can achieve even a rudimentary conduit, we won't need to worry about whether or not Kerista or the other mystics can read our thoughts. We can be in constant communication no matter where we are or what happens."

As they moved deeper into the woods, Ulmaen still felt irritated by their earlier altercation. He wasn't able to shake it off the way Navalis had.

The aggression, no matter how justified, breached his good nature.

He no longer wanted to consult with Navalis over every decision. At the thought, his very being was flooded with a brilliance of unlimited possibilities. He'd continue to learn new abilities, but when it came to when and how he'd apply these skills, he would decide. His decisions were his own now.

Master yourself from now on, Ulmaen thought. We're done.

✳ CHAPTER 29 ✳

Nostalgia consumed Ulmaen as he squeezed between the desks scattered across the upper loft of the Library. He didn't remember the work stations being so small or the ceiling so low and angled. The air was thick and warm, unlike the cool, spacious Library below, where long rows of shelves were stacked with books.

The late morning sun lit the east-side windows in a blaze once it rose above the Inner Sanctum, and come midday, when the sun was positioned directly overhead, Ule used to look out a nearby window and watch the stained glass windows of the Inner Sanctum's glitter and sparkle.

He recalled sitting there as Ule, enjoying the warmth while copying merchant ledgers; always feeling lucky when Mbjard occasionally assigned her to copy some old journal in a foreign language on the verge of decay.

Most days, the desks in the room disappeared beneath piles of parchment and books as apprentice and adept scribes deeply immersed themselves in work—writing, copying, reading and, now and again, remembering to straighten their spines and stretch.

Ule had been one of them, so Ulmaen was certain to become one, too,. This time around, he intended not to convey nearly as much skill and knowledge as his former self had shown.

At the far end of the room, Mbjard sat hunkered over a desk far too large for his stature. He turned a page in a thick book he was reading.

Ulmaen felt a tremendous sense of relief knowing Mbjard wasn't the spy he had thought him to be, but given the circumstance of Ule's murder, he had to consider it, if just for a little while.

In the silence, Mbjard must have heard footfalls, for he spoke while continuing to read.

"There aren't any scribes for hire," he said. "They're interviewing and writing biographies of the thirty-three electoral candidates."

"I'm here to apply for apprenticeship." He slouched a little more, as a way to make the room return to the size he remembered.

Mbjard glanced up, promptly tucked a ribbon into the crease of the book and closed it.

"Your name, it's Ulmaen, correct?"

Ulmaen nodded and sat in a chair just the other side of the desk. "Yes, it is," he replied, and in a rush, he added, "I'd like to become an apprentice. Honestly, I don't have the talent to be a servant."

Mbjard tilted his head and smiled. "Many would agree with you." His smile crinkled his face, nearly squeezing his eyes shut.

By sheer reflex, one Ulmaen couldn't seem to get under control, he laughed.

Mbjard appreciated the mirth for the briefest of moments then became serious again. "Other than speaking a bit of Diminished Eelsee, what other skills do you possess?"

When Ulmaen had been a woman, Mbjard had seemed meek and mild, his title being his only source of power and respect.

"I speak a lot of Diminished Eelsee," he replied.

As a man, Mbjard now seemed small and pathetic, hiding behind his position, and although Ule might not have minded being questioned, Ulmaen did. He wanted to grab Mbjard by the collar and earn his position through the old custom of stealing rank by way of a good fight. It wouldn't take much, except...

Mbjard turned toward a shelf on the wall behind him and retrieved a glass pen filled with black ink. He poised it over a blank parchment tucked partially beneath the book he was reading and glanced up.

...There! Inflexible authority beamed through Mbjard's every pore. He had assumed some mental stance. He was unmovable and unnerving.

He nodded once and spoke. "First, tell me how many other languages you know and which ones." His hand rested on the parchment, waiting.

"Well, I'm from the North," Ulmaen began, remembering the incident in Fehran's Hall, when Mbjard had spoken to him in Diminished Eelsee. The dialect contained a fusion of elements from other dialects and languages as well.

"Yes, you can speak the trade language of that region. Very good, and what else?"

The background Ulmaen had prepared for himself, one with limited knowledge that he had painstakingly created to be dissimilar from Ule's breadth of knowledge, laid itself out in his mind. Lying came easier than it ever had.

"The North," he repeated. He scratched at his arm when he was struck with a pang of guilt.

"You've no need to be nervous," Mbjard assured him. "You know what you know. This isn't a test or a competition. I merely want to know what you have to offer."

"Okay," Ulmaen agreed, now pretending to feel nervous. He took a deep breath and began again. "Like I said, I was born in the North, so I'm familiar mostly with Gulilic."

Lowering his hand, the arch scribe sighed, all excitement expelled in one breath. "Unless you know all six dialects of Gulilic, you don't possess enough skills to work for us directly, and even then, I don't know. Most of our scribes know a minimum of three distinct language families."

"Since when?" Ulmaen bit his tongue.

Mbjard tilted his head to the side, stared over the rim of his spectacles. "What was that?"

Ulmaen remembered the requirements for apprenticeship by heart. There had never been a minimum language requirement. All that mattered was that you had an aptitude. And besides, there were more than six dialects of Gulilic. Had Mbjard just lied to him? Was this a test?

"Actually," Ulmaen said slowly, doing his best to conceal his annoyance. "I was told otherwise, about the requirements for apprenticeship."

"You were misinformed."

Irritation got the better of Ulmaen and he blurted again. "And there are nine known dialects of Gulilic, not six."

The arch mystic sat upright, blinking profusely. He set down the glass pen and folded his hands together over the blank parchment.

"Yes," he said carefully. "The other three are dead and no longer spoken." He licked his lips, an odd expression embittering his features. "Is there anything else?"

Ulmaen shook his head. He wasn't sure if he should stick to his original lie or risk creating discontinuity by altering it in some way.

Mbjard, however, had a desire to leave. He stood and nodded.

Ulmaen's desperation to acquire apprenticeship eclipsed his prideful ego. His instincts took over. "I know all of them, all nine of them."

Mbjard stared down through his round spectacles and smiled politely. "I only know of two scribes who are familiar with those dead languages, and they're—"

"Felsut and Belurod," Ulmaen said the names quickly. "And they're both dead, yeah, I know."

Mbjard sat down again, and leaned forward over the desk. "How's this possible?"

"I've read everything they've written," Ulmaen flexed the lie, being careful not to make leaps. The lie would only be convincing if he pushed the details little by little. "I studied their work three, four times over at the libraries in Woedshor when I was younger."

"How long did it take you to study these dead languages?"

Ulmaen feigned thinking by rolling his eyes upward to mentally count. "A little over seven months," he finally said, hoping the amount of time was long enough to be plausible, yet short enough to be impressive.

Mbjard bowed his head in contemplation.

"I may not know a lot of languages yet," Ulmaen implored, "but I do have a, uh, I know a lot about the North. Not just languages. History and culture and customs."

Nodding, Mbjard stood again. "I'll give this consideration."

"And if you say yes, I can be apprenticed?"

Mbjard gathered up the thick book he had been reading and pressed it against his chest, above his heart, like a shield.

"I would need to test you on your knowledge, to be sure. It'll take time."

Ulmaen's ego flared again. He didn't have time to wait for the man to come to a decision, to prove himself. There was a murderer hiding among them, hiding somewhere in the castle grounds. He or she might be planning to kill someone else.

Mbjard stepped around the desk and began making his way across the loft. "In the meantime," he said, "I welcome you to peruse the Library. Perhaps begin studying a second language to prove this quick learning ability of yours."

"Wait!"

Mbjard stopped.

Ulmaen struggled to find some way to connect with the man, anything that might persuade him to reconsider taking Ulmaen on as an apprentice immediately. He needed access to restricted areas of the Library to search certain sales ledgers, and he hadn't the time to waste.

"I'm something of a treasure hunter," Ulmaen blurted, hoping to pique Mbjard's curiosity.

Mbjard stood still a moment, and finally nipped at the bait, his mood souring.

"What kind of treasure?"

"Old treasure," he answered. "The oldest. I love history."

Mbjard stared at him a moment, then his expression relaxed. "Good for you," he said. "The past is certainly fascinating. We have an excellent collection you'll find most satisfying."

Ulmaen cocked an eyebrow, feigning surprise over what he already knew. "Anything in the Archive on the treasure that's supposed to be hidden here in Sondshor?"

Mbjard chuckled. "Do you think you're the first to come here hunting for it? Besides, that type of information is in the restricted areas, which aren't available to the public." His eyes momentarily lit up, then he nodded repeatedly, knowingly. "That's the true reason you want to become a scribe, is it?"

"No, no." Ulmaen felt his attempt to connect with him backfiring, and he wondered what might happen if he was honest. "Please!" He nearly threw himself on the ground, a giant on his knees before this diminutive man. "I'll help you find the treasure."

Mbjard froze. He stared a long hard moment.

Ulmaen realized his error. Only a few people knew of Mbjard's ongoing hunt for the treasure, and he wasn't supposed to be one of them. "I'm a servant," he began another lie. "People talk. I listen when I shouldn't."

This seemed to ease Mbjard's paranoia. "You're smarter than I thought. Good for you." He pushed his spectacles back onto the bridge of his nose. "It's an interest. Nothing more."

Ulmaen knew that wasn't true. Based on the nature of their

conversations, Mbjard was obsessed with the treasure, striving to learn more about it as an object, understanding its meaning, and more importantly, determining its location.

"I'll make you an offer," Ulmaen said, hoping to find some leverage in the situation. Perhaps if Mbjard knew the real reason, the truth about his search for evidence, he might be compassionate and willing to agree. "I'll tell you everything I know about the treasure, help you research it, if you permit me access to the financial records."

Mbjard peered above the rims of his spectacles again. "What do you want with those? There's nothing in them about the treasure. "

Ulmaen stepped a little closer and hunched. He lowered his voice. "No, but there may be information about the ownership of the gloves, the ones used to poison Ule."

Mbjard stood in silent rumination. After several moments, he blinked a few times and asked, "Ule died before you started working here. How do you know her?"

"I... uh..." Ulmaen winced. "I-I don't. It's..."

In his new form, he didn't have any direct association with Ule. When he thought about it, he could only know anything about her based on what he had heard from others. He'd need to shift the focus of his investigation away from Ule onto something or someone else that made more sense, if he was to convince Mbjard.

He straightened himself, searching his mind for a solution, and then it came to him.

"I've been serving food in the Prison," he explained. "Rozafel isn't handling it very well. I've never seen someone so... distressed." He shook his head. "I did a foolish thing."

"What did you do?"

"I promised her I'd find evidence to prove her story. I always keep my word. Will you help her by helping me? Let me search the financial ledgers."

Mbjard turned away. He stared out through a nearby window.

The silence was unnerving, and Ulmaen caught himself holding his breath as he waited. The approach had been direct and abrupt, and in hindsight, he realized nothing would come of it. Mbjard was a compassionate man, but perhaps he had asked too much of him. Despite being the arch scribe, he still had limitations within his position. Ulmaen simply needed to be patient about becoming a scribe.

"What you promised Rozafel was very kind," Mbjard finally said, turning back toward Ulmaen. "Yes, let's help her."

Ulmaen shook his head in disbelief. "What?"

"I accept your offer. You help me with researching the treasure, and you can have access to the Archive, but there are conditions you must agree to."

Stunned, Ulmaen fumbled for words. "Name it, I'll do it."

"First, you can't tell anyone. It's our secret, understood?"

Ulmaen quickly nodded. He agreed that the fewer people who knew what he was doing, the less likely anyone, including the murdere, could undermine his work.

"Second, you search the Archive only under my supervision. If I'm not available, then you must wait until I am."

Ulmaen sucked in his breath at the prospect. With another watching him, he'd have to pretend he knew nothing about their Archive or how to search them, and that was going to slow him down.

Perhaps he should have shifted his body to infiltrate the Archive. It was a simpler more direct approach, but he risked draining his energy reserve. He didn't want to deathmorph prematurely and be forced to return in another form, to start all over again establishing himself in the castle, pretending not to know anyone.

He also risked being seen in his shifted state. He'd appear like a phantom, and he didn't want to raise suspicion or frighten the scribes who worked in shifts throughout the night. There was enough gossip being slung about on account of the election.

Ulmaen grabbed Mbjard's hand and shook it. "Thank you."

"You're not a scribe," Mbjard reminded him, pulling his hand away. "Not yet. I'd like to observe how you work first. Understood?"

"Understood," Ulmaen agreed reluctantly, feeling oddly satisfied with himself. Yet again, he'd successfully negotiated and maneuvered himself into the very place he needed to be.

✳ CHAPTER 30 ✳

Between the Temple and the Inner Sanctum stood a two-level L-shaped building, a remnant of a structure from long ago. The steps were cracked and broken. The door squeaked when it was opened and groaned as it shut. Inside, Ulmaen walked a dark hallway draped in tapestries and dark paintings of nearly-forgotten Magnisi.

Distracted by their regal countenances and squared postures, he immediately understood these men and women had been people of great power. He wondered if any of them had ever experienced doubt regarding their decisions, having to act alone even after considering the counsel of their advisers.

Doubt stirred within him as he struggled to accept the decision he had made to apply for scribe apprenticeship. Was he being foolish to regain the position he had lost as Ule? Although he was naturally inclined toward seeking guidance from Navalis, their last training session had broke Ulmaen of the habit. Then he questioned if doing so had been a mistake. Perhaps it wasn't his Master's wisdom he sought, but rather the comfort of confiding in him.

Somehow, he needed to dispel his doubt. Sure, it had come about after being denied apprenticeship as a scribe, yet he still had managed to acquire access to the Archive. This ability to maneuver in the world with mind and might both excited and terrified him. What if he made a misstep somewhere?

Determined to steady his nerves, he inhaled deeply. Fumes from mildew and linseed oil filled his nostrils, as he entered the large studio. The windows were wide open, yet the fresh air hadn't completely eradicated the smell of solvents and oil paints.

Diffused daylight cast subtle cool shadows over the easels, chairs, and paintings. In the far corner, Laere stood on a stool, scrubbing paint into the background of a portrait, absorbed in the push and pull of blending colors on canvas.

As Ulmaen neared, he recognized the face of his former self. Ule stared back at him, captured in a moment of haughty superiority—unyielding, defiant, graceful, elegant even. Whatever had been sketched of her had now been fully rendered in life-like color.

He had forgotten about the portrait, but he hadn't forgotten about Laere or their conversation at the Colonnade. She had heard him project his thoughts toward Istok during Sabien's show.

Since then, he'd gone drinking with Laere several times, and she seemed to have forgotten the incident for they talked mostly nonsense when they got drunk. Still, he wondered. He'd been meaning to talk with her again, mostly because he rather liked talking with her.

He tugged on her brown cotton skirt and broke her concentration. She spun around, shocked at first until she saw him. For the first time, they stood eye to eye.

"After what happened near the fountain," he said, "I figured you'd given up on that." He pointed at the painting.

She smiled weakly. "I wanted to." She set down the palette and brush on a nearby table littered with other used brushes, then continued standing on the stool.

Now, he thought, she was a little too tall, having grown accustomed to stooping in her presence.

"Lyan examines my progress every day. You should see him when he does, the way his eyes glaze. I think he might marry the painting." Her eyes lit up. She was on the verge of laughter at her own remark.

He regarded the painting, feeling a little nostalgic as he compared who he used to be to what he had become.

"So? Are you an apprentice?" she asked. "Shall we celebrate?"

He winced and shook his head. "Not exactly."

Her mirth transformed into remorse. "Do you want to talk about it?"

He tore his eyes away from the painting. "If it's alright with you, I'd rather drink about it."

"There's not a lick of spirits back in my room," she told him. "We'll need to find more."

After instructing her assistant to clean brushes and preserve the palette for her next painting session, she led Ulmaen from the building, along the Colonnade, past the Starry Rise.

After they passed beneath the covered walkway, she let out a laugh and bolted ahead, passed in front of the Dining Hall's main doors and did a playful twirl as she rounded the north side of the Kitchen. There, they waited at the side entrance, and when no one was looking, they darted inside, ducking behind the stoves all the way to the main pantry, where they nearly tumbled down a narrow stairwell into the cellar below, grabbed a bottle of wine, and sneaked back out again.

They returned to Laere's room in Kugilla Hall, where they sat on the floor in the corner, her against one wall, him against the other. They popped the cork and took turns swigging from the heady, thick red nectar which left Ulmaen feeling only slightly numb half-way through the bottle. Next time, he reminded himself to bring a bottle of whiskey.

Laere dabbed a bit of red wine on her lips, tinting them a darker shade. "Kiss me," she demanded.

It was the sort of thing Bethereel would do, and he saw Bethereel laying there instead, her arms outstretched, her long dark hair entangled about her arms.

He kissed her.

Their kisses were exploratory at first. Ulmaen deepened them, and when Laere slipped out of her shirt and guided his hands to her breasts, he recovered his senses and sat upright.

"Don't you want to?" She smiled her crooked smiled. Something in the way she tilted her head also reminded him of Bethereel.

Yes, he very much wanted to.

"There's always a parade of people through here," he complained, sitting upright. "No privacy here. No privacy in my room either." He gestured to the cots. "The beds are too small for two people..."

Laere's smile deepened. Her eyes twinkled. "Come on, help me with the dresser."

They pulled a heavy oak cabinet across the closed door. It scraped the floor with faint lines, and he noticed similar markings, indicating the furniture had been moved to block the door many times before. Then they pulled mattresses from several cots and threw them together on the ground to make a larger one.

Laere scrambled to pull off her clothes. Dressed in only her long hair, she tended to his clothes with an effortless grace.

Gone were the teasing kisses, soft caresses, and whispers he had been accustomed to as Ule. Despite the lack of foreplay, his flesh woke up on its own, burning where her fingers dug into his muscles.

The rattling door failed to break his concentration, for he hadn't any thoughts. His body was in control. He heard harsh words but couldn't make out what exactly had been said.

Fierce energy boiled inside and drove down toward his pelvis. There was no slow, spiraling rise of arousal like he remembered the last time he made love, when he had been a woman. Instead, he felt a coursing of energy in one direction, a fierce downward pushing toward the head of his shaft which he aimed toward her.

Bethereel.

Although he didn't mind the way she ground beneath him, he preferred the bucking, the long pulling and especially the pushing back inside her. No matter how unusual the quickening pulse of his arousal felt, he was glad to be with her again.

Flushed and breathless, Bethereel moaned. "Stop, just a sec."

He slowed, and shook his head. "What?"

Bethereel caught her breath. She gripped his arms, arched her back. A noisy orgasm shook her. He felt her muscles tighten about him. She was beautiful. So different in the throes of her release, but he had to expect that from her now. He was a man.

She urged him to continue. She relaxed into his thrusts, enjoying them more. The flesh around his erection swelled, the urge for release quickening.

The energy in his abdomen surged downward, and he pushed, and the energy burst and rushed from him. It was exquisite, and a relief, and familiar. Just when he thought there were no similarities between the sexual energies of each gender, he experienced the same abandonment of his senses that he had as a woman.

The world disappeared.

His nerves numbed.

His flesh melted and fused with the air and the mattress and most wonderful of all, with Bethereel.

He remained inside her a moment, struggling to regain his breath, his senses. All at once, the world returned, and with it the harsh sounds, vibrant light, and the hardness of their bodies against each other.

His love.

Except Bethereel didn't lay beneath him.

Hastily, he pulled free of Laere and settled next to her, mindful of the itch of the straw against his backside and the twitches in his groin. He wondered if he could ever get used to its autonomous nature.

"Hmm," Laere moaned. "See!" She waved at the room. "Privacy. We made that happen." She sat upright and retrieved the discarded bottle of wine. She drank a bit of it then held out the bottle to him.

Ulmaen shook his head, trying very hard not to fall asleep, which he had done as a woman, too. He breathed shakily, waiting for the rush of blood to his brain to settle.

"You okay?"

Ulmaen nodded.

"You were married, right?"

Squeezing his eyes shut, he thought of Bethereel instead of his make believe wife. "Yeah."

"It's just the way you're acting, you look like you never..." Laere laid a hand on his chest. "Wait, you haven't have you, not since your wife?"

Her gentle empathy began to soothe him.

"That's the real reason you were so sad at Bethee's funeral. It brought back memories of her."

A whip of anger lashed through his mind when Laere mentioned Bethereel. He pinched the bridge of his nose, waited for the pain to subside.

Laere settled back. "I won't tell anyone," she promised. "And just to prove my word is good, I'll tell you something about myself, something I've never told anyone."

She laid back down again, balancing the wine bottle on her belly. "I can't have children," she said. "Oh how I've tried!" She laughed. "A lot of people suspect I'm lacking in some way. I guess what I can't bring myself to tell anyone is that I know why."

She stretched out on the makeshift bed, her toes kicking at her skirt crumpled in a pile on the floor.

"To be honest, I've always felt like there's something I'm not getting that everyone else knows."

He regarded her, trying to understand her drunken ramblings, wishing instead he was somewhere else, and he saw her body was smaller than he first thought. Or, had he worked so hard to impress the image of Bethereel onto her that he saw what he had wanted to?

Laere smiled. Her smile was deeply crooked; Bethereel's only a little. Laere's eyes were too large for her head. Bethereel's were smaller. Laere looked nothing at all like Bethereel.

Reaching forward, Laere trailed a finger along his chest. "It's like..." But she didn't finish the sentence immediately. She smacked her lips and blinked. "It's like there's something missing inside. An emptiness."

Laere jabbed him in the stomach, trying to get his attention. "Do you ever feel, you know, deep down in your gut, that all of this," she waved at the air, "is made up?"

Ulmaen rolled onto his back. Regret wriggled into his mind. Laere wasn't Bethereel, no matter how much he had wanted her to be. Laere was Laere, and she was reaching out to him, trying to make a connection he didn't want to make.

"What's wrong?"

He sat upright. "Nothing," he mumbled. He swung around to the side of the mattress, his knees pulled to his chest. He needed to leave before the anxiety ticking inside his chest exploded. "I need to go."

Another rap at the door. Another one of Laere's roommates cursing in anger, demanding to be admitted. The bureau rocked. Laere cursed back.

"No, stay," she insisted. "I love talking with you."

At the touch of her fingers on his lower back, he jumped up and searched for his pants, yanking them on leg by leg. The words spilled out before he could understand why he said them.

"It was just sex, right?"

Laere bolted upright. "Of course it was." Annoyance furrowed her brow. "But you don't have to be weird about it. I'm not asking you to marry me."

A pang shot through his heart at the mention of marriage. He'd had a wife once; Laere wasn't her.

What had he just done? What kind of person was he to use Laere like this? Plenty of people enjoyed sex for no other reason than physical release. There wasn't anything wrong with that, but he'd known what it felt like once to be a woman, to be misled into believing there was an emotional connection where none existed.

Did he like Laere? Did he care about her? If he was honest with himself, he barely knew her, yet he took pleasure in her. What he truly wanted was Bethereel.

Partially dressed, he wiped his bare head.

There had been hair there once. Long blond hair. He had been a woman, someone who now seemed so alien and strange. Ule had always been free spirited, but she had always felt some emotion for whomever she was with, even if it was for a night. Then Bethereel changed all that. With Bethereel there was a connection beyond just the physical. There was freedom and bliss, a never ending dance where Ule forgot sometimes where she ended and Bethereel began.

What he had experienced with Laere was fantasy, and beyond the fantasy, it had felt cool and carnal, like an itch in his body that needed to be scratched.

Ule would never have done something like this, so why had he? Weren't they the same on the inside?

Struck by the question, Ulmaen's heart skipped a beat as an answer came to him. Whatever was at his core was being expressed in a very different way than when he had been a woman. And for the first time since becoming a man, he hated himself.

❋ CHAPTER 31 ❋

In the early dawn, Navalis slipped from bed and woke Boriag with a hard shove. He had one task to accomplish before he got on with his daily duties and studies, and if Boriag hadn't begged to tag along, he'd have the task accomplished much quicker.

They dressed and tip-toed downstairs to the main laboratory, where a few exhausted apprentices still worked at their benches. Outside, Navalis led Boriag along the rear wall of the plain, two-level Treasury. The path at the eastern edge of the field offered a quick route to Eastgate, but very few ever walked the steep rocks there anymore and instead took the safer route, any one the three sets of stairs set into the retaining wall.

They veered around the corner of the Treasury, and strolled past the Granary, guarded water wells, and Mareel's Gatehouse, where broken spinning wheels littered the arched door and several tower windows were lit, indicating some of the clothiers had worked through the night.

Questions wove into Navalis's mind, the kind that scratched at him like wool and kept him up at night—Why did demons roam the Root Dimension instead of passing through the Nexus to the Chthonic Dimension? And why did his kind know so little about demons and the realm they existed within? For all his power and experience, he felt as though there was still so much more to learn.

"Hey, want to hear a fun fact?" Boriag asked.

Navalis preferred the silence.

Boriag, however, didn't and rattled on. "Did you know, even though Magnes Mareel built built the gatehouse on the hill, so she'd have somewhere to sit and watch the sunsets."

Navalis nodded, as he headed for the retaining wall and descended the stairs into the courtyard of Fehran's Hall.

Boriag followed at his heels. "And when Mareel built her ramparts down there, mostly around the Starry Rise, she excluded Kugilla Hall on purpose, 'cause she detested his violent character. But this, what I'm going to tell you next, this is the fun part. After Mareel passed and her castle fell to ruin, evident by that nonsense pile of rubble by the old Mystics Tower and the others near Northgate, someone decided to repair Kugilla Hall, using guess what?"

Boriag laughed. "Stones from Mareel's Hall. All of them. I swear, she's got to be throwing fits of rage in Mxalem."

Navalis grunted again. For a moment, he considered what Boriag had to say, giving his inquiries a rest. As far as he knew, materials from the ruins of Mareel's old castle continued to be recycled into newer structures, including the new southern rampart. Everything around them had been repurposed at one time or another.

Boriag nudged him. "Thanks for letting me come along with you."

Beyond Fehran's Hall, they followed the Colonnade eastward. Past Kugilla Hall, the pink marble covering above them ceased, yet evidence of it remained behind in slabs that had been carved into benches or statues. The marble turned to quarry stone and merged with a roadway that ran from Eastgate and south along the old rampart. Soon, they passed beneath the archway of the outermost rampart wall, where shacks and buildings butted against one another.

"You alright?" Boriag finally asked.

Navalis nodded again.

"Hey, you interested in hearing about my balm?"

"Sure," Navalis replied, and Boriag perked up a bit.

"It isn't fully tested yet," he reported. "Based on my observations, the tensile strength imbued into that armor may have been entirely the result of my tweaking the old white ray machine. The one made by Fehran's Mystic—

"Goyas," Navalis said. If questions about the demons weren't enough, his mind reconsidered who might want to eat the old mystic's corpse.

"The formula's being a fusswart, and all the masters go cloudy when they look at my notes, tell me they've faith I'll figure it out. If they don't know, how can I know—"

"None of us know," Navalis interrupted, irritated by the response. "Listen, I'll help you as much as you've been helping me, understood?"

Boriag gratefully nodded and grew worried. "We're not supposed to do that though, not at our skill level. Apprentices teaching apprentices?" Boriag shook his head. "What if Kerista finds out what we're up to?"

"She won't." A hardness overcame Navalis, a natural inclination toward warding off predators in the derelict area they walked through. The road wound through small markets where anyone could sell their wares, whether it be stale fish, used trinkets, or sex.

"Just be sure to get what you need for several batches of balm," Navalis urged. "I'd like you to fortify a gauntlet for me."

Boriag lit up at the prospect. "Oh, so that's how you're going to dissect the next demon. Clever."

Navalis thought so, too. With fortified metal protecting his hands, he'd finally be able to explore what lay deep within a demon's physiology.

"Can't promise it'll work. What if you get hurt again? Or worse, what if I've got to rescue you and I get hurt?"

Navalis laughed. "I have more faith in you than you do, my friend." He wrapped an arm around Boriag's neck, forcing him to stoop. "You've got tenacity. You try things regardless of what anyone thinks. You've got a lot more going for you than most. Believe in that, okay?"

"I suppose," Boriag mumbled. "Don't you think Kerista would be better suited to help you?"

"No." Navalis let go of him. Kerista would only stop him.

Alleyways intersected the main road, snaking between taverns and inns. Past a row of smithies, a warehouse of great height reeked of yeast and old ale. They'd walked for a little less than an hour from the time they departed the Mystics Tower and finally came to a stop in the first quarter of Eastgate.

"The apothecary I told you about is just behind that distillery," Boriag said, pointing toward a barn like building stained in oil and smoke. "It's got the best laurel. I'll get some of that for sure, 'cause it bends light. Come on, now."

"Tell you what," Navalis backed away, heading toward a sidestreet. "Why don't you go and buy the ingredients you need."

Boriag frowned, narrowing his eyes at him. "Why? Where're you going?"

"I've got a date." Navalis gave a stern nod, the kind that demanded adherence or else. "Meet me back here when you're done. There's someone I need to see. And not a word to anyone."

Boriag froze, his mouth agape. After a second, he stomped his foot and called after him angrily. "Can't you find someone at the castle to bump?"

Navalis smiled. It wasn't anything like that.

Boriag reluctantly gave a nod and turned down an alleyway alongside the distillery. Once he was well out of sight, Navalis followed the sidestreet a ways then ducked between a dilapidated playhouse and an inn.

At the back of the inn was a seedy little tavern with narrow iron grated windows and a sign made of black painted wood in the shape of a horse—The Black Horse.

At the corner of the tavern, a couple of roughers stood near a urine-drenched post, their shirt sleeves rolled up to show their overworked muscles and a number of scars tallying their many fights and kills.

The bigger one cast a sneer, asked for a tussle, winner takes a sil. For a moment, Navalis considered the offer. A fight was tempting, a great way to numb his raw nerves instead of sex.

"Another time," he told the rougher, as he opened the rickety door to the tavern and entered.

Inside, the air was thick with smoke, a mingling of sweet tobacco and the oils of mind altering euphorias. Beneath the haze, the stink of musk and sweat and dirty feet clung to the floors and walls.

He squeezed between the small tables, scrutinizing the patrons. Though their eyes were bloodshot, they seemed too lucid for any of them to be the man he sought. At the bar, an older lady weighed down by a leather clothier smock tottered on her stool, her head nodding off into sleep over a half dozen empty mead glasses.

Beyond her, in the far corner, an old man with a gray frizz of unkempt beard, stared unblinkingly across the room, rocking slightly.

Navalis wandered over to the table and slipped onto a stool across from the man.

"You Rolen?" he asked.

The man's eyes brightened a little. "Maybe," he mumbled.

"Used to be a farmer, right?" Navalis motioned to the barkeep for two ales, then fished a coin from the pouch he wore around his neck and kept hidden beneath his shirt and tunic.

"Ah huh, somethin' like that." The man's eyes drifted downward. He placed a shaky hand on the table. His fingers twitched as he brushed them against his thumb. "Worked the land, I think."

The barkeep called out, and Navalis fetched two tankards topped with froth. He offered one to the farmer. "Will this help you remember?"

The man's hand opened to grasp the tankard. "I'd say," he replied with a nod. "Yeah, it helps. Except for getting work." He sipped at the ale. "Used to be married, too, you know."

"A friend told me, he said your farm was special." Navalis hoped to encourage Rolen to speak.

"Uh huh." The man's eyes darkened a little.

"He said you like tilling bones and such." Navalis tried to stay connected with Rolen's gaze as it began to sink. "What kind of bones?"

"Demon kind," Rolen sputtered. His head bolted upright, his face tense. "That baby, it wasn't right. Not since the beginning."

"What baby?"

Rolen sighed. With both hands, he brought the mug to his lips and drank. He sniffed. "I loved it. It's hard not to love a child."

"How come the child wasn't right?" Navalis drank from his mug in a show of camaraderie.

Rolen approved and he drank again. After a moment, he wiped his mouth. "I'd turn the soil in the morning, the way you ought to. When I'd found the one bone, didn't think much of it. Just assumed the dog buried it there. The next morning, there were more. Tiny little bones. I remember thinking they looked like chicken bones, but we didn't eat chicken the night before and we didn't keep them."

He wheezed, sucking in his breath, before he let out a series of dry coughs. He drank again and spilled some of the ale down his stained shirt.

"Held them up to the sun, to see a little closer, but they just turned to ash, one by one."

"How long ago did this happen?"

"I don't know." Looking sidelong, Rolen muttered to himself. "The child be grown up now, I suppose." He nodded, turning his attention back to Navalis. "Could've been some twenty-five years or more when I first saw those bones."

Navalis wasn't quite following the man's meaning. He leaned forward and asked, "What do the bones have to do with the child?"

"They are the child!" Rolen slammed his hand on the small table, making it wobble. "Aren't you listening?" He leaned forward, his wiry fingers wrapping around the fabric of Navalis's tunic.

"The bones, they came back the next morning and the morning after. And every time I held them up to the sun, they turned to ash, see?"

Navalis recalled what Sabien had told him about the farmer, about what he had always been heard chanting: *Tilling and turning the soil at night made that baby demon's bones grow bright.*

"So you waited until nightfall," he surmised.

Rolen nodded, his eyes growing sullen. "The bones shone in the moonlight, they did. I thought it strange, but I was curious too. I picked through all the bones and I should've tossed them, but something in my gut said leave them be, see what happens come morning."

"What happened?"

Rolen paused. His attention drifted back through time. "They'd grown. I saw them easier then. A ribcage, a leg bone, a jaw bone, all scattered through the potatoes."

Navalis tried determining if what he was being told was truth or the result of an active and inebriated imagination.

"They grew," Rolen continued. "Every night, a little larger, just like the tomatoes and the potatoes and carrots too. And I tried to hide it from my wife as best I could. She's always asked why I was tilling at sundown." He paused a moment, and when he looked up, his eyes watered. "Ever known a woman who can't bear children?"

Navalis shook his head.

"They get crazy desperate when they've got nothing to love, nothing to coddle. It's in their bones to fuss. That's why I couldn't tell her. At least not until I had to."

Navalis drank again from his beer, appreciating the way the alcohol numbed his nerves. He pushed through the stupor it created and remained clear headed.

"One night, I saw the bones were knitting together, the way my wife knits a sweater. Right before my eyes, they did. And I could see them for what they were. Arms and legs, a ribcage, a big head, curling up the way slugs do in the sunlight."

Rolen coughed again. He huffed a few times, his eyes tearing up. "I'm a humble man. Don't mean none no harm, but I buried that *thing*. It wasn't right. I knew that then, and I buried it, packed it in hard soil what was certain to smother it. But the next night, my wife and I heard it. We heard it wail. When Pordre asked, I told her it was an animal hurt that's all, and I took up an axe and a shovel and saw to taking care of it."

"And it was this creature, this baby?"

Rolen nodded. A tear slid down his cheek. "I tried hard to kill it, I did. No child deserves that. When it grew up, it was sweet at first, but it wasn't right coming into the world the way it did. Not natural, and my wife, she didn't care. She only ever wanted a child."

Navalis noted how the man never acknowledged the child's gender and how the story contained familiar elements from folktales he had been told, ones Sabien had whispered to him during their long nights together back when Navalis had been Avn, back when he had been a battle weary blacksmith, when he had been trapped in the world and needed companionship.

Rolen nodded again. "Pordre, she saw the child as a gift. But the child wasn't right." He drank the last of his ale, wiped his beard, and held out the empty tankard and shook it.

Navalis procured another, and the farmer held onto it with all his strength.

"When I went out that first night, the babe hadn't been fully formed yet. It glistened beneath the soil, all insides. Tendons and meat and sinew. It mewled something sad, like it needed nursing. I buried it even deeper."

A shift overcame Rolen. He sucked in his trembling lower lip. "I was sure I killed it that time, but the next night, we heard it calling again, crying out, mewling and howling something fierce. I tried to stop Pordre, but she wouldn't listen. Told her it was just an animal and to ignore it, but she wouldn't believe me. She found the child curled up next to the tomatoes, trying to suckle on them. She saw nothing wrong with it."

"Did she take care of the child?" Navalis had heard this story before, at least variations of it. They had been older stories, though, and not as current as this one.

"Hmm, we both did." Rolen began to sag at the table, the ale finally numbing his senses. "Pordre cared for the child like it was her own, but her blessing became my curse."

Navalis nodded. He understood. "No one wanted to buy your food anymore."

Nodding profusely, Rolen pointed a finger. "Not a one of them ever asked. They just assumed we'd stolen the child, and I told 'em, the thing was born in my own potato patch. It broke Pordre's heart, and after she passed, I was left to raising the child on my own, but I was bitter and harsh and the damned thing ran away."

Reaching beneath his tunic, Navalis pulled out the pouch again and fished out a couple of sils, placed them on the table before the old man, and stood.

"You're like them, quick to judge." The old farmer shook with rage.

"Go see for yourself."

Navalis turned to leave but stopped at what the farmer said next.

"I feared that child. I loved it, but I feared it more. I've never feared no one before, ever, except for the puppets Adinav made of some of us."

The event, this birth, Navalis realized coincided with the final years of the war. Not the days prior to Adinav's demise when he re-animated the bodies of the recently deceased to restore his diminishing army. No, the birth occurred years before that, when Adinav's army was at its peak, a massive military force comprised of both Elishians and demons, bodies usurped and controlled by Adinav's powerful abilities.

Adinav had hollowed people out, used them to build an army, turned the Elishians against one another in a way never before experienced in the history of this world. Navalis imagined people waking to stare into the eyes of their loved ones and not recognizing them. Still, trust hadn't been breached, not yet. They trusted these shells of people only to be abandoned or killed by them. This must have bred a new kind of fear.

Navalis rubbed his face at the possibility of a new fear manifesting in the world, a demon far different from any of the others that walked the Root Dimension.

He addressed the farmer again. "You said I could see the farm for myself?"

Rolen nodded. "There's not much to see. No one goes near it anymore. They think it's cursed. Couldn't even sell the place."

"Where is it?"

"Didn't you hear me? I said it's cursed!"

Regardless, there was something to be learned from the farm. If there was any truth to the story, something about this place had brought forth a demon. Not a vapor, but a solid, humanoid form that had grown and evolved like any other Elishian.

Navalis reached beneath the neckline of his shirt and again pulled out the small leather pouch. This time, he poured out a small pile of coins.

Rolen reached across the table. Eyes wide, his hand shook as he picked up the largest of the coins and held it up.

"You value directions this much?"

Navalis shook his head. "That's to pay for the farm. Now, why don't you tell me where *my* farm is located?"

A grin spread across Rolen's face, revealing empty spaces instead of front teeth.

✳ CHAPTER 32 ✳

The food basket weighed heavily, rocking side to side against Ulmaen's thigh. He endured the weight with extra zeal as he approached the steps to the Prison, for this morning was his final day for serving food there—one last round through the Core.

Thankfully he needn't bother with the Pit this time, for Ilgaud and his buddies had been returned to the quarry, where they no doubt plotted to escape again. What made the morning the sunniest of them all was his hopeful news for Rozafel.

His research in the Archive had been a slow process, mostly because Mbjard had overseen every step, except for a few stretches of time when he was immersed in a thick tome entitled *The Collected Histories of Sondsee* or when he was conducting research on behalf of Kerista, who had expressed an interest in local blacksmiths going back several years. During these times, Ulmaen took the opportunity to push his perception and scan many ledger pages at once so that when he turned each page, he needn't bother to scrutinize every entry.

His speed, focus, and determination still impressed Mbjard, even though it took several evenings to find the smallest amount of information. Although more research was still required, at least he could assure Rozafel that he was fulfilling his promise to help her.

At the top of the steps to the Prison, he was struck by General Gorlen barking a long list of instructions. Cautiously, Ulmaen descended and paused a moment inside the entrance.

Gorlen stood before three young women, each standing at attention—the daughters of some of Lyan's generals. They were young, disheveled, and sullied. Stiff with fear, they paled before Gorlen's tirade, regret for whatever they had done making their eyes dark and teary.

Ulmaen shuddered at Gorlen's bracing tone and hastily padded toward the opening to the hallway on his right. His walkabout of the Core always began to the left of the counter, then he'd circle around and come back to where he started on the other side, but today he couldn't wait to tell Rozafel the good news.

At the first cell, he quickly delivered breakfast to the complainer, as he liked to call him. The complainer snatched the food and, after taking a bite of bread, grumbled about never being first. Ulmaen ignored him and hurried to Rozafel's cell. As he approached, he reached into the basket and pulled out a bundle of papers.

"Good news, Rozafel." He turned at the gate. "My research so far will prove—" He stopped and searched the cell. It was empty. In the far corner, where Rozafel had kept a tidy pile of apple cores, the floor had been swept clean. Not even the dreads she worked free from her head were anywhere to be seen.

Ulmaen wasn't sure what to make of her absence. Had Mbjard gone ahead and presented the information to the Council? Had Lyan and Gorlen finally come to their senses and approved her release?

Gorlen's voice thundered down the corridor, berating while simultaneously informing the young women of the details of their punishments. The clop of boot heels added to the din, then laughter and voices—loud, gregarious, and distinctly feminine.

Ulmaen was suddenly transported to a time in his past when he had been Ule and had danced to music, under the influence of ale and honey mead at the tavern of Sunset House. He shook off the memory in haste.

He carefully returned the papers to the basket, then carried on delivering food to the other cells. Returning to the main entrance in the south arm, he stood to the side, just out of sight.

Gorlen reminded the young women to meet with the Drill Marshall for combat training, for if they were going to start fights in public taverns, then they should prepare themselves for careers as soldiers. When he dismissed them, the young women scrambled over one another for the exit.

Ulmaen stepped forward until the counter came into view. Standing in front of it were two women just shy of twenty years. He smiled, understanding why their laughter had evoked such specific memories. Although, he had never been in direct contact with either of them, back when he had been Ule, they all had frequented Sunset House.

Aesa and Mera were identical twins, the daughters of Hazias, a blacksmith in Sondshor Market. They were as tall as Ulmaen, clad in long tan skirts and short-sleeved indigo work shirts, which were covered by heavily marked black leather smith aprons.

Aesa, who Ulmaen identified by the burn scar on her bottom lip, leaned against the counter, her arms folded beneath her diminutive chest. The sleeve of the shirt she wore cut into her thick biceps. She wore her black hair short in the back and long enough in the front to tuck behind her ears, unlike Mera who wore hers short and spiked on top.

Ulmaen returned to the shadows of the corridor behind the counter and hugged the wall. From this vantage, he could see the sisters well, and Gorlen from the side, as he lingered at the edge of the counter.

"Well?" Aesa asked Gorlen. "Are you satisfied?"

Gorlen bowed his head and began flipping through a ledger. "With what? You'll need to be more specific?"

Maliciousness overcame him. It was in his tone and the way he attempted a smile yet managed a subtle sneer instead.

"The sword," Aesa replied. "You know, the one you commissioned us to make."

Ulmaen remembered the sword Gorlen had lain out on the counter, the one he oiled and polished with great care, the one he wrapped in soft tawny leather and kept tucked away on the lowest shelf beneath the counter.

"Such a shame for you two," Gorlen told the girls. "Such a shame truly."

Mera snorted. "What is?" She clenched her jaw, trying to appear more intimidating, but the roundness of her soft cheeks made her look more like a child play fighting.

"One day you'll both be out of work," Gorlen said. "You haven't seen the cannons, have you?"

"They're alright for long distance," Mera retorted. "If you've got the patience."

Aesa tilted her head back and snarled. A strand of hair caught at the edge of her lip, but she ignored it. "People will always need a good sword."

"For now," Gorlen said.

The girls remained silent. Mera's leg began to twitch, and Aesa bit the faded scar on her lower lip.

"I hear they're making smaller versions of the canons," Gorlen continued to goad them. "So small they'll fit in the palm of your hand. No need for two men to load it. We'll be able to kill from a ways off, without getting ourselves dirty."

Mera tsked. "Where's the fun in that?"

"That's the future," Aesa said. "What matters is now." She rapped the top of the counter with her knuckles. "Now tell us if you're pleased with the sword and pay up. Otherwise, give it back."

"Oh, that!" He shook his head sadly. "It was stolen."

Liar! Ulmaen's sudden irritation prickled his flesh.

The sisters regarded one another briefly. An unspoken message passed between them. They didn't believe the general either. Together, simultaneously and synchronized, their mirth turned acidic.

Aesa unfolded her arms. "Pay us for the work we've done!"

"Things around here go missing. It's unfortunate, but that's the hard truth ladies." He regarded them briefly. "I won't pay for something that isn't in my possession," he told them, then smirked to make sure he had made his point.

Aesa leaned forward on the counter until her head was close to the general's. In a low, sweet voice she asked, "How's that wife of yours by the way?"

Gorlen's head snapped up. His eyes bulged, and his lower lip trembled.

"Who is it she's got two little ones with now?" Aesa continued to goad him. "An *actor*?"

Gorlen's response was reflexive, automatic—he backhanded her across the face.

"Hey!" Ulmaen rushed forward from the shadows to intervene, and he positioned himself between Gorlen and the twins.

Mera raised both her arms, one toward him and the other toward Gorlen, each hand held with palms facing out. It was an old wartime gesture, one that meant *stop and back away*.

Gorlen stepped back from the counter, his hands raised as though he had just touched fire.

Aesa rubbed the side of her face. A sneer melted away her sweetness. Then she laughed at him.

Mera lowered her arms. "Come on," she said, reaching across Aesa's chest and giving her a slight nudge. "We won't solve anything like this."

The sisters retreated from the Prison, Aesa all the while rubbing her cheek. When they departed, an odd smile spread over Gorlen's face.

Ulmaen's distaste for the man escalated. Still, he needed to play nice with the general, if he was ever going to help Rozafel and find some resolution about Ule's murder.

Gorlen snapped his head around. "What do you want?"

Ulmaen stepped backward. "Any chance Rozafel was released?"

"What are you going on about?"

"Rozafel," Ulmaen repeated her name. "She isn't in her cell."

Gorlen glanced sideways, his tongue jabbing at the inside of his cheek. The intensity of his lingering rage had left him flush. After a moment, he refocused his attention on the ledger. "She's working the quarry," he finally said.

Liar, he thought, except this time around, the observation wasn't a shock.

Rozafel may have been stronger when she was younger, when she used to climb trees, but she was older now. And why hadn't she been put to work in the quarry earlier?

Instinct wasn't enough to prove Gorlen was lying, Ulmaen realized. He had just witnessed him withhold funds for a missing sword, which sat on a shelf beneath the counter. The man couldn't be trusted.

Ulmaen chuckled to lighten the tension and soothe Gorlen's mood, but his voice cracked. "I didn't realize she possessed the kind of strength required for breaking rocks with pike and hammer."

Gorlen shrugged. "She's stouter than you think. Besides, she asked for it."

Ulmaen was uncertain of what to make of Gorlen's meaning. Had Rozafel done something to warrant punishment? Or had she asked to be worked to the bone? The thought was ludicrous. She wouldn't. She couldn't. She seemed so frail the last time he delivered her breakfast.

"You might as well send a guard to fetch her," he told Gorlen. "It's just a matter of time now."

"What is?"

"Her release." Ulmaen retrieved his research from the basket. He placed the bundle of parchment on the counter.

"See there," he said, and pointed to the bottom of the first page. "That's Mbjard's signature. He's my witness."

Gorlen began thumbing through the papers, impatience making his cheeks twitch. "What am I looking at?"

"Proof to support Rozafel's story."

Even though Ulmaen had a rough estimate of the time when Rozafel had sold the gloves, Mbjard was quick to remind him of not believing what she had told him. There was always the chance she had lied. Ulmaen didn't believe her capable. Still, he did as he was told and conducted a thorough search, starting with the day of Rozafel's incarceration and working backward through the years.

"See here, this is a copy of the entry in Rozafel's merchant ledger, when she ran a textile shop in Eastgate. It's dated six years ago. She sold the gloves to a textile merchant from Sondshor Market for four sils."

Gorlen read the text in the column next to a summary of the item description. "Elusis." And without giving any consideration to the research in front of him, he decided on a course of action. "So then, I'll bring him in for questioning."

Several years ago, Ulmaen had personally ensured Elusis stay alive by letting him be charmed into a blissful amnesia, which made him forget his past. He currently lived in a grove in the desert governed by a cat demon. According to gossip, everyone believed Elusis had gone missing in the same way many women had back then.

"He disappeared," Ulmaen offered, knowing he couldn't elaborate on what happened to the man. He turned to the next page. "See, this is an Auction Notice for the contents of his store, but there is no listing for the gloves there. It's possible he sold them before the shop was auctioned."

"So what's this nonsense all mean? Who bought the gloves?" Gorlen jabbed the papers and they crinkled beneath his finger.

Hastily Ulmaen retrieved the papers. "I-I'm still searching for Elusis's Sales Records."

"What if Rozafel bought the gloves back?" Gorlen's mood was shifting again, his temper rising. "What if they were a gift to someone else?"

"Uh, those are both possibilities. I suppose Rozafel would have them listed in her Purchase Ledgers, and if the gloves were a gift, that'd be difficult to track."

Gorlen laughed sharply. "So, you still don't know anything, not for certain, eh?"

Ulmaen grimaced.

"Stop wasting my time." Gorlen snatched the papers back, and began thumbing through them. After he finished, he grunted. "All Mbjard's handwriting too. At least that's impressive." Gradually he began to show some interest in the research and slowed to scrutinize every page.

"Ownership of the gloves would be helpful," he grumbled. "I'd tell you to leave this to us, but you're not going to, are you?"

Ulmaen shook his head and reached for the paperwork.

"I'll hold onto this."

"But I need it—"

Gorlen grinned. It was toothy and unnerving. He looked like an angry dog baring its teeth. "Go on now."

Ulmaen wanted to hurt the man—a good, hard, hammer punch across the top of his head. The urge was strong, and Ulmaen tasted bile as he resisted giving into the impulse. He backed away from the counter and tried to smile, but couldn't. His left eye twitched. Quietly, he crossed the room and flew up the stairs.

Outside, at the top of the stairs, he curled his fingers into fists, but there was no time to find something to pummel into dust. Instead, his voice erupted in a fury, desperate to express the ball of anger and frustration.

"Fuck!"

As the tension in his head subsided, he heard more curse words. He wasn't alone. The twins loitered about in the field. Aesa stood still while patting her red cheek. Mera paced back and forth. They each took turns cursing in the direction of the Prison entrance.

"Aesa! Mera!" He called out to them. Both sisters halted their outbursts.

As he neared them, he noticed they eyed him suspiciously.

A red welt had begun to swell on the peak of Aesa's cheekbone, looking even angrier than she did.

"Do we know you?" Mera asked.

Ulmaen laughed at what could potentially have been a big error. Of course he'd be a complete stranger to them. He'd need to work on learning to keep track of his current relationships and let go of the ones from Ule's lifetime. Thankfully the twins had a reputation in Sondshor, and everyone knew of them.

"What do you want?" Aesa asked.

Feeling a little cocky, he began to walk between them. Smiling, he winked at Aesa. She snorted in disbelief at the gesture. As he passed Mera, he gave her a once over. Well beyond their reach, he turned to regard both of them. "Your sword," he told them, walking backward in the tall grass.

"What about it?" Mera snapped. This time her child like cheeks found their edge, and he still found her beautiful.

"It's on a shelf beneath that counter where Gorlen keeps watch."

Both sisters' faces slackened at the information. They regarded one another in awe at the revelation, but their moods switched, again in an eerie synchronicity. Words were exchanged. Afterward, they both smiled at one another.

Aesa aimed herself toward the entrance of the Prison while Mera turned toward him and bowed. She mouthed a silent thank you, then joined her sister, and pulled a leather mallet from a side pocket of her smith apron.

✳ CHAPTER 33 ✳

As a ghost, there are an infinite number of ways to enter a building, but Ulmaen didn't want to spook anyone and stir rumors within the castle that were certain to be heard by Navalis. His Master would know what he had been up to and disapprove of his carelessness at being seen, then remind him about the necessity of reserving his inner energy.

Losing time from his current generation was the only part of the plan Ulmaen didn't like. He wasn't willing to give up a lot of energy and considered two ways to limit the damage. First, that evening he ate heavily of high energy foods, irritating Senaga when he returned twice for more portions of mashed potatoes. And second, he planned to limit his shifting to times of need, like avoiding guards and getting in and out of the Prison.

Navalis would never know.

Oddly, the desire to appease his Master had begun fading. Every day, he thought less of Navalis's needs and more of his own. If he was meant to be a Sentinel, he needed to start acting on his own instincts and accept the consequences, regardless of what they might be.

At this moment, he needed to recover his research. He had considered other ways to accomplish his goal, but each scenario ended the same way—him fighting Gorlen and then being arrested for assault. He couldn't waste time being locked away in a cell, not even for a day.

He knew he risked the chance of being seen in his shifted form as an ethereal vapor haunting the Prison, so he wore dark clothing and black sandals to mute his appearance. Keeping to the shadows, he wandered through less traveled courtyards until he made it to the ruins along the northern Colonnade. He hid by a lookout tower near the Northgate until yard by the Bath House had emptied.

Then skirted the woods behind the Bath House, and half way toward the stable, he turned into the field and waded into the high grass. He spied the north arm of the Prison where large doors were heavily guarded. Rows of carts lined the outer walls and dirt paths ran past the stable, through the woods, and down into Warfield.

He ducked in the tall grass and inched his way toward the east arm of the Prison, careful to keep the movement of the grass to a minimum. At the wall, he crouched at where he estimated the secondary stairs to the Pit existed on the other side of the stonework.

He had considered the many places where Gorlen might have stored his research, but decided the first place to search was the counter where Aesa and Mera's sword had been hidden. If Gorlen had hidden that there, why not the research?

Ulmaen pushed the energy within his body. His arms and legs blurred as he dove into the ground. He expected to find a thick section of solid earth and rocks. Instead, he emerged into a collapsed cell. He pushed onward, slowing down as he passed through a thick iron wall and onto the lower steps of the stairs.

When he was certain there weren't any guards making their rounds, he returned to a solid state and quietly scrambled up the steps. When the landing on the main floor was level with his eyes, he peeked around the corner down the block of cells and saw that every one was occupied.

He crept back down the stairs, peering as far down the tunnel as possible, for it inclined downward and curved, and at any time, a guard might turn the bend and come into view.

He hugged the wall as he treaded down the corridor, preparing to shift at any moment. Around the bend, he approached the cell that had been occupied by one of Ilgaud's buddies but was empty now. He crept along till the end and emerged into the larger tunnel which led to Mithreel's cell.

A soft swoosh, footsteps, and the light scraping of metal against metal set off Ulmaen's nerves. Trying not to panic, he shifted and pushed himself too deeply into a wall, for he emerged in an empty cell on the other side. He scrambled to push himself into the next wall and found safety engulfed in solid earth spotted with rocks. He stayed hidden there until the sound of footfalls faded.

"I hear you."

Ulmaen followed the voice, slipping through the sidewall of a familiar cell.

Mithreel sat upright and swung his shackled legs over the edge of the cot. One of his uppermost arms reached out, and the cupped end and the chain fastened to it passed through Ulmaen.

A tingle came over Ulmaen at the presence of the demon's unusual energy. He returned to a solid form.

"Ule!" A pleasant expression softened the demon's face.

"I'm called Ulmaen now," he whispered. He looked over his shoulder toward the window in the cell door. The guard had moved on.

"You've come to reminisce." Mithreel stood, the chains clanking as he joined Ulmaen in the middle of the room. "It'll be different this time, I promise. I'm different."

Ulmaen tried to figure out what Mithreel meant, until the demon raised one of his bound hands.

"I would touch you, but..." He raised all six hands, making all the chains rattle. "Would you mind?" He extended his upper right hand more than the others.

At this angle, Ulmaen examined the mystical symbols on the cups, interpreting more of their meaning than what he had the last time he had saw them. He wondered if the glyphs and the ritual that accompanied them had been responsible for the tingling sensation he experienced when Mithreel's shackled hand made contact with his shifted form.

"I'd rather not," he said, knowing there must be a good reason for the demon to be bound in this way.

A flash of anger interrupted Mithreel's serenity. He regained his composure swiftly. "So it is the treasure you seek." He nodded at first, then shook his head. "I won't tell you."

"Tell me what?!"

"Where to find the treasure."

"Oh, that again? I don't care about any treasure."

Mithreel recoiled. He softly muttered, "You used to."

The spider demon's eyes were murky and blue and unsettling. They didn't bulge. They weren't large or almond shaped. They were like his, and Ulmaen's curiosity got the better of him. He leaned in closer, pressed his hand against Mithreel's bare chest to determine what his flesh felt like. In response, Mithreel flexed his pectoral muscle. Laces of energy whipped through the muscle.

"It has taken what seems like forever," Mithreel said. He tilted his head, peered up at Ulmaen. "Perhaps now, you find me attractive?"

Ulmaen carefully retracted his hand from the demon's chest, once again uncertain of his meaning.

"You no longer serve food here." Mithreel smiled. "I miss your sound."

Ulmaen stepped backward. "What? I don't understand what you're saying."

"Words travel," Mithreel said. He tilted his head, extending his well formed ear toward the cell door. "I hear everything. At this moment, upstairs Ilgaud smacks his lips. The day old leg of ham must be good. On the west side of the Core, a fat man snores."

Ulmaen knew the prisoner Mithreel referred to, the slovenly fellow who had always seemed to be asleep whenever he delivered breakfast.

Mithreel continued. "The soft whisk of hair being braided. The slap of feet climbing stone walls, the way she used to climb trees when she was little. She grunted when she tied off the rope, did you know?"

"What are you talking about?"

"Shhh."

Ulmaen looked over his shoulder, through the window in the door, and saw the tunnel was empty. Struck by the reference to tree climbing, he asked, "Do you mean Rozafel?"

Mithreel slowly nodded.

"What happened to her?"

"She gurgled as she breathed her last bit of air." Mithreel's eyes rolled upward, nearly disappearing in the back of his head. "I heard her death rattle against the bars. Then grunts and groans as guards struggled to take her down, the slap of limp arms on the floor as she was dragged, footfalls clump-clumping on the stairs, in the tunnel, to that cell with the door locked tight, click, click-click." Mithreel restored his eyes and gazed at Ulmaen. "Somebody doesn't want her to be found."

"She—" A pang of grief tore through Ulmaen. He tried to dispel the imagery of Mithreel's words, hoping there was another interpretation. "She hung herself?"

"By a rope of her own hair." Mithreel smiled briefly, then stopped. "Feytleel told me that. She knows such things." He returned to the edge of his cot and sat there. "Her whispers crawl along the walls every day. She spoke of the end of times and your friend's death and how she misses the days from long ago, when we used to walk the shores of an old river. We were free then, and we'd gather the bones of the dead and mark the ground where they had fallen."

Ulmaen struggled with accepting that Rozafel had taken her life and grew irritated by Mithreel's nostalgic reflections. "I don't know about old rivers," he snapped. "And I don't want to know what you and the death demon used to do together."

Dread pressed in on him, threatening to crush his spirits, but he wouldn't let it in and instinctively questioned the veracity of Mithreel's story.

"Don't believe me?" Mithreel shrugged. "See for yourself!"

Ulmaen wanted to, but he had come for his research, which he hoped would free Rozafel and bring him closer to answers about Ule's death. Without it, he'd have to explain to Mbjard what had happened to it, and he didn't want to trouble Mbjard with the labor of making duplicates or worse, create conflict between Mbjard and General Gorlen.

Shifting his form, Ulmaen peered through the barred window and checked the tunnel one more time for guards, then passed through the door. On the other side, he stopped, returned to solid form, and told Mithreel, "I will, old friend."

He tiptoed along the tunnels, ignoring comments uttered by other demons, and kept vigilant watch for movement, being prepared to shift and duck into a wall at any moment.

The tunnel remained clear, and he made it to the stairs leading up to the main floor behind the counter. He crept up a few steps at a time, straining to see above the top. A pair of boots clopped against the floor, and their close proximity made his heart race. He ducked down and wiped sweat from his brow.

After a minute, he flattened against the wall and crept up a few more steps, wondering if he should drain his inner reserve of energy to shape shift into a small animal. He didn't want to, for he knew he risked being caught or killed.

From his vantage point, he saw two figures standing at the counter.

Sabien stood on the far side, grim and somber. Every few minutes, he hugged himself and paced a bit.

Gorlen stood opposite him, where he hunched over as he wrote on parchment with a chunk of lead wrapped in cloth. His left arm jerked in an animated manner as he wrote, and Ulmaen realized he didn't normally write with that hand. No, the hand he normally wrote with was slung at his side, swaddled with thick cotton bandages and splints along several of his fingers.

Immediately, Ulmaen thought of Aesa and Mera and wondered if they'd been the ones to cause Gorlen's injuries. He imagined the sisters rather enjoyed using their forging tools to pound on Gorlen till he gave up his coin pouch.

Amused by the little fantasy, Ulmaen extended the range of his vision and searched the shelves beneath the counter. The leather swaddled sword was nowhere to be seen, yet amid the piles of chains, shackles, and belts, he spied a stack of parchment—his research.

"When was it stolen?" Gorlen asked Sabien.

Sabien sighed and closed his eyes briefly. "The last I saw it... yesterday." He shrugged. "Some time last night maybe?"

"Describe the box again."

"About this size." Sabien gestured with his hands, indicating a small box. "Plain and simple. Made from cast iron."

"And the stone?" Gorlen stopped writing a moment. "It was a precious stone right?"

Sabien blanched. "Sentimental value. A family heirloom." His lips pinched together. "Its value is in its reputation. It would sell well in any market." Then Sabien began to describe the kornerupine that had once been a demon.

Ulmaen's mind reeled at the notion of Istok in the hands of another. Why would anyone want to steal something that filled them with rage? How could Sabien have let it happen? Why hadn't he been more careful?

Annoyed by the discovery, Ulmaen knew he should tell Navalis about it, but to do so meant telling him about the infiltration of the Prison or some other cover story. Ulmaen pushed the issue from his mind, determined to tell Navalis something eventually, when he was ready.

He settled against the wall, prepared to shift in case either of the guards nearby bothered to step away from their posts and examine the stairwell.

Sabien retreated from the counter, his footfalls receding. The stone walls amplified and distorted the sound, and Ulmaen couldn't quite tell in which direction he had gone and assumed Sabien had departed through the main entrance.

Gorlen continued writing, scratching notes onto the parchment. Ulmaen waited for him to retreat from the counter, where directly within his line of vision he saw the papers, very easily within arm's reach.

Finally, Gorlen set down the chunk of lead. As he backed away from the counter, Ulmaen readied himself to spring up the remaining steps at the first opportunity.

Gorlen stepped aside, almost out of view. Ulmaen was ready to move, already pushing himself forward until Gorlen returned and clumsily wrote a few more words on the parchment.

Ulmaen ceased his forward momentum. His heart raced at a maddening pace. His breath shallowed, and while he tried to calm himself, a voice of reason—a voice that had once been a blue flame he used to talk with in times of need—pulsed inside.

"Why are you doing this to yourself?" the blue flame asked. "Shift and then flee. No one will see if you're quick-quick about it. You'll use little of your time for this generation. A year, maybe two. You're compromising yourself. You're being unnecessarily cautious. You're still young."

The inner voice should have calmed Ulmaen. Instead, it geared him up. His heart beat faster. His thoughts grew frantic.

Grab the paper. Shift. Run.

That's all he needed to do. If he had done this from the outset and not worried about the shifting draining time from his current generation, he'd have been in and out by now, the research filed away in the Archive.

Gorlen backed away from the counter again. Ulmaen waited only a second for the general's footfalls to diminish. He ducked low, lunged forward, his arm outstretched toward the shelf.

His fingers curled around the edges of the paper, squeezing tight. He shifted himself and the parchmenbt and dove through the floor and returned to the stairwell. He shot through earth and tunnel with ease in a mad panicked rush, giving little consideration to what stood in his way, not the iron grates, not the thick stone walls, not Feytleel, the death demon, who sat on the floor hunched in stillness.

He expected material with a high density of molecules to be more difficult to pass through than matter containing fewer molecules. Upon passing through the death demon, a force pulled at Ulmaen that slowed his momentum and speed by a fraction. The sensation was odd. He felt as though he had traveled a long way for a very long time, yet only less than a second had passed.

He snapped away from the death demon and hurried along, through another row of cells. He avoided Mithreel altogether and pushed headlong into the earth beyond the iron wall and into the field. Not caring if anyone saw him—he just wanted to find a safe place to recollect himself— he emerged from the ground, shot across toward the stables near the woods, and found an empty space among the haystacks.

There, he stopped. Returning to solid form, Ulmaen's mind tilted. He lost his balance and reached out to support himself against a bale. His hand slipped and he collapsed on the ground. Papers fluttered all about him.

Blinking profusely at the clouded sky, he focused on bringing his breath to a calm, even pace. He turned his perception inward; his vitals were fine, his physiology as well. Nothing had changed, except he felt an absence, as if something were missing, and he frantically scanned his body. Every molecule was accounted for, the integrity of their energy and bonds intact.

Upon closer examination, he felt the absence within his essence. The shifting, what normally would have taken a year or two of energy from his current generation, had drained an unprecedented amount of time.

He couldn't understand how it was possible. Matter simply did not affect his kind in this way. He assessed the damage and counted twenty-two years of life gone in an instant. An ache coursed through his head. He rubbed his face, forcing back the urge to scream.

✳ CHAPTER 34 ✳

Navalis wore Boriag's imbued gauntlet. Whatever process had strengthened the metal hadn't yet been fully tested. Although Boriag had conducted some experiments, Navalis still wanted to see if it held up against the innards of a demon, except what remained of his current specimen was in the process of spoiling.

He sat on the floor, his back against the wall, and observed the accelerated decay of the snake demon across the laboratory. The last of the creature's skin bubbled into green gelatin until what remained solid in form jiggled. Then it began to bubble and drip and spill from the dissection table onto the floor.

This snake demon had lasted longer than the previous one, probably because it was considerably older, as indicated by the complexity of its form. Somehow the age of the demon and the stage of its evolution affected how long the body took to decay.

Analysis plagued Navalis as he watched the accumulation of slop on the floor begin to thin into a fluid—Why did demons strive for Elishian form at all? What did they hope to accomplish by doing that? And what would it mean to them, to the world, once they had achieved their goal?

He wondered, too, how long it would take before hunters captured another and what he would do in the meantime. He needed to continue with his inquiries and studies.

He recalled his conversation with the farmer, Rolen. If there was any truth to the man's story, he needed to persuade Kerista to let him travel to the Woedshor Steppes and investigate the farm, providing the hunters at least a week to trap a new specimen. Deep down, he suspected investigating Rolen's story was a waste of time.

He expected resistance from Kerista, who would think of some way to stop him. Only magic and science mattered to her, not the unsubstantiated drivel of drunken farm folk. However, he owned the farm now, and she didn't seem the type to deny him the need to check out his new property. Kerista never need know the true reason for his travels.

It'll take too long, he thought.

Time. He was tired of it. Tired of rushing and tired of waiting, tired of withholding. He was Xiinisi. The most powerful of his kind—a Master of the Masters.

He didn't want to risk being seen in a shifted state or using his inner energy to morph into a creature. However, he saw he had little choice if he wanted answers quickly. He'd need to be careful again, about withholding whatever information he discovered, this time from Kerista instead of the Xiinisi Council.

A pang shot through his mind. A dull, throbbing tightened the tendons in his neck. Withholding was lying, and here he was doing the very thing he had hoped to avoid. He'd constantly lied during his previous incarnation as a blacksmith. Lies spun more lies, spiraling out like a thick web that both shielded him and disconnected him from the world. He hated that feeling.

It's not fabrication, only withholding, he told himself. *Nothing to get worried about.*

He removed the gauntlet and set it down on the floor beside him. Pulling his knees to his chest, he sat and waited. When he felt the pull of the moon deep within strengthen as it began its ascent, he knew night had come.

He shifted the molecules in his body. For a moment, his body shimmered and hovered above the floor, then he propelled himself across the room, shot out the door, up the spiral tower, through stone and mortar and terra cotta tiles, through dirt and pipes and rushing water, and up into the sky, where he hovered like a ghostly cloud.

High above the Starry Rise, the rush of fountain water was like a trickle. Above him, the stars twinkled, fixed lights in a sky that reflected all the worlds stored in The Vault back in his realm. He noticed a few more stars had been added to the sky since the last time he looked, and he wondered what those new worlds were like and who had made them.

He hurtled through the air, not bothering to transform into a bird. He crossed the border into Woedshor in mere minutes instead of the several days required had he traveled by horse.

Below, the thick forest blurred, a swell of foliage that appeared to rise and fall like a dark green sea. He steered toward the distant mountains, where stepped cliffs topped by glens and meadows rose toward the base of a long extinct volcano. Here, the fertile land was dotted by farms.

Navalis slowed and descended. He searched for a water tower with a terra cotta shingled roof and spotted it below. It was as Rolen had described—a teetering beast straddling water. Navalis swooped toward it, following the thin river that cut down through the Steppes, then broke into two streams. He followed the one that curved toward a small woods, and there, just the other side, nestled between a sheer rise of rock jutting from the ground and another woods, he saw the shadow of the farm.

He descended in a rush and landed without sound, his feet hovering just above the ground. He maintained his shifted form, not caring if anyone passing by saw a shimmering man walking the abandoned farm. He'd rather be prepared to hide or flee if needed.

Rolen's farm had been small compared to the ones south of the castle. What garden beds had once existed were now covered by a carpet of quack grass, and the suggestion of a small tilled field was made evident by clusters of sun-seared corn husks poking through tall flowering weeds.

Nothing had been tended to in years yet everything insisted on growing, vying for space and sun.

A small barn had collapsed, yet nearby the house remained intact, though the windows were soiled and broken and the roof caved in slightly. Surprisingly, the front door remained shut.

Navalis knelt in the place where he assumed Rolen had grown his potatoes and carrots. Projecting his mind, he looked past the mess of weeds and the grubs and worms beneath the soil. The chemistry of the soil was consistent and expected for a land that had been farmed.

He tried the house next, pushing through the wall with ease. Inside, he discovered a spindle chair set before a small cast iron stove, as though it waited for someone to return and stoke the fire, to restore warmth and vitality to what had once been a home.

Little furnishing remained in the front room, and off the back of the house were two more rooms. In one, what remained of a bed had collapsed, the straw mattress strewn about the room. In the other, he discovered the bed still intact, smaller than the first, one intended for a child.

The wood panels had been drawn on, marked by many different hands over the years. The room had obviously been a haven for adolescents, a place of refuge for some, allowing them to express their hostility and rage through harsh, thick lines spelling out a myriad of vulgarities. For others, the room was a place for them to safely explore their awakening sexual urges and desires, to share their love with another.

Navalis walked the room, his hand trailing over a promise of eternal devotion, two names tied together inside the image of a knot. There were other drawings too, ones less bawdy, depictions of faces instead of genitalia. The faces were faded, the lines tenuous and uncertain, as though drawn by a child. As he walked the room, he noticed the images were depicting narratives.

He knelt before the drawing of what appeared to be the farm. Beside it was a man, a woman, a young child, and next to the child a white flame. He couldn't be certain of the child's gender. There was nothing to indicate what it might be. Next to it were more drawings, scratch marks depicting the farm and the young child, always a white flame nearby.

By the bed, Navalis discovered a series of images piled on top of one another. The first depicted an older child walking above the horizon, and beneath the child, hovering close to the ground, the white flame again. In the second image, the man struck the child in the head with an arrow. Beneath both of these images, another of the child lay curled up below the horizon, on the ground, eyes open, mouth shut. Next to it, the white flame was also curled up, with cross-marks for eyes and mouth open as though it were dead.

Rising again, Navalis walked the perimeter of the room, convinced the images had some significance. His understanding of what they depicted was that the child may have been possessed by a demon, which he didn't think possible.

The notion, however, suggested a possible theory for how demons had achieved physical form in the Root Dimension—they took them. Whatever the nature of the fear the vapor was created from, it sought out the representation of that fear in the world and possessed the object. Once they had, somehow they affected change in that body. How else could a cat demon talk or a cactus demon walk!

The only way he could test his theory was to find this child, the one who had drawn the simple stick figures. He wondered if the child made it into adulthood. Being a demon possessing an Elishian body, the feat was a possibility.

He flitted throughout the house, pushing through the walls. In the child's bedroom, a hiding place in the wall behind the bed revealed a small, hand bound book filled with meticulous diagrams, maps of the area, and drawings of animals, the farm, and people.

Onward he searched and found a locked trunk in a crawlspace beneath the house. He scanned the contents and found ledgers, and beneath a stack of contracts was a bound book of parchment. He shifted it to extract it from the trunk.

As he flipped through the pages, the images, the maps and diagrams were more sophisticated, more intentional, more stylized and distinct, and unexpectedly familiar. He dropped the book. It returned to its original solid form and struck the ground.

He shot upward through earth and wood, into the sky, and returned to the castle in haste, for in the last few pages of the book, he recognized the child. He knew exactly who the child had become.

* CHAPTER 35 *

Ulmaen woke with vigor. He expected lethargy, depression even, after having his current generation nearly come to an end in an instant. Contact with the death demon had affected him in a way he hadn't expected, and the anxiety regarding the experience motivated him into great action.

He buzzed through his new daily tasks of disinfecting the men's portion of the Bath House, then sped along to the Library, where he tidied stacks of books. By late evening, persistent belly growls reminded him that sustenance was a necessity and he really should eat, and he realized what he thought was vim was actually panic.

Dizzied from the experience, no amount of food or sleep could ever restore the time drained from him. Still, he needed to ease his discomfort. He clutched at his stomach as it gurgled again. His hunger was fierce. His body ached, too. He bid Mbjard farewell and hastily made his way to the Kitchen.

He hurried between the Library and the Inner Sanctum, then west along the Colonnade, grateful the few people wandering there paid him little attention. Passed the Starry Rise, he skirted the end of the Armory, bolted beneath the arch of the covered walkway and aimed for the servants' entrance of the Scullery behind the Dining Hall and Kitchen.

Once inside, he followed the corridor at his leisure. To his left, he peered into a large room filled with overstock from the pantry and extra tables and stools. To his right, he passed the archways leading to the podium where the head table overlooked the Dining Hall. Most of the stools were stacked on top of tables, except for the odd one here and there which was still in use by someone, sitting in solitude hunched over a bowl of food.

He was surprised to see anyone eating at this time of night. The last of the evening cooks and bakers had retired, gone to get a good long rest. In a couple of hours, the next crew would arrive and begin preparing the morning meal, which gave him the opportunity to eat without engaging with anyone.

He neared the end of the hall, past the stone brick wall belonging to the pantry, and detected movement beyond the doorway. At the farthest serving window, Senaga stood near a fire pit. She wrung her hands through a cloth while scrutinizing the room.

He hung back in the shadows. The whoosh-whoosh of her hands against the rag and the soft, low hiss of embers in the nearby oven, did little to obscure his belly growls.

"Whoever you are," she called out, "there's a bit of stew left." When he didn't reply, she said, "Be sure to clean up after yourself then."

He poked his head around the edge of the doorway.

Senaga squinted. "It's you," she declared. She tossed the rag across the room into a basket heaped high with other soiled cloths.

He approached the only pot idling on the closest fire pit.

"Listen, when you're done here, be sure to put the last of the stools up," Senaga said. "And there's a puddle of pickle juice in the pantry that didn't get cleaned up right. Take care of it. And wash your dishes too. We get enough bugs in here. We don't need any more."

Her instructions were like spear jabs in his ribs, stirring him to defend himself. He wanted a sword to raise, a troop to lead into battle with an ear-splitting war cry, but when Senaga started toward the exit to the Dining Hall, his mind stepped back from the fantasy. He sighed in relief.

Senaga paused in the doorway a moment. "By the way," she said, "good on you."

He wasn't sure what she meant. He only wanted to eat. He grabbed a ladle from a wash bin on the floor next to the fire pit.

"I'm hard on the servants for a reason, did you know that?"

He blinked at her. His stomach had given up growling and ached instead.

"If I'm not, they stay stupid," she said. "They think this is all there is to life. Riding them hard makes 'em smarten up and realize they want something else for themselves. Usually. Then they get a move on, right out of here. I hate seeing people getting stuck somewhere they don't belong. What a waste of life!"

"What about you?"

"Think you're smarter than me, do ya?"

"Nothing like that," he replied. "Just curious about why you stay on in the Kitchen. With your talent, you could easily open your own bakery or public house?"

"The baking's a cover for my true talent." She shook her head. "No, what I'm real good at is lighting fires under people's arses!" She gave him a wink.

She continued on her way, and half way toward the main doors of the Dining Hall, she turned around and told him, "When you need a good word for getting in with the scribes, you let me know."

A spark of hope eased his anxiety and discomfort. His mood began to lift. After Senaga left the Dining Hall, he cleaned a bowl then filled it with what remained in the stew spot. He grabbed a spoon and began eating. His stomach heaved at the first few bites, but afterward, as he ambled into the Dining Hall, it settled down.

At the nearest table, Laere peeked out between stool legs. He walked past her, and at the next table he pulled down a stool, sat down, and began to eat.

Several moments passed in silence before Laere spoke up. "You're always so... preoccupied."

Ulmaen remained silent. Although he'd rather not engage with her, a part of him missed having a confidante, someone with whom he could discuss his intimate feelings and concerns. It was difficult holding back. When it came to issues with Elish, Bethereel had listened attentively. For Xiinisi issues he went to Navalis. Neither were available any more.

"Lots on my mind," he finally replied. "Nothing for you to worry about."

"Oh, I'm not worried." Laere's stool scraped against the floor as she backed away from her table. In an instant, she stood across from him, pulled a stool down, and sat. She reached out and touched the back of his hand. She smiled her crooked smile and winked. "Your secrets are safe with me."

"It's nothing, really."

"Is it your wife?"

"Yeah," he said, realizing too late he referenced Bethereel and not the fictitious wife everyone else believed he always spoke about. "And other concerns," he added quickly.

She waited a moment, but when he said nothing else, she smiled then shoved a piece of bread into her mouth.

He debated confiding in her, for it threatened to deepen a bond with her he didn't necessarily want to encourage. However, her insights as someone who worked daily reconciling a blank canvas and who had a keen eye for capturing people realistically, promised to be beneficial.

Leaning forward, his hunger not yet sated, he tapped her bowl with his spoon and in low voice said, "I'm searching for evidence to help free Rozafel. Don't tell anyone. Shhh."

Laere blinked at first. She brought another piece of bread to her mouth. It lingered at her lips. "Oh," she said, her eyes widening. Her expression was caught somewhere between awe and shock, and it made her appear more innocent. Abandoning the bread, she jumped to her feet, skirted the end of the table, pulled down another stool, and sat next to him.

"That is so... That's so..." Consumed by awe, she struggled to find words. When none came to her, she grabbed him by the collar, pulled him down toward her and planted her lips on his. When she finally released him and regained her senses, a flurry of questions arose.

"What do you know so far? How do you know where to look? Do you know the murderer? Do you have any theories?"

No. The single word had become a complete thought in his mind. He heard himself think it again. *No, I haven't figured out who the murderer is. No, I don't want to be lovers.* Each no that rushed into his mind became a stone used to build a wall.

He shook his head, hiding his frustration.

Her smiled faded. She sat back, staring at him. "You don't have any feelings for me, do you?"

He wiped his mouth, surprised at the turn in their conversation. Then he remembered—woman's intuition. He had had that once.

"You're just like the others. You have no feelings whatsoever?"

"Yeah, I have feelings," he said, slightly perturbed by the suggestion. Without his emotions, even if they were a bit distant at times, he wouldn't be compelled to search for a murderer, he wouldn't feel the need to avenge the deaths of Bethereel and Ule. He wouldn't act on anything. He simply wouldn't care, but he did. His feelings weren't always a priority anymore.

His primary care, his greatest responsibility, was maintaining the integrity of the world Elish. Beyond this responsibility were his old loves, when he had been Ule. Long ago, there had been Ibe and his unrequited love. Then there was Milos, an Elishian whose stupidity and lack of social graces landed him with a broken nose. He had deserved it, though. His words were the same as a punch, and an apology would have gone a long way to soothe Ule's bruised ego.

Ulmaen paused in his reflection.

He hadn't been as rude to Laere as Milos had been to Ule, but he'd discarded Laere just the same. That hadn't been his intention. He wanted her to be Bethereel, and he had gone down that path only to realize he'd made a mistake.

Wondering if Laere might benefit from him acknowledging the suffering he had caused her, he took both of her hands in his.

"I'm sorry," he said and genuinely meant it.

"Sorry? Sorry!" Laere pulled a hand free and struck him across the face.

He laughed at how little pain he felt from the blow, trying to figure out where his reasoning had failed him.

She struck him again, harder this time, then sprang to her feet and headed toward the main doors. She glanced back, her brows furrowed and cheeks etched by anger. "I'll make you sorry!"

Once she had gone, the silence of the Dining Hall became a deep contrast to his mind, where his thoughts rambled on, reviewing the sharp rejections from his past, and he realized his error. He'd regarded Laere as only a woman, one that could be substituted for another. There was a much broader understanding of her he'd overlooked, that he'd forgotten. Above all else, Laere was a person, unique in her ways and reactions. While someone might cry and another punch, Laere made threats.

I'll make you sorry.

He was certain the threat was idle. Laere just needed a bit of time to cool down. Still, her words hooked onto a memory and reeled it to the surface of his mind, and as it flip-flopped about within his perception, he saw that it was an old memory going back to a time when demons walked Elish as vapors and he'd been a young girl.

Ule had stabilized the An Energy in the south, where there had been groves and lush fields before desert prevailed. Rivulets had scarred the terrain, and she wandered farther north along the bank of one of the larger of those riverlets until she came upon a young forest thick with saplings to her west.

She knelt down on the bank to examine the bedrock beneath and began to push her mind into the ground.

"Whaaat beee thiiisss?"

The raspy words sounded in her mind instead of her ears. At first, she thought it belonged to her Master. Convinced the Council had reduced her sentence and sent him to free her, she joyfully withdrew her perception from the ground and found a demon instead.

This demon was the only one of all the vapors she had ever met in any world that projected thought and used a rudimentary language, sounding out each word in drawn out whispers in the manner of a child.

"Be more specific," she told it. If it was going to communicate, it might as well learn to do it well.

The vapor slid across the ground toward a small fissure in the air that floated above the soil near her feet. It motioned to the rippling distortion but knew well enough not to touch it.

"That is a Safeway," she explained.

The fissure was dark on the inside, a reflection of the other end of the portal—the Isolation Chamber where she was fulfilling her punishment. The portal to her realm provided a way to exit Elish without the need of the An Energy. It was a temporary safeguard used by young Xiinisi should anything happen to prevent them from Ascending.

"What be ssssafeway?"

The demon's curiosity was unusual for its kind, but she didn't worry about what it learned during its brief existence in the Root Dimension. Once the An Energy started to recede, all the demons eventually passed through the Nexus into the Chthonic Dimension, a place better suited to them and separate from the rest of the world.

"A shortcut back home," she replied.

"Can I goooo?"

Ule shook her head. "You won't like it. Time moves slower in my realm compared to here. Even if you survived the shift, my realm wouldn't sustain your... vaporiness. And if I made you corporeal, you wouldn't survive long, unless I made you exactly like me in every way. You can only truly exist here."

"I be heeere."

Intrigued by the sensation of joy that permeated from the vapor, she asked it, "Do you like it here?"

The vapor crawled toward her, climbed into the air and bowed slightly. The feeling intensified.

She recognized the feeling. "You *love* it?"

The vapor bowed again. "Looove," it repeated. From then on, the demon had learned new words quickly.

She sat back and admired the fields of saplings which would one day grow into a forest that spanned well beyond the riverlet.

"Me too," she agreed. "It's beautiful."

The vapor returned to the ground and pulled along the grass until it brushed against her leg. A coldness permeated her and the flesh across her shoulders prickled.

"Go away little demon!" She waved her hand through the vapor. The contact made her shiver again.

The demon unfurled smoky tendrils and pulled itself along the ground, beyond her reach. "But I looove," it said.

She stared after it, unsure of the sentiment it had tried to convey.

"I looove... Ule."

She had been young, unaccustomed to understanding fully the explosions of emotions that consumed her. They had always been there, except for the brief time during which her memories had been temporarily suppressed by the Council as part of her early incarceration. Only then had she felt a reprieve from their chaos.

"Well don't!"

The intensity of the reply propelled the demon across the ground. It curled into a ball until her rage ceased.

"I can't love you back. You're not like me. You're a demon, and one day you'll be gone like all the others."

At a great distance, the demon shot out eight tendrils of smoke and crawled along the ground toward an outcropping of rock, where it spoke again.

"You'll beee soooreeey..."

Ulmaen's mind snapped back to the present, to the spider demon locked away in the Pit. He shook his head at the absurdity of Mithreel expressing love—any demon for that matter. Although, at one time, he had heard a demon speak of his love for another, that same demon issued threats, subjected others to violence, and had killed hundreds, more likely thousands of Elishians since the dawn of civilization. He found it difficult to believe that any creature that felt love could be so destructive.

✴ CHAPTER 36 ✴

This time, Ulmaen walked toward the Prison in broad daylight. Without slowing his pace, he broke away from the dirt path through the tall grass and steered away from the south arm's entrance. He cast a final glance at the guards in the corner watchtowers. No one took notice of him heading into the woods.

The west arm of the Prison looked the same as the east arm. He wanted a better vantage point, so he wove between the trees, along the edge of the woods, until the entire west side of the Prison came into view. He estimated and marked an entry point in the wall.

He didn't want to waste what little of his generation remained, but he needed to know what had happened to Rozafel. As long as he was careful, as long as he found answers, losing a couple of years from his reserve of energy was worth it.

Aiming himself at his destination, he shifted and bolted across the field, zooming through the tips of the long grass, grazing the taller stalks that had gone to seed.

Nearing the wall, he steered himself downward into the ground, pushing through the soil and the iron shell of the old Prison, being careful to avoid contact with any of the demons.

He aimed for the cell with the door inside, but when he stopped, he found himself inside another.

"You're beautiful when you play, Ule," the tree demon said. She blinked sleepily laying curled up in the corner. "Play with me?"

Ulmaen scanned the length of the tunnel for roaming guards. The passage was clear in both directions. He passed through the gate and hesitated, recalling his memory of Mithreel and the cavalier way he had dismissed him so long ago.

"Perhaps another time," he told her. "I've got to find my friend."

He saw a flicker of rage in her eyes as she bowed her head. "Another time," she said.

Ulmaen flew down the tunnel a short way and pushed through a gate. Inside the cell, he stopped to examine the peculiarity of the cast iron door on the far stone wall. Not only was it secured by the gate, it bore two locks of its own.

Normally, he'd forge ahead, but he had learned his lesson. He reached through the door, an arm at a time, and felt his way onto a landing no more than a few feet in width.

Around him, a narrow tunnel had been dug into the earth and stone. Steep steps snaked down and curved to the right, and on every other step a blue crystal emitted a harsh white glow, lighting the way.

He slid down the steps and peered around the bend. More blue crystals dimly lit the space ahead, and he discovered a low-ceilinged underground cavern with most of the bottom filled with water.

The steps he slid along were supported by beams of wood and metal brackets until half way down. The remainder were carved into the cavern wall. High above, the ceiling of the cavern was supported by a network of thicker beams, except for an area to his left that was a heap of rubble and rotten wood, suggesting the cavern must have been bigger at one time.

On the far side of the water, derelict scaffolding hugged heavily striated layers of earth and stone. Intersecting those layers were walls and outlines of doors and window frames, the remnants of buildings trapped in fluvial sediment from thousands of years ago when the area had been heavily flooded.

Spanning the water, he noted a wide wooden bridge that was rotten and black from mold. Running adjacent to it was a pathway worn into the embankment of sediment along the curve of the water's edge, as though people walked there for many years. He wondered if they still walked there for he sensed the presence of several people nearby even though he couldn't see anyone.

There were no exits or entrances to the cavern that he could see, only the precarious steps that led back up to the door in the holding cell of the Pit.

From this vantage point, he realized the cavern was an excavation site; one that he assumed had been abandoned at some point, perhaps due to the water. A series of floods in the past had transformed the landscape considerably, perhaps even shifting the flow of an old river. No matter the reason, the water must have made it difficult to stabilize the scaffolding.

He followed the rock steps down to the very bottom, where they wound alongside the remnants of a large temple partially fused with the cavern wall. It remained mostly intact, except for the uppermost level, what must have been a peaked roof. The front doors were shut, the windows dark and empty.

He floated along the dirt pathway, noticing sediment deposits along outcroppings of limestone as well as the roofs of buildings that receded into the water. On the far side of the cavern, the tiered pattern of houses on top of houses suggested the settlement had been on both sides of a small ravine.

The buildings above water were mostly one and two level buildings with doors and windows worn smooth and round at the corners. Some had been entirely unearthed while others remained partially recessed in stone and rubble. In some of them, he detected flickers of light.

He looked both ways along the edge of the water and then peered beneath its surface. He wasn't sure how the water was entering or exiting the cavern, but it didn't smell bad, which meant it wasn't spill off from the Sewers.

The squeal of old hinges broke the silence. The door to the temple eased open.

He dove into the water of the river, and because he had no true form to make a splash, the water stayed calm. A bald man in a mystic's robe emerged from the temple. He lightly patted his braided beard while he waited.

Eventually, another mystic emerged from the temple, and he immediately recognized Kerista with her signature pursed lips. She shut the door to the temple, waved her hand over the handle as she muttered to herself, then walked beside her companion along the dirt path.

As Kerista and her companion walked past where Ulmaen hid in the water, they both stopped a moment and squinted directly at him. Finally, the man urged Kerista along, and they rounded the temple and climbed the steps to the Prison.

Ulmaen remained in the water, waiting to be sure no one else was around, wondering what business mystics had in a place like this. He felt a gentle current tugging at him and sank into the water, where he found more buildings stacked on top of one another, both sides of the ravine.

The current moved in a southerly direction, pulling him toward a heap of rubble in the collapsed portion of the cavern, and he clung to the rush of water. The debris was extensive, and he could have passed through all of it, but as he dove farther, he saw the chasm was deeper than he initially thought. Near the bottom, a stone archway still intact was tilted at an angle and offered an unobstructed passageway.

He eased through the archway, interrupting a gathering of small yellow fish. As he came close to a wall of packed earth, a silver and black dappled eel bolted from a small cave. The eel dove at him several times before twisting about and slipping back into its home.

The water was fresh with little algae, and as Ulmaen was about to rise to find the surface of the water, he noticed unusual plant life tangled about a bent nail in a giant beam of wood.

He reached to touch the dark, stringy tubular seaweed, the kind that usually grew in clusters. Here, it managed to somehow thrive on its own.

He looked closer.

The texture was finer than he first observed, darker too. The current caused it to undulate, and the seaweed swelled. Ulmaen shuddered. What he had thought was seaweed was a length of knotted black hair.

His mind darkened. He didn't want to believe what Mithreel had told him was true, but he began searching the underground river to be certain.

He dove into the cave, hovering in and out with the eel, both of them occupying the same space until the eel, slipped out and lingered in the underground river.

Ulmaen found nothing in the cave and returned to the river, where the eel curled over the current and side-winded at his side, joining him for the journey.

The cavern shrank and expanded. Buildings forever fossilized in the sediment and rock grew fewer. He scanned the riverbed for nooks and caves and for anything that might tell him how Rozafel's hair had come to be in the water.

The river dipped downward, funneling through a long channel. Nothing could survive the pressure of the current or the flat yet wide cave it connected to, which was entirely submerged in water. Even with his natural ability to see in the dark, he struggled to make out dark shapes on the cavern floor.

Upon closer examination, he discovered the remnants of ancient statues. Floating among them, pulled along by the current yet stuck in place next to the broken face of a giant man, he saw her.

He bolted toward Rozafel. She swayed in the current yet remained still. A length of her woven hair was caught at one end by the crown of a statue; the other was wrapped about her neck.

She floated, otherworldly and weightless, defying the current. If not for the pull on what remained of her hair, her soiled dress, and her bare feet, he would've thought her alive with the way her eyes remained opened.

His mind reeled in confusion. Gorlen had lied. Mithreel hadn't. He shot upward through the bedrock, through the layers of sediment, breaking the surface in the middle of a farmer's cornfield. He bolted into the sky and only when everything on the surface of the world looked small and distant did he stop.

The bird's eye view of the sprawling castle grounds did little to ease his disappointment or his sadness—he'd not only failed Bethereel, but Rozafel, too.

Below, tilled farmland butted against one another. Roads snaked through the golden and green fields, merging into one road which gouged the shanty town markets near Southgate.

"Ulmaen."

He ignored the voice resonating within his chest.

He stared at the castle. No, not one castle, not really. It was several castles, wasn't it. Halls built by different Magnisi, all wanting to stand apart from those who came before them and those who would come after them. Buildings standing on the ruins of previous buildings; rulers standing on the graves of previous rulers. As Ule, he understood the castle differently from the one Ulmaen had discovered.

"Ulmaen, what's wrong?"

Nothing, he thought. Everything.

His mind grappled with how reality as he had always understood it had started to fracture. There were many realities, and he sought a way to fit them back together into one again.

"I'm fine," he projected, realizing that every one of his thoughts and feelings were open to Navalis's scrutiny.

"That's not what I sense. Where are you?"

Ulmaen looked past the castle, at the sprawl of Eastgate, then to the north past Warfield. In the distance, the Woedshor Steppes graduated into mountain. The landscape displayed variation but nothing seemed separate. Buildings fused with forests, farms with rivers, fields into rock—all different yet connected.

"I'll be fine," he assured Navalis.

He wanted his privacy. No, he needed it. He wanted to hear his thoughts alone instead of having them filtered through someone else's. He needed to find his own wisdom. to experience firsthand the profound impact of an epiphany instead of being told what to think and what to feel.

He considered a barrier around his mind, but Navalis was stronger and knew ways to break through it, so he started focusing his thoughts and emotions into other areas of his body, the way he had been taught.

As he floated above the world, he realized reality wasn't fractured; it was simply flexible, taking on forms and shapes and colors for what was required in different regions. Like a painting, he thought. Like the landscape below.

When he grew bored with the vista and with his thoughts and feelings, he pushed through a layer of converging clouds, returned to the woods by the Prison, and shifted back into solid form.

His sadness hadn't lifted, only receded. He knew now that every part of reality, regardless of how it appeared, cast a shadow. Knowing that, he found it difficult to look anyone in the eye, to smile, but he couldn't continue behaving this way without raising suspicion.

Somehow, he forced himself to smile, to laugh as well, and felt his own shadow begin to grow.

❊ CHAPTER 37 ❊

Navalis stooped as he followed Kerista through the low-ceilinged Catacomb tunnel. She had others helping investigate the collapsed gallery, but today, for some reason, she wanted his assistance. Wary of her reasons, he kept at a safe distance.

"I dreamed about you the other night," she told him when they had moved past the last few workers reinforcing beams.

Her confession unnerved him. Was she expressing a desire for a certain type of intimacy? Or had she convinced herself that a relationship already existed between them?

The tunnel grew a little smaller in circumference. By reflex, he breathed in deeply, even though he didn't need to, for fresh air was being piped in along the tunnels and through the galleries above.

Kerista looked over her shoulder toward him, waiting for a reaction.

He had other priorities that needed attending, like acquiring another specimen, but he recognized the game she wanted to play. In response, he scratched the back of his neck, then shrugged.

"Any word on an older demon yet?" he asked, hoping to change the subject.

She stopped and blocked the way. "We've the oldest demons alive according to our records, all tucked away in the Pit, if you really want an *old* one."

All this time he'd been waiting, when he could have chosen one first hand. Why had she sent hunters to catch them when they had already been caught? Why had they been imprisoned and not killed?

"When you say the oldest, how old exactly?"

Kerista stepped aside as best she could in the narrow tunnel, motioning to him to take the lead down a flight of steps.

As he squeezed by, their chests brushing each other, Kerista smirked, and he couldn't tell if she was amused by this question or by their touching.

"I figured you knew about them," she said.

"Why?"

"You and your brother-in-law don't discuss everything after all."

He remained quiet as he descended the steps. Something in the way she spoke felt accusatory.

"If Ulmaen is a demon-sympathizer, which I suspect he is, that won't bode well for your reputation here."

Had Kerista asked him to join her today to discuss politics? At the bottom of the steps, he turned round to face her. "What makes you say he's a sympathizer?"

She winced, not caring at all for the way he refused to be cowed by her threat. "I have a source that says he lingers in the Pit, he's been seen talking with the demons."

Here the tunnel was wider, and Kerista slipped by him and down the last few steps. His step faltered as he followed her again. He'd been so preoccupied with his own studies, he only now realized Ulmaen had been servicing the Prison and hadn't said a word to him about demons being held there.

His mind clamped down; his jaw, too. His desire to specialize in demons as a mystic had been mentioned casually during conversation, but he had never directly discussed his true agenda with Ulmaen, as per the instructions of the Xiinisi Council.

Surely, Ulmaen must have detected his sincere interest in the subject matter, but lately he hadn't been as forthcoming as usual. He'd always go on about his latest discoveries, no matter how insignificant they were. There must have been something of interest worth mentioning about the Pit, yet Ulmaen had said nothing.

Navalis decided to remain silent on the subject.

"This isn't why I asked you here," Kerista assured him. "Aren't you curious about my dream?" She ducked beneath a partially fallen beam and stepped over another strewn across the ground.

"No offense," he told her, "but it's been my experience that dreams are only interesting to the ones who dreamed them."

Kerista laughed, not in her usual way. It was short and sharp, a little too harsh. "Perhaps," she said. "Still, as mystics you must admit we acquire unique insights during our dream states."

"True." He agreed with the sentiment, aware that all states of consciousness were valued by the mystics, as well as the Xiinisi. He mentally noted the similarity between Elish and his own realm and the unsettling way it made him feel.

Kerista stood aside from the mouth of the collapsed gallery, the one where Ule had harvested her first new molecular array without discretion. The masons had done a great job clearing out debris. What remained of the ceiling had been reinforced, and he could see into the gallery above.

Nearby, the wreckage had been tidied into a pile close to where Goyas's body had lain. The tile floor had been swept clean and what remained of Goyas's robe was neatly folded. As he changed his vantage point, he saw something peculiar beside the robe. Drawn with salt on the ground was a circle altar. Inside sat four half burned candles marking each cardinal direction, and at the very center lay a silver ring.

The circle didn't conform to any ritual he knew, and he wondered if this was how arch mystics honored their predecessors.

Kerista gestured to him to enter the gallery, and he did so with great care, stepping over piles of broken wood, stone, and plaster. The number of bodies had diminished compared to what he had witnessed before the gallery collapsed, and he surmised they were being relocated.

At the moment, only he and Kerista were present.

"I assure you, I'm not in the habit of sharing my dreams with apprentices," she told him. "However, this dream seemed significant. You see, in it you weren't a mystic. No, you had another profession. You were a blacksmith."

A stab of fear—just a cautionary pinprick really—drove deep into his gut. He tried to shield his worry with amusement. How had she seen that image in her dreams?

"That's interesting," he told her. "Perhaps you're developing a talent for determining previous lives."

Kerista moved into the mouth of the gallery. "Perhaps," she agreed. "Know what else I found curious about the dream? Everyone called you Navalis, except you. Do you know what you called yourself?"

He dreaded hearing the answer.

"Avn."

The name shook through him. He shuddered.

"It's an unusual name, don't you think?"

There was no way she could know the name. He'd made sure Avn the blacksmith had been seen traveling south, long past the desert, heading out in a boat on the Attalaga Sea. Once the boat reached port, he disembarked and disappeared into the mountains, where he Ascended back to his realm.

"You also called yourself Xiin... Xiinisi."

Navalis froze at the reference to his people. Recovering himself, he cleared his throat. "What's that?"

"What? You don't know that word?" She drew closer to him. "How odd. Entire sections of Goyas's journals are dedicated to his attempts at speaking to one. Didn't you read the journals I lent to you?"

He had read them. He should have known about the reference. Unsure of what to say, he turned toward her and asked, "How do you spell—"

"Don't play with me!" Kerista grew rigid and tense. "I asked around. There was a blacksmith named Avn. He had a smithy in Sondshor Market a few years back, but before then? He worked for Adinav."

"You must've heard of him before—"

"Never."

Tentative and cautious, she drew closer to him.

He'd never seen her afraid.

"I know what you are." Her gaze roved over him again, as it had done before, and he understood now why she had asked him here. She knew what he was and sought some indication, a physical trait, anything at all that indicated he was a god.

She began to shake. Her eyes, wide and frantic, swam with desire. "It's true then. You're Xiinisi, just like the one trapped inside that stone!"

Navalis stilled his rising anxiety at the mention of a stone. He momentarily forgot he was pretending to be a mystic, pretending to be an Elishian. "What stone?"

"The one that horrible little man kept in his show," she told him. "I thought it was a soul bound to a stone, an old soul, but no matter how I tried, I couldn't release the poor thing. I tried communicating with it the way Goyas had with his."

She laid the palm of her hand on his chest, carefully at first.

"I thought I might accomplish what he couldn't, but I gave up, kept the stone by my bed, and every night since, whatever is inside has been feeding my dreams with notions of you; different faces, different names, yet everyone is the same on the inside somehow."

Her fingers curled into the fabric of his tunic, touching him with a reverence he didn't know she was capable of. "Acquiring power comes so easy to some. It's been a struggle, but I'm willing. Teach me." Her breath shallowed. "Whatever it takes. I'll do your bidding."

Her thirst for knowledge was strong, her hunger for power even stronger. Navalis admired her conviction, yet pitied her desperation. He understood now what had motivated her to investigate the fallen gallery. Goyas.

She was the one who had relocated his body. She had eaten his flesh, an ancient form of magic he'd seen in many cultures on many worlds. By ingesting an object, the eater would then take on the traits of that object.

Kerista had intended to imbue herself with the old mystic's Clear Sight. She'd accomplished the ability through sorcery and not in the manner of honing perception the way Goyas had. It explained why her ability only worked occasionally. It explained her migraines too—withdrawal from the potions made from ingested flesh.

Pretending he wasn't Xiinisi was futile, he realized. He straightened himself, disengaging her from his robe.

Kerista squeezed her eyes shut. "Don't kill me. I won't tell anyone what you are." Her voice was plaintive and diminished. "I've still got so much to learn."

"Why do you learn?"

Kerista backed away. She held up a hand in defense. "To be more powerful. To assure my position, regardless of who is elected."

"Lyan is your Magnes."

She found strength in her voice again. "One of many who will vie for the Chair in the years to come. Do you honestly think anyone will honor the election results?"

"They must. It's law."

She tilted her head. "They'll do what they've been doing for thousands of years—fight! And the winner will take power. When another Magnes like Adinav comes along, I'll be ready. I won't be a puppet. Ever the na, I swear."

"Have more faith in Lyan—"

"What does it matter to you. You're a god. The workings of this world must be trivial to your kind."

They weren't, he realized. At least not when it came to this world. Elish and its demons were of great significance, something to be both truly curious and concerned about.

"Please!" She fell to her knees.

He found her peculiar in that moment. The strength and tenacity she was known for vanished. She fussed and fiddled with the hem of his tunic, and he found it distracting.

He gagged. Vinegar and mint stung his nostrils, and he recognized Kerista's magic scent. The gallery began to fill with smoke that billowed from beneath his robe, the collar, and the ends of his sleeves. He stumbled back, clutching at the hem, where he found she had written an unusual symbol with blood from the tip of one of her fingers.

The smoke swirled and began to turn into tendrils, smaller and tighter around him, pulling him over the ground.

Kerista's lower lip trembled. Her eyes narrowed as she tightened a fist. She mouthed the words of an incantation. The tendrils obeyed her and dug into his flesh as they dragged him toward the circle altar, intending to bind him to the ring there.

Kerista's perception sharpened and twisted. The smoke transformed into fine, fierce ropes of energy that exceeded his strength—even his Xiinisi strength.

Instinctively, he knew a way to defeat the binding spell. He calmed himself, cast Kerista a dark look, and shifted. The tension between his molecules became phantoms in the world. Her lasso, finding nothing to hold onto, dissintegrated.

He bolted across the room till he stood before Kerista then rematerialized. The force slammed her against what remained of a pillar. Pinned there, the span of his hand pressed against her forehead, his palm aligned with the location of her pineal gland.

Frightened, she struggled against his strength, and when she realized she couldn't move, she succumbed.

"Please," she said again, struggling for air. This time, her plea was genuine, for he felt her tremble.

He loathed her in that moment. So vulnerable, so pathetic. She couldn't continue on with knowledge of him, knowledge of the Xiinisi, not with her abilities. Though he admired her desire for autonomy over herself, it had been born out of fear, and that fear made her a threat.

He regarded the dilation of her pupils, the wild way her eyes darted, and he leaned in close and told her, "I'm sorry." He pressed his palm against her forehead and released a jolt of energy from his inner reserve.

The pulse was strong enough to interrupt the flow of oxygen to her brain, long enough for memory cells to begin dying.

Kerista's body began to convulse as the damage set in. He released her head, and cradled her body as she spasmed.

He could have veiled some of her memories using his mind, but given her power of perception, she'd eventually detect those veils. This way was harsher but more effective.

After a couple of forced deep breaths, he slung her across one of his shoulders. He stopped a moment to destroy the circle altar and scatter the candles and Goyas's robe, then hurried from the gallery, hollering for the nearest worker.

He rushed from the tunnel into the Mortuary, where he carefully laid her across one of the redstone slabs.

A guard on duty left his post by the entrance.

"She's had some sort of seizure," Navalis told the young man.

The guard's boyish face paled at the small bubbling of froth forming at the side of Kerista's mouth.

"Fetch Osblod now!"

She spasmed again, and the young guard froze a moment. Finding himself, he dashed from the chamber to make his way across the castle grounds to the Infirmary in search of assistance.

Navalis cradled Kerista's head in his hands. He sensed her presence completely disconnected from the neural network of her brain. Communication with the outside world was well beyond her ability now.

"I won't let you die," he projected into what remained of her conscious mind. "But if you want authentic power, then your mind must find a way back on its own."

❋ CHAPTER 38 ❋

Ulmaen set out to explore the shadows and discovered they were well guarded. Overheard conversations were the most difficult to infiltrate, now that he was truly listening, and he was stunned at how many people wrapped themselves in verbal veils to shield some aspect of their lives, usually a lover on the side or some sordid event from the past.

Everyone had secrets.

The shadows themselves banded together into a wall, and Ulmaen searched for a doorway through them. He wanted answers, and somewhere on the other side of those shadows was illumination to a dark, treacherous secret—the confession of a murderer.

He drained time and energy from his current generation to begin a swift, methodical search of the castle grounds. He hoped he wouldn't deathmorph too soon. If he found what he was looking for, the sacrifice would be worth it.

He chose the early morning, that quiet time when those celebrating Kerista's illness had passed out from exhaustion and the servants hadn't yet woken to begin their day. His chances of being seen by anyone then were few.

He laid on his mattress, listening to servants squirm and shuffle in their beds, waiting for their heavy breathing and deep snores. Once they were asleep, he shifted his body, pushed through the straw and the floor beneath, and came to a stop inside a storage room. From there, he began his search.

Every morning thereafter, he shifted and systematically explored the castle grounds. He searched for anything that might provide clues to the identity of Ule's murderer.

He began on the east side of the castle and worked his way west, knowing the farther he roamed from Kugilla Hall, the less time he'd have to search before returning to begin his duties for the day.

He searched every broom closet and the tower of every building. He slid through walls and furniture, peeked into drawers and cupboards, then moved on to the next unexplored space. After several mornings, he discovered certain buildings had sub-cellars, which led to tunnels and rooms beneath the ground, including the Sewers.

Beneath the ground was mostly soil and boulders, but when he breezed through an old stone wall, he hadn't expected to find a hollow tower on the other side. The tower belonged to an old castle, which he estimated spanned the area from the Starry Rise to the Old Slate Tower by the Dining Hall and the Armory.

He scrutinized every room that hadn't been filled in with earth or rubble, and discovered that some of them were still in use, though he didn't know why.

In one room, he watched an apprentice mystic copy glyphs from a stash of old parchments. In another, three master mystics were huddled together, speaking in whispers. When they sensed something nearby, they fell silent and only resumed their whispering again once Ulmaen retreated.

He moved back and forth, layer by layer through the rudimentary architecture—the square towers, the small rooms, the simple archways. Most of the chambers were empty or stacked with miscellaneous furniture.

Occasionally, he found small laboratories. One in particular captured his curiosity for jars of green liquid lined the walls near a metal table, and the workbench and cupboards were filled to the brim with all sorts of crystals, scopes, and tools.

He moved down through the lower levels of the castle, discovered discarded treasures locked away in abandoned wardrobes or sealed in walls. In the collapsed dungeon of the castle, he passed through a floor of iron.

Below that, blocks of marble were buried under thick layers of sediment, and farther down he saw a great mound of black rocks piled in a symmetrical pattern. Between the rocks, small streams of water trickled into the soil.

He aimed upward again, pushing past the layer of iron. As he began another pass of the underground world, he rose up to the base of a tower in the old castle. As he was about to whiz by, he spied a break in the wall, where the steps to the main floor had collapsed. Something within the darkness shimmered.

He zoomed toward the small alcove, and recognized a flat stone dais, the kind used to support a figurine or statue. What he saw there was something else entirely.

He gazed in awe at a fissure that warped and bent the air. Light oscillated along the edge of the rift.

My Safeway, he thought. It can't be!

The gateway to his realm had been dismantled long ago. It must have been. After the An Energy had receded from Elish, Ule hadn't any need for it anymore. She was incarcerated at that time, and the Safeway reflected the Isolation Chamber—a dark place curtained with matter-infused An Energy, dark threads waiting to be woven into new creations. Seeing it day to day had pained her.

When the An Energy was abundant, she had laced together molecular patterns to create different types of rock, vegetation, and striations of gas to create an atmosphere. The biological inhabitants of the world at that time often had many concerns, questions, and later on fears.

For a while, she had been afraid, too. Once the An Energy had receded and the world stabilized, she had felt safer. She'd wandered off, distancing herself from the Safeway, especially when she had been preoccupied with playing games with Elishevera.

For a time, she kept the Safeway open, waiting and hoping to see something other than a ripple of darkness in the air. At the first glimpse of another vista, she'd planned to jump through and be among her kind again, for on her realm's end, the Safeway was anchored in proximity to Elish and she'd emerge in whatever location the planet was being kept.

In Elish, the Safeway could be half way round the world, yet she'd be able to will it to her side in an instant. Since no one waited for her— no friends, no Mentors or Masters, no one to love—Ule must have wandered off, immersed in world building, forgetting all about it.

Now, here it was. So much smaller than what he remembered. The edges of the rift glowed, alternating between gold and silver. Sprigs of blue light crawled over the opening. What truly captured his attention was the image he saw in the rupture.

He'd only ever seen darkness through the fissure. Now, he watched images from his realm. Students skirted the perimeter of a dais containing a similar world to Elish. Their faces were distorted by the thin barrier which separated the dimension of Elish from that of Xii, but it was beautiful.

Lined in gold and silver...

Words drifted through his mind, and he recalled conversations with Mbjard stuck in his head. He fought the intrusion of the man's voice, but something Mbjard had once said demanded attention, and he vocalized the description.

"Lined in gold and silver and sapphires..."

... like water, he thought. Contained water? A sea or an ocean? Or was it a mirror? Yes, like a mirror.

"Lined in gold and silver and sapphires, and within a shimmering reflection, a rolling sea of mystery."

That was it. That was what Mbjard was always muttering under his breath. The very treasure Mbjard sought—the one Istok had referred to, and Mithreel, too—wasn't some jeweled mirror or a scrying cup; the treasure was the Safeway.

Perhaps to someone long ago it seemed mystical, inspiring them to write of its beauty. Over the years the description was re-interpreted again and again, understanding flipping back and forth between the literal and the metaphorical. Ultimately, the treasure was just a conduit between two dimensions.

He dared not use it. There was no guarantee it hadn't degraded over time in the absence of the An Energy, even though it seemed fully intact. He wondered if he should dismantle it, but without an abundance of An

Energy, he wouldn't be able to restore it. It was a relic, and for that reason alone, he decided to let it be.

I should tell Navalis about this at least, he thought. Then he realized, the entire time they had been trapped in the world—hundreds of Elishian years—they could have easily returned home had he known about the Safeway. Given his Master's temper, he decided to stay quiet about it— keep it a secret.

Ulmaen looked about, peered up into the main tower of the old castle beneath the ground. He wouldn't have left it behind here, he realized. The castle hadn't existed then, which meant someone else must have taken great care to hide it in the wall.

He bolted up the stairwell a ways and looked back the way he had come. The rubble hid the Safeway well from this vantage point, and since no one came from below anymore, because the main floor was filled in with earth and rubble, he didn't feel the need to move it.

He wound around the tower, rising high. He passed the laboratory with the strange green liquid, then the entrance to the tunnel leading to Fehran's Hall. He bolted through the ground and the rush of water from the Starry Rise, and shot into the air until he hovered high above.

Dawn had come. He needed to return to begin his morning service duties, then later, his studies in the library. Come next day, he'd continue where he left off, moving west over and under and through the grounds Sondshor Castle.

✳ CHAPTER 39 ✳

Soldiers loitered about the barracks. Some hung about open doorways chatting to one another, and although they didn't have to, some cooked breakfast over small fire pits set in the yard.

Navalis walked among them. He avoided their cheery gazes, reeled at their hangover breaths, and whenever he bumped into one, his own breathing shallowed. Vulgar jokes were bandied about, their battle-trained voices beating into him, reminding him of the war.

Some of the soldiers milling about were old enough to have fought during the last ten years of Adinav's reign. The older ones, a bit longer. Navalis had fought in the entire war, all one hundred years of it, regenerating over and over. He could have crawled into a cave somewhere and waited it out, but someone had to stop Adinav before he ripped the world apart in his determination to get to the realm beyond Elish.

They hadn't been at war now for several years, he reminded himself. Still, anxiety tore through him, and he breathed a heavy sigh of relief as he entered the Infirmary. Inside the door, he glanced into the Examination Room where he had watched over Ule's body. The room hadn't changed much since then—the same cupboards with the same specimens floating in amber jars. This time, the shutters to the windows had been swung wide open, letting in sunlight.

As he softly treaded past the room and along the wide corridor, he hoped to avoid anyone else, worrying he'd be forced to create an elaborate fiction to explain his actions. When it came to lying, omissions were easy to manage. Presenting false information, however, had always been problematic. No matter how many possible contingencies he imagined developing from his lies, in this world there was a random element he couldn't predict.

Navigating the truth was challenging at times, simply because it produced unpredictable outcomes. Lies, however, had a way of growing into more lies which made them difficult to track. That's why he kept to himself, so he wouldn't be forced to invent too much about his past. He only wanted to fulfill his mandate: Study demons and train Ulmaen as Sentinel. Instead, he had two issues to settle.

First, he needed to recover the Stone of Istok. On two occasions, he had sneaked into Kerista's sleeping quarter, and worried someone else had found it and their dreams were being manipulated by the demon.

Second, he needed to determine the extent of the damage he had inflicted on Kerista, to be certain she was silenced, at least for a little while. There was no way to know how she'd respond to the injury. She might be in a genuine catatonic state or she might be honing her perception skills.

If so, he wanted to know the rate at which she was healing.

He'd already used a considerable amount of time from his current generation. He had shifted to visit Rolen's farm, and he had restored himself after being oxygen deprived in a Catacomb gallery, where Ule had deathmorphed into a man. These events had had a cumulative effect, sapping time from his reserve of energy, and he didn't want to waste any more of it on anything that didn't absolutely require it. The search for the stone could be done manually, as an Elishian. Seeing into Kerista, however, required his Xiinisi abilities.

He turned the corner and passed through a doorway which opened up into a long room at the back of the building. The straw beds were lined up along the plastered walls. most of them empty. He neared the only one surrounded by a green curtain, and slipped behind it.

Kerista laid neatly tucked between pristine sheets, her face paler than before. Her eyes widened and bulged at the sight of him.

Worried that her cognitive abilities were far better than he initially thought, he sat on a stool next to the bed and inhaled deeply, preparing to push his perception into her body. His vision turned microscopic as it descended through folded layers of her neural tissue. He pushed farther, until he saw the neural network on a cellular level.

She was conscious, her thoughts forming and remaining trapped with no means of expression. Her mind struggled against its physical restrictions, experimenting with patterns and potency. She was honing her thoughts but with no effect, at least not yet.

"Who's there?"

He recognized Osblod's distinguished voice. He reacted quickly, cradling Kerista's hand in his, to give the impression that he cared for her.

Osblod peeked through the curtain.

"Just come to see how she's doing," Navalis told him.

Osblod frowned. He pulled back the curtain with a fierce tug. "You were there with her when this happened, eh? You sure there isn't a detail you've overlooked?"

In moments like these, Navalis might consider lying, but the truth offered an intriguing opportunity to determine, once and for all, Osblod's true character.

Navalis stared down at Kerista. "The master mystics sometimes get involved in clandestine practices. She never talked to anyone about them."

Osblod remained silent.

"Just... It could be..."

Osblod must have sensed his hesitation because he patted him on the shoulder. "Tell me anything," he urged.

"I don't have any proof."

Navalis rested Kerista's hand back on the bed alongside her body.

He stood and drew Osblod away from the curtain. "I think she's been..."

"Come now, spit it out."

Navalis lowered his voice. "She's been eating the dead."

Osblod cocked an eyebrow. "Interesting. And illegal."

"It's believed to imbue the eater with the abilities the deceased possessed when they were alive," Navalis explained.

Osblod winced. "Perhaps." He rubbed his chin. "I suppose she would believe that, even though the practice was banned a long time ago."

Navalis nodded. "True," he agreed and then added, "Because the deceased would not arrive in Mxalem intact."

Osblod shook his head. "No, no. Vultures might be able to stomach rotting flesh, but even they know when to quit. *Spreading disease* was the true reason for passing the law against it." He tsked in the direction of Kerista. "Could be something in the decayed flesh that's affected her. Any idea who she's been eating?"

Navalis shook his head, even though he knew. The body of Goyas had been picked at, then later harvested by Ulmaen and incorporated into his Student's new molecular array. There was no body to be found, nothing to examine.

"Most likely a mystic," he suggested. "Which one is anyone's guess."

"A shame this happened." Osblod sighed. "If word of this gets around..."

Navalis wondered if Osblod would keep the information to himself. Or would he convey yet another unfortunate bit of news that promised to further taint Lyan's already sullied campaign?

As he watched Osblod stand in silence, his head bowed in thought, one of those unpredictable outcomes wiggled into Navalis's mind. If the truth got out and Kerista's intentions came under question, there was a possibility that everyone under Kerista's guidance, every apprentice and adept mystic, even the masters, would be treated the same.

Osblod pointed a thick finger at him. "No evidence, eh?"

Navalis shrugged, already thinking of ways to stall a future investigation of the mystics.

"None whatsoever?" Osblod blinked in astonishment. "I mean, have you looked for any?"

Other than the Stone of Istok, Navalis hadn't looked for anything else. Kerista's sleeping quarters had lacked many personal belongings and none of her professional paraphernalia revealed anything.

"No, I haven't," he answered.

"Maybe you should, eh?" He paused a moment. "Think you could do that?"

"The thing about eating the dead," Navalis began to explain, "is that the evidence gets destroyed in the process."

Osblod chuckled at the comment. "Think you're smart, eh? How about you head back to that tower of yours and start looking for the parts she hasn't eaten yet. Or how about the formula or ritual or any personal notes she might have made."

"And what if I don't?" Navalis regretted the words the moment he spoke them. He hadn't meant to challenge Osblod; he was simply curious.

"Could be I tell Gorlen, and you know how he gets. Do you want inspections of the tower? There'd be inquiries with every single one of you. Mneos only knows what your kind get up to in there. If Lyan found out anything untoward he'd let go of the lot of you."

Navalis hadn't expected threats from Osblod, although he agreed with the scenario Osblod presented. Lyan would deem every mystic in his employ compromised and then fire them all.

"I'll make it worth your while to stay quiet," he told Osblod, hoping he was the kind of man to negotiate. "I'll look for evidence, but I need more time. What do you say?"

Osblod wiped the side of his head and sighed. "I have to tell Gorlen. It's my obligation."

Navalis panicked. "Think of Lyan and what this might do to his campaign."

"Ah, sacking all the mystics might work in his favor," Osblod proposed, "given that nobody likes your kind very much. Did you see how everyone celebrated when Kerista fell ill?"

The truth suddenly became a challenge. At first, Navalis didn't care if all the mystics were expelled from the castle. Then he realized that without access to their laboratories and their instruments, his demon studies would be more difficult to pursue. He needed to protect the mystics somehow.

"Give me a couple of days," he demanded.

Osblod licked his lips. "Can't do it, friend. Your kind are slippery. You might make up evidence. I figure by the time I see Gorlen, it'll be nightfall. If you find something before then, I'll stay quiet a little longer."

Navalis was about to protest when Osblod raised his hand and said, "Take the offer."

Navalis departed the Infirmary with haste. Outside again, he was struck by anxiety, but it wasn't the kind stirred by memories of the war. Instead, he was struggling to figure out how to protect the mystics and secure their positions once Kerista's cannibalistic activities became known.

He rushed across the southern Colonnade and navigated through courtyards, skirted the Inner Sanctum, crossed the eastern Colonnade into the courtyard of Fehran's Hall and climbed the steps of the retaining wall two at a time. The entire time he mentally played with ways to distort the truth, to add to it what hadn't been there before, and prepared himself for the lies he'd need to tell.

No, stay within the truth, he reminded himself. Even though the truth had complicated his situation, he began to see that the truth contained a solution as well.

He ran past the Gatehouse and the Treasury, picking up speed in the field where the Mystics Tower stood, so that when he burst into the main laboratory and climbed onto a chair, he struggled for breath.

Adepts and apprentices milled around their work stations. Only Boriag looked up from his workbench and acknowledged him with a curt nod. He blinked a few times, as though struck by curiosity, and he meandered over to where Navalis stood on the chair.

"How's Kerista doing?" he asked.

Navalis inhaled violently through his nostrils as he answered. "About the same."

Boriag pouted a moment, then looked up again. "Soooo, why are you standing on that chair?"

Breathing easily again, Navalis brought his fingers to his lips and whistled loud and hard. The laboratory fell silent. All heads turned toward him, including two master mystics who sat at the long table.

"I just came back from the Infirmary," he announced. "There's a theory, a rumor, that Kerista has been eating the dead to imbue herself with powers."

"Eeeewww," Boriag whined. "She wouldn't. It's... It's gross! I wouldn't even do that, and that says a lot, doesn't it?"

"It doesn't matter if the rumor is true or not," Navalis told everyone. "What matters is that by nightfall this place is going to be crawling with Gorlen's guards searching for evidence to support this rumored behavior."

The master mystics stood abruptly, their chairs scraping the floor. They paled as they muttered amongst themselves.

"I know some of you with unofficial studies are stationed elsewhere, off the castle grounds, but for those of you concealing anything in this tower, we need to be rid of it or we'll be gotten rid of."

The master mystics both began shouting orders. Apprentices and adepts scrambled about the lab gathering up materials. Everyone grew frenzied and manic.

Navalis stepped down from the chair and approached the masters. "If you permit it, I'll search Kerista's laboratory and hide anything there, unless you feel you should."

The older of the master mystics trembled. He agreed to Navalis's offer, and made it clear that anything unusual be hidden immediately and they would examine it themselves once the investigation had finished.

Navalis ducked inside the doorway to Kerista's laboratory, and began to search, scanning the shelves and bookcases and sliding open every drawer in the cupboards.

Boriag had followed him into the room and stood by the door, his mouth agape. Stunned, he didn't dare move but he hadn't lost his voice. "W-what's going on? What are you doing?"

Misgivings about Boriag made Navalis avert his gaze. "Searching for anything that might incriminate Kerista and indirectly us," he replied.

He pulled open a small drawer and discovered small vials of blue amber and lenses wrapped in soft cloth. So far, nothing out of the ordinary.

Boriag lowered his voice. "If she's done something wrong, they should know, don't you think?"

Navalis considered his role as mystic in the Elishian world, and how a mystic might respond to such a rumor. They'd see it as a threat, and they'd do what they could to protect their own kind. His actions were justified and authentic.

"Think about it," he snapped. "If Kerista's been up to no good, why wouldn't we be up to no good?"

"But some of us *are* up to no good."

Navalis shuddered at Boriag's admission. Now that he knew the story about the demon born at Rolen's farm, the eventual impact of that knowledge, if it were true, might end their friendship.

"We're under her guidance," he explained. "Suspicion is going to come down on all of us. Even if Lyan keeps the Chair, he won't be able to trust us. We won't be just out of work and unable to study, we'll never be trusted again. Ever! Anywhere! By anyone!"

The truth, embellished with a little drama, sunk into Boriag with great speed.

"I didn't think." He looked back toward the main laboratory, then at the bookshelf. "What can I do?"

"Do you have anything you're hiding?"

"Nope."

"Then start searching." Navalis returned to rummaging through another drawer.

Boriag stood upright, trying to act casual, but fidgeted instead. "She keeps something up on the shelf behind the stack of blue books."

Navalis paused a moment. "How do you know that?"

"Walked in on her once. She wasn't too happy about it. Come to think of it, I've walked in on her a lot. She's got a cot stashed away behind that shelf, did you know? She sleeps in here most nights."

Navalis hadn't known she slept in her laboratory, and he realized the Stone of Istok must be in here somewhere. He spotted the stack of blue books. He reached for them but they were too high. He pulled a stool toward the shelf, and once he climbed onto it, could see faint lines where fingers had trailed through the dust on top of the bookcase. Behind the blue books he found a large iron key blackened by age.

He searched the room and found a small bureau with a drawer tucked beneath her laboratory worktable. He tried the key in it and the locked clicked. The drawer slid open, revealing a number of items wrapped in cloth.

He picked up the closest object wrapped in blue satin. The fabric slipped away, revealing a dark green kornerupine with a fine line of pink through the middle.

"Ah, it's you again!" Istok's disembodied voice thundered in Navalis's mind. "Tried to warn that lady about you, but you're still here. Didn't work, did it?"

"No," Navalis replied.

"What's that?" Boriag called out.

Navalis peered over his shoulder and noticed Boriag had finally regained mobility. He was feeling the backs of each bookcase along each shelf. Every now and again, he pulled out a thin journal tucked behind the other books.

"Nothing," Navalis mumbled. He returned his attention to the other items in the drawer.

"Such a shame," Istok continued. "I killed you once, almost twice. But you can't die, can you? You know, once I'm out of this stone, I can kill you again and again, forever, if you'd like."

What Istok didn't know, and didn't need to know, was that their kind could die. They all eventually experienced the Quietus, the relinquishing of their final generation.

Navalis fished out the pouch that hung from his neck and stuffed the kornerupine deep inside.

"So what's happened to the old girl?" Istok asked. "I've never been able to muck about in people's minds till her. Thankfully she ditched that iron box and I was free to cast my thoughts. Oh, and did I ever tell you, when I'm whole again, I'm going to fucking kill you? Again and again..."

Satisfied with finding Istok, Navalis searched the drawer. He detected a glint of light, something soulful and sentient peeking from beneath a beige handkerchief. He lifted the fabric and regarded a humanoid eyeball.

"You listening to me?"

Navalis ignored the demon and picked up a glass sphere containing a well-preserved crystal blue eye floating in amber resin.

Istok squealed in disgust, exaggerating the sound. "Who keeps an eye in a drawer? Eh, do you think she killed the guy and carved out that eye herself?"

Navalis couldn't say who the eye belonged to. He held it up and pushed his perception into the tissue. A flash of white pierced his vision. If he had to make an educated guess? It had belonged to a mystic, hopefully one that had been dead and not alive during the extraction.

He cradled it in his one palm, along with the stone, and pulled out another object wrapped in soft black leather. Inside was a large glass lens.

Something in the interior moved. When he examined it closer, he discovered the glass lens was hollow and was filled with fluid.

"She's got a Lilamon Eye, too!" Boriag's complaint was shrill and whiny.

A Lilamon Eye was a remnant from ancient times that involved extracting eye fluid from powerful and living mystics. The glass lens increased the power of perception for anyone who looked through it. The extraction process usually resulted in blinding and death for the targeted mystic, so the manufacturing or possession of one had been outlawed in Sondshor and Woedshor.

Navalis found more items in the drawer, eyes and fingers and other strange objects. He figured the pieces had all belonged to mystics, and possession of them was illegal. He wondered how Kerista had come to own them. Had she procured them herself?

"Oh, hey!" Boriag said unusually loud. "He blocked the doorway with his arms. "What brings you here?"

Hastily, Navalis emptied the contents of the drawer, dispersing the contraband into various pockets within his tunic. He was about to ask who Boriag was talking to when he heard a strong, earthy, feminine voice.

"We're looking for a mystic. The one who got clobbered by a horse a while back?"

"Oh yeah, that's me!" Boriag grew excited. "Um!" He looked back over his shoulder, at Navalis. "Everything taken care of?"

Navalis nodded, straightening his tunic.

Boriag barreled through the door, and Navalis followed him this time, keeping a wide space between them.

Back in the main laboratory, only a couple of apprentices remained. They were clearly confused by everything that was happening and probably had no inclination of doing or possessing anything illegal, so they went about their work. The other mystics, however, had retreated to their private quarters in upper floors to hide their secrets.

Two women stood in the main entrance. Navalis recognized Hazias's daughters from back when he had been a blacksmith in Sondshor Market. Back then, they'd been younger, a little shorter, and less intimidating.

"Aesa," he said to the one peering from behind her messy hair. "Mera," he addressed the other, who stood behind her sister, hand on hip, short hair spiked like a burr.

Aesa sighed. Leaning back toward Mera, she said, "He knows us. How grand!"

Mera wrinkled her nose. Her words came swift and curt. "We're here about a commission." She winked at Navalis. "Please tell me you're the one. I'd definitely pay to see you struck down by a horse again. Maybe make you feel better after—"

"Me!" Boriag blurted. "It's me. I'm the one. Me. That's right."

"I'll be in Kerista's room," Navalis told Boriag, as he carefully made his way to the stairwell landing. "If any mystics return, you tell them what I told everyone here about Kerista. They'll know what to do." He patted his tunic to convey to Boriag he'd found plenty of incriminating objects.

Boriag nodded to indicate he understood.

"Well?" Mera demanded.

Boriag's attention snapped back the sisters. "I need a knife," he told them. "Two of them. Identical to one another." He lunged toward his desk and rifled through a pile of parchment. "One to keep as is, the other for imbuing. You know, for demonstrating a comparison."

Aesa shook her head. "No, I don't know. And I don't want to know."

Mera regarded her sister. "Sounds like we should ask for money up front. He smells like anise seed."

"Oh that's just my magic scent," Boriag told them. "You should smell some of the other guys."

Navalis motioned silently to the apprentices, indicating he meant to continue his search upstairs. They nodded to convey they understood. He paused on the first step, looked back toward Boriag showing the sisters a design he'd drawn.

"Like this, thin and narrow. Not a traditional blade. A spike, see? With a hilt."

Aesa took the drawing and examined it. "You want two spike daggers then?"

"Is that what they're called?" Boriag asked.

"Yeah," Mera said.

Boriag nodded excitedly, seeming to have forgotten everything that had happened, everything he'd been told.

Navalis climbed the stairs, two at a time. His intention of searching Kerista's room was a ruse. He'd already done it several times. He went there again and shut the door, grateful he had stuck to telling the truth, for it had proved bountiful.

He was especially satisfied with the way the truth had led him directly to the Stone of Istok, which he slipped into the pouch about his neck before anyone could see.

* CHAPTER 40 *

Ulmaen counted the shadows during his predawn searches. By the end of fifteen excursions, he'd witnessed seven romantic trysts, four bribes, seven thefts (mostly clothes) and eighteen fights (mostly soldiers). His concern about being seen proved frivolous; everyone was so deeply caught up in themselves, they hadn't noticed a ghost flitting about the castle grounds.

So far, he'd found nothing to help identify Ule's murderer. Yet, he persisted.

On an excursion to the northern castle grounds, he made several passes through the Mystics Tower, where a trio of masters mystics always seemed to be barking instructions at the others. He searched every nook and cranny there, expecting to find all kinds of strange tools and potions secreted away, but every hiding hole was empty.

He expected the master mystics to sense his presence, but they were preoccupied with their own affairs. From what he overheard, the mystics were worried about being replaced with others, a tactic often used by new Magnisi to assure the loyalty of those responsible for their protection.

Dawn turned to morning, and he abandoned the Mystics Tower. He flew above the buildings, skipping areas he had searched before, and focused on the southwestern region of the castle grounds, where barracks lined the edge of a field. There he hid in the walls of each barrack, waiting until the soldiers had woken and departed for their assignments. Then he looked in every cupboard and trunk, beneath every cot, and saw that nearly every soldier possessed fighting gear, riding gear, armor, bottles of whiskey or wine, a few coins, and bits of jewelry.

Bored by Soldier Alley, Ulmaen slipped through the glass of a window and into the Infirmary. He regarded the empty table where Ule's body had been stripped and examined. Any sentiment he had for her was overshadowed by a deepening impulse to find out who had killed her.

He searched cupboards and shelves, found rusted bone saws and knives of all sorts. Bottles sat idle, filled with fluid and animals at various stages of life. None of it offered any help.

He dove through a wall, crossed the corridor, and dove through another into a room filled with beds. Lying in one was a soldier with a burn that ran the length of her arm. Her right hand was bandaged thickly, and her eyes were glazed over. She was in far too much pain to notice a ghost hovering above him.

Ulmaen looked beneath the cots and along the shelves until he came to a green curtain. When he passed through the fabric, he regarded Kerista lying in a well kept bed.

Her face was slack, eyes open. They widened a moment then relaxed, as though she sensed someone watching her. Her head twitched but the rest of her body remained immobile, and deep in her throat, a sound softly gurgled. Did she try to say something?

Beyond the curtain, a multitude of footsteps marched into the room. Ulmaen propelled upward and disappeared into a beam of wood, where he watched Osblod guide Lyan and his four guards toward Kerista's bed.

Osblod pulled back the curtain and leaned over Kerista, passing his hands over her eyes. "There's still some movement."

Lyan motioned the guards to step aside, and they obeyed. He joined Osblod and watched him do it again.

"Is there a reaction?" Lyan wondered.

Osblod shrugged. "A little."

Sound struggled to form within Kerista's throat again, as she peered straight above her, directly at Ulmaen. Osblod leaned in to listen.

"Do you hear this?"

Lyan nodded. "What do you make of it?"

"Remember in the war," Osblod began to speculate, "how some of the bodies we carried from the field weren't as dead as we believed them to be?"

Lyan nodded again. "Some of them recovered. Do you think this paralysis is temporary then?"

"Possibly." Osblod straightened the blanket covering Kerista. "It's truly too soon to tell how much damage she's done to herself."

Weariness was a standard expression for Lyan these days. He backed away from the bed, motioning to Osblod to follow.

"Is she suffering?"

Osblod shook his head. "Can't say for certain. She seems comfortable enough." And he launched into theories about what had happened to her.

Ulmaen observed their cordial familiarity with one another, the ease with which they discussed Kerista. Their friendliness contrasted with their public displays of antagonistic discourse. Had Osblod's public attacks of Lyan been a charade, and now, without an audience, he didn't bother to play his part? Were they truly campaigning against each other, or were they working together to ensure Lyan stay in power?

Ulmaen shushed his curiosity. The questions were distracting, and the conversation, like so many others he'd overheard, was lacking the information he required. He was already late and should be at Kugilla Hall washing floors, but his instincts urged him to keep looking for a little while longer.

He dove toward the floor, slid through the coarse wood, and emerged into a sub cellar, where large cabinets lined the walls. One by one he scanned them, then began exploring other rooms.

He slipped through a shut door into a storage area. There, lying on a table, he saw the white gloves he had worn. They were bits of fabric and thread and spider poison. He had thought them dainty. They'd been deadly. He wanted to examine them, but after what they had done to Ule, he didn't want to risk contact with them again.

He shifted into solid form. Under usual circumstances, he'd simply will the object into the air with his mind, but he didn't want Navalis detecting him. Lately, he had been keeping his thoughts and feelings nestled deeply within his solar plexus, so Navalis couldn't know the depth of his disdain toward him.

On a whim, Ulmaen wondered if he could move the gloves by channeling his will through his body instead of through his mind. He gave it a try, and a conduit ripped open from the fierce pressure, and he winced at the sharp pain in his chest.

Before him, the glove suddenly jerked about and rose into the air.

Deeply satisfied by his cleverness, he bent forward to examine the glove closer, but his mood began to shift as memories of what he endured from the poisoning returned. His anger flared. In the same instant, a finger on the glove began to smolder.

He recoiled, his will instantly withdrew, and the glove fell to the floor. He became a ghost again, staring at the smoke gathering about the glove. Then he was gone, pushing past the foundation wall into the field beyond, weaving back and forth through the earth. He passed through a tunnel, and then another that had caved in long ago; he saw the remnants of ancient stone houses, small farm yards, and a few skeletons curled in fetal positions.

He neared the Prison. Avoiding the demons, he searched every niche and cupboard. He saw a sword and a knife, even a mace, made for killing people overtly, directly. Nowhere did he find a pair of elegant gloves laced with poison, because gloves weren't intended to be weapons. Whoever his murderer was, they had been creative with their approach, and they had known Ule well.

Ule would never have cooed over a weapon given to her as a wedding gift. The gloves were a perfect choice, now that he thought about it. They were elegant and beautiful, and they had appealed to her vanity. And yes, Ule had been vain, hadn't she?

Well below ground Ulmaen couldn't see the moon, but he felt its subtle pull wane as it passed the horizon of the planet. He quickened his pace, moving through the ground through the ancient town toward the excavated cavern.

He ignored any rooms or huts filled with sediment and rock, since no one could possibly have physical access to them. Among the excavated buildings, he slowed his search, picking over every storehouse, dwelling, and especially the temple. At first, he thought the buildings were easily accessible, but many had locks on their doors. The temple had been well barricaded with barrier spells at the main doors and every window.

Inside the temple, additional barrier spells had been cast over most of the interior doors. With the matter of his body phased out of the world's Root Dimension, he passed through them with ease, feeling a tingle as he did so.

Most of the temple rooms contained tables and chairs. A few hid secret compartments in the walls or beneath the floors. He passed through rooms stacked with books, scrolls of parchment, lanterns, and curious contraptions made from wires, lenses, and glass vessels filled with moving luminescent liquids.

Some rooms were bare, others small and cramped. One had walls plastered with maps. In another, located in a sub level far away from the others, he glimpsed a glass box that contained a creature which glowed white. It must have sensed a presence in the room for it scrabbled from a hunched position and rolled tightly into a ball.

Ulmaen pushed on, but in the middle of the foundation wall he stopped. His instincts told him to go back, there was something he'd overlooked, and he returned to the room with the caged creature.

He examined the cramped space closely. The door had been fitted with two locks. A table, a chair, and several bookshelves butted up against one another. There were books and parchments, scopes, small machines that looked like they produced electricity, clamps, lenses, and an assortment of surgical tools.

On a shelf behind him, he heard a tick-tick-tick as something scuttled across a hard surface. He turned about and leaned toward the glass box, which was not much bigger than his head. Here and there, tiny holes had been drilled into the top, and a barrier had been placed around it, too.

Tick-tick-tickety-tick.

The creature scuttled from one side of the glass box to the other. It was about the size of a man's hand and covered in a brilliant white bioluminescent exoskeleton that flared and sparked fine whips of energy along its outer body. Beneath the exoskeleton, the body was black. He counted eight legs and staggered clusters of black eyes, and although he sensed something familiar about the creature, he couldn't figure out what.

On a nearby table, he saw an assortment of personal objects. A beautiful hair comb encrusted with tiny diamonds, a triangular silver pendant set with a topaz, a bracelet of small rubies. Next to them he found small vials filled with clear fluid near a microscope, a glass nib pen, and a small paint brush.

Ulmaen regarded the spider again. It hooked the ends of its legs into the holes of the box and hung upside down.

Someone has an interest in spiders, he thought. I wonder who?

"Was it your venom that killed me then?"

The spider jumped to the other side of the box and slid down to the bottom.

Ulmaen retreated to the middle of the room, taking in the sight of everything, allowing his imagination to run wild and speculate. Who knew how to extract venom from a spider? Who had access to medical and alchemy tools, as well as a scribe's pen and an artist's brush? Who was capable of creating and navigating energy barriers?

He thought of everyone, the most unlikely suspects first. There was Bethereel, sweet Bethee, who had no reason to kill Ule; at least, none he could imagine. And if she did, she didn't have access to the equipment in the room.

There was Laere, the artist with her keen insight, but her privileges in the castle were limited, too, and based on what he knew about her, she wasn't interested in anything beyond art.

There was Gorlen, who for unknown reasons despised Ule. He was capable, but was he smart enough to know how to extract venom from a spider?

He suspected Mithreel most of all, the spider demon locked away in the dungeon, and questioned if the shackles were for show. Had he lied about never having had them removed? Perhaps he knew how to slip in and out of his cell without being detected. He had been infatuated with Ule since the beginning of the world, and could have killed her out of spite. That was a good enough motive.

Based on the remote location of the temple room, the lenses and scopes and beakers, the books and parchment, he knew Ule's murderer was someone with accessibility, someone of high authority within the castle. He thought of the highest authority of all.

What of Magnes Lyan? He had access to everything within the castle, and the power to instruct those with knowledge to do his bidding and keep it secret. But why would he?

"Because he *loooved* her," Ulmaen said aloud, mimicking the way Mithreel had said it to him long, long ago. If Lyan couldn't have her, no one could.

Yet, from what he knew about Lyan, he was a warrior and didn't know the most rudimentary uses for loupes, scopes, and electrical current devices. The person who used this room had a scientifically inclined mind.

He considered Mbjard with his extensive book knowledge. As an arch scribe he'd be knowledgeable and influential and privy to just about anything if he asked. Understanding why he'd murdered Ule was easy. He had never agreed with Ule's promotion to adept. Unable to overturn Lyan's authority on the matter might have stirred him to eliminate the cause of what defied his authority—Ule. And perhaps guilt over inadvertently harming an innocent explained why he agreed to the research to help free Rozafel.

Next, Osblod came to mind. He had learned to be calculating, practical, resourceful, and manipulative as a physician during the wars. Again, the question arose. What did he stand to gain from getting rid of Ule?

The Chair.

He'd made it clear since the beginning of the election how much he doubted Lyan's ability. He challenged Lyan publicly. Removing Lyan's primary translator would undermine the Magnes's ability to communicate effectively and efficiently with foreign allies, just as Kerista had once suggested.

If Osblod knew about Lyan's affection for Ule, her death might have been meant to disable him on a personal level as well. He had the knowhow, access to resources, perhaps a connection to a mystic.

Finally, Ulmaen thought of the mystics. Any of them could be suspect, all of them possessed a flexible morality, all in the pursuit of knowledge, skill, and power. If he had to guess among them, he'd point a finger at Kerista, on account of the sudden emergence of her ability to read minds.

Kerista assisted in nearly all facets of castle life for the simple reason that she was head of security. She had knowledge of medical tools and mystical devices. She might have been gifted one of Mbjard's famous glass nib pens. And anyone could buy paintbrushes in Eastgate.

But why kill Ule?

Of all the suspects, Kerista seemed the only one with the power to do so. Yet, he didn't understand why she'd murder Ule, unless... Unless she had succeeded in reading someone's thoughts. Had she sensed in Ule something otherworldly? Had she feared for the safety of Lyan?

Ulmaen dove upward through the sub-cellar and the upper floors of the temple, through the ground, and into a bright sunny morning well underway. He returned to the broom closet in Kugilla Hall, where he shifted back into solid form and gathered up a mop and a bucket. He immersed himself in washing floors, and did his best to settle the anxiety churning in his chest.

* CHAPTER 41 *

The stillness of the laboratory unsettled Navalis. He inhaled a deep labored breath. He was wasting time.

He reclined on a stool near the work table, back pressed against the wall. Around him, the floor was strewn with half-melted tools and books, since both the table and the cupboard were stuffed with equipment and testing paraphernalia they had borrowed from the main laboratory.

His efforts were being wasted, too. He needed to persist with studying demons in more depth, but his supply of dissection specimens had ceased now that Kerista was no longer arch mystic.

As per Osblod's word, he had informed Gorlen of Kerista's cannibalistic activity, prompting Gorlen and a troop of guards to thoroughly search Kerista's laboratory. Gorlen couldn't find anything to support Osblod's claim and eventually stood down.

Although the mystics remained unnerved by the search, life within the tower had gone back to their kind of normal, for three master mystics had been temporarily appointed by Lyan to manage their affairs until after the election. Unfortunately, none of them approved of Navalis's specialty and refused to co-operate on acquiring another specification for him.

He should have appreciated Kerista more for giving into his needs, for urging him to dissect demons instead of pursue anecdotal evidence, but back then he hadn't known the extent of information he'd cull from cutting open a demon.

Now, he had more questions, wanted to observe and understand what resided within their forms. The sooner he determined the underlying nature of demon corporeality, the sooner he could assuage the curiosity of the Xiinisi Council and return to Xii to resume his world building projects.

He had thought of visiting the Prison, to see if demons were being held there like Kerista had said. Without her approval, he'd be forced to sneak one out, and he didn't want to risk it escaping. He'd fought a demon before and lost.

Sitting upright, he swiveled toward the table and picked up the kornerupine he had confiscated from Kerista's lab. He turned the familiar stone over in his hand, held it up to the light of a crystal lantern. The pink line in the middle of the stone seemed to move depending on how the light reflected off the smooth surface.

Istok's disembodied voice rose from the stone. "Don't look at me like that!"

Ignoring the demon, Navalis pushed aside scopes and lanterns to clear a space on the table. Only one item remained in place, a dagger buried to the hilt inside a small anvil. He regarded the shiv-like weapon inside the block of metal, then saw a duplicate of the dagger laying nearby, the spike blade crumpled to the hilt.

The two spike daggers were the ones Boriag had had custom made for a demonstration, which had been entertaining and unsettling. Although Boriag tried hard to explain his work, he was met with blank, questioning stares. The masters recognized he'd delivered what he'd promised, but even they were unnerved by their failure to understand what he had accomplished.

Boriag had a gift, an ability no one else had. He might very well suffer for it, being held at arm's length by the other mystics. He'd need to find a way to comfort himself, especially once everyone found out the truth. Perhaps the truth wouldn't have to be known, not by Boriag, not by anyone, if the farmer's story proved to be false.

With a strength that exceeded his body's ability, Navalis pulled the spike dagger from the anvil and set it on the table next to the fortified gauntlet. As it rolled back and forth, he wondered if the gauntlet would hold up as well as the spike dagger had, for he still hadn't tested it yet.

In the space he cleared on the table, he set down the kornerupine beneath the fortified spike dagger and alongside the Lilamon Eye, which at a distance looked more like a crystal then a lens. The remaining space was occupied by other paraphernalia he had taken from Kerista's lab, each object unwrapped and evenly placed from one another.

A low hum broke the silence.

Navalis cocked his head toward the closed door, but as the hum grew louder, he realized the sound was coming from inside the room.

The hum turned into a rattle—something hard butting against something else that was hard. The dagger began to shimmy along the table.

Navalis grabbed the dagger and examined the spike closely. Instantly it became still and quiet. Unsure of what to make of the change, he set it back down again and watched as it began to vibrate across the table. It moved slowly, in tiny increments, toward the Stone of Istok.

He lifted the kornerupine and examined it. "Are you doing that?" he asked Istok.

"Oh, you're talking to me now. How gracious of you!"

"Are you making that noise, making the dagger rattle?"

"No! Fuck off!"

Navalis picked up both the dagger and the kornerupine and held them in proximity to one another. The vibration and hum ceased. He tried the dagger with the Lilamon Eye. Still no effect. One by one he held each object on its own and then next to the dagger. Nothing.

"It must be a combination of three or more objects causing this," he reasoned. He returned all the objects, including the dagger, to the table and waited for the dagger to resume its vibration. One by one, he removed each item and set it far across the room on the dissection table.

The absence of mystic fingers and eyes made no difference. The dagger still vibrated toward Istok's Stone. After he removed all objects consisting of pure biological matter, he started extracting objects made primarily of mineral. As soon as he removed a rock laced with iron and nickel, the dagger stopped rattling.

He held the dagger and the rock together again. They remained still and silent, and he grew frustrated. He returned them to the table. All that remained was the dagger, the rock, the Lilamon Eye, and the kornerupine. He removed the Lilamon Eye. The vibration stopped. As soon as he returned it, the vibration started again.

After he pulled away the kornerupine and noted the silence, he knew something about *all four* objects: being near one another created the vibration.

He set the kornerupine down again. Immediately the hum returned, making the dagger rattle against the table. After a while, he heard a new sound—a low musical tone that grew louder and louder. He'd heard it before, long ago, emanating from a weapon.

Years before, the sword of Kaleel the Rex had come into close proximity with a tear in the fabric of the world, the same sword that had released both him and Ule from being trapped by Istok's magic. Kaleel had told him the sword had been forged from metals in a quarry near a tear in the fabric of the world long ago.

The sound rose in volume, and the metals in both the dagger and the rock began to glow. He pushed them far apart until they stopped affecting one another, and asked out loud, "What about this combination of objects is producing the same effect as Kaleel's sword?"

"Ugh," Istok replied. "Don't mention that scat again!"

Navalis softly shushed the demon. He pushed his perception deeply into each object, examining the chemical makeup. By morning he had discovered that saturated currents of An Energy ran in tandem with the iron and nickel of the stone. The kornerupine and the Lilamon Eye both contained crystals reinforced by An energy. And the dagger had a thick coating of it encasing the spike, no doubt the result of Boriag's imbuing process.

"An Energy," he muttered to himself.

His kind called upon the An Energy for moving between dimensions and for creating their worlds. This energy had one key nature. It facilitated change well. In other words, it was slippery, at least that's how he liked to describe the primary energy to his Students. Elements stuck to it, and its natural state was to flow.

The beginnings of new worlds were abundant with An Energy, but once the building of a world was completed, any excess energy not bound to matter receded. Then two dimensional states were created: the Root Dimension, which was the material expression of the world; and the Chthonic Dimension, the immaterial expression.

The fixed nature of the Root Dimension always repelled the An Energy due to its natural tendency to flow. From what Navalis observed in the objects, however, an excess of An Energy had found a way to stick around in the world, and when enough objects containing this excess came into proximity with one another, its slippery side re-emerged.

He picked up the Stone of Istok and rolled it about his fingers, examining every facet and finally understood how both he and Ule had been released from Istok's magic. It hadn't been Kaleel's sword coming into contact with Istok's magic that had rescued them from their gemstone prisons. It had been the high concentration of An Energy in the sword's refined metals.

He held up the kornerupine and smiled. He'd love more than anything to dysmutate Istok, take him apart thread by thread, but he'd learn more if he dissected Istok instead. He had found his next specimen, but he'd need to release him from the stone first.

The only problem he could foresee was detaining Istok, who had been and probably still was very strong and clever. Navalis would just have to be more clever. He'd need to be quick too, predetermining the kind of strike that would instantly kill the demon. And he knew what weapons to use.

Unfortunately, he didn't possess anything containing the cactus demon's magic. No blood. No hair from the head of a creature supermutated by him. A red spine or one of his pups or flowers would do, but his physicality was contained within the kornerupine.

Navalis knew where to look to find some of Istok's magic, but the journey would take too long as an Elishian. He simply didn't have the patience to make the journey by horse, and so he began to change, and for the first time in Elish, he willingly and with great pleasure gave up a considerable amount of time from his current generation, knowing it would be well worth it.

The mosquito hovered a moment, wings a blur. The laboratory reflected a multitude of times in its massive black eyes, each ringed with a halo of green.

It dove through the laboratory doorway, up the stairwell of the old castle, along the tunnel toward Fehran's Hall, and out through a window on the main floor. Outside, it flew high into the humid air above the crowds and meandered across the Colonnade, weaving in and out among the maze of courtyards toward Southgate.

It buzzed past the ruin of the old gate, and flew between the pillars of the new one being built. High above the markets and shanty towns, it avoided contact with farmhands and farmers, and when the markets turned into farmland, it dodged the whip tails of cows and horses.

The road to Sondshor Market snaked through fields of wheat and corn, and eventually all roads hooked toward the east around a small, dense forest of blue pines and hills. The mosquito headed westerly until flatland ended and the thick of Woedshor Forest began. It followed the edge of the forest, along a valley, toward a vast stretch of sand, aiming itself toward a small grove that looked like a deserted island in a tawny sea.

There, the mosquito dove through a gap between two bowed saplings, and on the inside, the tiny woods opened up into the heart of a lush forest. The trees were taller and wider in girth, not the kind normally associated with the desert. Pine needles and leaves blanketed the ground, and the canopy far above cast rippling shadows.

The mosquito buzzed along, and at a barrier of green energy, it effortlessly dove through and followed the path on the other side. There, it ascended to avoid the flailing hands of children, their wrists glinting from bracelets that kept them forgetful and bound to the woods.

Farther along, a starling snapped at the mosquito, and the mosquito dove sharply, escaping the sharp beak as it searched for a young woman with long black hair and oddly shaped brown marks on her pale flesh.

Many paths were scanned, some of the shanties along the way, too, but the woman wasn't anywhere to be found, until a familiar hut with a covered porch came into view.

The porch was empty except for a chair and the beast that sat in it. The cat demon, who called himself Kaleel the Rex, hadn't changed much over the years. His wrinkled, fur-less flesh was still riddled with battle scars, and one of his triangular ears remained torn. What had changed was that he wore brown trousers instead of black ones, yet they were still being held up by a belt covered in jaw fragments and finger bones.

Beneath the shade of the porch, which was sheltered by the forest above, Kaleel's naked, humanoid like chest beaded with sweat. He lightly dozed, one leg crossed over the other.

The mosquito flew onto the porch and hovered there.

Kaleel's almond-shaped eyes snapped opened. Ice blue disks glowered a moment, then he bolted upright, looking around as though he had expected to see someone there and was surprised to find no one. He raised a lean muscular arm and scratched his head with a black taloned finger.

The mosquito buzzed through the open doorway to the hut, buoying across the room, searching for the woman. She had been slender before. Long before that she'd had more girth, and long before that she had been a cow that had been transformed into an Elishian by Istok.

Mulga was her name, and when the mosquito found her in a room at the back of the hut, she was fast asleep beneath a blanket in a small bed.

She laid flat on her back, a hand curled by her face, her lips slightly parted. She softly snored and occasionally mumbled in her sleep.

The mosquito searched for a spot of flesh to land on. Her neck was covered with a mess of long black hair and the blanket was bundled at her naked breasts. All that remained was the hand curled by her face.

The mosquito landed on her smallest finger near the bend of the mid joint. It crawled toward her knuckle, where it slid its proboscis into her flesh and began to saw gently, back and forth, searching for a blood capillary.

Blood gushed over the mosquito's proboscis. It pulled at the warm fluid, siphoning it inside, feeling its belly swell, all the while mindful of someone other than Mulga in the room, someone who was watching.

Mulga stirred and mumbled again.

A shadow fell across the bed.

Somewhere from beneath the blanket her other hand popped out and slapped the one curled by her face. The mosquito pulled free just in time, darting to the side, only a set of its wings bruised by the blow. Regaining its balance, it rose into the air before another blow could burst open the sanguine trove it now possessed.

Kaleel glared down at Mulga a moment, then he looked about the room again. He rubbed his chin as he sat on the edge of the bed.

Mulga shifted. Sleepily, she turned on her side and opened her eyes. "What is it?" she asked, her voice thick.

"Nothing," he told her. He looked around the room once more to be sure. "I hope." He brushed her cheek with his finger, pushing a strand of hair from her cheek. "Go back to sleep."

Mulga yawned. "Join me?"

"Perhaps."

The mosquito flew from the room, mindful of its bloated gut. As it retraced the journey through the forest, back out into the desert where the forest became a small woods again, it repaired its bruised wing and zoomed back through the desert toward Sondshor Castle.

Back in the laboratory, in the castle beneath the ground, the mosquito settled onto a glass plate on the table.

Smoke spilled out of the insect's proboscis and eyes, pouring into black and gray tendrils that swirled and flashed green. The volume of smoke grew, swirling about flashes of green energy, while the mosquito remained still and whole.

The smoke began coalescing into an inky mass, taking the shape of a humanoid, a man. Slowly, the form solidified, taking on the features associated with Navalis. The only part of him missing was the tip of a fingernail.

He regarded the angular small insect, still intact on the dish. The mosquito turned slightly to look at him, and they recognized one another as being one and the same.

A bit of blood was all he needed. The part of him that was humanoid, whole, and fully solid, raised a hand and with the tip of his finger squished the mosquito.

He felt the creature's abdominal wall burst. The pain was infinitesimal, barely registering as a pinprick.

The corpse of the insect dematerialized, the matter restoring the very tip of Navalis's incomplete fingernail. He then took the blood on his finger and smeared it on the Stone of Istok, soiling the bright pink line.

"Hmm," Istok said, breaking the silence. "Smells like Mulga. What are you up to?"

❋

Navalis waited until the middle of the night, when he knew Boriag and most of the castle would be asleep and no one was likely to come wandering into the laboratory. He ignored Istok's incessant questions and laughed when the demon hurled curses at him.

He considered using the old ray device Goyas had invented, the one with the mystical lens and the soft white light, to increase the concentration of the An Energy in one of the objects, perhaps the rock. The notion stirred up an old memory, and the voice of his Master from long ago resonated through his mind.

Hethn hadn't been as old then. As a Student, Navalis had felt quite satisfied by a liquid world he had created. It thrived, yet, for some reason, he still wanted to do more with it.

"Let it be," Hethn had told him. "Do not fix anything that is already functioning. Come now, let it be."

The advice echoed in his mind. He recalled saying something similar to Ule when she was younger. He applied the advice and chose to work with what he had.

With a large wad of tree gum, he fixed the Lilamon Eye to one end of the nickel and iron laced rock. Leaving the dagger free, he stacked it onto the rock. Three items in one hand, the kornerupine sullied by blood infused with Istok's magic in his other, he brought them to the dissection table.

He set down the kornerupine and the trio of objects nearby. Then the dagger began to vibrate.

He recalled the explosion that had resulted from Kaleel's sword striking Istok's magic, but he came prepared, having donned the armor Boriag had imbued with more tensile strength.

He'd be protected well enough, for the armor not only provided a layer of defense against Istok's power, but it stood a chance at repelling the red spines Istok wielded along the backs of his forearms and calves. Navalis feared those red spines the most, for they possessed powers that changed the state of whatever they came into contact with, making the object transform into something less complex in form, usually a stone.

On his right hand, he wore the imbued gauntlet, determined to test its strength. On his left hand, he wore one of his leather surgery gloves. And Boriag had been kind enough to bring him a helmet, too, the kind the guards wore.

He lowered the visor on the helmet, then grabbed the rock. It butted against the metal of the gauntlet's palm, as he raised his arm, positioning it above the kornerupine. His left hand held the dagger firmly, poised and ready to strike.

The plan was simple in his mind. As soon as Istok manifested, he'd stab him in the chest, and although he hoped the demon's death came swiftly, he prepared himself for a fight.

The humming increased in volume. The metal of the dagger began to glow blue. He steadied his hand above the bloodied kornerupine, drew back the stone. After a deep breath, he raised the stone a bit higher and brought it down toward the kornerupine.

A loud crack pierced the air.

The explosion he expected didn't happen. The kornerupine remained whole.

He raised his arm again. This time he brought it down with a strength that exceeded his body's ability. He pulled a day's worth from his inner reserve of energy. He aimed for the wavering pink line of the stone.

Kaboooom!

He struck the wall across the lab near the work table. When he regained his sight, it was clouded by falling plaster and dust. The armor weighed him down as he struggled to stand. His right hand flexed. The stone and Lilamon Eye were gone. Also missing was the spike dagger.

Tiny bright lights flickered around the edge of the room. Each light was a shard of the kornerupine. One by one, each fragment shot back toward the dissection table where they fell into place along the invisible outline of a large humanoid figure. The outline had one arm folded across its chest and the other extended alongside its thigh.

Navalis knelt down and frantically searched the debris. Fed up with the awkwardness of the gauntlet, he shook it free and ran his bare fingers beneath the plaster and along the floor.

On the table, the fragments twitched and turned, their light dimming into spots of darkness. The room about him began to dim. He blinked profusely, adjusting his perception, but he saw nothing.

There was always light, even in the darkest of caves. Unsettled by the loss of his sight, he listened instead. From the direction of the dissection table, Navalis discerned a low mumble. His fingers pushed through the debris, blindly feeling out the shape of the objects he encountered. When he discerned the long, thin spike of the dagger, he sighed in relief.

As he clutched the dagger to his chest, he heard heavy breathing. Was it his or did it belong to the cactus demon? He swiped at whatever was before him, but the spike blade swooshed through empty air. Then, in a rush, the light returned, burning his retinas. Struggling against the pain, he glimpsed the figure of something large and green standing before him.

Something long and solid struck him across the side of the head. He flew sideways from the impact, his helmet catching the edge of a small table. A tray of scalpels and pincers clattered to the floor and disappeared beneath the plaster dust. Pooling in his lap were several red spines. Panicked, he checked his armor but all of it remained intact. He clutched the spike dagger, threw himself upward, and lunged.

Istok's beady black eyes glowered. The glean of his black teeth snapped, once, and then again. He pulled himself to his full height, a good head or two above Navalis. His flesh was thick and ribbed. Although his features and form were mostly humanoid, he still resembled a pipe cactus.

His nudity was bold and brazen. His eyes were slightly skewed. He was proportionate but not quite properly aligned, if you dared look close enough. He hadn't changed since being submutated into a kornerupine. He'd one good arm then, and still did now.

Navalis regarded the demon's half arm, open at the elbow, oozing with green blood. The wound was as fresh as the day he'd torn it off, a couple of years ago, back when they had fought one another in the desert. Istok had defeated him back then. If not for the quick thinking of Ule, he might have been turned back into a gemstone.

Istok carried the severed forearm with his good one, holding it by the wrist.

Determined to detain the demon this time, Navalis scrambled to his feet, fisting the hilt of the dagger in his hand. He lunged forward.

Istok wielded his severed forearm like a club at first, then he brought it in front of him and rolled it forward to expose the red spines and aimed them at Navalis. Several shot out.

Navalis dove for cover beside the table, but it was too late. The spines struck his chest. The metal of his armor vibrated where the spines stuck. Beneath the embedded projectiles, the armor began to melt into gray sand and pour onto the floor.

He shuddered. He wouldn't let the demon transform him again, by any means necessary, even if it meant tapping into his abilities and depleting his inner reserve of energy. He pushed the molecular structure of his body and the clothing he wore beneath the dissolving armor. The dagger phased out of the material plane, and he held onto it, shifting everything but the armor he wore.

Istok frowned as what remained of the chest plate and the helmet fell in a tumble and clanked on the floor. He squinted at the phantom image of Navalis and stepped backward.

Navalis pushed forward, extending the spike dagger.

Istok swung his detached arm upward and to the side, and stumbled when the arm struck empty air. "Tricks," he grumbled.

Navalis lunged forward, the dagger and his body solidifying in an instant. He sank the point of the blade into Istok's flesh just beneath where a ribcage might be.

A howl of pain erupted from the cactus demon. He flung backward, dislodging himself from the dagger. He bent the elbow of his detached arm again, but this time he aimed it toward the door. A red spine sunk into the wood, and the wood instantly exploded into ash. He dove through the gray cloud and took to the stairs.

Navalis returned to an ethereal state and dove through the doorway, a little unnerved by the demon's desire to flee. He expected Istok to rage with blood lust and revenge after being subjected to his own submutative powers and trapped in a stone. Instead, he fled up the stairwell.

Such an odd choice of direction, Navalis thought. They were in a tower. His instincts would have lead him down, if he hadn't known the tower was underground, which meant Istok was aware of their surroundings.

Panicked, Navalis shot up the stairwell, determined to block the exit to the tunnel, but as he ascended, he noticed that Istok had gone well past it, climbing toward the tower's peak.

He laughed, his nerves calming. The uppermost part of the tower was a lookout that had been filled in with rubble and earth, and the entrance boarded up with wood. There was nowhere for Istok to go.

Navalis whipped along the steps. As he caught up with the demon getting closer to the lookout, Istok fired another red spine. This time he aimed it into the wood slats covering the lookout doorway. The wood exploded into puffs of brown ash.

Istok bent his elbow again, firing a spine into the boulder that blocked the other side of the doorway, and it disintegrated into a waterfall of sand. Beyond that was packed earth dotted with large and small boulders. He'd need a million spines to disintegrate it all.

Navalis raised the spike dagger, preparing to shift back into solid form and finally put an end to Istok. There was much to be learned from him as a specimen, more than what Navalis had gleaned from the younger snake demons.

Istok turned to peer down the stairwell as he dabbed the forefinger of the severed forearm in the green blood oozing from his elbow.

What's this? What's he trying to do? Navalis wondered, feeling his thoughts spin. What does he think he can do? There's no escape here.

The panic returned. He raised the dagger, watched with dread as Istok drew a mark with his blood on two stones, one on each side of the doorway.

Navalis's body began to solidify; the dagger, too. He aimed it toward the space between Istok's shoulder blades.

Istok turned back round again. His upper lipped curled. The smile was smug, his actions quick.

Just as the point of the blade pressed against Istok's flesh, the demon stepped forward and vanished. The space of earth between the two stones shimmered briefly, as though it were liquid, then grew still.

Navalis struck out with the dagger and it grazed the earth. He shifted the dagger and his body again. He passed through the earth, pushing through large boulders and black sediment. He searched and searched and found only a lingering scent of iron and decay.

Grimness overcame him as he returned to the tower stairwell and resumed solid form. He descended back to his lab. Inside, he whipped the dagger across the room with a grunt. As the dagger careened off a wall and disappeared beneath the plaster on the floor, Navalis sank against the dissection table.

He had thought of ways to protect himself with armor, made sure the location was isolated and contained, but what he had never considered was that Istok was aware of his surroundings, that he had been watching the entire time Navalis was preparing for their encounter.

✳ CHAPTER 42 ✳

The moon was expected to be at its zenith this evening, an auspicious time to work spells and rituals. Every mystic who occupied the tower scrambled to prepare their formulas, many sharing workbenches on the main floor for lack of space. Frustrations bubbled and flared as egos clashed.

Navalis sat at the main table, near the open doors. The morning air was cool and soothing. He rubbed the base of his skull, doing his best to ignore the arguments and focus on the pages of parchment strewn before him. He tried to make sense of the tiny script of Boriag's notes, but his mind kept wandering.

He was desperate for a demon specimen. He needed to move forward somehow, regarding what he had learned while exploring Rolen's farm. A demon walked among them. Flesh the color and texture of an Elishian, with a humanoid head, balanced eyes, a proportionate body.

He'd been thinking long and hard about *that* demon, but was having difficulty believing it existed. He needed something other than a story told to him by a drunken farmer who might be vilifying a willful child as a way to explain his inability to control that child. Disinclined to believe the story, Navalis wasn't quite willing to dismiss it either, for some of the most fantastical tales were based on some truth.

A strong breeze made the pages before him rustle. The words and diagrams written on them rippled as though they were alive.

Voices rose above the thrum, each a temper rising in pitch and volume determined to outshout the other. A trio of adepts quarreled over the proper interpretation of an equation they'd developed together, slinging hurtful words back and forth, until Boriag interrupted them.

A loud thump-thump of his fist pounded the workbench, preventing him from turning around to face the adepts. In a shrill, warbling voice he began to yell.

"Shuuut uuup! For the love of Mxalem, shut up, or I'll seal your mouths with, with... mortar! That doesn't require any fucking magic!"

In the wake of his outburst, a silence lingered. Navalis welcomed the reprieve, even if it was temporary.

The adepts yelled back: *I dare ya ta try it. I'll see you in the Pit for it. Eat me!*

Boriag spun around to face them. "Don't test me!" He shook his fist in the air. "Without any magic scent, you won't be able to prove it was me. I'll deny it, I will!"

Normally, Navalis found Boriag's outbursts amusing, but at the mention of magic scent, his mind clung to the idea.

Demons had some ability that exuded magic scent. He hadn't met one that didn't have a lingering smell. The snake demons had it. Istok's had been earth and iron. Kaleel the Rex, his smelled of piss and burnt sugar.

Unfortunately, mystics exuded magic scent also. Goyas's had been onion and sandalwood. Even Adinav smelled, the worst of them all, like wine and radishes and rotten meat.

A voice at the door cut through his mind chatter. It was soft and hushed. "Boriag," it called out. "Boriag!" A little louder this time. The voice still failed to capture Boriag's attention.

Navalis turned toward the source and saw Laere. She looked small standing in the arched doorway, and the full brown skirt she wore dwarfed her further. The morning sun glinted off her white shirt, causing him to wince. Her nose wrinkled up at the magic scent that thickened the air.

Laere pointed at Boriag. "I just wanted..." She held up her hand and showed him a bundle of pencils. "... to give him these?" Bravely, she sucked in a deep breath and embraced the pungent smells.

Navalis shrugged. He pointed at Boriag, encouraging her to approach him. "Come in, if you dare."

The adepts continued to argue, in harsh whispers, and the noise in the tower returned to its original volume.

Navalis resumed his thoughts about the nature of magic scent, and began mentally documenting every occurrence of it he'd encountered and was intrigued when a pattern began to emerge.

The mystics had recognizable scents. Goyas's had been onion and sandalwood. Boriag smelled like anise seed, and Kerista like vinegar and mint. Their scent was always something strong and distinct and sometimes intolerable to the non-mystic.

Every demon he'd encountered so far, no matter what pleasant smells they exuded, possessed a repugnant undertone—decay, rotten meat, urine. No one ever enjoyed those smells, no matter which other ones accompanied them.

As for the Xiinisi, their scents were similar to the mystics and tended to be culinary in nature. Ulmaen's was apples and ginger. Another Student of his smelled of orange and cinnamon. His own magic scent was radish and black pepper.

If given a chance to smell the magic scent of the demon that looked exactly like an Elishian, he was certain he'd detect a hint of foulness, no matter how well-mannered or good natured the creature.

He checked on his assistant again. Boriag was far too immersed in writing formulas on a block of paper to notice that Laere stood beside him, so he called for his attention.

"Hey, Boriag!"

"What?" Boriag snapped, then nearly jumped out of his skin when he noticed Laere. "Oh, hey!"

"I didn't mean to interrupt," Laere said. "Is it alright for me to be here?"

Boriag nodded enthusiastically with a face splitting grin.

Very few regular folk had the nerve to visit the tower, and several curious mystics strained to listen in on the conversation, Navalis included.

Laere held up the bundle of pencils. "Just wanted to give you these." She began pointing to different ones. "There's a couple softs, a few mediums, and a hard."

An apprentice mystic nearby snickered at the comment, no doubt thinking lewd thoughts.

Boriag grabbed them, his large hand engulfing hers, and he apologized three times for touching her.

Laere glanced about the tower, then returned a smile. It was forced and wanting, and Navalis grew more curious. He was certain she had an ulterior reason for being here. He extended his hearing, mindful of the pull it had on his energy. Discreetly he listened as he watched them from the corner of his eye.

Laere leaned back a little to meet Boriag's gaze. "Do you mind if I ask you something?"

Wide-eyed and suddenly eager, Boriag shook his head. "I'm free to go out any time," he blurted.

"Huh?" She bit her lip. She stared at him, a little stunned. "I... but I... I'm sort of involved with somebody."

Boriag saddened at the response. "Sort of?"

"I..." She huffed and rolled her eyes. "It's Ulmaen."

Navalis frowned at the information. Ulmaen had been distraught over Bethereel when last they spoke. Had he finally let her go? Had Ulmaen finally started exploring his new form, learning to adapt to a different outlook, a different state of existence?

The moment Laere spoke the name, she seemed to regret it. "Or at least I *was* involved with him." She became defensive then. Stepping backward, she raised a hand. "I shouldn't have said anything—"

"That's fine," Boriag told her. "You need some time to get over him. I get it."

"Yes!" She pointed at him. "That's it exactly." Relaxing a bit, she leaned toward him again. "There is something I do need to ask you, though, and you're the only one I know to ask, who I can... trust."

Still wide-eyed and eager, Boriag clutched the pencils in both hands now.

"But I'm not sure if I should be asking," she rambled.

"You're confusing me," Boriag said. "I like that about you."

Across the room, the trio of adepts exploded into heated arguments again. Navalis flinched at the shatter of breaking glass. He ducked just in time to avoid a beaker being cast across the room at nothing in particular. The beaker exploded once it hit the stone floor, glass fragments spraying everywhere, stirring outrage in the other mystics.

In that moment, Laere leaned into Boriag. Their lips moved, but he heard nothing of what they said. Boriag patted her shoulder in a reassuring way, then steered her toward the doorway.

Other mystics followed them, retreating to the outdoors to be away from the argument. Navalis joined them. Outside, he followed the wall of the tower, walked along an outcropping that contained Kerista's laboratory. There, he leaned against the brick and watched Boriag and Laere walk side by side through the field toward the stables. He extended his hearing a bit more.

"It's different for everyone," Boriag said. His voice sounded as though it were at the other end of a long tube.

Laere nodded, as though she understood. "Is it a trade that calls to you... in the literal way?"

Boriag motioned her to stop, and she did, her arms tightly folded in front of her. As they faced one another, Laere twitched. Even at this distance, Navalis could tell she was nervous and uncomfortable by the way she stood, the way she rambled.

"You know, it's probably some artistic fugue state I experienced. Too much whiskey or something. Not enough sleep. Or the chemicals in the paint thinners..."

Boriag reached for her hair, to brush it out of the way perhaps, but stopped himself. He mirrored her instead, folding his arms across his chest, and asked, "Has something happened?"

She tossed her head back and laughed. "Something's always happening!" She went quiet a moment then peered up. "Do you ever hear voices?"

"Yeah, everyone's got one," Boriag replied.

"No, not real voices. I mean—" She struggled for a deep breath. "I mean the kind of voices that aren't coming from anyone who's speaking."

"Well, yeah." Boriag touched the base of his skull. "I've got this voice back here, see. It tells me to try this and do that, then I do it." He shrugged. "'Cause it's fun and I end up making really interesting things happen—"

Their conversation abruptly went silent as the adepts burst through the archway. Flying fists had been exchanged for the flinging of words and glassware. Navalis backed away from the gathering crowd. No one wanted to be near the conflict yet they stayed close enough to watch. Some of the apprentices tried to break up the fight but without any luck.

Navalis remained at a distance, keeping to himself. He pondered what life had been like for the Elishian demon. If it had grown from a babe into adult form, had it experienced growth spurts and phases of awkwardness? Had it ever broken a limb or cried? Had it struggled with the same conflicts as other Elishians? Had it ever been in a fist fight?

He regarded Boriag and Laere, whose conversation came to an abrupt end. Laere turned about and walked away, her arms still across her belly.

Had the demon ever fallen in love? Did it thrive on others' fears, like other demons he knew of? Would it know to? Was it aware of itself? Did this creature that looked and behaved and felt just like anyone else, realize it had power at all? Was it even aware it was a demon?

Boriag returned. Sadness lingered in his eyes.

Navalis imagined that sadness two fold, three fold, or more. He imagined Boriag's face twisted in anger, the despair he was certain to feel, the suffering, because regardless of whether or not the Elishian demon was aware of itself, Navalis needed to trick it somehow.

Yes, he needed to force it to express its signature magic ability, to trigger its magic scent. If he could get a whiff of it, he'd know for certain if he was dealing with a demon.

Regardless of the outcome, Boriag would be forever changed.

❋ CHAPTER 43 ❋

The stiff capelet rubbed against Ulmaen's neck as he lifted a stack of books and cradled them in an arm. He walked the stone floor of the Archive, his new boots growing dusty. The massive room with its mess of documentation soothed him; the capelet did not, even though it indicated his new position as apprentice scribe.

He thought back to his final day working in the Kitchen. Senaga and the others had given him a proper farewell, complete with sweet pastries. Senaga had mock kicked his arse as he departed through the side door. Then, he attended the Library where he knelt, his lips still sticky with pistachio and vanilla glaze, and Mbjard swore him in as a scribe.

The memory was fleeting. Ever since discovering the room tucked away in the excavated temple, he thought mostly of Kerista. He imagined her in her secret room, milking the spider of its venom. His hand clenched into a fist of its own accord. He wanted satisfaction yet felt denied of what? Revenge? Retribution? Justice?

He marched along a row of bookshelves, mindful to skirt the ledgers piled in random spots on the floor. Above him, boot heels clumped across the wooden floor of the main Library. At least down here in the Archive, paper and cloth and leather dampened his huffing, grunting, and cursing. No one need hear him, and since he was alone, he needn't pretend to be happy.

He appreciated the many rows of books and scrolls, the way their spines were embossed with tiny glyphs that fished for his attention. Unfortunately, his curiosity wasn't biting today. He no longer had a need to conduct research. Bethereel had died, and Rozafel, too. Finding closure for them no longer mattered. He, at least, knew who had killed Ule. What he didn't know was why?

He searched for gaps between the thick tomes stacked there, found space next to a hand bound stack of parchment documenting Armory Inventory for the past year. None of the books he carried suited the category. He huffed and moved on to the next gap on the shelves.

At a bookcase tucked away in the back corner, he stopped and skimmed a series of blackened leather journals. Next to them, a belted stack of parchment teetered, and high above, in a niche in the stone wall, books had been stacked every which way.

He needed a ladder to access them, but wasn't in the mood to fetch one. He looked about the room, making sure he was alone before focusing on his solar plexus. A small portion of it began to spin fast. He cringed at the ache as a conduit formed, and when the opening was wide enough, he projected his will through it. He scanned the books in the niche, chose the only red one, and pulled at it with his mind.

The book shuddered, then settled into stillness again.

He adjusted the conduit, made it a little wider, and tried again.

The book shook, slid off the shelf, and whizzed through the air toward him, settling into his outstretched hand.

Ulmaen laughed at his success. He'd been practicing at channeling his will through his body instead of his mind, with little effect. For the first time, he accomplished his intent—the book hadn't fallen in mid flight, it hadn't burst into flame—and as he began flipping through the pages, he sighed with satisfaction.

The pages contained long lists of sold items: dresses, suits, shirts. Some lists indicated services, such as hemming and size modifications, and others reflected inventory and custom orders for table clothes, bedding, and drapery. He'd seen many of these kinds of sales ledgers while searching for Rozafel's.

Once he had found the sales ledger for her Eastgate business, he was surprised to discover the gloves had been sold to Elusis, someone he had once known; someone who at one time had much preferred that his niece, Yensilva, befriend anyone other than Ule.

Elusis had been a bitter man who had barely tolerated Ule at best, and when his niece had disappeared, he'd blamed Ule. When he was at his worst, passed out in the desert from too much whiskey, Ule had helped him to a nearby magical woods, where he was made to forget his life and his misery.

With no memory of the world beyond the woods, Elusis had no need to leave them unless he somehow remembered and returned to Sondshor, where he'd discover his livelihood had been auctioned off to another merchant.

Ulmaen imagined Elusis angrier than ever, recalling a time when his niece had disappeared and he had evicted Ule from the farm without hesitation. He was capable of cruelty, but was he capable of murdering someone? Ulmaen didn't know, but Elusis had a reason to hurt her, even if his animosity toward her was misplaced.

Ulmaen shook his head free of the sudden thought. He knew who Ule's murderer was—Kerista. She had the ability and the knowhow, and he had a theory as to her reason. She must have somehow figured out what Ule was and acted according to her duties as head of security to ensure Lyan's protection.

The knowledge was supposed to ease Ulmaen's anger, to appease his curiosity, but he remained unsettled. Given Kerista's current condition, she would never be identified as the murderer or held accountable for her crime. That bothered him most of all.

After discovering the room within the excavated temple, he had visited her in the Infirmary, hoping to find answers. He pressed his perception into her body, saw the damage to her neural pathways and made little sense of her jumbled, disjointed thoughts.

Ulmaen flipped through the pages of the ledger, scanning the headings of each page, and wondered if there was any evidence in the Archive to help prove Kerista's crime. He no longer had Rozafel as a cover to explain his research, and Mbjard would want to know why he was reading Kerista's journals and ledgers.

"What do you have there?"

Ulmaen nearly dropped the book. He had been so deeply engrossed in his thoughts, he hadn't heard Mbjard enter the Archive. He laughed off his jittery nerves and shrugged. Pointing to the list, he replied, "A misfiled ledger."

Mbjard stood next to him to examine the page and mumbled. "We've a lot of those here. Any further luck investigating Rozafel's gloves?"

"Yeah," Ulmaen lied, and pretended to be searching the book he held. He flipped through the pages again, and his eyes snapped to a familiar name—Elusis.

He re-examined the listings. They were sales records for Elusis's store. After several pages, Ulmaen was drawn to an entry for a pair of gloves: *White gloves, 1 pair, white silk, white fine embroidery, wrist length, female; sold to...*

He anticipated the name Kerista to be printed there, but found instead: *sold to Lishadru, for the amount of seven sils.*

Mbjard patted him on the shoulder again. "Find anything?"

Ulmaen's confusion betrayed him.

"What's the matter?" Mbjard asked, growing concerned.

"Who's Lishadru?!"

"Lovely," Mbjard answered.

Ulmaen read the name again, fighting his disappointment. The name printed there had to be Kerista. "What's lovely about it," he complained.

"The name, it means *lovely*," Mbjard explained.

No it didn't, Ulmaen almost blurted out loud. When he had created the first language of the world, the root word for love was *elish*, the name by which the world was now called.

"Do you know who she is?"

Mbjard rubbed his chin. "Can't say I do. She could be anyone, though if I had to make a guess by the sound of her name, she was probably from Woedshor."

He wandered from the table, both forefingers pressed to his lips, lost in deep thought. He nodded occasionally, turned back toward the table, and lowered his hands.

"Out of curiosity, when was the date of the sale?"

Ulmaen read it out, indicating the gloves had been resold nearly five years ago.

"The war," Mbjard said. "The war was still raging then. Ah, yes, we can narrow this down."

"How?" Ulmaen's mood turned dark. More than ever, he wanted to find a way to connect Kerista to the gloves. "If she's from Woedshor, we won't have any records—"

"Shhh," Mbjard attempted to calm Ulmaen. "At that time, Sondshor was the least desirable of locations to travel to. Anyone who was from away, settled down somewhere in Sondshor to wait out the war. This means she had to have some kind of livelihood to survive, and Adinav was diligent about tracking monies within the shor."

Ulmaen frowned.

"If this woman is still alive," Mbjard continued, "or she's among the unfortunate who were slaughtered during the war, she'll be in the Identity records. I suggest you start there." He chuckled. "I don't pity you *that* task."

Ulmaen had seen the state of the Identity Records. He estimated the search would take many hours of thumbing through parchment, interpreting handwriting, and reading the faded ink. If he was left unattended, he'd find the information in a fraction of the time.

Mbjard patted him gently on the shoulder. "Your desire to do this for Rozafel is commendable," he told him. "However, I sense your hesitancy. I'll understand if you want to stop."

Ulmaen bit his tongue. He needed to tell someone the truth about Rozafel. Her friends needed to know she was gone, and Gorlen needed to be reprimanded in some way for his neglect of her. Yet, if he said anything about seeing Rozafel's body, he'd have to explain how he'd gotten into that cavern beside the Pit.

"She's dead." The words escaped his lips like prisoners bolting for freedom.

Mbjard tilted his head. His features narrowed in every conceivable way. "Who's dead?"

"Rozafel."

Ulmaen momentarily chastised himself for telling Mbjard, though he hadn't any reason to distrust him. He'd told the truth once before and that honesty had worked to his benefit by assuring Mbjard of Ulmaen's character.

Ulmaen took a deep breath to calm himself. He didn't have to convey every detail of his experience finding Rozafel's bloated body floating in the underground river. He just needed to be careful.

Mbjard peered up at him with scrutiny and softly asked, "Don't be afraid. Tell me how you know this."

"When I was serving in the Pit," Ulmaen replied. "The other prisoners, they heard her hang herself."

As though stung by a fever bee, Mbjard spun around and began pacing the room. Eventually he stopped and said, "You are very brave to confide in me this way," he said. "A tragic shame about Rozafel."

"Why won't Gorlen tell anyone?" Ulmaen suddenly asked, grateful not to have to go into details about what the prisoners saw, about the eerie conversation he'd had with Mithreel.

"To protect Ule's investigation, perhaps. Rozafel was a suspect," Mbjard suggested.

"She was innocent."

Mbjard nodded. "Yes, as indicated by your research. Could be Gorlen is considering what effect this will have on the electoral proceedings, or..."

The silence lingered. Ulmaen waited for Mbjard to continue but his patience was limited. "Or what?"

"Or, Gorlen fears that her death under his care might cause him to lose his position as head of Prison. You see, in conjunction with the arch mystic, he can remove a Magnes from the Chair. He stands to lose a lot of power. "

Ulmaen understood. Long ago, when he'd been Ule, a cactus spine had transformed her into a gemstone, making her Xiinisi powers ineffectual. He never wanted to lose his power again, and he shook his head.

"People ask me about Rozafel all the time, and I tell them what Gorlen told me, that she's working in the quarry." He sighed deeply. "Everyone wants to know. And everyone should know."

Mbjard drew close to him again. "This burden, I ask you to carry it a little while longer, until we know more about why Gorlen has hidden her death. Understood?"

Ulmaen nodded.

"You're not alone in this now," Mbjard said as he wandered toward the door of the Archive. "I trust you can do whatever research you require on your own then?"

"What? You're not going to observe?"

"You know what you're doing." Mbjard stopped at the door. "This research is important, for security reasons. Therefore, I grant you access to the entire Archive, including restricted materials. If the other apprentices complain, send them to me." He bowed and exited the room.

Alone in the Archive, Ulmaen quickly filed away the pile of books left in his care. He returned the Sales Ledger to a better location, on a shelf within easy reach, then he started hunting through the Identity Records.

"Who's Lishadru?" he repeated to himself, over and over again.

He wouldn't be satisfied until he knew the answer, until he found some documented proof of Kerista's involvement.

The Identity Records showed remnants of a system—a few books here and there were still in order, especially anything that dated from more than twenty years ago. The messiest records were those maintained during the last ten years of Adinav's reign.

Ulmaen sacrificed a bit of time from his inner reserve to quicken the process. Holding in his mind the pattern of characters for the name he sought, Lishadru, he began scanning ledgers.

There. Lishadru. He had found her.

He pulled out a tall, narrow ledger and flipped to the page containing her name. It listed her and her family, and he noted several comments and descriptions marked there by different people over the years.

He read quickly, learning that Lishadru had been married to an ambassador from Woedshor who had defected during the war. Knowing Adinav and his ability to manipulate others, Ulmaen wondered if Lishadru's family remained of their own accord or if they had been threatened or forced by Adinav to do so.

The document listed Lishadru's birth date. She'd been in her early thirties while she lived in the castle. She had been married to a man considerably older than herself, and together they were raising a son aged three. At the very end, a simple note had been left following the entries for each family member, the same word with every entry: Deceased.

He turned to the Death Records. He pushed his perception through the books until he found several entries which coincided with that time in history. Among them, he found Lishadru and read:

Impaled by sword. Evidence of one resurrection (post mortem wounds). Found outside Council Chamber. Interment: Mass Burial. Content of Body: 1 yellow shawl, 1 green dress, 2 brown leather riding boots, 1 silver necklace with blue topaz, 2 white gloves, 1 hair comb...

Half-heartedly he read about her husband. He too had died from being impaled by a sword. He also had been resurrected. As for their child, all the record stated was: *Body not found. Assumed dead.*

Ulmaen sucked at his teeth, wondering how Kerista had come to possess Lishadru's gloves, and how exactly these two women were connected with one another.

✳

Drips of water fell onto the beige and turquoise tiles at Ulmaen's feet, and he relished in the sensation of washing away the dust and dirt that had gathered on him during his search through the Identity Records.

Water lapped at the sides of many basins recessed in the floor. Occasionally the squeal of a tap turning on and the rush of water interrupted the steamy silence of the Bath House.

A couple of men soaked in a nearby basin and kept to themselves. A few others came and went; he paid them no attention. When he'd dried enough, he reached for his clothes and discovered a note tucked in the fold of his shirt.

Tiny lettering printed on a square of parchment read: *Meet me in my studio, please. It's important. I won't slap, promise! L—*

He recognized Laere's handwriting and wasn't sure if he wanted to meet with her again. She'd misunderstood him when they last talked, and he worried she intended to lecture him, or perhaps subject him to a hostile rant.

When he arrived at her studio, she jumped down from her stool by the easel and approached him carefully.

"I'm sorry," she said immediately. "I shouldn't have slapped you." She wiped paint from her hands on the apron covering her long skirt. "I don't think sometimes, you know." Her eyes fluttered. "I say things I shouldn't. Things I should keep to myself and regret later."

She was a passionate woman. That much he knew. Her passion wasn't the same as Bethereel's, who had directed that swell of fierce energy the way a trainer herded a pride of sand lionsl. Laere's passion was different, ferocious yet scattered.

"Yeah," he said. "I get that."

Laere let out a huge sigh. "I'm still sore about what *won't* happen between us, but I understand. Besides, there are more important things going on, like an election and you solving a murder."

The murder had already been solved, but he couldn't tell her that.

Carefully, she took him by the hand. "Relax, I don't mean anything by this. I got to thinking about how I could help you out. Wracked my brain for days." She led him from the studio and down the hallway, where she began to ramble.

"Those white gloves, the ones that poisoned Ule, they were fine work. Rozafel would have asked a large sum for them."

Based on what he saw in Rozafel's sales ledger, she hadn't asked enough for the gloves. Laere couldn't know that, of course, and he didn't feel the need to squash her speculation.

"So I asked myself," Laere continued, "who could afford such expensive gloves? Someone with lots of money, of course."

Ulmaen appreciated the turn in her reasoning. Elusis had a habit of buying product from other clothiers then reselling it for considerably more than what he had paid. Lishadru, the one who bought the gloves from Elusis, had to have been fairly wealthy at least. Come the morning, he'd discuss with Mbjard how to research the moneyed citizens of Sondshor.

"I thought it would take me longer," Laere started again. "I wasn't certain if there'd even be one, but I followed your example and conducted a thorough search through portrait galleries downstairs. It's the least I could do to make up for my outburst."

As usual, he didn't understand the jumble of Laere's words and softly asked, "What are you talking about?"

"Portraits." She pushed through a door, and pulled him along. As she led him down steep steps, she paused a moment to peer over her shoulder.

She pouted slightly, and the gesture pulled at his flesh and his muscles, arousing him slightly even though he didn't want to feel that way about her. Gently, he released her hand.

"Over here." She led him through a short doorway.

He ducked to make it through, and found that in the room his head grazed the beams of the floor above.

Paintings packed the room. Some were small and stacked in piles. Others were as long as Laere, leaning in stacks against the walls, the painted side faced down, well protected from dust and dirt.

"Portraits of Magnisi are mandatory," Laere explained. "And generals too, if they show exemplary performance or conduct during their duty. Those are on the Treasury's account. Importants usually commission us to have their portraits done. Not all of them do. Sometimes they take advantage of independent artists in Eastgate or Sondshor Market."

He listened to her, wondering where her reasoning was taking him. He ducked beneath a double thick beam in the ceiling, wiped a cobweb away, and followed her toward the far wall.

"Artists can make a few coin for portraits," Laere admitted.

From what he had seen of the portraits hanging in the halls and corridors around the castle grounds, the high quality of craftsmanship indicated the artists deserved more than a few coin for their talent and skill.

"You should be getting a few gols," he told her.

She laughed and shook her head. "You don't know a thing about being an artist, do you?"

He did know something about being an artist. Ulmaen valued creativity above all, just like every other Xiines.

"Every day since we last talked, I've been spending some time going through the old portraits down here, keeping watch for anyone wearing white gloves."

She gestured to the paintings around her. "These were all abandoned during the war." She pointed toward a stack on the wall ahead of them. "This lot was found in the rubble of the building near the old Mystics Tower. Found a diary tucked behind one of the paintings. Couldn't help myself, I read a few parts."

"Only a few?" Ulmaen asked, watching not to step on any of the paintings.

"I wanted to, 'til I got to the part that described how Adinav kept the importants, their entire families, locked up in the Inner Sanctum with him for days. They'd huddle in the hall outside the tower room and not let soldiers pass. Adinav had taken over their minds, so they stayed willingly, slowly starving to death. For the few who weren't controllable, Adinav made them watch."

Laere saddened, and her voice trembled when she spoke again.

"He'd made the ones he controlled use their bodies like shields to protect him. And when they died, he'd resurrect them." She turned on the spot, her head bowed in shame. "I had no idea. I thought those stories were exaggerations. Ule was right to destroy all traces of his existence. I never appreciated what she was trying to do."

Ulmaen rejoiced at hearing Laere admit it had been wrong for her to hold onto reminders of Adinav. He delighted in her speaking kindly about Ule for once, but his joy was short-lived. He suddenly saw the error in Ule's ways.

"You're wrong," he told Laere, disappointed in himself. "Ule was wrong to take history away from people. Think about it. Without that documentation, you'd have gone on thinking the stories about Adinav weren't true, and you wouldn't have had a change of heart, you wouldn't have gotten to see him through someone else's eyes."

Laere nodded slowly at first. "I think you're right, but I also think Ule meant well. I see that now." Though she still seemed a little sullen, Laere turned back around, took a few more steps, than motioned toward a painting, which was the only one turned upright.

"I'd like you to meet Lishadru *and* her family. All of their names are written on the backside, if you need them. Isn't the boy cute?"

The portrait was of an older man in a chair. He looked uncomfortable, as though the suit he wore was stiff and itchy. Sitting on his lap was a young boy dressed in blue velvet. Next to them, Lishadru stood in a yellow dress.

The pictorial reference of the woman who had bought the white gloves from Elusis's shop was stunning. He stared at Lishadru, feeling a familiarity about her. They had both lived in the castle together, except he had been a gemstone at the time. Perhaps their paths had crossed. Then Lishadru died, was resurrected, then died again.

The portrait was inferior to anything Laere had painted, but it still captured certain details well. Lishadru wore a multitude of thin bracelets on both wrists. Poking out from her short-cropped hair was some form of jewelry, and around her neck, cradled on the flat of her chest above her cleavage, was a silver necklace with a blue pendant.

He reached out and touched the image of the necklace. His thumb glided over the blue pendant and he muttered, "Topaz."

"What's that?"

He stepped back and pointed. "Does that look like a triangle to you?"

Laere stepped forward and squinted her eyes. After a few seconds, she pulled away and nodded. "Yeah, that's a triangle. Is that important? I thought the gloves were."

Yes, the gloves were important, but so was the necklace. It had been listed in Lishadru's death record.

"Is this a common kind of necklace?"

"I don't think so." Laere shrugged, looking at the portrait again. "People in their position want to stand out from everyone else. What better way than custom jewelry? I mean, did you like your wife looking just like every other woman?"

"No!" He thought of Bethereel, and for an instant, he believed Bethereel needed to be set apart from other women, even though deep down he knew no one could be exactly like her and doing so wasn't necessary. Why did he need to prove to others what he knew in his heart to be true?

He remembered how he used to be when he had been a woman. Ule didn't need to set Bethereel apart from others. She only had to look into Bethereel's eyes, and the rest of the world fell away. It didn't matter what anyone else thought or believed.

Once Ulmaen's ego settled, he realized he was full of nonsense. Ule, despite some misjudgments, had the right attitude. He'd exchange all the necklaces, jewelry, and clothes for more time with Bethereel, to kiss her, to feel the pulse of her life again.

Laere stepped back a little farther to examine the overall painting. "What was she like?"

"Who?"

"Your wife." Laere gazed at him. "Did she look like her brother?"

Bethereel didn't have a brother, only a cousin, he thought as he struggled to understand Laere's departure from their topic.

Laere closed her eyes. "I'm trying to imagine a female version of Navalis. Was her hair short or long?"

Panic twisted his chest. He'd forgotten his Elishian identity again. Yes, he was supposed to have been married to Navalis's sister.

"Long," he told her, not giving any consideration to how the women from that area of Elish dressed.

"Was she... buried?" Laere's face softened. "That's the custom where you're from, isn't it? Do you bury them in clothing like we do? Are they buried with their favorite possessions?"

An onset of numbness dulled Ulmaen's pangs of grief, until the last of Laere's questions sheered him from his emotions. His mind burst with revelation: A silver necklace. A blue pendant. Topaz to be exact. Triangular in shape. And there was a hair comb, too.

The hairs on his neck prickled his flesh. A twinge of excitement fueled his memories. He recalled the room with the strange spider and what he had found there—a silver necklace with a triangular pendant set with topaz, an ornate hair comb. All of the items he saw there belonged to Lishadru. They were the same items he saw listed on her death record, and wondered if Kerista had robbed Lishadru's grave.

✳ CHAPTER 44 ✳

At the top of the retaining wall near Mareel's Gatehouse, Navalis stopped a moment at the stairs that led down into the courtyard of Fehran's Hall below. People spilled into the courtyard, some trickling in from the northern courtyards while most streamed through the archway from the Colonnade.

"Whoa!" Boriag said, standing beside him. "That's a lot of people in one place."

Farther along the wall, a couple of young boys eyed the corner roof line of the Hall, looking for a way to climb up onto the roof. After a few moments, they thought better of it and sat on the wall with their feet dangling over the edge.

Navalis stepped back to let a small group of clothiers access the stairs. As they descended, he followed their lead, mindful of Boriag being close behind him.

The clothiers chattered among themselves, occasionally patting along the straps of their marigold overdresses where rows of sewing needles and pins had been stuck. Their clothes were dusted in textile lint and snippets of black thread, reminding him of matter-infused An Energy, the very energy his kind used to create worlds, creatures, as well as their Xiinisi forms.

Demons, too.

Always, in the forefront of his mind, the physical nature of demons cast a veil over everything he saw. Questions nagged at him. What had caused a demon to take the form of an Elishian? Since there was one among them, could there be another?

The clothiers disembarked from the stairs, then he and Boriag did the same. As he scanned the crowds, Boriag came up beside him, and dug an elbow into his side.

"A bunch of farmers dropped out, did you hear?" Boriag asked.

No, he hadn't heard. In fact, he'd been so preoccupied with reviewing what he knew of demons, he had only bothered to attend a few of the candidates' campaign speeches.

Their rhetoric had reeked of lies, changes they hoped to make, like improving the conditions in the ever-deteriorating Eastgate with its rundown buildings and infestations, and suggesting better ways to deal with farmers setting up their shanty markets at Southgate. Unfortunately, greed and the desire for power smeared their faces with slippery smiles, and Navalis didn't trust a word of anything they had said.

He had listened to Osblod, too, who droned on about earning the right to rule, of honoring the needs of everyone, no matter their station in life.

His notions were idealistic and perhaps not practical, and he had regarded Lyan the entire time he spoke, as though he were imparting some secret message to him.

"Betcha those farmers' knees were knocking, eh?" Boriag said. "Can't say I blame 'em. So close to voting. Lots dropped out. Now's the time for all the scaredies to run back to their homes and shiver." He began to nod, his lips pressed together—a firm expression assuring his seriousness. "This election... it's important, you know. Not for people playing games."

Navalis glanced at Boriag again. Ruddy sunlight gleaned along the bridge of his bulbous nose and long neck, both features disproportionate to his others. The awkwardness and improbability of his features reminded Navalis of certain demons, the older ones who had spent thousands of years pushing themselves to look more like Elishians.

For a demon to resemble an Elishian exactly, then a large number of Elishians must have developed a fear of their own kind. But how? And why? When—

"Laere!" Boriag waved his arm high in the air. "Laere?"

Ahead of them, Navalis caught a glimpse of the back of Laere's long black hair swinging in one direction as she turned in another. Then she was gone.

"How's your love affair with her coming along?" Navalis asked.

Boriag guffawed. "She's not... I'm not in..." Finally he sighed. "She's scared."

Navalis laughed. "Of you?"

"Nooo." Boriag's face scrunched up. "Okay, maybe."

"Relax," Navalis told him. "Be yourself." From the corner of his eye, he waited for Boriag's reaction.

"It's not that," Boriag complained. "She thinks she's a mystic, wanted to know if there was a way to find out."

As the crowds pressed in around them, Navalis grew more mindful of his step, having already kicked the heels of a clothier in front of him, causing his shoe to fall off.

"She wouldn't be the first artist to become a mystic," Navalis said.

"Like I said, she's scared." Boriag straightened his tunic, craning his neck. "It's not like there's a test for it. You just have to want to be one."

A test.

Navalis mulled over the idea, for he had been trying to find ways to assuage his doubts about Rolen's story, to be sure the Elishian he intended to confront was indeed a demon.

He squared his shoulders, resisting the flow of people squeezing in around him. Window shutters had been bolted open, offering an alternate way for the servants, farmers, and soldiers lingering outside to hear Magnes Lyan give the last of the campaign speeches.

The sheer enormity of the gathering impressed upon him the importance of the event, and he grew impatient with the distraction. His impulse toward satisfying his curiosity was often difficult to curb.

Creating worlds to explore and study was the primary activity for his kind. They learned about themselves, and whenever a world expressed a new system or construct generated by a world's inhabitants which proved intriguing, they incorporated the construct into their own realm.

The model designation for Elish was based on one of those constructs— a method of timekeeping that had developed in another world consisting of a solar system, in which only one planet and its inhabitants had evolved. That planet, which the inhabitants called Earth, was the progenitor for all 24-60-60 model planets. Although the twenty four hour system wasn't a perfect clock, somehow it had been embraced globally by Earth's inhabitants, and had sparked a trend among the Xiinisi for building similar worlds.

Earth's early history had inspired many constructs, which they absorbed into their own realm, in particular the artful brilliance of architecture that arose in this world's ancient past in a region called Middle Land, what the ancient Earthlings had called the Mediterranean. Earth had offered them plenty to explore, and now they were learning from Elish.

"Push through now," Boriag insisted. "We were supposed to be with the others inside half an hour ago."

Navalis squeezed through the open doorway, Boriag slipping in behind. When those nearest recognized their formal teal tunics, they recoiled or swore. Anyone who had detested mystics before now had reason to justify their reactions toward them, for rumors of Kerista's cannibalism validated their beliefs.

Navalis scanned the Hall. On the north and south sides, tapestries had been rolled up to allow people to stand beneath the mezzanines and view the front of the hall. Farmers, merchants, and importants stood squeezed together, and somewhere he imagined Laere standing on her tip toes trying to see above the crowd.

The mystics had gathered by the south mezzanine, clustered on one end of the stage. On the north side were the scribes, and he glimpsed Ulmaen standing among them. He wore the same black capelet as they did, and Navalis wondered when Ulmaen had been inducted into their profession and why he hadn't mentioned it.

Lyan stood in the middle of the stage, where other candidates had on previous days. He leaned against a wooden podium, his hands clutching either side, waiting to commence his speech.

Before the stage, directly in front of the podium, Osblod towered above those on the front edge of the crowd. His mood was solemn, and he stood with arms crossed in front of his chest.

At the back of the stage, near the scribes, General Gorlen braced himself in an informal stance, his hands folded behind his back. His entourage of guards formed a wide circle around the Magnes to ensure his safety.

Near the podium, Mbjard stood, adjusting the stiff collar of his capelet. When he was comfortable, he stepped toward the edge of the stage and raised both hands to signal for silence.

The rush of conversation throughout Fehran's Hall began to diminish. He held his arms upward and waited until complete silence was established before lowering them again. He returned to his original position near a guard, withdrew a small scroll of parchment from within his tunic and held it out toward Lyan.

Mbjard frowned when Lyan refused to accept it. He extended the scroll a little farther, and Lyan, who seemed frozen in thought, finally responded. He turned away, steadied himself at the podium, and addressed the assembly.

"We gather here on the eve of voting," he began, "campaigning nearly at an end except for my final words. I assure you, my closing remarks are few."

Mbjard lowered the roll of parchment, his cheeks gone flushed. Panic made the whites of his eyes more pronounced, and he stood riveted in place.

Children's laughter and the wails of young babes drifted in through the open doors from the courtyard, where mothers tended to their young, and the faces of latecomers peered through the open windows, straining to hear what the Magnes had to say.

Within the hall, feet shuffled yet no one uttered a sound. Smoke hung in the air, and Navalis smelled a familiar sweet cherry tobacco. Instantly, he spotted Sabien near Osblod.

Sabien craned his head to listen, brows furrowed. A puff of pale smoke rose from a thin pipe clenched between his teeth, as he gave his full attention to Lyan.

Navalis retreated into his thoughts. He'd cared about Sabien as a lover once. He'd never meant to hurt him. He never meant to hurt anyone, but he always seemed to. Now, he had a choice to make, consequences to consider, as he figured out how to engage with the Elishian demon. Doing so meant hurting someone again.

He glanced at Boriag, dreading what he had to.

"I could list my achievements, if you want." Lyan's voice carried throughout the hall. "My mistakes as well. If ruling a shor was about keeping score, I'd be in the lead by my mistakes alone."

Navalis cocked his head to one side, intrigued by the unusual opening of the speech. A leader admitting their flaws was unheard of in any of their worlds' histories. Rulers commonly demanded recognition of their perfection, and anyone who denied it was punished.

Across the podium, Mbjard frowned. Some of the soldiers regarded one another in confusion. Throughout the hall, people leaned into one another to whisper.

"The truth is," Lyan continued, and the hall fell silent again, "everyone here has benefited from the end of the war. Any one of you could've sat in the Chair. Anyone."

A smattering of voices droned throughout the hall.

"I'll have it then!" Boriag called out in jest.

Navalis coughed to dispel his mirth at the outburst. He appreciated Boriag's humor, for it wouldn't last. Not after what he intended to do soon.

While others snickered, Mbjard's displeasure deepened at the outburst.

Lyan smirked at the comment, mildly amused, but as the laughter faded, he grew serious again.

Osblod clamped a hand over his mouth and kept it there. His expression matched those of some of the advisers—a look of sheer perplexity, of worry and fear.

On the far side of the stage, Ulmaen appeared disinterested in what Lyan had to say.

Mbjard brought his arms above his head again, and the assembly quieted down.

"No matter who, no matter how they ruled," Lyan continued, "the world became a better place the moment Adinav was executed, his hold on the world released."

Light applause rose and fell, even though most didn't fully understand or appreciate what the Magnes had just said.

Adinav. The name stuck in Navalis's mind. How long had it been since he and Kaleel the Rex fought their way through the undead to overthrow and kill the Grand Magnes? It had been a little more than two years since he stood at the side of that cat demon—his form the manifestation of a collective fear of cats.

That's what demons were, after all—manifestations of fear. But they weren't meant to be anything more than vapors, so how and when did they finally learn to take on the shape of an Elishian?

"As of late," Lyan continued, "I've been considering whether or not I've truly *earned* the position of Magnes, to sit in the Chair, to begin a new lineage." He curled his hands around the edge of the podium.

"What's that?" Boriag muttered under his breath.

Navalis ignored him as he reviewed events from the end of the war, the numerous people who had been made into puppets, hollowed out, forced to fight, and once dead, brought back as the undead to fight again.

The war, he realized, this demon must have been born during the war. There had been other wars before, but none commanded by a supernatural Magnes, none lasting over a hundred years, none that pitted Elishians against empty shells of their own kind. That alone would be enough to cause fear on a massive level. Fear of other Elishians.

The revelation was a dreadful thought, yet he remained fixated on Lyan, who sagged against the podium as though he'd given in to defeat already. He spoke again.

"I must confess..."

Osblod rushed to the stage, releasing his hand from his mouth. He reached toward the podium, tried to grab at Lyan's leg, but a guard pushed him back.

"Don't do this!" Osblod called out.

Mbjard stepped forward. "What is this?"

Lyan shook his head at Osblod, and told them both, "The truth matters."

Whispers spread throughout the Hall again. Lyan didn't bother to wait for Mbjard to calm everyone, and resumed his speech.

"After Adinav was defeated and executed, I skirmished with undead soldiers in the courtyard beyond that one."

Yes, yes, Navalis thought. Undead soldiers. So many soldiers had run at first, their legs trembling, screams stuck in their throats. When did Adinav's puppets start appearing on the battlefields? Five, six, seven years before then? Yes, those were the days of the resurrected dead, but those who had been hollowed out, made into living puppets, they'd been on the battlefield far longer.

Outside, the howl of an unhappy baby grew loud and shrill, then stopped with a choking gurgle.

More than enough time, he realized, for a collective fear to grow and spark into a vaporous life, to solidify into bone, to become a babe and grow to maturity, confirming what he suspected. The demon was an adult in physical development.

"Yes, I admit it," Lyan continued, braving the scrutiny of the assembly. He straightened himself at the podium. "I had no hand in stopping Adinav. I did not fight him. I did not kill him. I wasn't even there to watch him die. I'm not a hero."

Gasps and mutterings exploded throughout the room.

Osblod trembled. He lowered his head, as though he grieved some great loss.

"I stumbled across the Chair Room." Lyan's eyes lost contact with the crowd, as though he were reliving that day in his mind. "It was empty and I was exhausted and injured badly. I waited, but Adinav didn't come. No one came. I sat on the Chair, half expecting to die from my wounds. That is how I became Magnes."

If ever a truth had been told in the history of Elish, this was by far the most accurate, perhaps the first by a leader. Suddenly, Navalis felt privileged to have witnessed this confession.

The assembly remained silent. Even Ulmaen had snapped out of his daze and paid attention now.

"To this day, whoever killed my predecessor remains unknown. Whoever they might be, *they* deserve accolades and honors, they *deserve* the Chair for ridding the world of his destructive force."

Osblod straightened himself. Navalis expected him to interrupt as he had done so many times before during Lyan's public speeches, but he remained quiet.

"As we try to forget Adinav, even my poor attempts to erase him from the record proved an impossible task." Lyan shook his head. "We cannot forget. We should *never* forget. We must remember Adinav for what he truly was—selfish, power-driven, a cautionary tale of how men can become monsters when charmed by power. He's a reminder that this world needs a leader with less personal ambition and more willingness to consider the welfare of everyone."

Lyan stood back from the podium, no longer requiring its support.

"I may not deserve the Chair, but when I took it, I took it on behalf of those like me. Those who were tired. Those who were pained by the war and by a Magnes who cared nothing for the world he lived in."

The mood within the room shifted. Nods animated the crowd. For many, their eyes glistened with sadness and a lingering fear.

"When I sat in that Chair, I chose to defend it against anyone who wanted it for purely selfish reasons." Anger tinged his weariness. Whatever was weighing him down vanished.

"I *chose* to accept the responsibility to ensure that stability and prosperity returned to Sondshor in a peaceful way. And if you should *choose* me, I will continue to accept and honor that responsibility, and teach it to my sons and daughters, and their sons and daughters, so that future generations of Magnisi understand that ruling a shor is difficult and challenging."

Lyan's anger subsided. "Anyone might be able to sit in the Chair, but it takes a certain type of person to rule a shor and to rule it well." He paused again, his eyes making contact with as many people as possible, including Osblod.

The tension in Lyan's demeanor lessened. In fact, he seemed more energetic than he had when he started. He raised his voice, and his words had recovered their firmness and strength.

"Sondshor is a reflection of all *our* hard work. Remember that when you vote."

With a final nod, Lyan stepped back from the podium. Guards immediately surrounded him and escorted him across the stage toward the north mezzanine, where he retreated into a room to wait for the assembly to disband.

Applause thundered throughout the hall, followed by farmers calling out for Lyan's instatement. Soldiers joined in next, their voices booming in unison. Caterwauls turned into a rhythmic chant accompanied by stomping feet as they called out Lyan's name again and again.

The appreciation for Lyan, however, did not extend throughout the entire hall. There were many who seemed unimpressed or irritated by the revelation of Lyan not having a direct hand in Adinav's demise.

Osblod, for example, had leaned over and pressed hard-knuckled fists against the wood. His eyes were squeezed shut. Navalis couldn't make out if Osblod was anguished or amused until he finally stood, let out a long whoop, and grinned with satisfaction.

Next to Navalis, Boriag finally shook himself out of his shock. "What was that?!" He craned his head, peering over the crowd. "Was that his speech? Holy Mneos!" He shook his head. "No wonder Osblod's happy, he and everyone else's chance at Magnes just got better. Guess we'll be out of jobs soon."

Navalis regarded Boriag's annoyance, appreciated his unique personality and spirit. Though he seemed glum, Navalis knew a worse kind of misery awaited him.

* CHAPTER 45 *

Ever since Istok's escape, whenever Navalis walked the castle grounds, he expected the cactus demon to lunge from a dark doorway or lane. Istok had been a gemstone for a couple of years, and skulking around the castle grounds in search of revenge or retaliation fit his nature. Although Navalis had good reason to be afraid for himself and for others, he reasoned that Istok had probably returned to the desert where he was enjoying his freedom, at least for a little while.

In the meantime, Navalis still needed to catch himself another demon, and he knew of one that walked freely among them. He'd considered how to lure it out and reveal its true nature. If it was indeed a demon, how would he feel prying open the guts of someone he knew?

He did his best to conceal his thoughts, for he wasn't alone on the eastern Colonnade, and he didn't want the subject matter to unsettle Laere, who walked quietly beside him.

"Thanks for meeting with me," he told her.

"Sure," she replied. She bit her lip and scooped up her braid to drape it over a shoulder. "This is about Boriag, isn't it? Is he getting you to ask me out for him? He seems that kind of guy. Or is this about me avoiding him? I'm not." She rolled her eyes. "Not really. I've been keeping myself busy on purpose."

She turned in at the Studio, skipped up the cracked steps turned and pulled open the rickety wooden door. He followed her inside, admiring old paintings and tapestries mounted on the walls. Her studio was spacious, the light dim due to an overcast sky, and the morning too early for other artists to tend to their work.

She approached a large painting on a podium and removed the covering, revealing what she had accomplished so far on her portrait of Ule.

Navalis was struck by the great depth and detail. Laere had captured Ule in many ways—her eyes, her posture, the lightness in the way she held herself, her personality, too—haughty, headstrong, impulsive, so sure of herself. Strange as it felt, he missed Ule's rawness, which also had been rendered well in the portrait.

Ule had been eager to share her experiences. She'd have been forthright about the demons in the Prison, offering insights no matter how superficial. At times, she'd even been funny or glib. Her biggest fault had been her honesty. But Ule was no more. She had become another.

Over time, Ulmaen had slowly obscured his previous feminine self, finding stability within masculine hormones. In every way, he behaved more and more like a man, expressing a quiet confidence, keeping observations to himself. He wasn't compelled to share anything. He didn't need to, since no one had asked him for a report and no one had told him about the experiments on demons.

At times, Ulmaen felt like a stranger, and the tether of responsibility Navalis felt for his Student snapped. He willingly let go, wishing that the trust between them hadn't been lost in the process.

"Nothing against Boriag," Laere said. "He's better than most guys I know."

Ulmaen shook himself free from the hold the painting had over him.

"Boriag doesn't know I'm here," he told her.

"Oh?" She paused at a small table, her hand settling on a colorful rag as she waited for further explanation.

"He told me about your... enquiry?"

Her lower lip trembled. She cast her eyes downward. Anyone might think she seemed ashamed, but Navalis sensed anger rising from her.

"He wasn't supposed to tell anyone," she said. "It was private."

"I know, but he cares about you, and you won't talk with him."

She remained quiet, and he continued.

"There are ways to determine whether or not you have talent to be a mystic."

Laere stood straight, raising her head in defiance. "What if I decide I don't want to?"

Navalis shrugged. "No one'll know any different. I won't tell." He paused a moment, understanding the nature of her hostility. "It's okay to be afraid. Having skills others don't can be unsettling."

Laere snorted. "Like I'm going to trust you when I can't trust Boriag."

He smirked. "We're a shady lot," he admitted, hoping to calm her a bit. "Everyone knows that we raise the dead and utter chants that can disintegrate a rock." He kept his mirth to a minimum, watched how it eased her temperament. "Besides, aren't you... curious?"

Her face froze. Lips parted, she stared unblinkingly.

"Don't you want to know what being a mystic's all about?" He tilted his head and smiled. "I've seen how you handle yourself. You like barking at people, pushing them back. You're assured enough to keep the apprentices and adepts in line. You're certain to rise through the ranks quickly for that. Wouldn't you enjoy a bit of power?"

Laere's lips twitched at first, then curled into a tentative smile. She stayed her ground. "I thought—"

He moved closer to the portrait of Ule, examining the details closer. "Occasionally there are people born a certain way. No one can deny that. Consider Adinav. He had skills far superior to any mystic's."

Laere's smile waned. "I always thought that about him," she admitted. "He must have been born a mystic. Is that possible?"

Navalis shrugged. "Some are. Most are made. Some experience what we like to call an awakening."

They spoke at length, he and Laere, about the history of mystics, their role in security and protecting the Magnes. She gradually found ease with the subject, showing intense interest in the rare ability of Clear Sight, the ability to detect auditory signals in others' minds.

Finally, he asked, "Do you want to know for sure, if becoming a mystic is right for you?"

She nodded several times. "When can I find out?"

"Now's as good a time as any, don't you think?"

She approached him near the portrait, and asked, "How do we begin?"

He looked about the studio. "When will the other artists arrive?"

"Whenever they've slept off the whiskey from last night," she replied.

"We need to be somewhere no one will interrupt us or distract you," he told her.

He led her away from the studio, and she willingly followed. Returning to the Colonnade, they walked eastward a little ways then north under the archway into the courtyard of Fehran's Hall.

"Won't there be lots of people there?" Laere asked as they entered the main doors to the Hall.

He shook his head. "As a mystic, you're given access to some of the less known places around here."

He steered her toward the back of the hall. Beneath a tapestry, he pushed open a wooden door revealing stairs that led down into a cellar. Within the cellar was another flight of steps made from worn stone.

Laere clung to the walls to stop herself from falling. "Are there many passages like this?" she asked, ducking into a tunnel that snaked and dipped on a steady decline, leading them deeper beneath the ground.

"The grounds are riddled with them," he explained to her, "as far as the Catacombs in the North."

"Really!"

"They're not all functional," he explained. "Some have collapsed and others, well, you could turn a corner and suddenly be out of oxygen and suffocate to death because the ventilation's been clogged."

The pitch in Laere's voice rose. "Really?"

Ahead of them, the tunnel split in two directions. He veered left and Laere followed.

"What's down there?" she asked, referring to the other tunnel.

"It goes to another part of the old castle," he replied.

"Wait, are you telling me there's a castle *beneath* the castle?"

Laere's footfalls grew louder as her muscles grew more fatigued. Emerging into the tower, she stopped to rub her lower back.

Instead of guiding her down the steps toward his lab, he led her up the stairwell. The higher Laere climbed, the quicker her breath came.

"There's... better ways... to woo... a girl," she joked.

He stopped closest to the lookout, where wood planks covered the dirt filled doorway and looked as rustic as the originals Istok had destroyed. He fought a bitterness toward his inability to overtake the demon and for the month of energy he drained from within to restore those planks, as well as his laboratory, and the wooden door.

He stopped and turned toward Laere.

Her cheeks were flushed, her lips parted. She fished for the loose braid of her hair, brought it forward over her shoulder again, and fanned the back of her neck to cool down.

"I thought you were taking me to your lab."

"After," he told her.

"After what?"

"A test."

Laere blinked at him, tilting her head in confusion. "Boriag said there wasn't any test he knew of?"

He stepped down, slipping past her.

Laere turned about on the step, and perhaps for the first time in her life of short stature, she looked down on someone. "Where are you going?"

"Stay still a moment," he told her.

She stopped smiling. "Is that the test?"

He didn't answer. He called on his strength, the kind that exceeded the limits of his form. He moved quickly. He gripped Laere on either side of the waist.

Annoyed, she pried at his fingers and tried to wriggle free, but it had no effect.

He lifted her high above the step she had been standing on. Her braid slipped from her shoulder and dangled. Her feet reached for the step beneath her until he flung her, high and far, casting her over his head and away from the steps.

She hurled into the air, her arms outstretched, grasping at nothing. Her skirt hiked up as her foot grazed the wall, pitching her at an odd angle. Eyes wide, her mouth opened.

A high wail erupted from her, tightening and rising in pitch as she reached for him. Her scream reverberated along the tower wall and down the steps as she began to descend.

Navalis anticipated that her fatigue from traveling through the tunnel combined with a sudden feeling of vulnerability—let's say, a threat to her life—might force her survival instincts to kick in, and along with it any defense mechanisms, such as latent magical ability.

As gravity took hold of her, he waited. If she had lied about her hearing ability or had notions of grandeur, she'd be seriously injured, perhaps even die. He wouldn't leave her to that fate; no, he'd heal her and wipe her memory of the incident, *if she was truly and simply just an Elishian.*

Her body was falling faster now, and when her head was mere inches away from cracking open against a step, she stopped. A few seconds later, she stopped screaming for she finally realized she'd stopped falling.

Navalis had a theory about her innate power, yet was still amazed to watch her hover in the air. Slowly, she turned in the air, arms occasionally reaching out to balance herself, and once upright, she remained suspended. Occasionally steadying herself, she rose toward him.

Lips downturned, eyes glistening, she floated high enough to glare down at him.

He met her gaze and inhaled the overpowering odors of magic scent—cherries and...

He inhaled deeply.

She smelled of cherries and something smoky—a combination of beef and pork burning along with something coppery and sweet. He recognized the smell from his time during the war, when bombs singed soldiers or lit oil sprayed their flesh. The undercurrent of her magic scent was the smell of burning bodies.

Navalis hadn't expected anything to come of this experiment. He honestly believed the farmer Rolen's story had been exaggerated. Now, he knew for certain.

Laere wasn't a mystic.

She hadn't any training or exposure to mystic practices, their rudimentary science, their rites and rituals, the summonings, imbuings, meditations, balms, and potions. Anyone could become a mystic as long as they agreed to be apprenticed. Those who developed their skills moved on to become adepts, and those who didn't found other professions.

Laere was something else.

Based on what others had told him about her, she was most skilled at capturing high degrees of realism in her subjects. She also had a reputation for being unruly, wild, and destructive. He knew she was an artist, but was she a demon?

He recalled his visit to the bedroom in the far away farm with the images on the wall. The one of a stick figure walking above the horizon, a clue to the nature of the demon's ability. As a child, she must have been frustrated, perhaps even scared of this power, especially if she had been punished for it.

Laere's voice trembled as she struggled to speak. "Why'd you do that?"

Navalis reached forward and gently touched her arm. Laere floated backward to avoid him, maintaining her balance. Her resistance to gravity was impressive.

"Levitation," he told her. "That's your innate ability."

Laere's anger persisted, reddening her cheeks. She lowered herself toward the steps, and when her feet touched them, fear consumed her. The way her legs buckled, how she clung to the wall for support, she seemed never to have walked before. Navalis offered to help her but she batted his hand away.

"You're safe here." He tried to ease her growing anxiety, but she began heaving for air, her eyes bulging wide.

"You just tried to kill me!"

"No, my intention was to threaten you," he insisted.

"But how did you know? I didn't even know."

He sensed a sincerity about her confusion, her fear toward herself. She had innate skill beyond transformative magic, something no mystic had ever accomplished in the history of Elish, including Goyas. Yet, Adinav had and he was Elishian in the beginning, and although his magic scent smelled rotten, he had become something unnatural, a being that had lived considerably longer than most.

Laere looked and acted Elishian, too. She was certainly not a mystic, yet doubt still needled him.

"Come on," he told her. "Let's discuss this in my laboratory. One last test will tell us for certain, then perhaps you can apply to become an apprentice mystic."

Laere's breath evened. She pushed herself from the wall. She glared at him again, daring him to be truthful. "Really?"

He nodded and held out his hand. Uncertain, Laere stared at it.

"It... my ability, it doesn't scare you?"

"No," he told her. "I'm fascinated by it."

She must have sensed his honesty, for her anger diminished a little. The trauma of what she had experienced was slowly being extinguished by curiosity. Though her face began to relax, she made no effort to touch his hand.

He led Laere down the steps, past the landing to the tunnel and another until they arrived at his laboratory. He unlocked the door and swung it wide.

The dim light of the crystal lanterns inside pulsed and flared bright at the presence of movement. Shadows vanished. Laere gasped as she entered the room.

Navalis lingered at the worktable littered with books and quills and polished surgical tools. He glimpsed a stack of Boriag's drawings and the pencil diagrams of demons on them, and casually flipped the top parchment over to hide it.

"Come inside and close the door," he told her.

Laere pushed the wooden door with some effort yet managed to shut it.

"Stay there."

Laere looked about her and asked, "Here, in front of the door like this?"

Her lack of confidence made him tremble with guilt. He nodded, afraid to look at her. She'd sounded familiar in that moment, like Ule so long ago, when she had been younger and more compliant.

"Is this test going to be scary too?"

He wished she wouldn't ask any more questions. They triggered memories of Ule, who had been innocent and eager to please.

"Perfect," he told her. He joined her at the door, positioning himself directly in front of her. He pushed a strand of hair from her flushed face. He searched for any glimmer of malformation in her form. Her ears were small and even, her eyes wide and level. Everything was balanced, level, proportionate, and aligned.

"Oh, so this is the part where the wooing starts?" Laere spoke in a cold, flat tone.

The comment jarred his focus. He stopped to look at her. "No," he assured her, his heart beating fast.

His other hand whipped from his side. In the light between them, the spike dagger cast a needle shadow.

Shuug!

Laere gasped. Her face slackened. Shock darkened her eyes and she shuddered.

"What—"

Shuug!

Navalis drove the blade into her solar plexus again.

Her face contorted with pain and rage. She tried to push him away. When she couldn't, she rose from the ground—

Shuug! Shuug! Shuug!

Again and again, Navalis drove the knife into her as though she were a source of frustration that he tried to hit but kept missing every time he stabbed at it.

Laere bucked against the door. Her feet searched for leverage against his legs but slipped as she grew weaker.

A rage overcame him and it found a rhythm. The dagger slid out and dove in again with quick ferocity. Struck by a brightness and a pain in his head, he stumbled backward.

The dagger stuck in Laere. Her head had tilted, eyes still wide. She'd found a way to relax into her death, for her arms went limp, her lips parted, and she slid down the doorway until her feet touched the floor.

Navalis caught her before she fell. When she breathed her last, he slid the dagger free and stared at the blood—blood as red as apples.

It shouldn't be! Demon's blood was green.

He stared long and hard, blinking occasionally, hoping his eyes were misreading the color. Suddenly doubtful, he set the dagger aside and moved Laere to the dissection table. As she laid there, red blood—Elishian blood—pooled in the folds of her dress.

He expected her to move, for her eyes to blink and the illusion of the demon to show itself. She remained still.

He backed away and sat on a stool at the far side of the room, where he waited. He'd learned to be patient that way, on account of Ule. He waited. And the blood dripped down, staining Laere's shirt and the table red.

For hours he sat staring at her, at times forcing himself to blink, worrying he had erred in judgment, until he saw the blood on the spike dagger nearby start to change. It bubbled and hissed, and he let out a deep breath when it turned green. On the dissection table, the blood oozing from Laere began to bubble and turn green as well.

Hastily, He slipped on a black leather smock and thick black leather gloves. He gathered a select few tools from around the room, and from the shelf he fetched the gauntlet Boriag had imbued.

When his nerves settled and his heartbeat recovered, he began to dissect the Elishian demon.

❋ CHAPTER 46 ❋

A lack of an assistant slowed down Navalis's progress. There was no one to fetch tools, to records his findings, and unlike the other specimens, this one wore clothing. He had methodically cut away Laere's skirt, blouse, and undergarments, making sure not to nick her flesh. Her nakedness—the droop of her breasts, the soft padding of flesh across her belly—demanded close examination before he cut her open.

Navalis expected her eyes to snap open at any moment, for her to bolt upright where she lay on the table. He knew he was being irrational, even though he was certain she was a demon. Dissecting her unnerved him at times, mostly because she still looked so alive.

He expected freckles, moles, and scars—every Elishian had a few—but her flesh was clear. Not a mark on her anywhere. And with the passing of every hour, the texture of the upper dermis smoothed out, losing detail. By the time he cut into her chest, the lines on her palms and fingerprints had vanished.

The smell was faint at first, undetectable once she died, but as he lengthened the incision in her chest, Laere's body released her magic scent. A copious fume engulfed him, stinging his eyes. The stench of burning bodies slicked his nostrils and mouth, and clung to the back of his throat.

He flung himself away from the table, gagging until he willed the flow of sensations within his nostrils to stop. He deadened his taste buds, too. In the absence of smell, he began to cough and his eyes watered as the cloud of magic scent thickened.

Reluctantly he opened the laboratory door, and the smoke curled out into the stairwell. His eyes stopped stinging, and he resumed the dissection. Scalpel pressed firmly between his fingers, the blade slid deeper into the tissue, revealing distinct layers of dermis. He eased the leather fingers of his gloved hand deeper into the fold and found bone.

He wanted to see more, so he made the incision longer, and folded back the flesh and secured it with large clamps. Like any ribcage, tendons and tissue were fixed to the textured bone. Still, he was careful. Her blood had turned green. Her body had emitted magic scent. Somewhere within he was sure to find an end to her Elishian body and the beginning of... What could he call it? A chasm? An abyss?

These words represented structures and failed to capture his meaning. The reference he intended was an inexplicable emptiness, a nothingness, a void.

He retrieved a pair of sheers and used them to crack the ribs. After the removal of the sternum, he anticipated the first glimpse of the emptiness within. Instead, he found organs—stomach, lungs, a heart.

Uncertain which of them to examine first, he chose the heart and carefully set the tip of the scalpel there. The light pressure was enough to slice through the outer flesh.

Black tendrils arched between the dark space inside the heart and along the scalpel. Navalis whipped his hand away as the blade began to disintegrate. The black tendrils clung to the scalpel, the metal bubbling then fraying into black threads as though something unraveled it.

The tendrils crawled closer to Navalis's gloved fingers and he dropped the scalpel, not wanting to chance any contact. What remained of the tool fell into the open cavity of the heart, where the tendrils ate the last bit of it then slithered back into the emptiness.

He retrieved another scalpel and set it against one of the lungs. The blade slid into the tissue and the lung gaped open like a fish sucking for air, revealing more of that emptiness. Tendrils squirmed from the opening and gobbled up the scalpel.

Navalis stepped back from Laere and from the table, reminded of the black filaments of matter they harvested to create their worlds. They were strings of molecules waiting for a pattern to be impressed upon them, dormant and immobile until manipulated by the will of a Xiinisi.

"Ho there! Ack, what a stink!"

Navalis flinched at the unexpected intrusion. From behind the partially opened door, Boriag emerged, his back to the dissection table as he aimed himself at the work table.

"Working late?" he asked. "You should've said something. I'd have given you a hand. Ah, there it is."

Navalis hastily skirted the dissection table, eyes fixed on Boriag, watching his every movement. If he acted quickly enough, Boriag might not have a chance to turn around and notice the specimen on the table.

Boriag picked up the spike dagger and ran his finger lightly along the blade. "Just woke from a dream with some inspiration. Eck, what's on this?" Boriag began to turn around, holding the dagger out before him.

Navalis pulled at him. "Come into the stairwell. We need to talk."

"If you don't mind," Boriag continued, ignoring him, "I'd like to experiment on... it..."

Navalis tried to shield the dissection table from his assistant's view.

Boriag blinked profusely. "Whoa, that's a big dem..." He never finished the last word. Upon recognizing the body, a paralyzing shock overcame him. His jaw slackened, and his lower lips quivered. "That's—" He pointed to the table with the dagger. "That's Laere!"

"She's doesn't look like one but I assure you, she's a demon," Navalis explained. He hadn't wanted to hurt Boriag but knew it was inevitable.

Boriag's faced paled. "But that's Laere!"

Navalis grabbed Boriag by both shoulders and shook him. "Listen to me."

Boriag continued gaping at the table. Confusion crinkled his brows.

"She's a demon, raised without knowing it," Navalis further explained, hoping to make Boriag understand. "She exhibited powers, the ability to levitate. She has magic scent. Why else do you think its smells like burning corpses in here?"

Tears welled up in Boriag's eyes. His lips pulled downward, his fingers tightening about the grip of the dagger. He screamed. *"But that's Laere!"* He pushed Navalis away with great ferocity, his voice straining with panic and grief. "What did you do, Nav? What did you do?"

Navalis braced himself. He brought the flats of his palms together before his chest, begging for him to understand. "What had to be done. You can help me now."

"Help you?" Boriag pointed his knife at the table. "I love her and you, you... *killed her!"* His voice reverberated throughout the room as he curled his free hand into a fist. He struck Navalis first in the chest, then in the face.

Navalis stumbled. Black dots flickered across his vision, the front of his tunic tightened, and when his vision returned, Boriag held him steady, his eyes darting back and forth, maniacally searching for some explanation.

"You can't just kill someone!" he shouted. "There's rules. We know her!" He held firm, a fistful of fabric pinning Navalis in place. He raised his other hand which held the dagger. "I love her!"

Navalis clutched Boriag's fist, holding it in place as he twisted to one side. Boriag's arm was forced to straighten, limiting his movement, but it didn't stop him. He pitched forward and swiped the dagger at Navalis. Boriag lost balance and tried again. Navalis blocked him, twisting further to the side, mindful that they had spun around and switched positions with one another. If they kept doing this, they'd just keep going in circles and Navalis hadn't the time to waste.

Pain and anguish erupted from Boriag in a scream. He shoved with all his might. Navalis fell backward against the edge of the table.

Reasoning with Boriag at this point was an impossibility. As long as he kept lashing out, he was certain to hurt someone, maybe even himself. He might tell someone, too.

Navalis needed to wipe Boriag's short term memory. Calling on his inner reserve of energy for more strength, he shoved his friend away.

Boriag stumbled backward, the momentum carrying him across the laboratory until the dissection table stopped him. He grimaced in pain upon contact, lost his balance, and fell against Laere. His rage shifted into sadness for a brief moment, then the rage returned. He swiped at the air with the dagger again.

Navalis needed to keep Boriag still to suppress his memories. He charged across the room and overpowered Boriag, pinning the dagger between them and Boriag against his beloved. Navalis began projecting his perception into Boriag's mind, sending a message of sleep.

A gurgle rose from Boriag.

"Sleep," Navalis whispered, pushing the message into Boriag's mind again.

The message was intended to immobilize Boriag. Instead, he squirmed and writhed. His gurgling grew louder. He shouted abruptly at nothing in particular, then he screamed.

Navalis flinched at the sight of the first black tendril writhing about Boriag's throat. He jumped back as others crept along the back of Boriag's head and neck.

Boriag flailed as a tendril snapped around his chest and yanked him back against the table. Keeping his wits, Boriag swiped at the tendril with the dagger. The blade sheared it in two, and the severed end evaporated into a line of fire that burned itself into nothing.

Seeing the effect Boriag's imbued weapon had on the phenomenon, Navalis began searching the room for the gauntlet, which stood the chance of holding up against the black tendrils as he helped free his friend. Across the room, he spied the metal glove on a shelf and bolted for it.

The remaining tendril wrapped tighter around Boriag's chest. Where it touched Boriag's tunic, it dissolved the fabric. Then it melted his shirt, and when it started to eat at his flesh, new tendrils shot out from the main tendril.

Boriag strained for release, like a trapped animal. "Get it off! Get it off!" The spike dagger fell and clattered against the floor. He pulled at the tendrils, and as he touched the creature, his fingers began to unravel, dissolving into the long black threads swirling and merging with the tendrils. His chest began to do the same, then the back of his head and neck. Wherever he was touched, tendrils grew and multiplied.

Boriag reached out with a stump of an arm, black tendrils unwinding and spiraling about him, pulling him into the cavity of Laere's corpse. His eyes bulged. Sharp, shrill screams erupted from him.

Navalis reached for the gauntlet, but a tendril blocked his way, forcing him into the corner near the workbench. There, he observed Boriag's face dissolve into a mass of writhing tendrils, silencing him. When the last of his friend faded, the tendrils retreated into the cavity of Laere's chest and hovered along the edges of the incision.

The mass of tendrils prodded at the air and the table and whatever was close by, blistering or pitting whatever it came into contact with. By evening, they began to recede, settling down inside the cavity in Laere's chest with some difficulty, for they seemed to have outgrown their shell.

Tendrils clung to the edges of the incisions. They pulsed as though alive with breath. Coiled like springs, they waited for another body to devour.

❇ CHAPTER 47 ❇

Ulmaen exited the northern most gate of the castle grounds near the Bath House. Here, he found the area more temperate and calm compared to the other gated areas.

In the east, industry had butted up against the old city wall and the sprawl of Eastgate had gotten out of control. In the south, shanty towns and markets were constantly being torn down to prevent the same from happening there. In the west, there was the Prison, like a scar in the grassy field, and where thick forest bordered on Woedshor, trees were being harvested and cut down.

Here, a recessed expanse of land spanned out into fields dotted with woods. He followed a path through a gap in the trees and came to the top of a ridge. He paused a moment to get his bearings.

To the east, loomed the Mystics Tower and the ruin of an older building on a hill sheered like a cliff overlooking Warfield. Ruins jutted at odd angles from the side of the hill, looking a jumble. To the northe east, the grade of the ridge became more gradual, rising up to meet another hill that arced around. Beyond that hill were the Catacombs.

Before him spanned a wide valley. In the distance, where the land began to rise again, swells of dark green forest ascended into foothills and rolled toward a volcanic mountain. Erupting from the forest to the west were the Woedshor Steppes, narrow tracts of fertile land which rose in sharp increments up the base of the mountain.

Based on what he'd learned from reading history books, the valley had been man-made. Over thousands of years, the area had been heavily mined and had provided building materials before it was partially filled in with fluvial sediment carried there by a series of floods.

Ulmaen followed the path, finding the angle of decline propelled him forward, and he picked up speed. Farther down, the path converged with others near Warfield, where he spotted a dozen soldiers on horses riding in a square defense formation.

The field hadn't changed much from a couple of years ago when he—or rather Ule—had rode a horse named Crank there. They'd crossed the field into another beyond a narrow patch of woods, where Crank had been startled. He'd reared up in distress, then bolted for safety, knocking Ule's memories back into her as she held on fiercely. When she had recovered her senses, remembered who and what she was, she had set the horse free.

"I'm Xiinisi," Ulmaen muttered to himself, remembering the sensation of identity and purpose that had flooded into every portion of his being.

Affirmation of his origin yet again helped ease the unsettled feeling he hadn't been able to shake since the evening Ule wore those gloves and raised a glass of wine in celebration of what she had accomplished since recovering her memory. Unfortunately, that's all the affirmation achieved.

Ulmaen still felt agitated by the thought of Kerista stealing objects from the dead to imbue them with poison. He had to be certain though. He needed to see if Lishadru's body had been disturbed, to see if Kerista had left behind anything to indicate it was she who had taken them, like a bite from Lishadru's corpse. Perhaps that kind of evidence would help ensure Kerista was held accountable for her actions. That way people could know the truth.

Much of the Xiinisi existence was about following their curiosity and learning, and though he had discovered intriguing comparisons between his current masculine form and his previous feminine one, he needed to do something to find peace, at least with regards to the little mystery of his death.

And it was little, he thought. *Wasn't it?*

He had a finite number of life cycles to live yet they were many; so many, that having one snatched from him wasn't such a big loss. He was young compared to Navalis, younger still compared to those on the Xiinisi Council, yet he was on the verge of full maturity. He wanted to enjoy what remained of his youthfulness, and without some resolution, he worried this life cycle would feel empty upon deathmorphing.

This little mystery had proved quite motivating. It had pushed every molecule of his being to figure out who had poisoned Ule. Although, he questioned if understanding why would be enough to satisfy him. Otherwise, why did he feel the need to hold Kerista up to the world and show everyone that eating the dead was the least of her crimes?

Once, long ago he had been held accountable for his transgressions. It was only fair that she be held accountable for hers, too.

He aimed himself toward a distant woods, crossing the east side of Warfield. At the west end, he made out a line of soldiers aiming strange weapons at far away targets. The weapons they held reminded him of matchlock pistols. He'd seen variations of this kind of weapon in other Xiinisi worlds, wherever a persistent culture of curiosity permitted experimenting with technology.

Saddened by the discovery, he realized Elish would never be the same again. The thought reminded him of how he wouldn't be the same again either. If being murdered wasn't enough, being a man had further expanded his awareness.

He focused on the woods ahead, and thought about how being a man had changed how he related to others and to the world. He no longer consulted with anyone. It unnerved him at first, but now he enjoyed being responsible for his own decisions. Though he felt isolated, as though the world were at a distance, it seemed to bend to him in times of need, as he had experienced with his research.

He had found Rozafel's sales ledger simply enough, but all he could find for Elusis's shop were auction papers. Only later, after he had given up and by accidental luck, had he found the sales ledger he needed. And the research in turn fulfilled another need.

He hadn't expected to become an apprentice scribe so soon, but his findings had deeply impressed Mbjard who hurried the apprenticeship initiation. Consequently, his new status permitted him access to restricted materials, making the search for the location of Lishadru's mass burial effortless.

His journey so far had led him here, pursuing one of many meanings of the term *mass burial*, for Lishadru and her family were part of one.

He crossed the wide field, keeping a consistent stride, grateful his long legs carried him a far distance in a short amount of time. He hit a stretch of ground that was circular in shape and sunk into the ground, and he wondered if it was one of the fire pits that Adinav had dug to cremate the dead.

A hundred years of war had assured the slaughter of thousands throughout the shors, and Adinav had chosen to preserve his resources instead of spending them on honoring the dead in the traditional way.

Anyone who had resided within the castle was burned over fire pits, their ashes stored in marked jars that lined the walls within some of the Catacomb galleries, *if they had been deemed loyal.* Everyone else had been thrown into a fire pit until the pits filled with ash and were finally covered with dirt.

He quickly crossed the patch of uneven ground, skirted a small narrow woods, and carried on into the next field, recalling another kind of mass burial he'd learned about.

Long trenches had been dug into the ground, and there farmers were buried next to thieves and murderers and demons. They were left to rot in an anonymous mess. If these trenches still scarred the field somewhere, the tall grass hid them well.

Then there was a more civilized mass burial, the kind that occurred after Adinav's reign, when authorities picked through and tried their hardest to account for every corpse within the castle. The ones they identified were interred and treated with their regular customs: the bathing and sealing of the body, confession, the wrapping, and the final procession.

Those who were original inhabitants of Sondshor were interred in the galleries closest to the castle, where they could be visited. Those who had originally belonged to another shor or area of Elish were merely bathed, dressed, and wrapped and interred elsewhere, should surviving family members come to claim them.

Elsewhere was here.

He pushed through a patch of grass stalks that reached his chest and breached the edge of a large woods. He wiped sweat from his head and face, welcoming the coolness of the shade.

He spied a large square structure with an archway built out of quarried stone. No doors barred the way to this alternate entrance to the extensive tunnels making up the Catacombs.

Based on numerous maps he had pieced together in his mind, he realized the Catacomb tunnels and galleries ran well beyond the hillside where the more recent dead were kept. If he had started his journey there, it would take days, maybe a week, of walking and navigating tunnels, some of which had little to no air. This entrance, however, provided a shorter route to his destination:

Beneath the ground, possibly as far as Warfield, was a hub of rooms built off of others in a circular formation, where each gallery and its offshoots were called a House. In each House was entombed a *mass burial* for those who had died in Sondshor but had been born elsewhere. This was the Nyeth Ossuary, where the largest of Houses contained the bodies of anyone who had originated from Woedshor, and one of its sub-galleries was dedicated to those whose bodies had been recovered after the fall of Adinav.

Lishadru rested here.

Ulmaen pushed through the foliage and emerged into a clearing at the archway. He noted a narrow path that snaked eastward through the woods, in the direction of the hill containing the Mortuary and back toward the castle.

Although the entrance had been recently cleared of creepers, he knew from speaking with Mbjard, it was seldom used and there was no guarantee the older galleries hadn't collapsed. However, this entrance offered the quickest way to the Nyeth Ossuary.

He'd considered searching for Lishadru by shifting and descending through the ground, but the time remaining of his current life cycle was coming to an end, and he didn't want to risk using any more of it unless he had to.

He ducked through the moss-covered archway and found the tunnels here were unusually narrow, as though time had stuck layers of mud to the walls and floors. They were steep too, and in places the steps had worn down and in their place were partially rotted ladders.

Along the ground large crystals glowed blue, lighting the path. Once he passed them, they grew dim again. He descended, moving through the tunnels, ducking to clear support beams.

Given the amount of mildew he smelled in the air, he thought it unlikely the environment was capable of preserving the dead, until he descended a little farther. The earthen walls gave way to tunnels carved into stone. The galleries were stone chambers with rounded ceilings reinforced by columns of block stones. Pipes dotted with small holes ran along the tops of the tunnels, letting in a minimal amount of air and moisture.

He consulted the map in his mind, and continued down the main tunnel a ways before veering to the left through a low archway.

The first gallery belonged to the House of Woedshor. Not a single carving or painting adorned the walls or the domed ceiling. Only a few bodies had been tucked away in alcoves. Off the chamber were six openings to tunnels leading to other galleries. He entered the second to his right and followed it down, noting that the tunnels, too, were rounded and much effort had gone into making the galleries symmetrical.

He followed more tunnels leading into more galleries, and the deeper he went, he discovered many had been sealed with stone and plaster, which meant no one visited them anymore.

Emerging into a seventh gallery, he stopped to read the map in his mind. He examined the room, nearly full to capacity with bodies wrapped in fabric. Their tight, darkened faces stared upward in their niches, eyes sealed tight, looking strikingly similar to every other gallery he'd walked through.

This one was different, for the first door on the right led to Lishadru's gallery, but he didn't know what to make of the mortar and stone that blocked the way.

He pressed a hand against it, wondering if Kerista had had it sealed as a way to hide her theft. Running his hand over the wall, plaster flaked off in places, and then he spotted an indent in the upper left corner, a stamp in the impediment indicating a date, and he flicked his hand away as though he'd been burned.

The date corresponded to a time shortly after Adinav's fall yet prior to Lyan's formal inauguration. Ulmaen backtracked through time, remembering when he had been Ule.

She had been on a farm, suffering amnesia. Eventually, she recovered her memories and moved to Eastgate, where she was rudely awoken one night and dragged by guards before Lyan to interpret a cipher. Later, after she was hired on as a translator and interpreter, Kerista still hadn't yet been summoned to her new appointment as arch mystic.

He considered turning back, but his instincts urged him to keep pushing forward. There was something he needed to see. Reluctantly, he shifted his body and pushed through the stone and mortar seal. On the other side, he continued down the tunnel, shifting back into corporeal form.

The air was stale and dusty. It burned his lungs as he searched the next gallery for the final opening, and it too was sealed with the same date as the other. He shifted again, pushing through the mortar and stone, and returned to corporeal form on the other side.

As he explored the final tunnel, a lightness entered his head and his chest began to tighten. The gallery was full, and he found Lishadru in an alcove midway up the wall. He stared at her, wiping his head again as sweat rolled down his face and dripped onto his cotton shirt.

Lishadru's wrapping had been loosened about the collar, as had others nearby. She hadn't been the only victim of theft. Unlike the others whose heads were tilted upward, Lishadru's had fallen to the side and rested on her swathed shoulder.

Ulmaen felt his lungs ache. His pulse began to race, pumping needed oxygen to other parts of his body.

He gazed at Lishadru. Her body hadn't been sealed. The dark flesh of her lips had parted and her eyelids hung midway over clouded eyes. He wanted her to talk, to tell him who really had done this to her, because he had begun to realize it couldn't have been Kerista.

Even if somehow with her mystical abilities, Kerista had found a way to walk through walls, there was no way she could walk the distance and remain in the chamber long enough to search for objects without suffocating.

Ulmaen straightened, hands curling into fists and opening again. He released a little of his energy to restore his vitals, repair the cells that were dying in his body.

No one, he realized, could survive being in the chamber more than a couple of minutes. No one.

Except...

Tension coursed through his body. His mood plummeted. Turning on the spot, he shifted his molecules and rushed back through the two sealed corridors. He rematerialized in an air-filled chamber, and doubled over heaving for air, struggling against the anxiety spinning wildly in his chest.

Oxygen soothed his lungs and ignited his mind.

It can't be, he thought.

The words failed to ease his confusion and disbelief. He blinked back a sting of tears. Rage ripped through him, firing every molecule within his being, threatening to incinerate his very body.

The gallery about him felt small. The constriction bothered him, and he could have easily shifted through the layers of rock and sediment back to the surface, but he'd used up too much of his life cycle now. Only a bit remained. That much he still cared about, and even though there was enough air to breathe, he struggled to catch his breath again.

He ran, back through the symmetrical galleries. He bent over and shouted in frustration when he got lost, and when he finally found the main tunnel, he ran until the worn steps and ladders forced him to slow down.

Scrambling up the last flight of steps, the cool white light of day poked through the entrance. Through his heavy breathing, he choked back a strange sound. He heard anguish and disbelief. Some part of him, something young and sweet and naive, forced itself out of him as though being this way had become poisonous.

He barreled through the underbrush of the shaded woods, and once fully bathed in sunlight, he collapsed on his knees. Hidden in the tall grass, he wiped in annoyance at the tears and sweat that streamed down his face, then doubled over in a desperate attempt to disgorge the knot of pain in his stomach.

In the distance, the new weapons being fired echoed along the hills.

Ulmaen wasn't sure how long he wept, or how long it took for what remained of Ule to be fully dispelled. She had died in body, but now, she had died in spirit as well. After releasing every last bit of her essence— her quirky humor, her innate trust in others, the way she gave those around her the benefit of the doubt—he made more room for rage.

The sudden discharge of many small projectiles thundered throughout the valley, until an explosion unlike the others cracked the air. Ulmaen shuddered at the shrill wail of pain that cut through the roar of amunition far across the field. The anonymous soldier's physical pain resonated with Ulmaen's distress, and he felt release, as though he had screamed himself.

A hush came over Warfield and the surrounding areas as the injured soldier suddenly fell quiet.

Ulmaen stood and brushed himself off, adjusting to the shift in his energy and perception. The field with its clusters of sapling trees and bushes, now seemed much smaller and less significant than it had before. He seemed smaller. Sondshor Castle, however, was more of a giant, and though the sun was high above marking midday, he felt the castle's shadow over him.

❋ CHAPTER 48 ❋

Ulmaen stretched out on the cot in the dank cell, where there was little room for anything. The cot was much longer than his regular bed in the servants' quarters, extending the length of his body. In one way, he was a bit more comfortable, but his girth surpassed its width, and he lay squished against the cold wall.

A pail of food had been left by the cell gate by someone, perhaps Senaga; he couldn't recall. At the end of the cot, in the far corner, sat a bucket rank with urine and excrement, but after the first several hours, his palate had numbed. The foulness of the Pit ceased to affect him.

Eyes shut to block out the closeness of the room, he brushed his fingertips over his brow, enjoying the light pressure against the ebb of rage lingering in his flesh. He paused a moment to flex his fingers and made the scabs along his knuckles crack.

After his breakdown near the Catacombs, where the memory of his former self dripped through his fingers, he surrendered to the slow draining of all that he had loved about Ule. When the last of her had evaporated, a hollow formed and the rage invaded it like a firestorm. Once it was filled, the storm settled into a constant pulse of pain.

Ule had been angry, too, but never to this extent. She had been spurned and rejected by her kind, never... *attacked*. She forgave them, eventually, and they her. This time, Ulmaen didn't want forgiveness, and that's when he had felt Ule pour from him.

At first, he thought she had been destroyed. Now, he realized, he had simply pushed her away and let her go for the sole purpose of keeping her safe, for if he couldn't protect her—protect himself!—how could he protect this world?

The loss of Ule's spirit was profound, more so than the loss of her body. She might as well have been another lover, for he felt the same grief he had when Bethereel died. Now, she and Ule were both phantoms, and their absence saddened him.

Being locked away in the Pit was fine by him. If he wanted to, he could shift his way to freedom, but he didn't. His desire for retaliation was stitching together schemes. Retreating into his body, he extended his toes, mindful of the pull of tendons across the bridge of his foot and the way the tiny bones popped back into alignment. He noted the way collagen bonded to calcium and determined how to extract what gave bones their flexibility.

Finding peace in honing his perception on a microscopic level, he retreated deeper into his mind, where recent events played over and over.

At the edge of the Warfield, he'd recovered a bit from the harsh realization of who had killed him. He wiped away the last of his tears and laughed deeply at the ridiculousness of his pursuit of justice. He thought that knowing who had killed Ule would make him feel better. It only made him feel vengeful.

Exhausted, he returned to the castle grounds to satisfy the grumble in his stomach and staggered into the Dining Hall just before dinner.

Halfway through a plate piled high with food, General Gorlen and two of his guards had surrounded him while he sat at a table.

"Need a word with you," Gorlen demanded. "When's the last time you saw Laere?"

The question prickled Ulmaen, made his flesh twitch. His respect for authority had burned off like the last bit of gas in a lantern.

"Don't remember," he snapped. Then he shoveled a fork full of potato mash into his mouth.

Gorlen smacked Ulmaen's hand hard. The fork flipped over in the air and clattered onto the table. Those eating nearby scrambled from their seats, taking their meal plates with them; they sat at a distance out of harm's way, yet close enough to hear the conversation.

"The story going 'round is you and Laere were involved." Gorlen leaned in closer. "As soon as you were in her, you wanted nothing to do with her. *That* must've bothered her. So what'd she do to get back at you, I wonder? What set you off?"

Ulmaen refused to respond, and preferred to chew leisurely on his mashed potato.

"I know what it's like," Gorlen had tried to sympathize. "Women cling. So, what'd you do to throw her off your back?"

Ulmaen swallowed.

Gorlen lowered his voice to a near whisper. "I know you're responsible for her disappearance." He smacked his lips.

Ulmaen shuddered.

"I don't have proof yet," Gorlen continued. "When I do, I'll—"

"You'll what?" Ulmaen's question was abrupt, his actions too. He swung around on his stool, his head thrown back in defiance as he locked eyes with Gorlen. He welcomed the ache in his clenched jaw. He wasn't going to cower before this man, not anyone, ever again.

Gorlen sneered. His voice turned to a whisper. "Give me a reason to—"

Ulmaen's fist slammed into the middle of Gorlen's face, a violent and brutal reaction to his close proximity. Ulmaen probably would have had more momentum had he punched Gorlen from a standing position, but he was satisfied with what he accomplished while sitting down.

The bridge of Gorlen's nose cracked. He staggered back, blood sputtering down onto his lips. He waved at the guards, and they each grabbed Ulmaen by an arm and dragged him to his feet.

"You just earned yourself a couple nights in the Core for that."

Gorlen spat blood onto the floor. "And that's because I like you."

Ulmaen flexed his chest and stepped backward, bearing down on his core muscles. He swung his arms together, and the guards, unprepared for the momentum created by his strength, hurled into one another with a clang.

The guards standing watch over the Dining Hall jumped in to help. Ulmaen managed a few uppercuts, and at some point, his fist attempted to drive through someone's chest plate, splitting his knuckles. He tired eventually, and they dragged him off to the Prison.

After Gorlen secured the gate, he grinned.

"The Pit suits you better, don't you think?" he asked.

The question must have been a rhetorical one, for Gorlen didn't bother to listen for an answer and led his guards away.

Ulmaen hadn't any answer then. He still didn't. The Pit was as good a place as any for what he wanted to do.

He fidgeted on the cot, working himself deeper into the straw mattress, relaxing into the sensation of being a body connected to a mind cocooned in rage. He wanted nothing to do with anyone, preferring the darkness behind closed eyes to any reminder of the shadow castle and its shadow people pretending to be all sunny and bright. He knew better now.

He focused on what he had control over, the energy within himself and the molecules that adhered to that energy. Once he figured out the best places within his body to create conduits, he began a list of all the Xiinisi laws he wanted to break.

They were many, and he expected to deplete his current generation of its remaining time once he finished, for he was done with his youth. He wanted nothing more to do with it.

If he was truly to be a Sentinel for the world, he needed to learn to protect himself—physically, emotionally, spiritually—by any means necessary from anyone, even his own kind. He needed to make sure they knew it, especially his Master whose teachings were no longer required.

Ulmaen adjusted himself on the cot, then smiled. He hadn't felt this comfortable for a very long time.

* CHAPTER 49 *

Navalis kept at a distance from Laere's body until the black tendrils, one by one, slowly receded into her organs. He'd lost track of time as he kept watch over her, evaluating the situation. The only assuring thought he possessed was that her body had to eventually decay the way the previous demons had. By the time he felt his nerves settle again, he suspected evening had come and gone

Boriag's screams echoed in his head. He wished his friend had stayed at the Mystics Tower, but Boriag had a habit of visiting the laboratory to show off his latest finds. Unlike the other mystics, Boriag also had the sense to hide his trophies in the lab, where they were less likely to be found and stolen by other mystics.

He regarded Boriag's legacy—all the trinkets and thingamabobs he'd squirreled away. Every worktable, shelf, and cupboard was stuffed with what looked like junk. Only Boriag knew what treasures were hidden here, and Navalis wondered if any of them might help protect him while he furthered his examination of Laere.

Navalis wiped the top of small wooden table clean, pushing everything there onto the floor. On the clean surface, he placed the spike dagger, for it had severed the tendrils residing inside Laere's body. Next to the dagger, he placed the imbued gauntlet. Though he still hand't tested it yet, he reasoned that it too should be effective at protecting him.

"Let's see what else is here?" he mumbled.

He conducted a thorough search, beginning with the cupboard by the door. At the back of a cabinet, he found a thin blanket. He tossed it on the floor along with everything else he deemed useless.

He found scissors, rolls of gauze, and bottles of alcohol. In another drawer were sets of lenses and a broken scope, and in the final drawer, he found tubes of gunpowder, confiscated whistle bombs, and several grenades.

He was struck by the familiarity of one of the weapons. It was made of white metal, and he picked up the spherical grenade to cradle it in his palm and compare it to another he had once held long ago. He turned it over and found the trigger, a tiny ball bearing inset within the surface.

He deciphered the intricate mystical symbols carved into the metal: Clear Fire, ten second delay. Smiling, Navalis set the sphere on the table.

A sharp rap-rap-rap rattled the laboratory door, jolting his nerves. The door began to glide open. He leapt toward the door and blocked the bottom corner with his foot as it opened.

"Stop!"

"Nav, is that you?"

Panic buzzed through Navalis upon recognizing Sabien's voice. "Hold on," he insisted.

He eased the door shut, the base of his skull beginning to ache. He didn't need this aggravation. He grabbed the blanket from the floor, shook it out, and threw it over the table, covering Laere completely. Satisfied, he opened the door only a bit and blocked the way.

"I need your services," Sabien blurted.

"You shouldn't be here."

Sabien leaned against the door, an attempt to push it farther open. "I called on you at the Tower. You weren't there, so I assumed you were here. I need to speak with you. There's no one else I trust."

A glance at the dissection table indicated the blanket remained intact yet wet green stains had begun bleeding through the fabric. At the foot of the table, a clear liquid with a thin viscosity dripped onto the floor, which hadn't happened with either of the snake demons. The new detail required his attention immediately.

"Another time," he told Sabien, then began to close the door.

"I'll only be a minute. It's important."

Navalis's instincts struggled with his emotions. They told him to shut the door, to send Sabien safely on his way, but his heart latched onto Sabien's desperation.

"Make it quick," he finally said.

He pulled the door open to escort Sabien back up the stairwell, but Sabien must have mistaken the gesture for an invitation. He strode in with a sharp nod, stopped short of the work table, and upon scanning the room, hesitated at the sight of the dissection table. Ever curious, he smacked his lips, no doubt wondering what was under the blanket.

"It's better you not ask about that," he told Sabien, trying not to sound alarmed as he tried to block Sabien's sight by standing between him and the dissection table.

Sabien stared a moment longer, shrugged, and returned his attention to Navalis. "Fair enough."

"What do you need, Sab?"

About to answer, Sabien stopped himself and blinked. He shook his head, as though perplexed. "Just for a moment, you reminded me of him again. The way you said my name."

The muscles in Navalis's neck tightened. "I don't have time for this."

Sabien frowned. "Neither do I.' He patted at his vest pockets, settling on the left one. He pulled out a piece of paper. "A valuable possession was stolen from me, here in the castle. I've tried searching for it myself, even reported the theft, but nothing. It looked like this." He unfolded the paper and held it out.

Navalis examined the rudimentary colored sketch of the kornerupine that he knew no longer existed.

"How am I supposed to help you?"

"Do you scry? I know most Mystics do. I'd pay well for your services."

Every moment Sabien stayed ruined any chance of documenting the new secretion from the demon, examining its cell decay, and became a potential threat to Sabien.

"I can't help you," Navalis lied, hoping to be rid of him. He motioned toward the open door, glad to know the nature of his distress and eager to end their interaction.

Sabien refolded the paper, remaining where he stood.

Navalis grabbed Sabien by the arm, intending to escort him from the laboratory, but Sabien resisted, keeping his ground.

"You don't understand. It may be just a rock to you, but it was entrusted to me by someone very important. I made a promise. I need to keep it. It's all... all I have."

Sabien lost his intensity. His focus shifted. Fear flickered in his eyes. Odd shapes reflected in their glassy surface, something thin and fine and dark.

Navalis lunged forward mindful of the explosive grunt that issued from Sabien when his backside hit the edge of the table. Ignoring him, Navalis scooped up the spike dagger and the grenade.

"Wh-what is *that*?"

Navalis spun around, the knife poised, and there on the dissection table, a mass of tendrils had started devouring the blanket and writhing down along the folds onto the floor. A braid of tendrils shot out across the room, and Navalis quickly slashed at it. The tip of the tendril burst into flames and the remainder recoiled to regenerate.

"Go! Now!" Navalis pushed at Sabien, who seemed rooted to the floor.

Sabien came to his senses and bolted through the open door just as another tendril shot out toward him. Navalis sliced at it. A long line of fire lit the air and vanished with a hiss.

He couldn't take the risk, he realized. He didn't know what Laere's body had unleashed, but it was unpredictable and unsafe for Elishians and for the world. As the mass of tendrils crept along the floor, up the walls of the lab, blistering or melting everything it touched, he fumbled with the grenade to find the button.

His thumb brushed across the tiny sphere. He pressed it in, started to count from ten, dropped it back on the table and ran for the doorway. Thicker tendrils had dissolved the first hinge of the door, and the wood released, swinging downward on an angle, blocking his way.

He wrenched it aside and dove through the doorway, avoiding the black filaments that had begun to crawl beyond the laboratory door and into the stairwell beyond.

Outside, he discovered Sabien had stopped half way to the next landing.

He stood there, frozen.

"You've six seconds to get to the tunnel!" Navalis raced up the stairs two steps at a time. "Five. Get going!"

Sabien turned and bolted up the stairs.

"Four."

Navalis wanted to extend his speed beyond his physical capacity or shift Sabien and himself into immaterial forms, but he would have to explain.

Sabien's foot slipped and he spilled down a few steps. Navalis caught up with him, grabbed him before he slipped any further, and together they hit a landing...

Three.

Explanations about his Xiinisi abilities to any Elishian meant he'd have to silence them. He'd rather not be forced to scramble Sabien's mind, or worse, kill him.

They started up the next flight of stairs...

Two.

They neared the next landing.

One.

Kabooom!

The blast of the Clear Fire grenade cracked sharp and loud. The sound whipped up and down the stairwell, thundering and crackling. A bright glow lit up the stairwell, shimmering across wall and stones. Navalis shoved Sabien hard into the tunnel on that landing before the light could engulf them and incinerate every part of their bodies, leaving behind only things made of metal or stone.

Sabien tripped into the tunnel. Navalis fell, too, and as they lay huddled on the dirt floor, blue and white light slithered into the entrance.

"Go! Farther in!" Navalis urged.

Sabien obeyed, crawling deeper into the tunnel until the blue and white light began to recede.

Catching his breath, Navalis pulled himself around and crawled toward Sabien. "Are you alright?"

Breathing heavily, Sabien nodded. His clothes were full of dirt and his hands trembled, but otherwise he didn't look hurt.

"What'd you say, Avn?"

Navalis caught his breath. He stood and dusted off his tunic. "Who—" The word caught in his mouth. He coughed to dislodge it and tried again. "Who's Avn?"

Sabien stood shakily and backed away. "I... I don't know how... or *what* you are, but I recognize you." He leaned against the wall, cradling his one arm against his chest.

Navalis saw blood drip from a cut across the back of Sabien's hand and stain his vest.

"You're injured." Quite by instinct, he stepped forward to examine the wound.

Sabien flinched at their contact. "Is that your name? Avn?" His voice grew shaky. "Or are you called something else entirely?"

"Hold still," Navalis demanded as he examined the gash, and tried to figure out some way to deflect their conversation. "Whoever it is you think—"

"It is you," Sabien insisted. "Avn. I see him in you, in your eyes. You're him, or he's you, I don't know how. Perhaps you're a master mystic in disguise or..." Sabien regarded him, scanning his face. "Or perhaps a demon."

Navalis laughed at the absurdity of the notion. He approached his old lover carefully. There had been many nights when he had wanted to tell Sabien the truth about what he truly was—I'm Xiinisi, he had practiced over and over.

He'd been a blacksmith back then, cut off from his kind, desperate and lonely, certain he would die in Elish. The desire to tell the truth had grown strong, but he denied the urge, for their kind only ever interacted covertly in the worlds they built. Most of them lost all remembrances of the Xiinisi, accept for Elish, which possessed documented historical recollections and long living demons who had retained memories of them.

Navalis regarded Sabien and said nothing, as in so many of their past conversations.

"If you told me," Sabien began to ask, mustering courage, "would you have to kill me then? Is that the kind of nonsense going through your head?"

The very thought pained Navalis. He should kill him but he wouldn't. "Yes." The word was reflexive, void of emotion.

Sabien's face grew grim. He clenched his jaw and softly whispered, "You still aren't very good at lying."

Navalis loathed the silence that followed. A part of him wanted to tell Sabien everything, but he knew the implications. Adinav had been privileged to a world beyond what he knew, and the world suffered greatly as a consequence.

A palatable and forceful pull remained between him and Sabien, reminding Navalis of the connections he felt with other Xiinisi. He loathed it, yet desire threatened to undermine this repulsion. He felt the pressure of it building inside him, and he pushed back at the fantasy of kissing Sabien one last time.

Furrowing his brow, he grabbed Sabien by the front of the vest and pushed him hard into the wall, mindful of how he flinched and squirmed within his grasp.

"Listen to me," Navalis growled. "Forget that promise! Forget the gemstone, forget what you saw here, and forget me, or you'll regret it."

Sabien shoved hard against Navalis's chest, and this time liberated himself. "Don't threaten me!"

Navalis ignored him and pinned him beneath one arm. With his free hand, he slammed the wall of the tunnel beside him. The earth rumbled. The tremor shook dirt from cracks in the mortar and the wooden beams supporting the tunnel walls.

At last, Sabien grew afraid. He struggled free and sidled along the wall, staring wide eyed as the ground grew still again. Straightening himself, he pinched his mouth, as though stopping himself from speaking. He backed away, farther and farther, not yet willing to turn his back.

Finally he stopped and said, "I'll do what you say." He licked his lips. "Just so you know, I'd rather you tell me the truth than kill me." After a curt nod, he turned his back on Navalis and hurried along the tunnel.

Navalis knew that the most logical tactic meant he should kill Sabien.

* CHAPTER 50 *

Navalis returned to the laboratory to ensure the Clear Fire had disintegrated the dark tendrils. He knew better than to hope for a part of Laere to remain unscathed by the grenade. Still, he searched, hoping to find the smallest of remnants to examine.

Outside the room, a pitted texture fanned out from the doorway, a scar across the stone and mortar from where the dark tendrils had crawled and eaten it.

Inside, tools and broken jars littered the floor, along with metal brackets, pins, and nails which had supported tables and shelves. The cupboards had vanished; the large table and stools, too. Anything made of organic material—parchment, leather, fabric, vegetation—had been disintegrated

All that remained of the door were iron brackets and bolts partially eroded by the dark tendrils. Patches of plaster on the walls, where the tendrils had touched, revealed lightly marred stonework. Over the floor were distorted scopes, crystals, surgical tools, and broken glass.

Laere's body was gone. Only a few stumps of metal remained of the table where she had lain. Gone too were the dark tendrils that had resided in her.

He felt a deep sense of loss at the potential Laere's body had to offer. Though he hadn't spent much time with her, he had gleaned enough to start developing a theory about how demons had become corporeal.

Fatigued from being awake a couple of days straight, he summoned the An Energy and gathered elements from other places within the castle. He rebuilt a door to the lab, fastened it in place with restored brackets, then locked it behind him as he departed.

He trekked through the tunnel, patting dirt from his tunic. Near Fehran's Hall, he lumbered up the cellar stairs and strolled through the Hall as though nothing had happened. Outside, he glimpsed the last light of day dip beneath the horizon as he hauled himself up stairs of the retaining wall nearby.

He needed rest, preferably somewhere calm and quiet, until the other apprentices retired for bed so he wouldn't need to explain his whereabouts for the past two days until the following morning.

He rounded Mareel's Gatehouse with its whir of spinning wheels and and sewing machines, and passed the ever quiet Treasury. Nearing the Mystics Tower, he glimpsed the darkening sky and knew exactly where he wanted to go.

Without a word to anyone, he slipped through the main laboratory and climbed the stairs to the top, where he stumbled out onto the

Observatory. Crystals lying about the floor flared at his movement, casting a soft blue light as he crossed to the lookout. He climbed a podium supporting a massive telescope, and fiddled with its brass knobs and levers, flipping lenses in and out of alignment, grateful for the distraction.

When the horizon darkened, he peeked through the telescope at the night sky and searched the Mirari for the presence of any new worlds. He found one of the new stars he had seen before, and he wondered how long it would take before a Mystic discovered it and change their understanding of the world?

Over time the mystics were destined to build stronger telescopes, peer deeper into their universe, change their theories and perceptions accordingly. Mathematical expressions would be amended and their universe would change to reflect their new understanding, for their sky was a mirror which reflected their evolving perceptions. That was the nature of any Mirari, for that was how the Xiinisi had designed them.

He turned another knob, adjusted his eyesight, and listened to phantom squabbling from an open window somewhere in the tower below. Then the clump of heavy boots up the stairwell to the Observatory and the soft rustle of fabric. A boot struck one of the blue crystals followed by footfalls, two sets of them walking out of sync. A cough and a sigh, each issuing from a different person.

He stared at the stars, preferring the quiet. Eventually, he addressed his visitors. "Good evening, Aesa , Mera. Can I help you?"

"Start by telling us the whereabouts of your friend, Boriag."

He recognized Mera's smoky voice.

"He's gone," he told her.

Something hard and cold pressed against the back of his thigh. He looked down and saw the head of Aesa's hammer pushing into his hamstring.

"Explain," she demanded.

He motioned to step down, but Aesa stayed where se stood, staring up at him. her hair flung back from her face. In the soft light, he barely saw the burn scars on her lip and neck. Behind her, Mera fiddled with the ball of a peen hammer.

Aesa eventually backed away, allowing him to climb down.

He appreciated not having to stoop or lower his gaze to speak with either of the sisters. He advanced on Aesa to show he wasn't intimidated by her. Made uncomfortable by their proximity, she laid her mallet against his chest and pushed him back.

"Where is he?" she asked again.

"He packed up his possessions and disappeared sometime yesterday," he improvised. The lie was necessary. He only wished he'd had a night to rest to better develop an explanation. For now, he only needed to remember to get rid of Boriag's belongings before sunrise.

"Just like that?" Mera wondered.

He shrugged.

Aesa lowered her mallet and let out a loud huff. "Two more blades lost!" Lovingly, she rubbed her thumb over the smooth metal of the mallet head.

Mera laughed. "No wonder everyone here's wealthy. No one ever pays for anything they custom order, even if we try beating it out of them."

Navalis reached beneath his tunic and withdrew Boriag's spike dagger from his belt.

"Is this one of those blades?" He pointed the tip of the spike toward her chest.

Aesa's reflexes were quick. She backed away and raised her hammer.

Navalis tossed the dagger in the air, making it flip over several times before the grip landed back in the palm of his hand. "It's a fine blade. Strange that he left it behind. I can tell you, the other one was destroyed in an experiment."

Aesa extended her free hand, motioning him to hand it over.

He returned it to his belt.

Her eyes narrowed, as her outstretched palm curled into a fist. "Is this a game? I'm sick of games."

He smiled and reached into his tunic again. This time he pulled out the pouch on the strap about his neck. He opened it and shook out a pile of sils and gols.

"How much is owed on the two daggers?"

She examined his outstretched hand and sniffed. Tentative and suspicious, she reached out, then stopped.

He shook the coins about, luring her, and finally Aesa found the courage to pull five gols from the pile. Satisfied by the transaction, she slipped the money into a pocket of her apron.

"It looks different," she said, relaxing a little.

"The metal's been imbued," he explained.

Mera scratched her pale cheek. He could tell she was unsure of his meaning.

"It's simply stronger," he explained. "I saw it pierce an anvil." Whatever Boriag had done to the dagger, had also made it capable of withstanding demon bound black tendrils. For that reason alone, he wanted to keep it.

Aesa and Mera exchanged disbelieving glances.

There wasn't any harm in demonstrating the dagger's ability. He owned it rightfully. He pulled it from his belt again.

Mera pushed her sister aside and snatched it from him. She set her peen hammer down on the floor. Kneeling over it, she raised the spike dagger high above her head and braced herself.

"This is probably going to hurt," she mumbled. "But I'm tired of everyone's bullshit!"

With a cry, she drove the dagger down against the metal head of the hammer and then fell back, her eyes staring wide.

The spike dagger pierced both the steel of the hammer head and the stone beneath.

Remembering how firmly lodged the spike had been in the anvil, Navalis lunged forward and wrenched it free with his Xiinisi strength, making sure they didn't try it first.

Scrambling forward, Mera slowly picked up the hammer to examine the hole. For the briefest of moments her face lit up. At the sight of her sister though, her delight faded.

"You had to take the money."

Aesa tilted her head, regarding the damage done to the hammer. "We've got to eat, and a new hammer to buy now. The horses need food, too. We can't forget those, or we'll have a difficult time getting back to Sondshor Market.

"I suppose there's paying work here after all," Mera mumbled, as she took to her feet, still examining her hammer from all sides.

"Come on!" Aesa tugged at Mera's apron. Together, they strode back across the Observatory, and as they descended the stairs, they both nodded farewells.

Navalis nodded in return, fighting the need to sleep, waiting for the tower to grow silent. When he sensed a pervasive stillness below, he returned to the main floor, and took advantage of being the only one there.

Remembering what he had told the sisters about Boriag, he gathered Boriag's personal ledgers and a small selection of his materials, began tearing them apart their molecular arrays and redistributed the elements into the bookcases, walls, and floor, making them a little thicker.

Back upstairs, where he roomed with several apprentices who were fast asleep, he padded about and gathered Boriag's personal possessions: soap, razors, a brush, and odd trinkets. He wrapped them in what little clothing Boriag possessed, but instead of redistributing their elements and risk being seen by someone should they wake up, he shifted the bundle from its solid state, and hid it inside a wall.

As he eased himself into bed, he shuddered at what had become of Boriag. Nothing of Boriag remained except memories, and Navalis acknowledged the small pang of nostalgia for his friend as he fell fast asleep.

✳

Navalis woke abruptly in the middle of the night. He listened for a noise or some indication of what had awakened him, but found nothing. The other apprentices remained asleep. Satisfied there wasn't any danger, he laid on his bed and closed his eyes.

"What was it like?"

Navalis touched his solar plexus. Words and thoughts that weren't his entered through an opening there.

"Your thoughts are strong," he projected in return. Ulmaen's previous attempts to project this way had been tickles and whispers at most, and he was impressed by the improvement in his ability.

"What was it like, sitting there right next to me while I lay on the slab in the Infirmary, knowing?"

Ulmaen's words trickled into him with a sickly tone. Though the rhythm of the phrasing was slow, each word came through stronger than the previous one. "And you did know. You knew the entire time."

"Know what?"

"Who killed me."

Navalis frowned, feeling an ache in his stomach as though each word was a punch. He waited for Ulmaen to project again, but felt him withdraw.

Unsettled by their brief exchange, Navalis meditated himself to sleep. He slept through the night and at midday, he rose from the bed, an ache in his jaw. He rubbed it as he descended toward the main floor, and discovered the mystics had gathered about the table in an informal meeting with General Gorlen, who was accompanied by a small troop of guards.

Navalis acknowledge the master mystics who urged him to join the gathering. As he sat on a stool at the table, he rubbed the left side of his face. The ache eased in the muscle yet settled into the bone of his lower jaw.

Besieged with a number of questions by the masters, Navalis patiently listened: *You knew the Laere girl, didn't you? Were you romantically involved with the girl? When did you last see her?*

Navalis stared about the room in confusion. "What's this all about?"

General Gorlen stepped forward, clearing his throat, his thumbs hooked over the edge of his belt.

"Could be I'm here about the tremor at the Starry Rise the other night. Your lot get up to a lot of weirdness. You sure spooked a lot of lovers at the fountain. What I want to know is, does anyone get hurt during... whatever it is you do down in that old castle? Like Laere for example. She's disappeared." He stared at each mystic in turn until he stopped at Navalis. "And you were seen with her last." He smirked. "Are you going to deny that?"

"I saw her," Navalis admitted to the truth. "She came to me for professional advice."

Gorlen winced at the response.

Navalis detected Gorlen's disbelief, and knew he ought to offer a little more detail about the encounter. "She wanted to know about our profession, if her skills of sensitivity were worth developing as a mystic instead of as an artist."

Gorlen skirted the table until he towered over Navalis and asked, "Were you seeing her romantically?"

A sharp pain engulfed one of Navalis's back molars. He flinched at the suddenness of it, but given the situation, he endured the pain until he could examine it later. He shook his head.

"No one here'll deny she had a certain reputation," he said, hoping the movement of his jaw would work out the pain. "But I'd never pursue anything with her."

The pain eased slightly.

"She not your type?"

Navalis wanted to smile, to express some appreciation for the turn of the conversation. He saw a way for spinning the truth, deflecting the investigation away from himself and onto someone else.

He shrugged. "Everyone here knows Boriag was sweet on her." The truth was reconfirmed by several mystics who nodded in agreement. "I'm not in the habit of bucking with who my friends fancy."

His back molar flared again, as though something were pushing at it from deep within his jaw. He sucked in his breath and slowly exhaled.

Gorlen grunted, and picking up on the new lead, he asked everybody, "Is Boriag here among you?"

The mystics shook their heads. One of the masters ordered an apprentice to search the Observatory, another to search Boriag's chamber, and a third to search the field where he sometimes conducted his experiments.

Gorlen stood back from the table. "Boriag? He's that weird one. The tall, skinny fellow who follows you around?"

Some of the younger mystics snickered at the description.

"That's him," Navalis confirmed, rubbing the side of his face again.

Gorlen paced the floor, scratching the side of his neck while he thought. "Can't see anyone wanting the affections of that gnat," he mumbled to himself. He circled the room and stopped again next to Navalis. "You were closest to him, then?"

Many of the apprentices nodded, and Navalis couldn't deny it. "Yeah, he was my assistant."

"Any chance you know if Laere returned his affection?"

"Can't say," he responded honestly, then began to remember Boriag's stories, the ones of his romantic rejections and desperation. It seemed unlikely Laere felt the same way.

He jerked his head back. Pain shot along his jawline again. He ran his tongue over the tooth and tasted blood.

"You alright?" Gorlen stared at him.

"Bad tooth," he admitted. As the pain dissipated, he gathered his recollections of his friend. "Boriag's not had much luck in the romance department. He once told me he, ah..."

"Spit it out!"

"That he had sex with a corpse."

Most of the apprentices twisted their faces in disgust, and the master mystics threw their heads back in annoyance.

"Well we've got no law against that," Gorlen said. He stood at attention and nearly shouted, "But we do have laws against murder."

The apprentice sent to look for Boriag in the chambers flew from the stairwell doorway. He caught his breath and explained that all of Boriag's belongings were gone.

Gorlen sneered at the news. "Are mystics in the habit of disappearing?"

The nods from the master mystics were reluctant. In truth, apprentices disappeared quite often, especially when they learned either they didn't have the talent for the studies or they lacked the stamina for the politics.

"It happens quite a bit," Navalis responded, fortifying the idea in everyone's minds. The deflection was nearly complete. He felt confident with the subtle manipulation and decided to plant one final idea in Gorlen's mind.

"What if Laere returned Boriag's affection?" he asked. The speculation stirred the imaginings of everyone in the room. "Could be they simply ran off together."

General Gorlen leaned over the chair again . "I'd be inclined to agree with you," he said. "If she hadn't left behind all of her things, including a hefty sum of coins."

Navalis frowned at his lack of foresight. He hadn't bothered to clean up after Laere. He'd been too absorbed in dissecting her.

Pain sheered throughout his mouth this time. His gum tore. Warm blood splashed the insides of his mouth. Something hard and smooth and bumpy rolled over his tongue. Grunting, he leaned forward and spit out both blood and one of his molars onto the main table.

Gasps abounded and whispers bandied back and forth among the apprentices and adepts, while the masters sat back in their chairs and scrutinized both Navalis and the tooth.

Gorlen straightened again and smacked Navalis on the back. "There, there," he said. "Old age hits us all eventually."

Confused, Navalis stared at his tooth. The slightly yellowed enamel was intact, the roots brilliant pink. Nothing about the tooth indicated rot or disease.

On Gorlen's signal, two of the guards marched toward the stairwell doorway and waited there.

"Could be your friend Boriag couldn't handle being rejected again," Gorlen speculated. "If you won't mind showing me where he sleeps,

I'd like to have a look."

Curling a fist around the tooth, Navalis rose from the stool, and although he worried, it didn't have anything to do with the guards finding evidence to incriminate Boriag. What truly worried him was the intrusion of Ulmaen projecting again, only this time, what came through his solar plexus was light-hearted laughter.

✳

Gorlen and his guards searched the entire floor where some of the apprentices slept and found no clues tying Boriag to Laere's disappearance or indicating where Boriag might have gone. After they cleared out of the room, Navalis laid back in his bed and held up the tooth his body had ejected.

The tooth had been pushed from his jaw. Pushed by a force beyond his own. There was only one other being in the world capable of such power.

"Ulmaen!" His projection was fierce and austere.

He waited for a response but none came.

"I know what you've done," he projected again. "There are laws against this type of behavior for a reason."

After several minutes, he heard Ulmaen's words filter into his chest, soft and slow.

"And I know what you've done, and how you did it—the chamber with the strange spider milked of its poison, the stolen artifacts from that poor girl's grave."

Navalis bolted upright.

How had Ulmaen found that room? No one in the world knew it was there. He'd concealed the entrance to the sub cellar. He'd made sure no one had seen him come or go.

He scrambled to his feet. "Where are you?"

Laughter filled his chest, causing a sharp shiver down his spine.

He focused on the direction from which Ulmaen's energy entered his solar plexus, slipped out of bed, and headed toward the stairs.

Ulmaen's voice returned, strong again. "What I really want to know is why you felt it necessary to kill me? No, actually, I want to know why you needed to kill me *that* way. So... violently."

By the time he descended to the main floor, he felt a persistent tingle in his right wrist. Once outside, he doubled over in extreme agony as the bone in his forearm sheered in two. A slight fracture only, for the bones remained in alignment.

For the sake of maintaining mental clarity, he interrupted the signal of pain to his nervous system, and stood again.

"Painful, isn't it?" Ulmaen's question had a curious innocence to it. "Not quite the same as emotional pain, but then I'm not a Master like you are. You do emotional pain very well, don't you?"

A clothier loitering in the yard ran to him, but Navalis pushed the young fellow away. He pulled energy from his reserve and healed the fracture, then resumed following the energy Ulmaen was emitting. As long as he kept his Student projecting, he'd be able to find him.

"You planned this. For how long?"

"A while," he admitted.

"Hmm, that spider. It's not even from this world, is it? You went to *that* much trouble. I... I didn't realize just how much you hate me."

Hate was a strong word. At times, Navalis felt a strong repulsion toward Ulmaen for not being willing to consider another perspective, but never hatred. Mostly, he resented Ule, ever since he'd been trapped in Elish, being forced to break certain rules. He hadn't the chance to release this feeling and it rushed from him in a blast.

"Adinav summoned that spider here with your help!" The release felt good, and he poured out more of his hostility. "When you were a gemstone, your combined efforts bridged dimensions. I discovered it. In the Catacombs, nesting in the chest of a corpse. I trapped it and hid it away."

The energy issuing from Ulmaen's communication had led Navalis around the Treasury, past Mareel's Gatehouse, down the stairs of the retaining wall, into the courtyard below, and as far as the eastern Colonnade before it faded away. He slipped into the lane between the Inner Sanctum and the Library and waited until Ulmaen projected again.

"What gave you any right to kill me?"

He detected a pull to the west, and returned to the Colonnade, hurrying toward the Starry Rise.

"Aren't laws supposed to protect all of us? Do you think that because you're my Master, you're an exception?"

"Yes," he told her. "But not because I'm your Master."

"I don't understand."

"That's always been your problem, hasn't it?"

At the Starry Rise, where the water still managed to glisten despite the overcast sky, he stopped to drink deeply. The cool water replenished his energy and dulled the ache from healing himself.

Ulmaen's projection grew stronger. "What makes you the exception?"

"The Council does," Navalis answered. He turned down the south pathway toward the Soldier Alley, determined to make it to the field beyond, where he could better navigate himself.

He felt a bubble inside him much lower than his solar plexus, in his stomach. Ulmaen was manipulating his body again, and he let him, wondering to what extent Ulmaen had developed his ability.

The bubble burned, making him cough up phlegm that tasted bitter.

He paused beneath the archway that lead out into a field and placed his hand on his abdomen.

"Why'd they make you above the law?"

"Can't say."

He knew Ulmaen had been practicing communicating through the body, and though affecting another's form beyond his own was a logical transition, it usually took a lot of training. Linking minds came naturally to their kind. Linking bodies? Merging? That took tremendous focus.

There were many ways to link their bodies, and there were rules of conduct that needed to be followed, usually with the the more experienced essence dominating the inexperienced. Consent was important in such situations, but what Ulmaen was doing was invasive and far beyond his ability to properly control.

"That's all you've got," he goaded Ulmaen. "Inflicting me with minor fractures and indigestion."

"I want to know."

"Tell me where you are and I'll tell you—"

He hadn't quite finished projecting when he felt Ulmaen pressing in on his mind. He stumbled, and a vein in his left arm ruptured. Instinctively he slapped a hand over it as though he were bleeding out, and laughed at himself for that.

As he stopped the internal bleeding, another vein popped, then another. He grew bored of chasing the internal bleeding inside him.

Like a flash of light, something invaded his nervous system. He tried to raise a barrier, but he was too late. Ulmaen slipped into his mind, invading memories in a way he had never experienced before.

He gasped at the speed with which Ulmaen scanned his neural network. Thankfully, Ulmaen took an interest only in memories laced with bitterness, hostility, and resentment, and hadn't noticed that they hid another layer of memories and emotions.

Those memories held the answers he was certain Ulmaen was searching for. He hadn't wanted Ulmaen to find out about Ule's death this way. He'd wanted to wait until Ulmaen entered full maturity, possessed more confidence and a well conditioned ego, so he could better handle the harshness of his new position.

Life as a Sentinel was difficult enough, always being on the lookout, being alone. In Elish, Ulmaen would have the added burden of also being under attack, never being able to hide from demons for very long. Given the degree of his rage after discovering the truth about his murder, Ulmaen still wasn't prepared to take on this responsibility.

In the field beyond Soldier's Alley, he followed the direction of Ulmaen's projected energy northwest, willing barriers in place around certain memories within his mind and hoping to find him before he attacked again.

✳ CHAPTER 51 ✳

Ulmaen shifted on the tiny cot. He unclenched his jaw, not realizing he had been grinding his teeth together. He tilted his head to gently crack his neck, then resumed his meditation.

He delighted in the way he had abruptly invaded his Master's mind and the panic it caused him. The brief thrill produced a euphoria finer than any ale or mead ever had, and it provided the few seconds' head start he needed to scan for information.

Barriers began to bubble around certain memories, one cluster in particular that was shaded by odd feelings.

You can guard those, if you want, Ulmaen thought bitterly.

It didn't take long for Navalis to start reclaiming his mind, and Ulmaen felt himself being pushed toward its perimeter. He clung to the closest memory cluster, scanning it for any clues. One in particular piqued his curiosity. He settled into the memory, ignoring the discomfort of taking on the role of his Master, being in his form, being addressed by his true name, observing from his perspective.

Avn, or at least what Ulmaen could feel of him, was a ball of nerves. He breathed deeply to settle his anxiety. Around him was the Lyceum, where the Xiinisi Council often met and merged minds.

This memory was connected to other memories, in which Avn had delivered a series of passionate arguments about Ule and her Mentor, Ibe, who had been demoted and toiled away as Student again.

Avn argued with the Xiinisi Council—nearly pleaded with them— for leniency on Ibe, who had undeniably misused his power. He'd instructed Ule to build a barrier, yet failed to oversee its progress in construction and had found himself trapped in the world of Elish.

Ulmaen returned to the original memory, where Avn worried about his arguments, about whether or not they had been persuasive enough.

Avn sat in the middle of the Lyceum. Above, the turn of the multi-coloured energy field soothed his nerves while he waited to discover what was to become of Ule and Ibe, and of himself as well. He was filled with hope, too, for he wanted to be the one convicted and punished.

Ulmaen was struck by how deep Avn's desire was to be locked away, for then he would truly be free—stripped of his duties, allowing him to be far, far away from *her*. With distance between him and Ule, he would have peace.

Ulmaen reeled at the revelation. He hadn't known his Master hated him, but it explained why he had murdered Ule.

The memory proceeded, and at the north end of the Lyceum, shadows shifted. The Xiinisi Council were huddled in an alcove. He thought it strange he didn't hear their thoughts within Avn's mind. They communicated instead among themselves, some sharing thoughts, others occasionally muttering words. Eventually, they withdrew from one another and returned to where Avn sat.

Oaxa and her frenzy of vipers arrived first, followed by Hethn, with his iridescent indigo feathers and austere posture.

"Do you feel that?" Oaxa asked out loud.

Hethn strode toward the middle of the room, chest raised and spine straight. A powerful Xiines, the most powerful of them all, and yet...

In this instance, Ulmaen realized he didn't envy Hethn, or feel inferior and inept the way he did around Avn.

Oaxa resumed her enquiry, pointing a paw at Avn. "How can our punishment be effective, if he sees it as a reprieve from his responsibilities?"

Emerging from the shadows, Gur padded toward Hethn and curled on the floor beside him. Veht, whose grace was surpassed by none among their kind, slunk forward and sat, her hundreds of eyes turned toward Avn.

Avn's breath shallowed as he continued guarding his emotions as well as his mind. Being within him, seeing from his perspective, began to stir Ulmaen's anxiety. The barrier Avn created for himself as a means of safety felt too much like a prison. Why speak when they could merge minds?

Hethn spoke, his tone raspy and withered. "We understand you have much to lose."

"I'm at your mercy," Avn told them.

He stared at every single Council member, as though daring them to have done any better than he had under the circumstances. Murder, possession—these were the laws he had broken while trapped in Elish, because of *her*, and he was willing to submit to their punishment.

"Being trapped in a world," Hethn began, "is unusual, yes, but not unheard of. We, of course, make exceptions about certain behaviors in these situations. This is especially true due to the nature of Elish, for the way in which it has breached our realm."

Hethn sat on the plinth and stared at his hands a moment. Ulmaen admired his wrinkled orange flesh, and the gentle curve of his talons. "On the matter of Ibe—"

Avn hastily interrupted. "I must impress upon all of you the extent to which I highly regard our codes of conduct."

Ulmaen recoiled at the passion behind Avn's words.

"As soon as Ibe's behavior proved obstructive, I imprisoned him. His impetuousness in his haste to help, combined with his first time experiencing Cleithrophobia—"

Hethn raised his hand. Avn immediately fell silent. Despite Avn's obedience, his ego lashed out. Ulmaen delighted in knowing he wasn't as mature as he led everyone to believe. He wasn't perfect after all.

"On the matter of Ibe," Hethn announced. "The imprisonment you imposed on him while in Elish was required. Non-consensual conduct cannot be ignored, and we've taken into account that, at times, he wasn't his usual self." His tongue clicked against his beak. "He needs to mature more before becoming a Mentor again. In the meantime, he is to be demoted and will undergo extensive re-evaluation."

Avn let out a shaky breath and was, Ulmaen realized, deeply relieved by the outcome of their discussion.

"I agree." Avn's breathing returned to normal, but his anxiety remained. Ulmaen felt Avn's musings about Ule as his own, and they were laced with concern and other emotions as well—annoyance, anger, resentment, and something else lingering beneath the surface of his conscious mind.

Avn yearned to be rid of *her*. He cared little if Ule wanted to remain in the world of Elish to live out the remainder of her life as Sentinel, as long as she stayed there. Perhaps then she'd cease wreaking chaos in their realm.

Avn's ego shifted, and the reasonable part of him intruded, recognizing this fantasy was a foolish wish, for Ule wasn't experienced or skilled enough to be a Sentinel.

Ulmaen grew dizzy as he listened in on his Master's thoughts and emotions, which swung from anger and annoyance to admiration. For a moment, Avn believed Ule possessed great potential. He also believed she required the guidance of a patient mind, and he considered three other Masters more qualified to work with her.

"On the matter of Ule," Hethn resumed.

Ulmaen listened intently.

"We grant her request."

"She—" Rage seized Avn's mind and tongue.

"She is formally assigned to Elish as a Sentinel in training," Hethn elaborated.

Avn struggled to regain focus. "She can't! She's not ready."

There, Ulmaen felt an odd sensation. Beneath his panic and frustration, his anger and anxiety, a slow plodding churn, an ache deep within him.

Hethn and Avn's minds linked together in a flash, and Ulmaen nearly rebounded as the thunder of Hethn's thoughts relayed the Council's final verdict telepathically.

Alert and focused, eager to know what would become of him, Avn welcomed the verdict, for he was willing to repeat the worst of his offenses to protect his Students. He was willing to be accountable for Ule's offenses, too. His desire to be separated from her was so great, the feeling must have been impressed upon Hethn in their exchange.

Hethn led the chorus of projected Xiinisi voices, just as he had when they condemned Ule as a child for the crime of destroying a world.

Their collective thoughts slid through Avn's mind like a cool salve, easing the tenderness of his disquietude.

"You are relieved of all current duties."

Relief flooded Avn; the tendril of obligation toward Ule had at last been severed.

Ulmaen's distaste for his Master became more embittered.

"We have been forced by your hand, do you understand?" Hethn warned him.

No, Ulmaen thought, I don't. If he's no longer my Master, then what is he doing in my world? Why is he training me?

Of course, Avn understood. Ulmaen felt him panic again. He had ended the lives of many of Elish's inhabitants. He had even possessed a few. These weren't actions to be dismissed lightly regardless of the fact that he had had no other recourse while trapped in Elish.

"You have survived and found escape from a world which has expressed a new phenomenon," the Council explained. "Elish is the first of our created worlds to give birth to demons in corporeal form. They exist in the Root Dimension where they should not. They have evolved. You have made contact with them. Most importantly, you are Master to the Student who is responsible for creating the environment in which this phenomenon occurs."

Avn frowned. "What do you want from me?"

"Your position is unique. You've surpassed us in experience and skill. In addition to world formation and destruction, you also have firsthand experience of a new phenomenon in world evolution, one that requires studying."

Avn's stomach clenched.

"We believe it is in the best interests of the Xiinisi that you be appointed Maven. The rank is a rare distinction. No one has been made Maven in nearly a millennium—"

Repulsed by the promotion, Ulmaen lashed out at the memory with a curse word, but the imprint of the past remained unaffected.

"My crimes," Avn insisted.

A murmur among the Council, then their mindspeak vanished, leaving Avn alone with his disappointment. After they fell silent, Hethn addressed him vocally.

"Our code of conduct was designed for common situations. For uncommon situations, we must consider other approaches." Hethn nodded. "You did what you needed to do to ensure the safety of your Students as well as the world of Elish as a whole. There are always casualties, Avn. Always."

Ulmaen raged. He felt his body in the cell squirm and fidget. Within his mind, a memory arose. At first, he thought it belonged to the cluster of memories he clung to, then realized it was one of his own—the voice of Mbjard from several months ago.

"There are rules," he had said. "The kinds created by those in power which give them permission to behave in ways others aren't permitted."

The memory continued, and Hethn spoke again.

"You are above us in position now. Codes of conduct are yours to bend when necessary. We trust you, Avn, and hope that one day you will teach all of the Masters what you know."

Ulmaen's resentment blossomed fully. Not only had Avn conspired to work against him, so had the Council.

"However," Hethn resumed, "since you insist on punishment, our reprimand is your new assignment."

Oaxa and Gur smiled brazenly at one another, their mirth mired in maliciousness. Veht remained expressionless, her multitude of eyes fixated on both Hethn and Avn.

"You are Xiinisi," Hethn began to explain. "You are not above or beyond receiving assignments." He sat upright, cocking his bird head to one side. "Knowing well your dislike for the world Elish…"

Ulmaen began to understand, relishing the way Avn trembled at the thought of returning to the world he'd been trapped in for hundreds of Elishian years, knowing what they intended for him.

"I'm to train Ule, aren't I?"

Ulmaen shared in Oaxa and Gur's laughter, simultaneously feeling Avn drown in his own broiling resentment.

"*That* is your primary mandate," Hethn replied. "To train Ule and only her. Your other Students have all been reassigned."

Ulmaen again delighted in Avn's misery.

Hethn nodded curtly. "By the mood I sense in you now, this reprimand is satisfactory. But, there is more."

Oaxa and Gur snickered like children until Veht shushed them. Gur sprang to all feet, leaned forward, and snarled at her, Oaxa goading him on. Veht swung around, jumping to her feet at his aggression. All of her eyes snapped toward Gur. She raised her salmon colored hand, grabbed him by the scruff of his neck and pinned him to the floor until he whined in pain.

Curling back on the floor, Gur stared at Veht until she released him. "Always a pleasure," he told her. She shrugged, then returned to her seat.

The incident hadn't amused Avn. Instead, he was consumed by dread.

Pleased by his discomfort, Hethn resumed describing the new assignment. "You're to conduct yourself discreetly in this world and learn everything you can about the demons. That is your secondary mandate. It is to be done covertly. Given Ule's level of discipline, she may do more harm than good if she assists you in any way. An exclusive focus on her Sentinel duties will do her good."

Avn remained silent. Oh, how in that very moment, he hated *her*. Ulmaen, however, had grown numb to the sting of his rejection.

Hethn tapped a talon against his thigh, indicating the end of their meeting, and as the Council began to exit the Lyceum, he paused. "I hope you find a way to make peace with her."

When Avn was alone again, he fought the urge to rant uncontrollably. A heat like no other stung his cheeks and eyes. His body trembled. His gaze remained fixated on the onyx floor that denied both him and Ulmaen a reflection—

Yanked from the memory, Ulmaen struggled to find orientation. He had been Avn in the Lyceum for what seemed like an hour, but only a fraction of a second had passed.

Other memories lingered nearby. About to peek into one, Ulmaen was violently shoved to the outer limits of his Master's mind, then beyond.

He opened his eyes. The ceiling of the Prison cell was marked with scratches and glyphs dating back centuries. That final push had exhausted him, and he waited until his heartbeat returned to a normal pace before planning another attack.

Ulmaen hadn't finished with Navalis yet.

✳

In. Out. In. Out. Ulmaen's breath found an even rhythm, and he re-established a connection with Navalis. He assumed Navalis kept his mind well guarded now, so he'd have to find another way in. He knew from his own experience how pain had a way of turning a person inside out.

He shifted his focus to his lower right lung, spun the energy there, and created a conduit. When it opened wide enough, he projected his thoughts into Navalis's right lung.

In. Out—

Ulmaen gasped. Deeply immersed within Navalis's body, he dove into a sea of seething the likes of which he'd never experienced before. Anger drenched every part of Navalis, no doubt a reaction to his mind being infiltrated.

"You think you're special, don't you *Maven*? How about now?" he goaded, then squeezed Navalis's lung and released it.

"You... Your behavior is unacceptable," Navalis projected. "When I find you—"

"Given the way you're talking to no one at the moment, I expect Osblod will have you locked away in the Infirmary to examine your insanity."

"I'm between the new and old ramparts. There's no one around. Besides, I don't care what they think of me at the moment. Only you."

"What? Do you want to kill me again?

Ulmaen wondered if he needed to make a second conduit, or if he could move the one he'd already created. With his will, he nudged the conduit in his lung and it slid a little. He pushed at it, and it slipped into the muscle beneath the ribcage. Satisfied with the new location, he hurled a strong blast of energy through it.

"If it's..." Navalis began.

Ulmaen sensed Navalis's lungs recoil from the blow as though his stomach had taken a hit.

On the exhale, Navalis finished his thought. "...necessary."

The projection felt weak, its message cold compared to the anger it was born out of. Ulmaen considered its meaning and hurled back a reply.

"Nobody's death is necessary!"

"Sometimes... it is."

Ulmaen struggled to keep his breath even. He wanted to respond, but Navalis kept projecting grim thoughts.

"Boriag's death was unfortunate," he told Ulmaen. "A victim of circumstance. Kerista's injury, too, but I couldn't kill her without creating suspicion. Laere..."

Ulmaen gulped at the mention of Laere. He dreaded asking. "What about her?"

"Did you know she was a demon? Or were you too busy falling in love again to notice?"

"I didn't love..." Ulmaen's focus faltered. He didn't love her, but he could have. "I could've loved her if not for Bethee."

"Yes, and Bethereel. What about her?" Navalis's thoughts oozed with contempt. "Leaving me to clean up the mess."

Ulmaen grew numb. "I... I don't understand. What mess?"

"There are consequences when we love our creations. The bond created is profound within the creation."

Ulmaen waited for Navalis to explain himself. The silence was agonizing, and he asked, "What did you do to Bethee?"

"When an Elishian dies, their essence ceases," Navalis responded calmly. "When we deathmorph our forms change, but... our essence always remains."

Ulmaen detected a hint of resentment. Pure and saturated, it dripped from the last few words Navalis uttered.

"Bethereel was certain you were dead," Navalis continued. "Yet she still felt connected to you. It was driving her insane, did you know that?"

Ulmaen had noticed Bethereel change, but he thought grief had been making her behave strangely.

"It isn't right to do that to your creations," Navalis persisted, his thoughts acrid and hurtful. "You should never have long term, intimate relationships with them."

"You did!" Ulmaen quickly retorted. "You and Sabien—"

"I believed I was going to die here," Navalis explained. "Once that barrier was dismantled, I knew I had to withdraw from him. Why else do you think I let him believe Avn had returned home instead of making him believe he was dead?"

Sickened by the notion, Ulmaen struggled to understand. He recalled what Osblod had said, about how Bethereel had been smothered in the way of mercy killings he had seen during the war. Had Navalis murdered Ule's lover, too? A chill trickled through him, and he imagined Navalis felt it also.

"Yes," Navalis said. "I smothered her."

Sickened by the admission, Ulmaen struggled for words, and Navalis continued projecting.

"You couldn't see the pain you were causing her, could you? You were so caught up in yourself."

"I was trying to get back to her," Ulmaen explained.

"You were dead!"

Ulmaen's mind whirred in a frenzy. Words failed him again.

"I made sure of that," Navalis admitted to a second crime. "You don't come back from the dead. Not here, not in this world."

"You could've—"

"No! You weren't listening," Navalis explained. "You were caught up in the minutiae of this world. You were compliant and comfortable and distracted. I had to."

In that instant, Ulmaen knew what he had to do, too.

He had trusted Navalis, implicitly, with deep conviction. Even when their bond had weakened, he had never considered Navalis capable of harm. Now, he knew otherwise, and he wanted to hurt Navalis back.

He created several conduits, one at a time until each was spinning and opened to the same degree—one in each thigh deep within the femur, another in the heart, and the last in the throat, beneath the chin.

He tried to push through all of them simultaneously. They resisted. He tried again and grew impatient. Stopping a moment, he breathed again—In. Out. In. Out.

His mind focused, and when he projected, his will slid through each conduit with ease. He sensed a trepidation rising in Navalis, as though he knew something was about to happen, but he wasn't sure what.

Ulmaen released his will.

He snapped Navalis's left femur first. Then the right. The bones broke with ease, and Ulmaen pushed on the fractures until the bones slid apart. He waited a moment, to make sure the nerve endings were firing pain signals to Navalis's brain. Then he focused on the throat conduit, splitting open the flesh and fracturing the bones there, making them splinter and splay and tear the main artery.

He waited again, felt Navalis begin to heal the wound.

Ulmaen hurled his will through the heart conduit. He gripped Navalis's heart, made it beat faster, pushing the blood along, hurrying it out the wound of the neck before it healed.

These wounds, however, hadn't felt sufficient. He'd envied Navalis once, but had eventually come to admire and love him. But now?

The pain ran deep. He needed to show Navalis he was no longer needed, wanted, or welcomed. He spun a conduit deep within his solar plexus, and when the connection was made, he took a deep breath.

Loud and clearly, he projected, "Be gone from my world!"

Ulmaen reinforced the command with a blast of energy that gained speed and momentum as it rushed from Ulmaen into Navalis's body, forcing his Master's molecules to expand, propelling him...

❋ CHAPTER 52 ❋

...into the sky.

The ground hurtled away beneath Navalis. He reached out reflexively, expecting to grab hold of the long grass. The field beyond the Infirmary grew smaller, the grass looking more like bristling fur.

He had followed Ulmaen's projected energy this far. On the verge of passing the Prison, he had realized his Student was somewhere within the structure and not in the woods like he first thought, when his left leg snapped. The disconnect between his mind and body had prevented him from experiencing any pain.

He had expected to fall. Instead, he hung suspended in the air. Then his right leg snapped. His heart thumped hard in his chest. Until blood sprayed from his neck, he hadn't been aware that it had been torn open.

Finally, there was the push. His reach was automatic and ineffective, no matter how much he willed his body to stop Ascending.

He gurgled as thick warm liquid rose into his mouth. He clutched at his slit throat, again a reflex that proved useless in stopping his blood from spilling down through the air. His legs flapped about, bent at odd angles. Though he felt no pain, the awkwardness of his alignment distracted him. The blood, too.

He tried to heal his body, at least partially. His will had no effect. The revelation struck Navalis hard and for the briefest of moments he wished his form didn't exist, that he could be pure immaterial thought, unaffected by material issues.

He was being expelled from the world. None of his fellow Xiinisi had experienced this in many eons, for Expulsion was a terrible offense and its punishment severe. Details of what transpired during the physical ejection were no longer known.

The force and momentum were beyond his control. His molecules, too, acted on their own, shifting to accommodate the transition between the dimensions of Elish and his home realm.

The speed of the Ascension troubled him most, for he was moving faster and faster instead of slowing down. He predicted complications, so he tried again to slow his Ascent. He summoned the An Energy, and it responded, remaining at a distance for a moment before flitting away. Any hope of anchoring to it vanished.

He blasted through the perimeter of the world into his own realm. His molecules coalesced of their own accord, maintaining an Elishian form instead of reverting to his Xiinisi form, and he was grateful his nerves were numb to the multitude of energy frequencies that now surrounded him. He tried again to exert control over some part of his existence—

Something hard cracked the base of his skull. He veered one way and glimpsed the onyx dais he had collided with. Despite its weight, it shifted from the impact, tipping and rolling, pitching the binary star system it held toward another dais containing a planet with seven moons. Then they were gone, replaced briefly by the vaulted ceiling with its numerous interconnecting arches. He had fully emerged into the Vault within his realm, struggling to regain control.

The worlds he had struck, their collision with one another was certain to be volatile. He focused, pushed his will to erect barriers around both of them, hoping to prevent them from colliding and possibly setting off a chain reaction. Although his will was there, it had no effect.

The worlds collided.

Their invisible perimeters resisted contact at first, spinning around the base of a pillar like two conjoined bubbles. Then, the barriers melted into one another, the dimensions within seeking equilibrium and fusion, which were an impossibility.

The explosion was deafening. The blast propelled him and other worlds nearby toward the outer wall of the Vault.

Being numb, Navalis *heard* the thump of his back against a marble pillar. The impact winded him, and he fell onto the floor in a crumpled mess, struggling to prop himself up.

Shouts pierced the silence. More explosions boomed.

Stunned, Navalis shook his head, trying to pull himself together. Blood ran down both arms, and he realized he must find a way to heal himself first before he could help the others.

He flinched as a chain of explosions went off. Their racket was muffled, as though shielded. Gur thundered throughout the room barking orders, erecting dampening barriers around the exploding planets.

Navalis pulled himself upright, determined to mend his body. He pushed his mind; his body didn't respond. He pushed again, falling back against the wall, feeling a pervasive urgency throughout him. His body was demanding food and water and sleep. He blinked away the darkness, trying to understand why he still existed in Elishian form.

Blood gurgled on his lips. He pressed against the gaping wound of his neck. Several Students stopped to kneel beside him. They were scared, but they asked if they could assist. Navalis tried, but couldn't project his thoughts or speak.

His mind reeled, and his eyelids grew heavy. Perhaps if he succumbed to his exhaustion, then he could communicate through dreams.

He jolted awake at the soft touch on his chest. He strained his eyes wide and regarded Veht kneeling before him. The black eyes across her cheekbones and along her arms were wide, flitting back and forth in alarm. She projected her thoughts.

"Are you alright, Avn?"

He shuddered.

"What happened?"

He tried to project but Veht could not hear him.

"Ul—" He began to speak. "Ule exp—" He sputtered and coughed as he gripped his throat. "Ex... pelled..."

The Students gasped and muttered among themselves: *That's wrong. Ule's going to Isolation again. What'd you do to deserve that?*

Veht hushed the Students, urging them to assist Gur. Reluctantly, they obeyed. Thankful for her presence, Navalis yearned for sensation to return to his body, just so he could enjoy her touch.

She continued to project her thoughts into his mind, and her soft tone soothed him.

"You're Maven now. I trust your actions were reasonable," she said. "Whatever transpired on Elish, whatever has caused your expulsion, the sooner you explain it, the sooner we can understand and fix it."

She touched the side of his face, a gentle caress he was sure of it.

"Ule is..." Veht began, then paused to search for an appropriate word. "Impetuous. Look around. Nine worlds destroyed so far. Students and Mentors injured. Ule has little regard for anyone. You can't protect her anymore."

A stillness pervaded Navalis. His double heartbeat slowed, and he longed to return to his Xiinisi form with its slow, single pulse.

"You've no need to hide anything from us." Veht's hand caressed his face again. "Will you link minds with us now? Tell us everything you've discovered and learned?"

With what little strength he possessed, he touched the back of her hand. Then his arm fell away and rested in his lap.

"No," he whispered. "I... can't."

Veht retracted her hand. Her many eyes began to glisten. After a moment, she placed her fingers on his forehead and a soft, gentle darkness overtook him, the kind in which dreams turned.

Avn feared what was to come, so he chose to dream of nothing.

✻

A thick veil of fog unfurled in Navalis's mind the moment he became aware again. Darkness lingered. There was a weightlessness to his being, a painlessness that defied explanation.

"Avn." Veht called out, her gentle voice threatening to lull him to sleep if he wasn't already asleep. "Do you know where you are?"

"In a dream."

"Yes, we are in your dream," she admitted. "Your body rests in the Sanatorium. We've done all we can. The damage..."

He listened, heard her sigh.

"The damage is extensive. We restored you to Xiines form, but..."

He tried to remember what had come before he lost consciousness, but only fragments floated around his mind—blood and explosions and Veht hovering above him. What he did remember was that he had been exhausted and broken.

Suddenly he knew what the Xiinisi had done, but not through his own experience. He sensed it through Veht. They had restored his body. His legs had been mended. His throat, too. Best of all, he was no longer Elishian, which meant he had fewer clusters of nerves.

His heart beat had returned to a single pulse that expanded outward and faded away. It pulsed again, so different to what he was accustomed to experiencing, for it sounded muffled.

He was whole again, in body and mind, except he couldn't sense it within his form. There was a gap, a space between his form and his essence, as though the bond that kept them attached had been pulled so long and so thin it could break at any moment.

"What's happened?"

Veht sighed. "You won't wake up."

Suddenly, he wasn't alone with Veht in his dream.

"I told you to wait until I was done," Veht complained as others presented themselves.

"Feel that?" Oaxa's mood was full of vitriol and disdain. "He's happy. Happy?! After what he's done." Her thoughts echoed in his mind, accompanied by a chorus of hisses from her vipers.

"How can he feel so satisfied?" growled Gur.

"Talk to me," Avn demanded of him. "Don't talk about me in my own dream as though I'm not here."

Gur howled with laughter. He projected his thoughts again. "How can you feel so satisfied? Nine worlds destroyed altogether. The An Energy is deeply affected by it. Roiled and... shamed."

Veht shushed Gur, as another presence breached the dream, someone the others yielded to. The primary members of Council were in Navalis's mind now. He wished none of them were here, except for Veht, for he'd rather be healing the bond between his essence and form.

"I understand your unique position," Hethn said. "We've observed some of your memories."

"Against my will?" Avn searched his mind and found some of his more recent memories had been prodded, split open, and devoured like fruit. Enraged by the violation, the darkness within his dream shimmered.

"You gave us little choice." Hethn's presence emanated a fierce magnetic pull, demanding attention. "You would not relay to us certain details, so we've been forced to interrogate you. We've only just begun."

He scanned his memories. No, they hadn't harvested all of them. They hadn't yet peeled open and picked through the ones involving his demon studies.

"I preferred you stay in stasis," Hethn said. "However, Veht insisted you have a right to be aware of our... trespassing."

Avn began willing barriers in place, securing his memories against intrusion. He couldn't allow it. He wouldn't let Hethn proceed. Hethn was older, but Avn, he was Maven and he'd try to overpower Hethn if he had to, regardless of his weakened state.

"What do you hide from us?!" Gur demanded. "See, he does it again!"

"We hope you will forgive us this trespass," Hethn continued. "The same forgiveness that you will ask of us for murdering your Student."

Oaxa's temper flared, a lick of flame intending to scorch him. "Disgusting!"

Gur and Oaxa's tempers subsided as Hethn's presence swelled. Veht was still there, too.

"You aspired to educate Ule," Hethn said. "You killed her to initiate a change in her form, one that could have been acquired through instruction without ending her current generation."

"He cannot be above our laws," Oaxa pleaded.

"Punish him!" Gur demanded.

Avn ignored their outbursts.

"I sensed a desperate compulsion in your memories," Hethn continued. "If you explain to us your urgency in quickening Ule's training, perhaps we can understand and absolve you of this crime."

"I hate her," he told them candidly. "Just as Oaxa and Gur and you hate me for being just a little different, a little more aware in a way you aren't. You'll be glad when I embrace the Quietus."

"Arrogance doesn't suit you," Hethn continued, seeing through Avn's lie. "We'll extract information from you by force. We all have a right to know what you know."

Oaxa and Gur each gave their opinions.

"Tear him open!"

"Gut him!"

Within the darkness, Veht stirred and asked her companions, "You would kill him?"

Avn laughed. He felt like he was dying, and he'd fight until the end. He'd fight them all to protect his knowledge, until he was ready.

Their threats motivated him to double barricade his memories, and he braced himself.

Veht spoke again, her softness hardening. "I won't be a part of this trespassing," she told Hethn. "Whatever Avn is keeping from us, I trust it is in the best interest and safety of the Xiinisi. I urge you not to do this."

Gur's thoughts boomed. "He's broken too many rules."

"Your mediation won't work this time," Oaxa sang, trying to antagonize Veht.

"Won't it?" Veht impressed her strength of will on all of them.

Avn reeled at the power she seldom exuded.

Veht withdrew her will. "As Council members, do we share with the others everything we know and learn?" she asked. "No, we don't, because what we know can confuse those of us who don't have the experience to understand."

"He still must answer to us," Hethn insisted.

Veht sighed. "What if the information he retains causes us confusion? We're the most experienced among our kind, and if we can't understand, how are we to make the others understand?"

Avn appreciated Veht's wisdom. She understood his situation as well as the situations of her peers. She knew they were afraid, even Hethn.

Within his essence, the bond weakened further, making his body seem farther away.

"Am I expected to treat his knowledge as privileged now?" Hethn asked. "What you're requesting, Veht, undermines our collective. How are we to trust him?"

"Avn, you must share what you know with at least one of us," Veht suggested. "As a way to stay connected to the collective. You risk excommunication otherwise."

He considered the compromise. It was... reasonable, and he wasn't sure if he had much time left. They felt him agree to the concession.

"Then let us be," Hethn projected, ordering the others to recede.

"No!" Avn resisted.

Sharing his knowledge about the demons of Elish with Hethn was the most logical choice, for Hethn was the oldest of their kind, the most experienced.

"Then who?" Oaxa asked.

"Veht," Avn requested.

"Why her?" Gur growled, demanding an immediate answer.

"She's the only one among us who regards other viewpoints as being just as valid as her own," Avn replied.

"She does possess a unique insight," Hethn admitted. "Would you agree to this, Veht?"

Avn trusted her most of all, for her discretion and confidence, and for her ability to stay calm and make sense of chaos in times of great conflict. Her perspective on the phenomenon he had been studying might ease his worries, and he could die peacefully knowing everything he knew was in her hands.

"Yes, I agree," Veht finally said.

Hethn's presence diminished immediately. Both Oaxa and Gur receded, too, taking their time, seemingly determined to overhear something of their conversation.

Veht remained quiet, and when hers was the only presence, Avn dismantled the barriers around his memories and offered them to her one by one, noticing how opening himself up made the bond between his essence and form a little stronger.

She conveyed no thoughts, only a pervasive sense of curiosity. With each memory she scanned, she exuded fear and anxiety and confusion. After setting the last memory aside, she remained reflective for a while, then finally spoke.

"This.... Emptiness? Absence?"

Emptiness was as good a name for the phenomenon as anything else, although the word *absence* was more accurate in meaning. He agreed to both of the terms.

"It unravels what we create?" she asked.

After a moment, he agreed again. He breathed easier having shared the knowledge with someone, but feared the depth of confusion he sensed spinning in Veht.

"It works against our will," he told her.

Veht laughed. "Just like Ule."

He hadn't thought of it that way, but yes, the presence of demons and the absence within them, these were all expressions of Ule's personality—both her creative and destructive tendencies.

"I sensed there was something in that darkness, something alive."

"I don't understand," she admitted.

Avn regretted having told her, yet was grateful she was willing to take on this burden.

"As long as the world Elish exists, it is a threat to its own dimension, especially ours if there's ever another breach in its Mirari."

"How?"

"I think somehow it's connected to the An Energy," he conjectured. "In Elish, the evolution of a demon is slow and gradual. Here, in our realm, immersed in the An Energy, I suspect these demons would evolve very quickly, into something beyond our control."

Veht considered what he had said, and asked, "Is this the reason for your harsh approach with Ule's training, why it was important to educate her with haste?"

Avn agreed with her sentiment, detecting a shift in her mood. He welcomed the growing bond between them, especially since the one between his essence and form had become so tenuous. There was no one else he'd rather be with when his final single heartbeat pulsed and faded away.

"What will become of her?" he asked.

"Do you care for her?"

"Of course I do." When he spoke of Ule, he felt a chill, the kind made from both dread and excitement, the kind that spun his curiosity with such force it left him wanting and desperate for answers.

"She's frustrating," he explained. "Difficult to instruct at times. She's impetuous, headstrong, and... impossible. I've learned more from her than from all of our Masters combined. Do you know, I push her to see how she reacts? I know it's against Conduct, but when Ule pushes back, it comes from somewhere beyond rules and laws. She isn't afraid."

"Do you think we're afraid?"

"What I think is that we're complacent."

Veht pondered the notion.

"This time around," he confided in her, "I chose to give Ule a taste of herself, to see what would happen, to learn."

"And what did you learn?"

"I learned that there's something beyond Xii, something we aren't seeing or don't want to see," he said. "And I've learned Ule's a fighter. My instincts tell me we may need her one day, but I'm not sure why."

Veht recoiled at Avn's admission.

"What is it?" he asked.

Sadness overcame her. After a moment she confided in him. "The Council has made a decision about her. Had I known what you just told me, I would have persuaded them to choose another way."

"What decision?"

Silence.

"Veht?"

Her thoughts came slowly. "To preserve ourselves against Ule's future actions, intentional or not, for our own protection, she has been excommunicated to Elish."

"That'll shorten her life! She'll die alone!"

"The world has already been placed in Isolation, in the event she breaches the barrier placed around the world, that way neither she nor the world can affect our realm ever again."

Avn understood the necessity of the quarantine to protect Xii, but he didn't agree with it. They'd need to be prepared for the Emptiness or the Absence, whatever Veht wanted to call it.

"This is what I know," he began. "We learn about each other and our environment, and this occurs by learning about ourselves first, through the worlds we build. These worlds contain different aspects of who and what we are. From the time we started establishing rules and codes of conduct, we've been creating within a contained space—"

Within the darkness of the dream, a second layer of darkness reached for him.

"Are you alright?" Veht's concern overshadowed her curiosity. "Can you continue?"

"The phenomenon of demons is a threat," he continued, pushing back the darkness. "I won't argue that, but it's also the product of Ule, who created without the limitations of our rules. She's tapped into something... else."

"It's highly unlikely," Veht said. "We know all there is to know."

"Really?" Avn laughed. "You, the Xiinisi Council, made me Maven. There hasn't been a Maven since our kind instated codes of conduct. I know, because I looked it up in our Archive. Hethn instructed me to bend the rules, and I did. I'm telling you, there's something we've cut ourselves off from because we haven't bothered to venture outside those rules for a very long time."

Veht's mind engulfed the revelation and clung to it. Her wonder flooded his mind.

"Those demons," he continued, "the Emptiness they harbor, that was created by Ule, and yes, they're a problem. However, it's been my experience that within the problem lies the solution."

"Ule?"

"Yes, Ule must be the source of the solution."

As Veht receded into the darkness, her flitting thoughts and emotions just beyond his detection, he focused on his sluggish breath and how the flow of his energy sounded like a whisper. He wished he could stay alive to see what Ule would become.

Veht returned. "You're the first appointed Maven in many, many eons, and under your guidance is a Student who is the first to bring about a new phenomenon in world building evolution. This is an interesting time for our kind, isn't it?"

Avn didn't share her wonderment.

"I understand now," she assured him. "Together, we *will* change their minds."

"You will," he corrected her.

"Keep the darkness away," she told him. "Stay in this dream and heal yourself, if you can. Do you feel any pain?"

"No," he told her. "I stopped the pain from transmitting."

"Then it is all on you to get better, to feel pain again." Then Veht was gone.

In the silence that ensued, he struggled to hear the pulse of his heart, as he tried to reign in the disconnect between his mind and body.

✳ CHAPTER 53 ✳

Ulmaen preferred silence to what he heard. The rush of his breath through his throat. The soft hiss of air filling his lungs. The voiceless whisper that brushed past his lips upon exhalation. Somewhere within The Pit water drip-dripped, and down the hall Mithreel shuffled in his cell, making his chains rattle.

Footfalls padded along the tunnel and grew louder. Each step caused a shudder through his chest, flaring his foul mood. He longed for his current generation to end and to begin deathmorphing, just to make the noises stop. Little noises, all of them, each striking at the rage until it threatened to spark into a long wailing scream.

He dragged his finger tips over his face and rested them on his lips. He considered the nature of that scream, the one that threatened to pour out of him, and wondered if it might do him good or if it, too, would be fleeting, like the delirious joy he had felt while he hurled Navalis back to their dimension. The satisfaction of that had started to wane, and the soreness of betrayal consumed him again.

Just one long strong scream...

"You look well."

He flinched at the intrusive voice. His eyes shot open. The little noises receded, and he barely heard them now, as he stared a moment at the low ceiling, then sat upright and swung his legs over the side of the cot.

His muscles were stiff and tight from laying in the same position for a couple of days. The exertion woke his body, making his stomach complain and growl.

Mbjard stood beyond the gate, his head tilted to one side. "Ready to go or would you rather continue meditating on that cot like you're a mystic?"

Ulmaen coughed to clear his dry throat. He stood and stumbled across the cell, disrupting a cloud of flies buzzing over several day's worth of food rotting in pails. He leaned against the gate and managed to speak despite the dryness in his throat.

"What are you doing here?"

Mbjard held up a large key, then slipped it into the lock of the gate. Though he tried to squash his smile, the light in his eyes expressed deep amusement. "It took me a while to figure out where you'd disappeared to. I knew you'd be a handful." The lock clicked. He withdrew the key and pulled the gate open with a tug.

Ulmaen hesitated at the door, wondering how long he had before his body died. He hadn't the clarity of mind to sense what was happening deep within his essence.

"So why do you bother with me?" he asked.

Mbjard tapped the tip of the key against the side of his spectacles. "Sometimes some instincts trump other instincts."

"How'd you get Gorlen to release me?"

"A private conversation," Mbjard replied. "A few well worded inquiries about Rozafel, and a mild threat that if he didn't release you, I'd have some of Lyan's advisers down to interview other prisoners about her whereabouts." He smiled again, as though his threat was as common and casual as breathing.

"We need to tell someone about Rozafel," Ulmaen suggested.

"Once the new Magnes is sworn in, I promise," Mbjard assured him. "One thing at a time. Come now. As long as we don't linger, you'll have time to clean up."

Ulmaen stepped out of the cell. His hamstrings fully released, and he stood a little taller. "Time for what?"

"Transcribing the Inaugural Ceremony, of course." Mbjard turned toward the cramped tunnel. "I know you've been locked down here, but surely you must've heard the voting results."

He hadn't. Perhaps a guard had told him, but he'd been preoccupied, his vengeful mood all consuming.

"Quick now," Mbjard insisted and took the lead down the hallway. "Gorlen's especially grumpy today, what with Lyan winning by a landslide. I'd always thought Gorlen an ally." He began to climb the main stairs. "Just goes to show, you never do really know someone. Could be he's grumpy with all the murders and disappearances."

Mbjard stopped on the stairs and turned back around. "Seems an apprentice mystic, that fellow who's always fluttering about your brother-in-law, has been responsible for some of it." Lowering his voice, he whispered, "There's something going on in the castle, but Gorlen hasn't figured it out yet."

Ulmaen agreed wholeheartedly with the comment. He rubbed a hand across his chest, expecting to feel his inner reserve of energy demanding fuel, but it remained satisfied. Only his body required sustenance.

"First there were the deaths," Mbjard continued. "Ule and Bethereel, now you didn't have anything to do with them, but the disappearances? Laere, then Boriag, and I hate to tell you this, but your brother-in-law can't be found now."

Ulmaen's cheek twitched at the mention of Navalis, then he blushed with satisfaction. As he started imagining how to celebrate being free of his Master, Mbjard began speaking again.

"The last to see him said he looked like he'd been in a brawl. Whatever is going on here, it's close to you, so watch yourself."

Ulmaen wasn't concerned. He'd defeated a Xiinisi. He was certain he could handle anything Elish threw at him, even its demons.

"We may never find out for certain what's been going on here," Mbjard said as he resumed climbing the stairs slowly, occasionally glancing back over his shoulder. "For the time being, Gorlen has soldiers searching for Boriag. Gorlen's convinced this fellow is responsible for Laere's disappearance and is now on the run. Let's hope he had nothing to do with your brother-in-law's disappearance."

He could tell Mbjard and the others what had happened to Laere, Boriag, and Navalis, but then he would have to explain. He wasn't sure why Navalis had killed Boriag or how he had come to believe Laere was a demon, but what he knew for certain was that Navalis had murdered his lover and deserved whatever happened to him during the expulsion from Elish.

As they emerged onto the main floor at the front of the Prison, Ulmaen was struck by the severe expression Gorlen wielded. His blazing glare and sharp curled sneer was enough to sheer through quarried stone.

"Watch yourself," Gorlen warned. "With a temper like yours, you'll be back in here."

Ulmaen wasn't afraid of anyone anymore, least of all Gorlen. Rage had become a reflex, and he hadn't even been aware that he'd aimed himself at Gorlen, hands fisted, until Mbjard steered him back toward the main door.

"There, there," Mbjard addressed Gorlen. "Your time is better served looking after your prisoners, don't you think?"

Gorlen's snarl waned at the gentle reminder of Mbjard's threat. In the wake of his silence, Ulmaen celebrated with overwhelming joy accompanied by a smirk.

Mbjard guided him toward the exit, determined to distract him. "I have a bit of news to lift your mood," he said.

Ulmaen wasn't sure why Mbjard changed the subject, but he went along with him, allowing the slight man to lead the way up the steps. Outside, a wind made the tall grass rustle. The sky above was clear, and he inhaled the freshness, enjoying the wild movement about him.

"I've found an important reference to our treasure."

Ulmaen shuddered.

"You want to talk about treasure?" The urge to tell Mbjard that the treasure didn't really exist nearly poured from him but he stopped himself.

"I find my obsession keeps me anchored during times of unease, or excitement."

Ulmaen felt he must tell Mbjard something, anything. "This treasure... Don't you worry you're chasing a phantom?"

Mbjard's eyes grew wide at the suggestion, signaling an interest.

"What if the treasure isn't anything of material value?" Ulmaen suggested, appreciating how the fresh air chased away the ache in his skull.

"What if it's something else? What if... the treasure is something abstract, like an idea?"

Mbjard nodded. "You mean a metaphor?"

"Sure." He went along with the suggestion, even though that wasn't what he truly meant.

"Those are the best kinds of treasure," Mbjard replied. "Those kind tend to contain wisdom instead of material wealth." He rested his hand on Ulmaen's arm, urging him to stop. "Sometimes wisdom is the better reward."

He laughed then, mostly to himself. "I'm not in need of wealth," Mbjard explained. "I'm very comfortable here. The pursuit of this treasure is really more of a quest for... mystery. The wondering keeps my mind limber. And when I've solved it, or have grown bored with it, I'll find another. There are so many unexplored realms to discover."

Ulmaen knew differently. There was only one realm. It lay beyond Elish, and he'd had quite enough of it.

Once bathed, dressed, and fed, Ulmaen felt revived. As he reveled in this moment of wellbeing, he realized that his reserve of energy was intact, and he didn't understand why the exertion of intensely directed will during moments of excruciating emotional pain hadn't shortened his life in any way. No answers came to him, just calm satisfaction which made him light-headed.

He cut through the courtyard by Fehran's Hall, and then the buildings behind it. He crossed the northern Colonnade, just above the Starry Rise near the ruins, and slipped into the Kitchen yard, where he found Senaga and thanked her for feeding him while he had been in Prison, even though he barely ate any of it. When he stole a large yellow and red apple from a barrell, Senaga swore at him as he raced back onto the Colonnade.

He bit into the flesh of the apple, tore away a mouthful of pulp and chewed with new found fervor. Something about the refreshing flesh felt cleansing, and for the briefest of moments, he felt pure.

Outside again, he hurried along the Colonnade toward the Starry Rise, where people gathered in small clusters. Most of the crowds had taken the southern path toward the Chair Room, and so he went east along the Colonnade, where the crowds were thinner.

Past the Inner Sanctum, he ran his fingers along the wall of Laere's studio. Anticipating the jutting corner of the building, he swung around, and saw that crowds gathering at the open windows of the Chair Room, some with young children sitting on their shoulders eager to witness Lyan's inauguration.

Ulmaen pushed through a cluster of people around the entrance, raising the apple high above their heads when he needed to turn sideways to squeeze between them. The guards at the door blocked him and told him no more could fit, until Mbjard waved him through.

"You made it, finally." Mbjard pulled him along, and sat him down at the end of a narrow table piled with parchment and ink filled glass pens.

To his left, three other scribes sat huddled close together, each with pens poised over blank parchment. Their tense, terse nods indicated either excitement or nervousness; he couldn't tell which.

"Begin writing a brief description of who's in attendance, and where they are located," Mbjard instructed. He placed a stack of paper before him, and topped it with a pen.

Ulmaen lifted the glass pen. It felt small against his fingers. He examined the chaos about him, wondering where to begin. Immediately, his eyes were drawn to Lyan.

He began to write:

If the crowd that came to hear Lyan's campaign speech was large, imagine a crowd threefold in size.

Lyan stands proudly, well dressed in formal Soldier's armor, his face shaved, his brown curls shorn. He keeps to the entrance of the stairwell of the Inner Sanctum, which lies on the north side of the square room, where restored plaster reliefs tell stories about the forest and have been beautifully painted. He surrounds himself with loyal Guards. Well protected, he is at ease. And so he should be.

The Chair intended for him gleams in the sun. Gone is the dark wood frame carved with leaves that extended the backrest and provided armrests. All that remains is the core of the Chair—worn blue marble that has been polished to a high gloss, a symbol of renewed tranquility, peace, and prosperity for Sondshor.

Council Advisers are dressed in their finery—lots of well polished armor for the Generals. They stand at attention in the northeast corner, gathered behind the Chair which is customarily angled to face west, to greet anyone who enters the main doors.

The Physician, Osblod, wears leather sparring gear from his old military days. He remains at the fringe of the group closest to Lyan. As one of many who campaigned against Lyan, I'd expect him to be jealous and bitter, but he accepts his defeat with grace and good sportsmanship, showing Lyan the utmost respect.

General Gorlen, however, stands on the other side of the Advisers, practically stuffed into the corner alongside a table of Scribes who are dutifully writing about this historic occasion. General Gorlen expresses a fit of sourness, his gaze fixed on Lyan.

Three Masters direct the Inaugural Ceremony, in the absence of a properly appointed Arch Mystic. On the left side of the Chair, a Master Mystic holds a gold crown. On the right side of the Chair, another holds the shor scepter, a masterfully faceted blue-green pegmatite set in a rod of etched iron.

General Gorlen shifts uncomfortably, flinching at the proximity of the Master Mystic who holds the scepter. It's a wonder what's going through General Gorlen's

*mind, given his great agitation. He repeatedly touches the grip of his sword and
tries to maneuver himself beside the Master Mystic without defying protocol.*

*Signaling the beginning of the ceremony, the third of the Master Mystics drapes
a red cloth embroidered with green leaves across the back of his shoulders...*

Ulmaen paused in his account. Someone's hand weighed on his shoulder,
and he acknowledged Mbjard as he leaned forward to read the account.

"How is it?" he asked Mbjard.

"Fine, very fine..." Mbjard lost himself in reading. "Your prose, it reminds
me of a previous apprentice I had. She passed away many months ago."

"I... I'm sorry," he said, not sure what he should say at the reference to
his former self.

"It's quite alright." Mbjard patted his shoulder. "It's nice to have
a reminder of her around. I suggest writing in code, something you're
familiar with, to help speed up your transcription."

"Will do," Ulmaen agreed to the suggestion.

He found himself torn by Mbjard's reflection. He thought of what Navalis
had said about getting too involved with his creations. If someone Ule had
only been friends with felt this way, he imagined Bethereel must have felt
this loss the deepest of anyone.

His rage was still too raw. He'd rather resume his writer duties, but
when he began to observe the unfolding events before him, General Gorlen
had moved again. Ulmaen leaned to the side, trying to glimpse the hilt of
the sword Gorlen pawed at.

Ulmean leaned a little farther. As Lyan stood before the Chair,
accompanied by the master mystic in the red cape. Lovingly, Ulmaen bit
into his apple—

Mbjard snatched it from his hand and whispered, "Have you no sense
of propriety?"

As Ulmaen was about to object, Mbjard disposed of the apple in a
nearby pail.

"Record Lyan's oath, first in short hand to capture it all, then later in
long hand, ten copies." He tapped the parchment on the desk. "Word for
word. Understood?"

Ulmaen gave in to the request, remembering that as long as he
remained in Elish, he needed to protect his true identity. His ability to
squash Mbjard like a bug would only raise suspicion. He had a role to play
in a significant historical event, and when the opportunity came, he'd slip
away discreetly. He'd go far away and become someone else for a while.

"Keep a personal account, as well," Mbjard suggested further,
"of everything you observe when you're not recording Lyan, in short hand
of course. Whichever code is quickest for you." He finally backed away and
stood beside the table, his arms neatly folded across the breast of his stiff
scribe capelet. After a moment, he raised an arm, showing it to the crowd.

In the courtyard, horns blasted. A hush swept through the crowd, beginning outside and rushing into the Chair Room, along the walls, and up to the mezzanine above. Ulmaen resumed writing.

Mbjard, our fussy Arch Scribe, announces the beginning of the ceremony, calling to Lyan to speak his intentions as leader. Outside, a second and third voice echo Mbjard's, informing those in the courtyard of what has been said.

Lyan steps forward, stands at attention, clears his throat. He raises his head to address his Advisers, nervous yet determined. About to speak, he stops. For a moment, his confidence fades. He shakes, the way a child shakes when faced with a nightmare. His eyes are fixed not on the Master Mystic before him, but on General Gorlen.

General Gorlen stands with both arms lifted straight out in front of him, both hands wrapped around a strange contraption. Attendees are curious about the device he holds. Among their murmurs, I hear them ask: What's that ugly thing? Is it part of the ceremony? What's he up to?

The Master Mystic holding the iron scepter, begins inscribing the air with a finger, calling on his powers. He focuses on General Gorlen, his eyes bulging, his face pressing forward as though his skull might burst his skin. He recognizes the device; so do the other Mystics, who seem confident in their comrade's ability to stop the General and stand by idly, waiting...

Ulmaen hadn't realized it, but he had been writing down everything he saw, everything he heard. His hand scratched shorthand code across the parchment, yet he felt frozen in the task. He knew what everyone else didn't, that if he tried to stop Gorlen, there would be questions. They'd want to know how he knew the device was dangerous, how Lyan knew what it was; the master mystics, too. So he wrote.

The Master Mystic isn't quick enough with whatever protective barrier he summons. Gorlen presses a button on the device. There is a click of metal hitting metal, then a pop and the smell of something hot burning—sulfur and carbon mixed with potassium nitrate...

Ulmaen flinched at the explosion and scored a deep line of ink across the parchment. He readied himself to stand up and wrestle Gorlen to the ground, but the room erupted into chaos and Gorlen was well beyond reach. The most he could do was sit back down, grab a blank piece of parchment and continue writing.

Osblod shoots across the room faster than the projectile from Gorlen's matchlock gun. That is what I've heard these weapons called by the soldiers practicing with them in Warfield. Osblod lunges to shield Magnes Lyan with his body. He falls to his knees on the floor clutching his shoulder.

Tension thickens the air. Some of the attendees scream. My fellow Scribes flee the table, seeking safety behind the aprons of Clothiers huddled together.

Osblod pitches to the floor, clutching his shoulder. His face twists in pain. He sucks in his breath, and Lyan shoves off the embrace of his guards to kneel at

Osblod's side.

"It burns," Osblod tells Lyan, pressing against the wound. Blood trickles between his fingers. "But I'm alright."

Lyan is deeply relieved and affected by Osblod's sacrifice. Lyan helps Osblod to his feet and faces him, securing both hands behind Osblod's head. Their foreheads meet in an ancient gesture indicating the highest expression of honor.

Let it be known here, on the eve of Lyan's Inauguration, that Lyan has chosen a spirit brother in Osblod.

"Thank you, my friend," Lyan says, releasing Osblod. "You'll always be treated like family."

Meanwhile, stunned guards finally mobilize themselves as they realize Osblod's injury was intended for the Magnes. They delight in wrestling Gorlen to the ground, calling him an assassin, demanding death...

Ulmaen kept writing, mindful of someone sitting down next to him. He glanced at Mbjard, who picked up a pen and began to transcribe events in lieu of the other apprentices, who must have fled for safety.

Mbjard nodded shakily, his dark skin gray. "Good on you," he told Ulmaen. "For keeping your wits about you." He breathed deeply to help settle his nerves.

Ulmaen wrote, aware that his thoughts split into two currents of thinking. One part recorded everything; the other asked, *Why?*

Why would Osblod protect Lyan? He had never outwardly supported Lyan during the campaign and had nothing to gain from protecting him, so why risk dying for him? Had their public debates been staged, in the manner of actors from Eastgate? Or had Osblod meant something else every time he challenged Lyan in public?

The guards forced Gorlen to endure the remainder of the Inaugural Ceremony, and Gorlen grunted and groaned against them as Lyan was led to the Chair by one master mystic, then fitted with the golden crown and the iron scepter by the others.

As protocol prescribed, Lyan was asked about his first order of business. Ulmaen expected him to have Gorlen executed for treason. Instead, Lyan announced the termination of the development and possession of firearms, and ordered all of the matchlock guns to be sealed away in the Vault until a time of true need.

Then Mbjard stood to address the Magnes. "I'd like to add testimony to the matter of General Gorlen, for the record." He snapped his fingers hastily at Ulmaen, to make sure everything he said was being recorded.

"I assure you, he will be dealt with," Lyan said. "Treason is punishable by death or excommunication, and I take his crime *very* seriously."

"My friend," Mbjard persisted. "Given what I know about recent events, I urge that General Gorlen be imprisoned in the very place he has been guarding."

Gorlen suddenly struggled against the soldiers who attempted to bind him in wrist shackles. His eyes bugged, and sweat ran down his cheeks.

"You see," Mbjard continued, "a prisoner in his care has gone missing. I've discreetly interviewed several other prisoners. In exchange for leniency with respect to their punishment, they are willing to testify that Rozafel hung herself and that Gorlen secreted the body away."

A wave of whispering rushed through the room. Gorlen finally collapsed onto his knees on the floor.

Lyan bowed his head, visibly disappointed by the news. "I will consider your counsel."

Ulmaen continued to write, his mind dazed. Confusion addled his thoughts, and after a moment, Mbjard nudged him.

"Be mindful of what you're writing there," he said.

Ulmaen stared down and read the parchment. For nearly half the page, he'd written the same word side by side, row after row: *Why? Why? Why?...*

He shuddered, for he'd had enough of asking that question.

✳ CHAPTER 54 ✳

Ulmaen regarded the stacks of parchment which had once been blank and were now heavily inked. Future generations perusing the Archive were likely to come across them bound as leather books, and within the pages, they'd read about the rare occurrence of Protos, the attempted act of treason, the instatement of the Lyanovmal lineage, and the advisers' demand that General Gorlen be dealt with during their assembly.

They'd read lengthy accounts of General Gorlen's confession of plotting to kill the elected Magnes and take the Chair for himself, his sentencing to life inside the Pit, and the autosurgical extraction of a small round projectile from the wound in Osblod's shoulder.

Future readers would discover discrepancies among the transcriptions of the Inaugural Ceremony, differing views expressed by differing scribes, which captured the gist of Lyan's overwhelming gratitude and the gracious manner in which he occupied the Chair and accepted the ruling scepter.

Ulmaen relayed the final details, transcribing the casual banter between Lyan and his advisers, describing their actions and reactions and how the setting sun beamed through the window, gilding everything and everyone who still lingered within the Chair Room.

Somewhere, filed away beneath the pages of parchment, future readers would also find a passage containing one repeating word.

Why? Why? Why...

Ulmaen's fingers ached and his palm throbbed. He'd lasted longer than the other scribes, who had returned to their regular duties an hour earlier, only because he'd healed the strain on the tendons and muscles.

"Well done," Mbjard praised him, as he gathered up empty glass pens.

"He could've been killed," Ulmaen muttered to himself, unable to release the memory of how Osblod used a knife to dig out the bullet in the front of his shoulder.

A warm hand cupped the back of Ulmaen's neck, making him flinch at first.

Mbjard leaned over, regarded him with concern, and asked, "Do you know you're repeating yourself?" He shook his head. "You've been writing for hours. Go, have some fun."

"Fun?"

Mbjard nodded. "When no one's around in the Library, I like to write couplets in Attalag about the scribes, something reflecting one of their skills or personality traits."

Ulmaen immediately thought of the strange writing Mbjard had inscribed on the inside of Ule's wrist:

The only tongue you need.

Beware, the multi-tongued beast!

He understood the inscription now. It was no more than a playful description of Ule's ability for speaking many languages.

"Go on," Mbjard encouraged him.

The idea of fun was savagely attacked by a pack of ideas growling deep within Ulmaen's mind. Once outside in the courtyard, where Lyan's most loyal advocates celebrated with drink and song and dance, he breathed easily again and his mind settled down.

He pushed his way toward the Colonnade, where the crowds were fewer. He slowed his pace near the Starry Rise, where the flicker of lanterns running low on oil cast dancing shadows over the fountain. The gurgle and splash of water lured him even closer.

The whiff of fresh water cleared his nostrils of alcohol and pipe smoke, and it cut through the chatter in his mind. He knelt at the fountain's edge, collapsing against the basin where he rested his chin on a folded arm and let the other dangle above the water.

He watched the moving water as one of his fingers dipped in and broke the surface. The water swirled about, ripples distorting the image of coins littered along the bottom of the fountain. The coins stretched and jumped, appearing like small copper fish circling about.

What he knew undermined what he saw. The coins were inanimate and smaller in size; the only movement, an exchange from one person's hand to another's. If he were to breach the water, reach down and grab one, he could prove it.

What he saw on the surface of the water was pure illusion, reflections of distorted images mesmerizing him, distracting him from seeing something else. Tthe truth, perhaps?

His thoughts kept returning to Osblod and the many times he had goaded Lyan in public during the election, the act of bravery and sacrifice he had made protecting Lyan.

Quite by reflex, Ulmaen summoned an old creation, one he hadn't spoken with in a while. He had first created it from black filaments long ago, then had learned to harness it from within. He felt its heat slide along the inside of his arm and emerge at the tip of his finger.

He let the blue flame sit there a moment before setting it adrift on the water.

"A copper for your thoughts?" the flame asked, as it drifted around large circles.

"They're called *cops* now," he corrected the flame.

The flame shrugged.

"Tell me, am I supposed to believe Osblod's head butting with Lyan during the election was for Lyan's benefit?"

"Think," the flame said.

"I am," Ulmaen grumbled.

"Push, push, push." The flame spun around on every word, gliding over the water. "They're brothers, can't you see?"

"Well, they are now."

A glimmer of a thought lit Ulmaen's mind. Perhaps Osblod and Lyan had always been brothers. Brothers in battle. Then later in government. Osblod had never intended to smear or destroy Lyan, had he? He had *pushed* Lyan, forced him to truly consider what he wanted to accomplish beyond simply resting from the war, because Osblod knew the Chair required something from Lyan in return—commitment.

Ulmaen gasped. "Osblod made Lyan fight for the Chair, because he hadn't fought for it when he first occupied it."

"He's more confident now," the flame said. "Can you see that? I know you can."

A pang shot through Ulmaen's mind, making him blink. Memories of his last encounter with Navalis sparked in his mind, demanding attention.

"Ouch," the flame complained. "You're almost there, though. Keep going. You'll make it."

"What?" Ulmaen snorted. "Are you saying that when Navalis killed me, he had other intentions besides acting out of sheer hatred? Are you insane?"

"Sometimes," the flame admitted. "Only when you're insane, but you know I can only know what you know."

The flame's attempt to explain that it was essentially a manifestation of his subconscious sounded ridiculous. Ulmaen tried to laugh. Instead, his stomach lurched.

The thought of his Master—No, what was he now? Maven?—the thought of *him* made Ulmaen ill. He punched at the water and it rocked about obliterating the images on the surface. The blue flame rose into the air and settled on a spout.

"Everyone hates," the flame said. "And lies and hides. There are always reasons. Your Master has reasons, too."

"Are you defending him?"

The flame shimmied. "No, you are."

"No, I'm not," he replied.

Ulmaen ran his fingers through the storm of water, waiting for the surface to calm, but it never would; not entirely. Navalis's hatred toward him made sure of that. What else could drive a Master to murder his Student?"

"Yes, you are."

"No—" Ulmaen caught himself before their arguing continued. "I care about him, but when I was inside Navalis's memory, I felt his contempt and irritation for me. It was very strong."

"It wasn't all you felt. Your Master had other memories. You must dive now. "The flame tittered, flickered briefly and faded away.

There had been other odd emotions, but he'd seen Navalis's agitation, anxiety, and anger as reflections of his own and had ignored the others. Those memories had been linked to others which had oozed with what? Affection? The feeling had been more profound than that, hadn't it?

Navalis cared for him very much. Ulmaen sagged against the fountain, annoyed by the revelation. Even within the memory of the trial, Navalis had defended his Students, protected them from reprimands and punishments issued by Hethn and the others. He also had been trapped in Elish for hundreds of years, waiting to ensure the safety and protection of Ule when he could have easily possessed her. In fact, Ule had begged him to possess her, so they could both return home, and he had refused.

Navalis's dedication was the true treasure hidden at the bottom of his emotions.

The notion leeched away some of Ulmaen's anger, as he dwelled on his memory of the past and how Navalis had refused to possess her under the most dire of circumstances.

"Yet he murders me when all is calm and well," he mumbled to himself. He tried to laugh at the humor of it, but only managed a snort. Like a reflex, more words slipped out of his mouth. "Unless there's something more dire going on than last time."

Ulmaen bolted upright. Shivers ran down along his arms. Was that possible? Was there some new danger in the world of Elish that Navalis knew about? He could understand his Master's motivations, if that were true.

He jumped to his feet, dried his hand on a pant leg, and began to pace. He didn't care for the possibility that some unknown threat lingered in the world. He wasn't fully trained as a Sentinel. He'd learned a lot recently, but there was still more to learn.

He stopped to gaze at the fountain, considering what thoughts had just transpired in his mind.

Yes, he had learned a lot. He had learned to live in the form of a man for the first time in his existence. Until then, his experience had been so limited and complacent compared to the way he felt now, that he was confident he'd never enjoy feeling comfortable again. But he needed to know for sure what Navalis had intended. Had Navalis chose to murder Ule himself? Or had the task been assigned to him by the Xiinisi Council? And why had it been so necessary?

Ulmaen set out along the Colonnade again, heading north past the Bath House and stables toward the nearest woods.

He recalled the warning Mbjard had given Ule, just before her demise, about how the rules change for people in power, allowing them privileges others don't have, and Ulmaen wondered what exactly Navalis was entitled to do as Maven.

The sun had set by the time Ulmaen found a secluded area in the woods. His gaze turned inward, toward the middle of his forehead. The An Energy snaked toward him, and with a slight push of his will, he latched on, allowing his molecules to expand as he Ascended.

The An Energy twitched and squirmed, then vanished. His molecular body snapped back into Elishian form. He steadied himself against the bare trunk of a nearby birch. He didn't need to look into the upper stratum of the atmosphere to see if the Council had placed a barrier there; he knew they had.

He was being punished again—confined to the world for ejecting Navalis from Elish. There were consequences for doing that, just as there were consequences for killing your own kind, depending on who you were.

Ulmaen rubbed the back of his neck, hoping to stop the rising tension as he wished for another way back home—

The Safeway.

The solution presented itself with ease, and he laughed out loud. He imagined his return to the Vault and the looks of shock on the Council's faces: Hethn's beak parted, Oaxa's vipers frozen still, Gur's growls silent, and Veht's eyes blinking all at once.

He checked on his inner reserves. What remained of his generation cycle was nearly at an end, a few weeks at the most. He had plenty of energy to return to Xii, sort out the truth behind Ule's murder and return better prepared to face whatever threat existed in the world.

He shifted and propelled himself down into the ground, then headed through the field and beyond. He passed through the sub level of the Bath House and along the sewer tunnels beneath the Colonnade. He breached the brick wall of the main tower of the underground castle, zoomed down the stairs, past the rubble, and settled down on a piece of broken stairwell before the hole in the wall, where he returned to solid form.

Blue crystals lined the steps of the stairwell above, casting a hint of cool light over the steps, and he detected a shimmer within the cavity of the wall. The Safeway assured him a safe return to Xii in close proximity to Elish, and he anticipated a vista of the Vault with pillars and worlds spinning on nearby daises, but when he looked into the rippling fissure, he saw only a flat patch of vibrant black

He stared long and hard into the fissure, waiting for some detail of the Vault beyond to manifest. The blackness buckled, the way a curtain does, and he recognized the Isolation Chamber beyond.

He forced himself to breathe against the rising dread. He had expected punishment for torturing and ejecting Navalis from the world, but placing a barrier in the world hadn't been enough. It hadn't been enough to exile just him. No, they had exiled Elish, too.

He laid down on the slab of stairwell, struck by dark thoughts. He wept and then slept. When he woke, he shuddered at the sight of the dark fissure. He waited for the slightest glimpse of another world, of an eye looking back, some assurance that someone had bothered to check in on him. He slept again, woke, and shuddered again.

He lost track of time peering into that darkness, waiting for some glimmer of light. Had it been days? Perhaps a week or two?

The darkness persisted.

As he lay there, his eyes eventually dried out. His flesh withered over his bones. The last of the energy in his reserve diminished completely. Relishing his last few breaths, he wanted to reach out toward the fissure, but he was too weak. His body cells had already begun to die, signaling the end of one generation and the beginning of the next.

Far below the Starry Rise, he stayed the change, held off deathmorphing for a month or more. He wasn't sure how much Elishian time had passed, but he was mindful of his current generation counting down until the end.

He simply wanted to go home, as he had wanted to when he was a child, except instead of yearning to be welcomed back in loving arms by his kind, he wanted answers and reasons and explanations. He wanted to yell at them and be heard, to tell them their behaviour wasn't acceptable, but if they had a good reason for doing what they did, if they could explain themselves, maybe then he'd understand.

Again, they denied him his rightful place in Xii. His anger bruned, numbing him. He felt like a monster. Finally, the urge to deathmorph became overpowering. As he began to reshape his molecular array, he wished for the Quietus—that final, eternal death.

❋ ❋ ❋

You have reached the end of *The Other Castle*...

But Ule's journey still isn't over yet!

Thank you for reading the second instalment of **A Xiinisi Trilogy**. Ule's journey continues in the third and final book, *The Starry Rise*, coming soon.

To learn more about *A Xiinisi Trilogy*, visit my website at **www.KitDaven.com,** and be sure to subscribe to my blog to stay up to date on all the latest news.

A Review Request

If you enjoyed reading **The Other Castle**, I'd greatly appreciate it if you'd take a few minutes to share this story with other readers and **review this book online**.

Reviews for indie writers are **the most powerful way to legitimize and support their work.** Regardless of whether you loved this book or hated it, be sure to tell others about it. **Your opinion matters.**

Acknowledgements

If not for the assistance from my biggest supporters, this book may have taken much longer to complete than it did. My deepest thanks, love, and appreciation to—

Sean Chappell, for yet again offering words of encouragement, feedback on content revisions and other edits, as well as creating kick ass cover art. Oh, and for feeding and watering me when I needed to hit deadlines.

Donna Stewart for her friendship, feedback, and keen eye during the edit and proofread of this book. If not for her eagle eyes, my characters would have *perennial* glands instead of *pineal* glands.

Monica Balastik for her generosity and undying belief in my ability... since high school.

A Xiinisi Trilogy—A SF&F Story About A World Builder Race
VOLUME ONE: THE FORGOTTEN GEMSTONE
VOLUME TWO: THE OTHER CASTLE

COMING SOON:

VOLUME THREE: THE STARRY RISE

About the Author

Kit Daven is the author of the otherworldly demon-infused fantasy novel *The Forgotten Gemstone*, the first book in *A Xiinisi Trilogy*. She continues the story in *The Other Castle*, and is already wrangling demons for the cosmic finale, *The Starry Rise*.

Always involved in creative activities, such as sculpting and dress making, Kit recently made her acting debut in the indie short film *Sidney*.

She currently resides in Cambridge, Ontario, along with her husband and two cats.

You can connect with Kit online at Facebook, Twitter, and Goodreads.

www.KitDaven.com
Email: Kit.Daven@gmail.com

Made in the USA
Charleston, SC
04 June 2016